Praise for the novels of Mindy L. Klasky

The Glasswrights' Test

"Rani is a first-class heroine with a nose for high adventure, making this adventure pretty fabulous." —*Booklist*

"Klasky tells a strong, straightforward, and convincing story full of entertaining twists and turns. Her first book marked her as a writer to be watched, and those that have followed have been every bit as good or better." —*Chronicle*

"A powerful entry to this series . . . *The Glasswrights' Test* is fantasy the way it was meant to be written. Mindy L. Klasky is a powerful world builder who creates a kingdom that is rich in culture and history, a place where a highborn princess can communicate with the gods. The heroine is a very independent and determined woman who sets a goal and lets nothing and nobody stand in her way." —*Midwest Book Review*

The Glasswrights' Journeyman

"A fast-paced adventure series featuring a passionate, heart-winning heroine." —*Booklist*

"The best book in the series. . . . A juicy epic fantasy that will appeal to fans of Mercedes Lackey." —*Midwest Book Review*

continued . . .

The Glasswrights' Progress

"A strong follow-up to Klasky's debut novel, building on the strengths of the first book without succumbing to repetition."
—SF Site

"This sequel . . . stands alone but will compel readers to read the first book."
—*VOYA*

"Ms. Klasky creates remarkably shaded characters."
—*Romantic Times*

The Glasswrights' Apprentice

"I wouldn't be surprised at all if Klasky moves quickly to the front rank of fantasy writers."
—*Chronicle*

"A fun and colorful adventure, and a solid first novel." —*Locus*

"A fine fantasy novel . . . a winner." —BookBrowser

"Klasky's future novels . . . will be worth waiting for."
—SF Site

"This is a splendid tale, one which captured me from start to finish. Bravo—nicely done." —Dennis L. McKiernan

"From its rich imagery to its all-too-believable class system, this first novel will absorb and intrigue you, right up to the unexpected ending." —Nancy Kress, author of *Maximum Light*

Season of Sacrifice

"A fine story of magic and adventure, this is a wonderful coming-of-age tale, too." —*Booklist*

"Entertaining, with a spectacular climax and satisfying conclusion." —*Locus*

"A very creative and colorful high fantasy novel [with] action and drama. . . . Klasky proves she is a super-talented author." —*Midwest Book Review*

"Klasky summons a medieval flavor for her descriptions of the kingdom, and she allows her well-rounded characters to display both frailties and courage." —*VOYA*

THE GLASSWRIGHTS' MASTER

Mindy L. Klasky

A ROC BOOK

ROC
Published by New American Library, a division of
Penguin Group (USA). Inc., 375 Hudson Street,
New York, New York, 10014, U.S.A.
Penguin Books Ltd, 80 Strand,
London, WC2R, 0RL, England
Penguin Books Australia Ltd, 250 Camberwell Road,
Camberwell, Victoria 3124, Australia
Penguin Books Canada Ltd, 10 Alcorn Avenue,
Toronto, Ontario, Canada M4V 3B2
Penguin Books (NZ), cnr Rosedale and Airborne Roads,
Albany, Auckland 1310, New Zealand

Penguin Books Ltd, Registered Offices:
80 Strand, London WC2R, 0RL, England

First published by Roc, an imprint of New American Library,
a division of Penguin Group (USA) Inc.

First Printing, June 2004
10 9 8 7 6 5 4 3 2 1

Cover art by Jerry Vanderstelt

Printed in the United States of America

PUBLISHER'S NOTE
This is a work of fiction. Names, characters, places, and incidents either are the product of the author's imagination or are used fictitiously, and any resemblance to actual persons, living or dead, business establishments, events, or locales is entirely coincidental.

To Bruce Sundrud,
First Reader extraordinaire,
with the patience, tact, and inspiration
of a Saint

ACKNOWLEDGMENTS

The Glasswrights' Master–indeed, the entire Glasswright series—would never have made it into print without the unflagging support of Richard Curtis (my agent), Laura Anne Gilman (my first editor), and Jennifer Heddle (my second editor, who received this manuscript with grace and charm). As always, I am indebted to my First Reader, Bruce Sundrud, who rose to the occasion despite my short deadlines and frantic schedule. I could not have finished this novel without the sympathy and understanding of my current boss—Sylvia Miller—and my coworkers at Collier Shannon Scott, or without the support of my former coworkers at Arent Fox (especially Bob Dickey). Jane Johnson remained on call throughout *Master*'s creation, even as she juggled her own new family responsibilities. As always, the Washington Area Writers Group and the Hatrack Tuesday-night gang kept me in good cheer and supported me at readings, signings, etc. Ben and Lisa provided me with the perfect writer's retreat (complete with fresh-off-the-vine cherry tomatoes!) when I needed to write the last three chapters, and Mom and Dad stood behind me with their constant confidence. And Mark . . . well, he listened to fears, hopes, concerns, laughter, and tears, all without running in the opposite direction, which is more than any bridegroom should need to do!

If you would like to learn more about the Glasswright series (including the story as it was told in earlier volumes of the series), participate in my newsgroup, or send me e-mail, come to my Web page: www.mindyklasky.com.

1

As the battering ram pounded against the city gates, Rani Trader prayed that the Thousand Gods would permit her to live until sunset. Hundreds of soldiers shuffled around her, making a holy sign with their mailed fists. A breeze swirled down the cathedral's marble aisle, a harbinger of autumn's chill, and Rani automatically looked at Mair, making sure that her Touched friend had settled a cloak around her too-thin shoulders.

Mair glared back at Rani, as if the cold breeze were a personal affront. Rani started to let herself believe that the Touched woman's old spirits had revived, that she had finally returned to her habit of ordering the world about. Before joy could boil around Rani's heart, though, Mair glanced at the silken square tied about her wrist. She whispered to the cloth in a voice almost too soft to make out in the echoing cathedral. "All'll be well, Lar. Fear not, son. Ye'll not grow too cold."

Rani shuddered against the chill that walked down her spine, a prickling that had nothing to do with the temperature in the House of the Thousand Gods. Mair had spent the better part of the past year speaking to her dead son, Laranifarso. She had convinced herself that he still rested in her arms, that she carried him wherever she went with the square of black cloth, cloth that had been ripped from the mask Mair wore when she attended clandestine meetings of the Fellowship of Jair.

Rani could still remember the sound of the fabric rending, Mair's rage against the Fellowship that had murdered her son. That day, Mair first crossed to the distant land of madness. That day, Mair first left sanity and stability and all the familiar world.

The battering ram continued to pound the gates in the city below the cathedral, and Rani tried to remember that entire days went by without the Touched woman speaking to the silk. But each time Rani's hopes climbed that Mair had been healed, the other woman would raise her wrist and mutter to the cloth as if it were a living, thinking creature, as if it could answer her more completely than Mair's infant son had ever managed in his too-short life. Rani forced herself to remain silent, to pretend that she did not see the imaginary child. And then Mair would go about her day as if there were nothing strange, nothing odd, nothing hideously, horribly wrong.

The ram increased its urgent tattoo as Mair rubbed her hand across the silk, as if she were smoothing a real boy's hair, as if she were gentling a fussy child. "Pay attention!" Rani whispered, unable to restrain herself.

"Mind yer own prayers, Rai," Mair growled, and Rani almost believed that the Touched woman was upset about nothing more than participating in a service that was designed to glorify the soldier caste. The old Mair would certainly chafe about wasting time in the House of the Thousand Gods while enemy Briantans camped outside the city walls, while Liantine ships blockaded the harbor. She would concentrate on keeping her fingers from roaming into the purses of the nobles who stood closest to her. She would focus on sparing the kneeling soldiers from her sharp tongue. She would glare at the priest who stood at the altar, blithely offering up prayers to gods that seemed always to ignore the Touched.

No, the new Mair acted nothing like the Touched woman that Rani had befriended more than nine years before. The new Mair ignored all the assembled worshipers around her—all of them but Rani. And Farsobalinti.

Rani caught a look flashed between the pair. Mair still wore the golden armband that Baron Farsobalinti had given her during their wedding ceremony. The nobleman, though, had set his aside, unable to bear the remembrance of easier times, of brighter days when his wife and his son had prospered. When Laranifarso had died, Mair was forced to disclose her secret loyalties, her involvement with the shadowy Fellowship. Farso had made it clear that Mair's silent betrayal hurt him even more than the murder of their son. Nevertheless, Rani could tell that he remained perfectly aware of Mair; the troubled nobleman darted frequent glances from the dais where he stood beside his king.

If only Mair and Farso could speak to each other in the easy way they had shared before Laranifarso was lost! If only they would say what they were thinking: how they ached, how they longed for vengeance against the secret forces that had killed their son!

But there would be no speaking, not today. Not with the War Rites only partially completed. Not with the steady pounding of a battering ram against Moren's gates. Not with a fleet of Liantine ships blockading the harbor, with all of King Halaravilli's enemies arrayed against him, ready to strike, ready to bring him down once and for all.

A Briantan army of priests had crested the hills near Moren on the same morning that Liantine ships blockaded the harbor. Hastily organized messengers had carried demands from the besieging army. The Briantans had come to Moren to burn out the corruption in the city's soul, a corruption that had led Halaravilli ben-Jair to offer sanctuary to Princess Berylina. The princess had been the strongest witch that the Briantans had executed in over a century of meting out religious death sentences.

Ironically, the Liantines were attacking Moren for the same princess. Berylina's father demanded compensation for the loss of his only daughter, for the strange child that he had only too willingly resigned to Moren nearly four years before. As a princess, Berylina had no value to the house of Thunderspear. As a martyr, she inspired dreams of revenge, dreams of recapturing the Liantines' longtime profits from monopolistic trade in spidersilk.

Religion and money—what better reasons for a war? What better reasons for Morenia to be caught in the vise of its neighbors to the east and to the west?

With aggravating deliberation, Father Siritalanu spread his green-clad arms and intoned, "And so we ask you, Arn, god of courage, to watch over Morenia. We ask you to guide our poor kingdom in these dark days. Arn, give us strength against all our enemies, from those known and unknown, from those seen and unseen."

Some of the soldiers were little more than boys; they had spent their entire lives practicing their caste's warrish obligations, but they had never marched to battle for their king. Nevertheless, they understood the War Rites; they knew what was expected of them in the ceremony. Taking their cue from the robed priest, the assembled soldiers bellowed their response from one united throat: "Arn, give us strength against all our enemies!"

Rani's eyes narrowed as she watched the priest. She had listened to him protest that morning. He had told King Halaravilli that he could not lead the Rites, that he could not prepare the men for battle, that they should wait for the missing Holy Father Dartulamino.

Dartulamino. No one had seen him in three days, since the Briantan soldiers had crested the distant ridge and poured onto the Morenian plain. The King's Men had searched throughout the city, demanding access to the cathedral close, but the Holy Father had vanished, as if he had been spirited away by the steady clang of the Pilgrims' Bell.

Rani bit the inside of her cheek, restraining herself from calling out Father Siritalanu's name, from urging the priest to skip large sections of the Rites. Couldn't he see that they were almost out of time? Didn't he realize that Moren needed the ceremony completed *now*?

Finishing their salute to Arn, the soldiers stamped their feet in a traditional military tattoo. Above the clattering noise, Rani recognized her own personal signature for Arn, the incongruous sound of a child suckling at its mother's breast. There was an urgency to that whisper, an earnestness that made Rani glance about the cathedral.

Arn was speaking to her. Little time remained. The god of courage would have grim work all too soon.

Next to Rani, Mair repeated the soldiers' vow mechanically: "Arn, give us strength against all our enemies."

Against the Fellowship, Rani knew Mair must be thinking. The Fellowship that had slain her son. Rani glanced about the cathedral, wondering who was spying for them even now. Had the hated Fellowship coerced the Liantines into setting siege to the harbor? Had they bought the Briantans, paid those western religious fanatics to close off all landward approaches to Moren?

On the dais, Father Siritalanu moved his hands in a holy symbol, and Rani's fingers reflexively followed. Perhaps the gods *would* help her. Perhaps they would calculate some escape from Moren's nearly inevitable destruction. Perhaps they would figure out a way that the city could slip free from the closing pincers of attacking armies.

After all, King Halaravilli had surrounded himself with his best advisors. When scouts first reported that the Briantans were marching, Hal had hurriedly recalled Duke Puladarati from distant Amanthia. When the Liantine ships appeared on the horizon, Hal had summoned Davin from the inventor's tower chamber, asking the old man to craft a system for breaking the blockade. Those advisors stood on the dais now, the lion-maned Puladarati brushing back his hair with his three-fingered hand, Davin squinting out at the soldiers through his deepest wrinkles.

The pounding of the battering ram echoed inside Rani's thoughts, squeezing her heart with its predictable rhythm.

Father Siritalanu swallowed hard, as if he were trying to drown his own hopeless desperation, and then he continued. "And let us pray in the name of Bon, the god of archers." In her mind, Rani immediately heard the powerful whinny of a stallion, the sound of Bon. In the past year, she had grown accustomed to meeting the gods this way, to gathering their introduction through her eyes or her ears, her mouth or her nose, through her very flesh. The gods came unannounced, pouncing on her as if she were a mouse daring to invade their feline domain.

She would offer herself up to Bon if that would help. She

would sanctify herself to the god of archers, if only Morenia's soldiers would be strengthened. The War Rites were designed to protect fighting men, to give them comfort and confidence as they prepared to chance their lives on a battlefield. Perhaps the sound of a stallion was precisely what they needed. Perhaps that was all they required to stave off the invaders.

"That's right, Lar," Mair crooned beside Rani, directing her words to the soiled silk. Her voice was loud enough that many people in the cathedral looked away, embarrassed. Rani scowled and stepped closer, knowing without looking at the dais that Farso's face would be carved with sorrow. Hal would be glaring at her, ordering her to keep Mair under control. He had wanted to forbid the Touched woman from attending the service altogether.

Rani had argued, though, that it would take an entire herd of stallions to keep Mair from the cathedral. She would not easily pass up the chance to gaze upon her husband, to study the new grey streaks in Farso's hair, to memorize the most recent lines etched into his face, into the face of the man who had fathered her poor, doomed son.

Now, that man looked straight at Father Siritalanu, raising his voice to proclaim, "Bon, give us strength against all our enemies!" The vow was shouted by hundreds of warrior voices, and the words echoed off the ceiling.

Almost, they drowned out the change of timbre in the battering ram. Almost, they hid the fact that the last *boom* was deeper. Almost, they obscured the sound of splintering oak, the roar of warriors on the distant plain. Rani could imagine the Briantan men maddened by their success; she could picture soldiers scrambling to enter the city, fighting to be the first to course through Moren's streets.

As if he were unaware of the encroaching disaster, Father Siritalanu moved his hands in another holy symbol, and his voice echoed off the cathedral ceiling. "And let us pray in the name of Doan, the god of hunters."

A flash of deep forest green blinded Rani. Would Doan protect them? Or would he shelter the Briantans and Liantines? Could Morenia possibly be the hunter, or was she doomed to be the hunted, the prey, the hapless victim?

The soldiers in the cathedral might never have thought to ask the question. Father Siritalanu raised his voice yet higher, and the cords of his neck stood out as he proclaimed: "We ask you Doan, god of hunters, to watch over Morenia. Doan, give us strength against all of our enemies!"

"Doan give us strength!" the soldiers cried, and their feet pounded out their military pattern upon the floor.

"Doan give us strength!" Rani added her voice to the melee. How many more gods would Father Siritalanu honor? How many more deities would he weave into the ancient Rites? How much more time did they have before the Briantans broke into the cathedral?

As if King Halaravilli heard Rani's impatience, he stepped forward, making his way to the center of the dais. The soldiers watched their king hungrily, pounding their mailed fists upon their shields. They stomped the stony floor as if they would crumble it into dust. Puladarati and Farso looked out with satisfaction, even as Davin cocked his head toward the cathedral doors.

"Soldiers of Morenia!" the king proclaimed, and Rani was struck by the realization that he was far more than simple Hal, much greater than the companion she had known for over eight years, than the friend who trusted her to advise him on matters of trade.

This was Halaravilli ben-Jair, king of all Morenia, founder of the Order of the Octolaris. This was a man who had held his throne for nearly a decade, despite conspirators of all kinds. This was a man who had fought his own demons, overcome his own doubts, fought to unify his kingdom against all threats.

As if Hal sensed the awe that Rani cast toward him, he raised his chin, setting his jaw as he stared out at his assembled soldiers. The men continued their clamor, a noise loud enough to drown out the roar of the successful Briantan soldiers, to wash away the tumult of foreign priests and warriors crowing victory in the Morenian streets.

Hal nodded slowly. His hands rose from his sides, and he looked like a priest himself, like one of the holiest men of the kingdom, summoning power and faith and devotion from his assembled warriors.

Then, just when Rani could not imagine the soldiers showing any more dedication, just when she could not fathom their demonstrating a greater love of their king, Hal took a single step forward. The motion brought him squarely into a beam of sunlight, a beacon that streamed from one of the highest windows in the cathedral wall.

Rani knew the window well. She had watched her glasswright masters crafting it when she had first joined their guild. She had scrubbed its clean lines from a whitewashed table when she was only an apprentice. She had studied every join of lead and solder; she had viewed it from inside the cathedral and from without.

Hal stepped into the cobalt stream of the Defender of the Faith.

Rani's guild had made that window for another descendant of Jair. They had fashioned the masterpiece for a man who was dead these nine long years, a man whom Rani had watched stand on the very same dais. Without glancing up, Rani knew that the window would reflect a near-perfect image of her king, the long lines of his face, the square shape of his jaw. She would see Hal's high cheekbones, his penetrating eyes. She would be looking at Hal's older brother, the prince who had been groomed to rule the kingdom, the glorious lord who had been cut down in the prime of his life, but she would see King Halaravilli ben-Jair captured there.

The riotous soldiers knew nothing of glasswork, of grozing irons or diamond knives. They had never heard of silver stain, or lead chains, or specially forged armatures to support the weight of a glass masterpiece. Their knowledge was limited to swords and maces, battle-axes and spears. They knew about long leagues marched down endless roads. They knew about blood and sweat and the salty stench of exhaustion.

And they knew about their king. They knew that their king was threatened, that he called upon them to rise up against invaders. They knew that they were about to be tested, that they were being asked to pledge their lives anew, to offer up the most personal of devotions.

Halaravilli ben-Jair raised his arms above his head, letting the cobalt light stream over his hands, down the ornate golden sleeves of his robe. He let the light envelop him, and when he was fully washed in its power, he proclaimed: "The house of ben-Jair needs you now! In the name of my glorious father, Shanoranvilli ben-Jair, in the name of my brother, Tuvashanoran, who once led you, I call you to stand beside me this day!"

Hal filled his lungs to continue his exhortation, but before he could speak again, there was a tremendous crash. The cathedral doors flew back on their massive hinges, and their oaken planks shattered against the marble walls.

Rani had expected chaos. She had thought that the Morenian soldiers would immediately unsheath their swords, that they would surge forward to slake their thirsty steel with the invaders' blood. She had pictured tumult in the side chapels, gore flowing from altars like wax from melting candles. She had imagined the reek of battle, the sickening pall of blood and fear and worse.

But there was none of that. There was none of the noise and the confusion, none of the heart-pounding horror. Instead, there was silence. And when Rani looked to the shattered doors of the House of the Thousand Gods, she could see why.

Holy Father Dartulamino stood clothed in robes of deepest green, gold trimmed, ermine lined, framed in the broken remnants of the cathedral doors.

And yet Dartulamino's power did not come solely from the fact that he was dressed in priestly robes; rather he had alloyed that force, forged a new core of faith. As if to symbolize his new strength, he wore a helmet on his head, a massive gold-washed construction. The headpiece fit him closely, accenting his cheeks, protecting his skull with the sharpest of metal points. Even down the length of the cathedral, Rani could make out the fierce glint of his noseguard and the sturdy metal flaps that came down over his ears.

As if the image of a warrior-priest were not enough, Rani realized that the Holy Father also wore a film of black gauze over his robes. She remembered the last priests she had seen wearing such shrouds, at the Curia in Brianta. Those men had used their holy office to sacrifice a woman; they had murdered Princess Berylina in service to their supposed gods. What could Dartulamino mean, donning such a garment in the House of the Thousand Gods? What evil did he think to work here?

As if in answer to her questions, men appeared in the church's shattered doorway—rank after rank of soldiers, all clad in dark Briantan cloaks. Rani knew those garments; she had worn one during the long summer months when she sought to complete a pilgrimage in the city of First Pilgrim Jair's birth, when she worked to become a master in her guild. Each Briantan warrior proclaimed his religious dedication with the Thousand-Pointed Star emblazoned on his chest. The brilliant gold splashes declared that the men dedicated their lives to all the Thousand Gods, to the First Pilgrim who had recognized the force of those deities. The Briantan soldiers were prepared to die to spread the fervor of their faith. They were ready to be martyrs for the Thousand.

Dartulamino strode down the aisle, looking neither to the left nor the right as he approached the great dais at the front of the cathedral. His warriors marched behind him in precise formation, their metal-shod boots clanging on the marble floor. The Briantans were well armed and fully rested; aside from manning the battering ram, they had spent their time on the plain outside the city recovering from their long march across Morenia.

Hal's soldiers shuffled as the enemy marched between them, and every hand moved closer to its weapon. Nevertheless, Rani sensed the superstitious fear that gripped the local men. They were present for the Rites; they had gathered to concentrate their power for a battle. That concecration was not complete; final blessings had not been bestowed. Hal had waited too long in summoning Father Siritalanu, and the Morenian soldiers were not fully prepared.

Beside Rani, Mair grew tense as Dartulamino approached. The Touched woman spread her fingers over her silk square, as if she could protect the fabric from rending blades. Her breath came fast, and her eyes flashed wildly. She reached one claw toward the man that she had wed, toward the father of her dead son, and it seemed that she was trying to signal Farsobalinti, trying to alert the nobleman to the evil in their midst.

A high keening tore at the back of her throat, a sound of terror annealed with rage. Rani remembered stallions she had heard, declaring their fury in hopeless battles, and she recognized Mair's passion.

Bon, Rani thought. The god of archers sounded like a stallion screaming.

But none of the archers inside this church had his weapons ready. And even if he had, not a single man would have dared to sight down a shaft. None would have been brave enough or ruthless enough or foolish enough to draw against the Holy Father of the Church of the Thousand Gods.

Dartulamino paused on the first step of the dais, and his men fell into formation behind him. He glared at Father Siritalanu, his gaze searing beneath his helmet as if it had the power to set the younger priest on fire. Father Siritalanu stood firm, but his plump face grew as pale as the marble altar behind him. The wind tore down the cathedral aisle, unimpeded by the ragged shards of the broken doors, and the younger priest's robes caught against him, outlining his body like a sad joke.

Father Siritalanu was no warrior. His legs were thin beneath his gown. His belly was soft. His arms had never been shaped by the weight of a sword, by the pressure of heavy labor. Nevertheless, he raised his chin, facing down the invaders as if he thought he could win this encounter.

Rani fought the urge to twist her hands in nervousness, to wring some confidence from her solemn gown. Why hadn't they started the ceremony earlier that morning? Why hadn't they completed the ritual swearing in of the soldiers the day before? Why were they unprepared in the face of this threat, in the swell of imminent danger?

Father Siritalanu's breath came faster, and Rani suspected that he was reciting the same catalog of failures. The poor man tried to draw himself up taller, straighter.

Beside Rani, Mair's lips curled back into a snarl. Dartulamino was perhaps the man Mair blamed most for the loss of her son. The priest was one of the strongest members of the Fellowship of Jair; he had long been instrumental in coordinating the cabal in Morenia. To this day, neither Mair nor Rani—nor Hal himself, for that matter—had learned who had given the actual order to steal away Laranifarso, who had commanded that the child be executed. Rani could still remember the moment when they learned of the infant's death, though, the instant that Mair had toppled from a shrewd, spirited advisor to a madwoman bent on revenge.

Rani reached out and grasped Mair's wrist, the bare one, the one not wrapped in silk.

Father Siritalanu called out, "Who are you that defiles the House of the Thousand Gods with your implements of violence and your warlike mask?" The priest's defiance might have inspired confidence among the loyal Morenian soldiers if his voice had not quaked.

"You know me, boy." Holy Father Dartulamino's voice echoed among the soldiers, as if he stood on a parade ground. "You know me, and you fear me."

"I f-fear no man who breaks into the House of the Thousand Gods!" Rani's heart was wrenched as the priest's brave defiance was hampered by his stammer, by the boyish curve of his cheeks. She pictured him kneeling beside the now-dead Berylina, speaking to the princess in reassuring tones. Siritalanu was meant to be a teacher, a guide, a peaceable man. He was not a warrior-priest.

"Stand down, boy, or I'll have you spitted on the dais."

"You would not do that, Dartulamino." Father Siritalanu's defiance was coated with incredulity. "Not here. Not in the House of the Thousand Gods. Not when my death would defile the church that you have worked so hard to build these many years."

For just an instant, Rani believed that Dartulamino might listen to reason. After all, he appeared in the church surrounded by religious warriors, by Briantans marked by the Thousand-Pointed Star. By their very costume, these men declared themselves devoted to the gods. Could they really mean to spill a priest's blood upon the altar? Could they truly intend to destroy a man consecrated to all the Thousand?

As if in answer to Rani's questions, Dartulamino raised one commanding hand. His fingers were jagged pokers, and fire jutted from his eyes. "Remove that man from the dais. Remove the taint from the House of the Thousand Gods!"

The Briantan soldiers sprang forward, but Hal's voice froze them in the aisle. "Halt!"

Dartulamino turned a sneering gaze on his king. "You do not have the right to command my Briantans."

Hal's voice was as bright as the edge of a sword. "I have every right, Father, for they are my men as well. I am Defender of the Faith, am I not? Was I not sanctified in that duty by your own predecessor's hand, in this very building, by the blessing of the self-same priest who elevated you to your post?"

At first, Rani thought that the Holy Father might be outsmarted that simply. He clearly had not anticipated Hal staking claim to any religious title; he had rallied his men around their rebellion against secular authority.

Silently bolstering his claim, Hal shifted the heavy necklace of J's that lay upon his shoulders. "I am the heir of First Pilgrim Jair, Father."

A part of Rani's mind objected to Hal granting the priest his religious title. After all, what sort of religious man would march an army into the cathedral? What sort of priest would raise angry steel in the very House of the Thousand Gods?

But then, Rani glanced at the Morenians who stood nearby, at the soldiers assembled for the Rites. These were men sworn to preserve order, to respect their liege lord and all that he stood for. These were men who acted to maintain the world as they understood it, who—even though they would not shrink back from fear or terror or pain in battle—would cower at the destruction of their religious faith.

Hal granted Dartulamino his proper title, but he demanded that the priest rise up to the responsibilities of that name. Hal bound the Holy Father to solemn obligation by acknowledging his strength.

"You have forfeited that claim, rebel," Dartulamino spat, and his Briantan fighters grew more tense. "You have deluded your people with your claims of right and wrong, with your attempts to steal diadems and gold that were not yours for the taking."

"What do you claim that I have stolen, Father?" Hal's challenge was hot and immediate. When he moved his hand to rest upon the hilt of his sword, his hair flashed in the cobalt light. Rani could not help but glance up at the window, could barely keep from choking out a word of warning. No. That had been another time. That had been another threat. That had been another test that she had taken, that she had failed, all unknowing. Hal repeated, "What do you claim?"

Dartulamino took three steady steps, mounting to the top of the dais. He pulled himself to his full height, a height made even taller by the helmet atop his head. Hal looked very young, as if he were a child playing at a game of war.

Beside Rani, Mair writhed like a possessed creature, pulling her silken square between her fingers, tugging at the fabric as if she could make it disappear. Rani longed to reach out for her, to gather her close, to protect her from the man they knew was a murderer.

Hal darted a glance at the Touched woman, then flicked his attention to the stone-faced Farsobalinti. Before Hal could speak, Dartulamino roared, "By Jair, you cannot claim innocence about the blood upon your hands!"

By Jair. Dartulamino was making this Fellowship business, then.

Despite Mair's strangled cry, Rani felt herself relax. She had not realized how difficult it was to fight a lifetime of teachings. She had not thought how hard it would be to take a stand against the highest priest in the land, against the leader of the very church that had nurtured her since infancy.

But Dartulamino did not stand on the dais as the emblem

of that church. Certainly, he bore its trappings, in his fine green robes, in his careful overgown of gauze. But he was not a priest, not today. He was a conspirator. He was a messenger from the Fellowship of Jair. He was a leader of the secret organization that was bent on ruling all the world, on taking over the kingdom of Morenia, and of Brianta as well, of Liantine and Amanthia and all the distant lands that it could reach.

Even as Rani clapped a hand on Mair's shoulder, she watched Hal measure out the same distinction; she sensed the certainty that settled over him as he accepted Dartulamino's oath. Of course, the Fellowship was hidden to most of those who stood in the cathedral. Those soldiers would not recognize the hidden meaning behind the traitor-priest's words. Even Father Siritalanu, even Puladarati and Davin were ignorant of the levels of betrayal that stood inside the church.

Rani glanced at the ranks of soldiers, Morenian and Briantan, and she knew that Hal must act quickly. His warriors were growing confused. They had been excited by Father Siritalanu's exhortations; they had collected their strength to rise up against the invaders, against the ships that blockaded the harbor, against the forces that besieged the city's walls. Now, though, they questioned the rightness of their fight.

And, looking out the broken doors of the cathedral, Rani wondered if the soldiers were not wise to quail. A giant plume of smoke rose from the city walls. Odd, Rani thought dispassionately. I never noticed that the gates were framed by these cathedral doors. I never thought that the Thousand Gods watched over all the comings and the goings of fair Moren. I never realized that they cared so much.

But the gates were indeed framed in the doorway, or what

was left of the gates. Staring out, Rani wondered what the invaders had done to create such billows of smoke, how they had managed to send such an incontrovertible signal.

She threw a quick glance to Davin, to see if the old man was working out what the Briantans had done, how they worked their war engines. The ancient advisor was nodding slowly, as if he had come to understand some secret, some arcane method of waging war that even he had not considered in his decades of military calculation.

What did it matter, though? What did it matter if the invaders had harnessed some Briantan trick, or merely received a healthy dollop of unholy luck? The city gates were burning.

And if the gates were burning, then the blockading vessels in the harbor would know that the end was near. The Liantines would land their boats and bolster the Briantan forces. They would force their own ships into the harbor, up to the docks. They would add their naval crossbows to the Briantans' weapons, and poor Moren would crumple under the weight.

Rani took a step forward, to advise Halaravilli ben-Jair of the full extent of his danger, in case he had not recognized the pattern. The king's jaw was tight as he glared back at Dartulamino. Had only seconds passed? Was Hal still formulating a response to the secret message that his enemy had delivered?

"Aye, Father," the king said. "In the name of Jair, the innocent must have clean hands."

And then, as if he were not threatened, as if there were not enemy armies before him, as if no navy waited to wade into his stronghold, Halaravilli ben-Jair turned his back on the invading priest. He raised his hand to Father Siritalanu and commanded, "Continue, Father. My men await your final blessing."

"Your men will be cursed if that so-called priest speaks a single word in the name of the Thousand!" Dartulamino's rage spattered across the cathedral floor.

"Continue," Hal said, refusing to grant the rebel his attention.

Father Siritalanu glanced once from his worldly lord to his spiritual one, and then his tongue darted out to moisten his lips. He raised his hands in a shaking holy gesture, and there was a long pause while pockets of men decided whether to settle to their knees to receive his blessing. "In the name of Arn and Bon, in the name of—"

"Will you risk your soul?" Dartulamino cried to Father Siritalanu. "Your soul and those of all the men who pray here?"

Many of the soldiers who had knelt scrambled to their feet, and more than one fist settled back on a weapon. Father Siritalanu managed to say, "The only souls risked in this house are those that do not bow before the Thousand Gods."

Holy Father Dartulamino's sallow face grew dark. Rani heard him catch his breath; the sound was amplified by his helmet. She felt the tension curl through his fingers, up his arms, into his gut. As if Mair were a mirror, the Touched woman stiffened as well, focusing all her anger and her grief upon the single man.

"First God Ait will spit upon you," Dartulamino said, and his voice quaked with fury, nearly as tremulous as poor Father Siritalanu's had been at the beginning of the ceremony. "First Pilgrim Jair will look upon you with outraged laughter. All of the Thousand will turn from you and glory in the ways that they can cause you grief. They will reach into your slumber; they will seize you while you are awake. They will strangle your minds and your hearts and leave you gasping like tiny children, abandoned in a winter storm."

As if in response to the Holy Father's exhortations, the sun moved behind a cloud bank, plunging both worshipers and invaders into shadows. At the same time, though, the cobalt light that came from the Defender's Window seemed to intensify, pulling in upon itself so that Halaravilli ben-Jair was more captivating, more controlling, more important than he had ever been in his life.

Hal stepped forward, raising his chin so that his necklace of J's was at the perfect angle to reflect the beam from the window. "Father Siritalanu," he said, and his voice was so soft, so even, that he might have been speaking to a child. "Finish with your service. Complete the War Rites so that my men will best be able to defend me with the strength of their arms and the faith in their hearts."

Father Siritalanu appeared unable to follow his king's command. The priest's boyish face trembled, and he might have been a child shamed before his elders. Then he flushed, and his cheeks reflected the crimson of Hal's royal raiment. The priest raised his hands in a familiar holy gesture, but he seemed to have forgotten all his words; he appeared doomed to eternal silence.

And in that instant, in that hesitation, in that pause where all the Thousand Gods seemed uncertain whether to rush in or abandon the rightful cause of Moren, Dartulamino raised his arms. He threw back his head, and he bellowed, "To me, Briantans! To all that is holy in this House of Gods! To me!"

For a heartbeat, Hal's loyal troops were frozen in shock. Then swords slipped from sheaths. Spears were leveled. Axes were hefted to shoulders, arrows nocked to bows.

Dartulamino tossed back his priest-green robes, revealing heavy sheets of chain mail. The man had never expected to parley in the House of the Thousand Gods. He had never expected to reach peace with his king. Dartulamino raised his hands and began to summon the gods, chanting through the decades of their names as if the very syllables filled him with power.

Rani's mind was filled with the presence of the gods; her senses were overwhelmed by sights and sounds, touches and tastes, by countless scents. How had Berylina borne this? How had the princess subjected herself to endless worship? How had she submitted to the Thousand, to their ever-changing, swirling emanations?

Rani shut her eyes against the nauseating array. Her knees buckled, and her breath came fast and sharp, as if she had run all through the city.

"Come along, then!" Suddenly, there was a strong hand beneath her arm, pulling her upright, forcing air back into her lungs. She opened her eyes and blinked hard, forcing herself to bring Mair into focus. "We'd best be leavin' this."

"Mair—" Rani struggled for words.

"Aye, 'n' Laranifarso, too." The girl gestured toward her silk square. "We came t' 'elp ye, since ye all seem unfit t' 'elp yerself."

"Help?" Rani asked, not comprehending. The battle boiled in the cathedral behind her. Horrible oaths echoed off the stone spine of the cathedral. When Rani dared a glance over one shoulder, she saw one of the Briantans stumble past a side chapel, pulling down an ornate curtain meant to honor Lor, the god of silk.

"Aye, Rai. Lar 'ere is a smart un. 'E knew there'd be trouble. 'E told me t' come prepared."

"How could he—" Rani started to protest, and then she looked at the scrap of black silk and fell silent. Mair was mad. She had been since returning from Brianta. Whatever fantasies her broken mind wove, whatever dreams she played out now . . .

"Dinna argue wi' me, Rai." The Touched woman certainly sounded reasonable, as sound as she ever had. "Ye'll do as I say, 'n' p'raps ye'll live through th' day."

A vicious clatter forced Rani to spin around, and she saw ranks of candelabra toppled to the floor, offerings to Tren flying. Soldiers jumped back from the burning wicks. One of the Briantans, discernible by the oversized Thousand-Pointed Star embroidered on his chest, picked up a sharp-pointed stand and lunged into a knot of Morenian soldiers. He was cut down, his blood spraying across the altar dedicated to the god of candles.

Mair laughed, and her cold glee was more frightening than anything she had said or done in all the days of her madness. "Are ye wi' us, then, Rai? Are ye wi' us, or d' ye plan t' stay 'ere 'n' be cut down?"

Another Briantan leaped into a group of soldiers loyal to Hal, and fierce blows echoed off shields. Oaths rang out in the cathedral, and the sickening stench of entrails wafted across on the wind that blew through the shattered door.

"I'm with you," Rani said, and she caught the victorious gleam in Mair's eye.

The Touched girl nodded once, and then she sprang past the dais. Rani never would have sought shelter there, away from the doors, away from the city, away from escape. Mair leaped, though, as if she had a plan, as if she had a destination. She moved with more certainty than she had in months.

Rani watched her friend move, and then she called out, "Sire!"

It was a sign of the devotion between them that Hal looked up at her cry. He did not hesitate to respond to the command in her one word; he trusted her, even in the midst of treachery and chaos. Against the battleground of the cathedral, she saw him measure her gesture. She watched him start to shake his head, to turn back to his soldiers, his pitiful, betrayed men.

But then the choice was taken from him. Farsobalinti bulled into his king, forcing his liege back one step, two, three. A group of soldiers swirled in front of the dais, as if they knew what Mair intended, and Farso took advantage of the chaos to push Hal forward even more forcefully.

Hal started to protest, to plant his feet, but he did not have a chance. Farso worked against him, and then Davin, and Puladarati and Father Siritalanu and a handful of loyal fighting men. All of them rolled past Rani, tumbled after Mair, through a doorway hidden in the floor behind the altar. Steps disappeared into darkness.

Rani hesitated on the threshold. Where was Mair taking them? What secret passage had she mastered years ago, during her misspent youth as a Touched wench who ransacked the city for her personal gain? What was to keep the invading soldiers from following them?

Rani bit back an oath as strong fingers wrapped around her arm. Mair had come back through the passage, come to pull her into the darkness. "Rai!" the Touched woman shouted. "Now! Or ye might as well prepare t' meet Tarn 'imself!"

Rani's eyes were clouded by the green-black wings of the god of death; he always hovered near. Before she could blink away his presence, Mair pulled her forward, into the darkness, into the relative quiet. And then Davin stood at the top of the stairs, resting his hands on the frame of the stone-cut door. He nodded once to himself, as if he had discovered some magic, some secret.

The old man cast one glance down the dim corridor, and then he twisted his wrists, manipulating some hidden latch. The door glided closed behind them, cutting off light, cutting off battle, sealing away Rani and Mair, Hal and Farsobalinti and Siritalanu, Puladarati and Davin and the handful of soldiers who remained loyal to their lost cause.

2

Kella leaned close over the fire, stirring the thick syrup in her iron cauldron. She had spent hours boiling down the moonbane, hours observing the Sisters' precepts. Following the ancient lore, she had harvested the herb in the dark of the first night after the crescent moon slipped from the sky. She had dug up the entire plant, snagging its splitting roots between her gnarled fingers, smoothing the wet earth from its gnarled bulbs. Moonbane looked like a man, her dam had said, and for years, Kella had believed that men had filth between their legs.

The herb-witch smiled at the memory. She had been naive once. Long ago. A lifetime ago.

Kella hefted her iron spoon, comforted by its weight. It had been a long time since she'd used the moonbane cauldron, a long time since she had called on this specific aspect of the Sisters' lore. People did not come to visit an herb-witch as often as they had in her dam's time. As often as they had when she was a young girl, and pretty.

"Isn't it ready yet?"

Kella should have waited longer, let the potion boil more. Certainly, there was pleasure in brewing the old herbs. Certainly, she enjoyed the power that coursed through her veins when she hefted the iron cauldron, when she stirred with the iron spoon.

But she had no desire to keep Jalina waiting any longer than necessary. The woman was a wildcat, nearly more trouble than she was worth. Of course, Kella had signed the handsel contract eagerly enough, sensing that Jalina had a deep purse. The ancient arrangement was simple: Jalina, as handsel, would pay Kella every copper of whatever price they agreed. In exchange, Kella would provide her herbs and keep the woman's identity a secret, her identity and the reasons that she sought an herb-witch's aid. The Sisters had developed the handsel arrangement generations back, and it served its purpose, soothing the wary, helping them to trust in herb-witches' skill.

Not that Jalina looked to frighten easily. She pretended to be an ordinary woman on an ordinary retreat in the forest. But she was something more. She was something powerful in the outside world, in the world of men. She ordered her retainers about as if she were accustomed to people meeting her needs.

If Kella wanted to, she could wipe that complaining expression from the girl's face, and she would not need the Sisters' magic to do it. Kella could simply mention the rider who had come through the woods a fortnight ago. She could say that there was money being offered for a woman of middling height, a dark woman with a northern accent, a stranger woman with a suckling babe.

But the handsel bound Kella to silence. She had said nothing to the rider, nothing to the twisted man who looked as if he should be cushioned on a litter rather than clinging to the mane of his warrior stallion. She had seen the pain etched across that one's face, seen his anger and his hurt, planted deep beneath the scar that glistened high on his cheekbone. She had seen the ghosts that he had left behind him, shed from his life as a soldier, certain as Kella was an herb-witch, born and raised.

That man would be back if he did not find Jalina. He'd be back, and he'd offer more for Kella's aid. By then Jalina might have moved on. The handsel might have ended. No reason for Kella to harvest the first green shoots of spring; better to wait until the plant had grown to summer height. Better to wait until she could turn a healthy profit on her information, her knowledge. That was the way of the herb-witch, after all, trading in knowledge. That was the way of the Sisters.

"Almost ready," she said to Jalina. "You wait and see. You give this potion to your son, and he'll grow strong as an oak. He'll have all the power of the moon in his veins. You've seen the moon, my dear. You've seen how it's strong enough to stay in the sky, even with the sun trying to drown it out."

Jalina nodded impatiently and shifted her sleeping child, clicking her tongue as she looked over her shoulder. She was a hurried one, like a spring crocus rushing out from under a snowbank. Well, crocuses froze sometimes. Crocuses lost their power.

The infant opened his mouth and mewled a protest. He was little, that babe. Kella had helped at his birthing, helped in her very own cottage. Even so, it had taken all her herb knowledge to keep both mother and son alive. In between contractions, Kella had asked Jalina about her other children, asked how many the slender woman had borne. Jalina's jaw had set firmly, as if her body were clenching in another birth throe. She'd insisted she had no other children.

Kella had gotten to the truth soon enough, though. She'd learned of the lost babes, left wandering in the twilight. The Heavenly Fields, Jalina had said. Even now, the herb-witch snorted. Those Heavenly Fields were fine for folk in the cities, fine for the noblemen and the merchants, the soldiers and the guildsmen who could take time to pray to their Thousand Gods.

The world's true power lived in the woods. Lived in herbs and trees, in secret streams. The Sisters found the true power, found it and harvested it.

Lost children would try to block a living sibling from entering the world. Kella had finally made Jalina understand. She'd made the woman recognize her lost babes—first a son, then a daughter, then twin boys. Kella had twisted a grass-babe for each of them, figures that represented the four lost bodies. She had sprinkled water over each knotted form, water that had been collected from dew on the first day of spring. She had tossed a handful of earth on top of the grass-babes, loam from the bank of the stream that fed the largest oak in the forest.

Kella had spoken the secret words, the mother words, the words the Sisters had taught her when she was young and fresh and new to her game. And during Jalina's next contraction, the young mother had gasped and clutched at the grass-babes. She had pulled them to her chest, staining her hands with grass and water and earth.

And then the new babe had been born.

He was a little slip of a thing. Jalina admitted that her time should not have come for another moon. Even so, the child had ten perfect fingers and ten perfect toes. He had soft ears, curved against his head like a mouse's. He had a tiny mouth and steady lungs, and he wasn't afraid to use them.

Marekanoran. That was what Jalina named her son. A hefty name for so small a babe. Kella refused to work her mouth around such a challenge. She called the child Mite. Jalina might have been displeased, but she would not speak out against the herb-witch midwife who had delivered her of a healthy son.

Kella poured the moonbane syrup into a thick clay jar, pushing in a cork stopper with all the force in her gnarled fingers. "Go, girl. Give Mite the potion." Jalina started to protest. "Twice a day, as the moon rises and as the moon sets, one swallow each time. He'll sleep through the night then. You'll both sleep, and he'll grow fat and happy."

The young mother looked too exhausted to complain. Instead, she folded her fingers about the jar. At first she looked as if she might thank the herb-witch, but then she seemed to remember her place. She turned on her heel and strode across the clearing.

Two shadows melted into the darkness after her. Oh, Jalina thought that she was crafty. She thought that she traveled with her guards all hidden. She thought that Kella was blind, or at least that the handsel bond would render the witch mute if anyone asked uncomfortable questions.

But Kella knew. Kella understood. Kella recognized King's Men when she saw them—soldiers from Sarmonia, from the north, it hardly mattered. She spat into her fire. King's Men were the same the world over. Quick to use their blades, they were, to cut down anything that stood in their way, be it herb or tree or living, growing body.

Kella felt hands on her shoulders, and she started in surprise. Even before she could dart her fingers into the patched pocket on her gown, though, she recognized the touch. No reason to attack this one. No reason to fight.

"I didn't mean to startle you." His voice was rich in the moonlight, complicated with the tones of lingering sunlight, of glinting amusement.

"You didn't." She huffed around to the fire, lifting up a stick to stir the burning wood. One working for each fire. That was the old way. That was the powerful way. Better to light another fire than to carry over leached power from one spell to another.

He took the stick from her, making short work of spreading out the glowing wood. Sparks leaped up, but he ignored them, as if he were accustomed to working with fire. As if he were immune to the touch of a flame. "You gave her what she wanted?" His voice was gruff, and she glanced suspiciously at his copper eyes.

"What is that to you? She's my handsel. It's enough for you to know that she came about a woman's matter."

"She came to you about the babe."

Why were so many interested in this woman and her child? Kella shrugged and snorted. "Babes. Mothers. It's all the same to an herb-witch like me."

He looked at her shrewdly, peering across the pool of glowing embers. "An herb-witch like you, eh?" He curled the words into a rough caress. "I've traveled in lands where those words could buy you death."

"So you say, traveling man. So you say." Still, his warning sent a shiver down her spine. Sarmonia might not honor its witches. It might not offer them power and prestige. But it protected the Sisters. No one was allowed to destroy Kella's possessions, to ride through her clearing and pillage her crops, her stores.

There were other places, though. Other lands. Other people who did not honor herb-witches properly. Kella shuddered as she thought of women wounded in the name of their craft. Murdered for sharing their power. She swallowed and licked her lips, suddenly aware of the breeze that whispered across the clearing.

The embers from her working fire glowed in the night. He'd done a good job spreading them. They were even, smooth. Balance. That was what she must maintain. Keep the fire balanced with the earth, with the air. Avoid the need for water to take away the heat and the color of the flames.

Grudgingly, Kella nodded toward the path from the clearing. "You were watching her, then?"

"Aye. I wonder why she comes here. Why she is in Sarmonia at all."

"The high road leads to many places," Kella quoted. His eyes still peered into the darkness, and a shadow had fallen across his cheeks. "Why, traveling man? Why do you care about her so?"

He shook himself, like a dog shedding rainwater. "Her?" His smile was easy. "I care not for her. I worry only that she takes you from me in the dark of the night."

Kella knew that she should not believe him. After all, he was young enough to be her son, and a late child at that. His hands were strong, his arms well muscled. The moonlight glinted on his cheekbones, silvering his hair even as his lips curved into a grin. "Easy words, traveling man."

"Hard ones," he grinned, and he closed the distance between them. She felt his hands across her back, firm and commanding. She breathed in the smell of him—wood smoke and sweat and a vague, unidentified dusting of spice. She held her body stiff for a moment, but then his lips warmed her; his hands melted her.

When she pulled back from his kiss, the embers were

dying in the night, flickering out the last of their orange life beneath the stars. The working was ended then. She had helped another deserving soul. She turned back to the man beside her and twined her fingers between his. "Very well, traveling man. Come speak to me of other things. Share more hard words with me, and I'll see what I can do to ease them."

He quirked a smile at her, and her heart raced faster. She was foolish to respond to him so. Her hair was grey; her joints ached. She was no girl. She should not let him manipulate her. She shook her head and bit off a laugh. "Come, Tovin. Come to bed."

And he did.

She awoke before dawn, smelling dew on the grass outside. The night must have been cool—much water had accumulated. That was good, for her purposes. The sweetvine would bloom with the sunrise. If she could pick the petals before they dried in the morning air, she could brew the strongest love draft in her books.

She slipped from beneath her sheets, and the scent of lavender followed her across the room, seeping from her mattress. There was no witchy power in the herb, but she had always been charmed by its fragrance.

Kella crouched by her hearth and began to poke in the ashes, burrowing down to the banked embers. There. A solid heart of orange, glowing in a grey silk bed. She filled her lungs and blew softly on the fire, encouraging it to strengthen, even as she squinted her eyes against a dusting of ash. Her fingers automatically reached for the dried deergrass she kept in a pot by the stove. She sprinkled the powdery stalks over the ember, waiting for them to kindle into tiny yellow flames.

Deergrass, to bring vision and caution to her day. She'd reached for it often since the traveling man came to her. She'd felt the need for careful steps around him, for delicate maneuvers. And she wasn't quite willing to ignore the Sisters' rumors that deergrass wove its way into a man's heart, bound him to the hearth where first he smelled the weed's clean sharpness.

She turned to look at Tovin, and she was not surprised to see him gazing back at her. She added a clutch of small twigs to the fire, and then she stood, brushing her hands against her apron. "Don't speak to me. Hold on to your thoughts."

"I would have helped you with the fire."

"Hush."

"I would have!"

"You would have made a mess." His young lungs were strong. He would have sent ash swirling across the floor. "You should be concentrating, not talking."

"Ah, yes. My morning interrogation."

"Interrogation?" Despite herself, despite her intention to keep him quiet and focused, she snorted. "Do all you northerners fear questions so?"

He smiled and shrugged. He was always relaxed when he awoke, lazy and soft, as if he only donned his sarcastic guise with his clothes. She crossed back to the lavender-scented pallet and stretched out beside him. His scarred hands folded around her, wandering down her flanks, but she stilled him with her own twisted fingers.

"Go ahead, then," she said. "Look into the flames." His fingers walked up her arm. "Don't try to distract me, traveling man." He sighed in mock frustration, but he directed his attention to the hearth. "Tell me," she urged. "Before you forget them."

He was silent for a long minute, and she forced herself to lie still beside him. She measured out her breath, slow and even. She was trying to support him, trying to assist. It was important for him to remember, to speak. After several deep breaths and silence, though, she could not keep herself from prompting: "Do you recall anything? Even images, if you can't remember an entire dream."

"I've told you, Kella. I don't dream."

"Everyone dreams. You must train yourself to remember what you see."

"I can tell you anything that I see with my waking eyes. I'm not some lazy child. I know how to use my senses."

"I know you're not lazy. I also know that you're not concentrating."

"Kella, why is this so important to you?"

Why? She wasn't sure how to answer him. Perhaps it was important because she had always shared her own dreams—first with her mother, then with her younger sister, then with her long-ago husband. Perhaps it was important because of the answers she had found to her own questions, answers lurking in the twisted hallways of sleep. Perhaps it was important because there was true witching power in dreams, true energy and force that could be helped along by wisely chosen herbs.

Perhaps it was important because she thrilled to hear the player man speak, thrilled to feel the rumble of his words rising in his chest, echoing down her spine.

"Look into the flames, Tovin. Concentrate, and remember your dreams."

Kella listened to him breathe beside her. She heard the fire whisper on the hearth, the nibble of the small flames as they worked their way through the dry wood. She heard a breeze pick up in the trees outside, the rustle of leaves and the rub of one branch against another. No words, though. No dreams. After a long silence, Tovin sighed. "Nothing."

"Nothing," she repeated.

"I've tried, Kella."

"Of course you have." She tried to keep her tone matter-of-fact.

"As well as you have," he countered, and she wasn't surprised to hear his argument begin. "It's only fair for *you* to try now, Kella. You promised."

She had, hadn't she? In some moment of weakness, when she'd been more intent on keeping the man beside her than on following her own common sense. What had she been thinking? The Sisters would laugh her out of their circle, if they saw her here, swayed by a handsome young man.

"There's nothing to be afraid of," he said easily, smiling as anger tensed her shoulders. He certainly knew how to get her to react. She watched the easy curve of his lips, and she reminded herself to be amused as well. After all, she wasn't doing anything she didn't want to do. Not really. And she might yet learn how to harness the power of his trick, use it in her own witchery.

She fell back on the bed, her arms rigid beside her body, close to her sides like the petals of a tight-wrapped rosebud. "Let's be quick about this, then. I've sweetvine to harvest."

"I'll help you with the sweetvine," he said. She snorted. He was as casually brutal as a child when he had anything to do with her plants. His hands were covered by a network of scars, thin white lines that crossed each other like straggling roots. He'd bruise the petals for sure. Nevertheless, she let his voice soothe her. "Sit back, Kella. Lie down on the pallet."

His hands passed over her sides, relaxing her as if she were a fine beeswax taper. She tried not to dwell on the warmth of his flesh. She was getting foolish, here, at the end of her middle passage. She should not let the thought of one boy turn her mind so. The sun would rise soon. The sweet-vine would dry out. She'd lose the petals for the entire year, have to make do with the dried stuff that already hung between the rafters of her cottage. No handsel would pay good coins for potions made solely of dried goods.

"Breathe deeply, Kella. Think of your most soothing herbs. Imagine them strewn upon the pallet. Breathe their scent. Smell them. Taste them at the back of your tongue. Remember, Kella. Remember the peacefulness that comes from your own working, from your own success."

Her own working. What did he presume to know about that? He had never joined with the Sisters. He could not understand her powers as she manipulated her herbs. He could not understand the balance between the fire herbs and ones of ice, between the earth plants and the airy ones.

"Relax, Kella. If you let me guide you, you can visit power you've only dreamed of. Follow my voice. Come with me when you're ready."

Follow his voice. The voice of a man half her age. If she had a son, he would have that voice. But she had never found the time to nurture a child-seed inside her. Her husband had left her because of that. She had been too busy tending her herbs. Her studies. She had been too busy traveling through the woods, meeting with the Sisters. Women like her, like her mother. Old women. Wise women. Women who did not prattle on about meaningless things.

"Kella, you need to let your thinking mind go. Stop counting out the days until the next harvest." Days? Hours! She needed to finish the harvest by the second hour after dawn. This traveling man knew nothing.

"Kella, you have the power to concentrate. I've seen you focus on your workings. Stop resisting what I'm saying, and let yourself travel to the soothing herbs, to the gentle ones." Soothing herbs. As if he could name a single one of them. As if he knew the first thing about her, about her workings.

She sat up on the pallet, pulling away from the gentling hand that he attempted to rest on her arm. "There's no strength in your Speaking, man."

She thought that he would be angry. He had been each other time that she had failed to follow him. This time, though, he only sighed. "I've strength, Kella. Strength enough for every Speaker who has ever come to my players. You've got more power than I, though. You can resist me more than any other I've tried to help."

Tried to help. She had never asked him for assistance. He seemed intent to get her to Speak, to harvest her story like she would harvest some precious herb in the forest. She forced her voice to be light. "I'm not resisting you, traveling man. I've merely got other things on my mind. Other problems. Other goals."

His sigh was deep enough that she cast a worried glance toward him. This was why no man had stayed with her for longer than a season. They tired of not understanding her. They tired of not being able to change her way of thinking. They wanted to redirect her energy toward their own projects, their own goals.

"And what would that be?" he asked, and the question was so wary that he might have been a coney darting from his burrow on a clear summer day.

"First off, harvesting the sweetvine. And since you've delayed me here with your mysterious Speaking, you can help me. We don't have long until the sun will be too high." He could carry the sack, at least. The sack and a water pouch. And a blanket, so that they could be comfortable when they took a break from their labors.

The traveling man rose from the pallet, bowing deeply before her. The fire glinted off his young skin, rippling from the normal array of scars and imperfections that men wore. "Your wish, my lady, is my sole desire."

She heard him slip into his player's tone, and she resisted the urge to tug him back beside her. After all, the sweetvine *might* not be at its height today. It might be best tomorrow. It might be best after she had fallen back on the pallet, after she had pulled him down beside her, after she had acted the part of a younger woman, a loving woman. . . .

She shook her head and made herself laugh out loud. This traveling man was dangerous; he threatened to overturn all that she had learned in her years of witching. "Come along, then. And leave your Speaking games behind."

"As you command, good lady." She scowled at the courtly words, but her disapproval merely let her move faster. She made quick work of shrugging on her overdress and cape and gathering up her close-woven sack. As she struck off down the forest path, she was pleased to hear Tovin's breathing grow sharp beside her. She still had strength left in her. Strength enough to keep ahead of a traveling man.

He remained silent throughout the morning, barely grunting as she indicated the clinging masses of sweetvine, the sticky lengths that needed to be tugged from the southern sides of oak trees. At the first clump, he watched her strip petals into her sack, and then he nodded twice, his eyes squinting into animal-wise slits. Perhaps she had not been fair. Perhaps he knew more than she thought. Or maybe he could learn.

He submitted to her inspection as he stripped his first vine, and he pretended that he did not notice her scrutiny as he attacked the second. He was actually doing a decent job, and she *could* accomplish more if she did not monitor his every move. After all, he was hardly a child; he was a man. The thicket was dense with sweetvine, and Kella knew that she could use it to turn a hearty profit from the village girls, come the boring days of winter. Thrusting down her misgivings, she gave Tovin his own collecting sack, and she began to count out in her mind how much potion she could brew from the sticky double harvest, how many handsels she could turn.

All too soon, the sun rose. The strong light began to pry apart the forest canopy, warming the earth at the base of the oaks. Kella felt the heat spread through the air, making each breath a little heavy.

The sweetvine petals began to shrivel on her fingers. Their dew started to dry, leaving behind an uncomfortable stickiness. Kella redoubled her efforts, determined to strip the last vine on the tree before her. She did not bother heading on to the next one, though. The magic was gone, burned away by the late summer-sun.

Instead, she cinched the mouth of her sack, sealing it closed against the heat's prying fingers. The petals would last fine, in the dark. They'd soak in their own juices, intensify their flavor. If she left them in the sack overnight, they would be even stronger for her potion. She smiled, thinking of the fragrance that would fill her cabin tomorrow afternoon, the heavy aroma of the sweetvine petals boiled down into syrup over long, quiet hours. The labor would be easier with Tovin to help. He would bring her wood, for as long as she needed to feed the flames.

Sighing contentedly, Kella led the way through the forest. They weren't far from the Great Clearing. She and Tovin could relax in the sun there. Perhaps if she let him fall asleep, she could prod him awake from the midst of a dream. Then he would be certain to remember something. Then he would be certain to share.

Kella stopped on the edge of the clearing, astonished by the sight of a platform on the far edge of the field, surrounded by a dozen brightly colored tents. She reached out one hand for Tovin's arm, scarcely managing to bite back her words of warning.

The player, though, strode into the center of the plain, oblivious to the wrongness, utterly unaware that things were not as they should be. "Gali!" he cried, and it took Kella a moment to realize that the strange syllables were the name of a woman, the woman who stood in the middle of the stark wooden platform.

She turned toward Tovin slowly, and Kella could see that she balanced the ends of two fine sticks upon her palms. Thin metal plates sat on top of the sticks. As Kella squinted, she realized that the sticks were spinning, twirling so rapidly that their motion was nearly invisible. The plates whirled on their narrow supports, catching glints of sunlight as if they were butterfly wings.

Gali inclined her head toward Tovin, but then she returned her attention to her sticks. With a studied concentration, she tossed the pole on her left palm to her right, so that the two sticks spun next to each other. The woman took a moment to verify that the plates were still in motion, and then she edged one foot forward. Kella saw that Gali wore strange slippers—odd shoes that curled up over her toes. The herb-witch blinked, and then she realized that the ends of the shoes were actually cloth-stuffed balls.

Gali watched her spinning plates with careful attention, the tip of her tongue caught between her teeth. When she perceived some invisible signal, she kicked forward with her right foot, and the motion tossed the cloth ball into the air. A quick shuffle brought the woman's plate-bearing hand beneath the bauble, and she managed to catch it on top of one of her plates.

She steadied the new configuration—one stick, plate, and ball, another stick and plate. Then she kicked her left foot into the air, sending its ball arcing into the sky.

The kick was too vigorous. Gali lunged for the ball, but it was too far beyond her reach. She stepped back, stilling her hand, steadying the spinning plates. Even that motion proved too extreme, though. The balance was gone. Sticks, plates, and balls came crashing down around her. A torrent of angry curses cut across Gali's lips.

Tovin laughed and reached down for the ball that had dropped off the edge of the wooden platform. He tossed it to the woman easily, nodding as she caught it. "Keep trying," he called. "You'll get the balance eventually."

Gali's eyes flashed fire, and Kella wondered that her traveling man could not see the true anger behind that gaze. Perhaps he did, though. Perhaps he merely laughed at the scarce-banked fury. Perhaps he did not care if a woman raged against him.

Tovin turned toward her with a deep bow, as if he were in the presence of royalty. "Kella Herb-Witch, may I present to you Gali Player."

Kella read the shrewd appraisal in the younger woman's face, realized that she was being measured against all sorts of speculation. *Aye,* she wanted to say. *Your player man has been keeping company with me, me with my grey hair and wrinkled flesh. I find more to entertain him than the spinning of a few plates.* Instead, Kella said, "You should not be here in the Clearing. If the King's Men come this way, they'll drive you away, after charging you kingspence for using the space."

Gali's response was immediate and frosty. "The King's Men will be entertained by my performance, goodwife."

"By throwing around some sticks and plates? If you run your mouth to the King's Men, you'll find yourself in a stone cell in the city." Kella knew that she was right. The king would never tolerate a company of vagabonds. Not here. Not near the groves where the stags ran, the ponds where the swans nested. Certainly not with this construction they had made—a wooden platform in the middle of the living forest.

Kella walked a narrow path inside the woods. She knew that she was mostly tolerated because she hid her presence. Hid her presence, and brewed a tincture or two, some that even found their way into the king's court.

But Kella would not waste time arguing with a child. She turned to Tovin. "You're borrowing trouble."

"We're plying our trade."

"You're trading in another man's market."

"It's not as if we're hunting here. We're practicing, and then we'll go into the city."

"The king will make no distinction! You should realize that. The forest is forbidden to all but nobles, the Clearing most of all." Another thought came to her, one that she suspected would hold more power than her warnings. "If the King's Men get wind of your troop here, they'll likely ride to see who else is in the forest. *All* the others who hide here."

She thought that Tovin would worry for her, that he would hesitate to place her in danger. The name that sprang to his lips, though, belonged to another. "Jalina."

Kella disciplined her face to a passive nod. Whatever it took to remove these invaders from her forest . . . "Jalina," she repeated.

Tovin's eyes narrowed, and he stopped to look at all the people arrayed across the clearing. There were six tents that Kella could see on the grass, and it looked as if a handful more were scattered beneath the canopy on the far side of the clearing. "We'll think about it, then," Tovin said. "Perhaps we'll move to the high road, just outside of the woods."

He looked to Kella, as if to seek her approval. She nodded once, exercising restraint so that she did not turn to Gali, did not gloat to the other woman. Kella had her power. She could best any city girl newly come to the woods.

Just then, one of the players called out to Tovin, summoning him across the grassy field by waving a white parchment scroll. Kella could just make out the ribbons that hung from the edge of the document, royal blue in the morning light. Tovin nodded and strode across the clearing, and the troop of performers gathered around him.

Kella could not hear the words they spoke; they were not

meant for her ears. She saw the scroll raised high, though, and she watched Tovin pore over it, nodding to himself.

She looked away from the knot of adults, and her attention was immediately captured by a cluster of children on the edge of the forest. A mere glance confirmed that these boys and girls belonged to the players' troop—they wore the same bright colors, carried themselves with the identical sense of entitled power.

And they were playing games on the edge of the Great Clearing. Games! Where the King's Men patrolled! Kella started to shake her head, started to cry out to the children, but even before she acted, she knew that she would be ignored.

Instead, she stepped back to watch the children play. A girl took the lead, a tall child with the willowy grace of a young girl soon to be a woman. Kella watched as the creature laughed and ran away from her peers, ran, trailing a white scarf.

Not a scarf, Kella realized. A length of silk. Spidersilk, that strange commodity brought by Tovin to Sarmonia. The fabric drifted on the air, hovering indecisively between floating away forever and settling down to earth.

The girl laughed as she ran, a metallic tinkle like bells whispering in the wind. The sound was infectious; other children laughed as well, and they began to run across the Great Clearing. As Kella watched, a boy trailed a length of cobalt silk, and then a girl ran, crimson floating from her hand.

Soon, the Clearing was full of children—laughing, running children, each followed by a length of silk. Kella's breath caught in her throat as she saw the images they wove, great sweeping circles, tight spins, impossible spirals. The ribbons trailed them as if the silk were some sort of trained beast; it circled in the air, billowing high, darting low.

Kella saw the strength there, the beauty, and a strong emotion rose inside her heart. These children were creating something new in the Great Clearing, something new in the forest. They were making a sort of magic that Kella could only imagine, that an herb-witch could only dream. They were weaving power out of empty air and wisps of cloth.

As Kella watched, she forgot the King's Men. She forgot the sweetvine petals stewing in her sack. She forgot all that she had lived and dreamed, all the lessons she had learned among the Sisters. She remembered only to watch and to breathe and to become the ribbon dance.

"So, you see the patterns."

Tovin's voice beside her made her jump, and she wanted to scream at him, to punish him for pulling her away from the perfection of the silk. She identified her rage, though, named it and shielded herself from it. "Aye," she said, and her voice was raw, as if she had been panting at hard labor for a day and a night.

"They're another of our tricks." Tovin shrugged. "Like Speaking."

Not like Speaking, Kella wanted to say. *Not like Speaking at all. There is true power in the ribbons, true power in the dance.* She shook her head and said, "They're children playing."

"They're players' children."

Kella forced herself to swallow hard and clear her throat. She pushed defiance into her tone, as if she mustn't let the traveling man know how the silk ribbons had affected her. "They'll still be cold and lonely in a Sarmonian prison if the King's Men catch them here."

Tovin laughed, throwing back his head and letting his chestnut curls reflect the sunlight. "You needn't worry about that. My players have just received a writ from King Hamid himself. It seems our reputation precedes us. Sarmonia has invited us to stay at the Great Clearing, to prepare a magnificent show. Come the last day of summer, we'll present ourselves to the court."

Immediately, Kella disbelieved the man. Commoners were not permitted in the Great Clearing, not without the company of the king. Commoners other than Kella, that was. Kella and the Sisters.

But times were changing. Sarmonia was no longer the kingdom she had known, no longer the home that had sheltered her with four familiar walls and a tight-woven roof. "The last day of summer," she said, and her voice scratched over the final word.

"Aye," Tovin agreed, nodding shrewdly. "Not long, now. But long enough. Long enough to do what must be done."

Kella caught the man's gaze drifting past the children, past the breathless ribbon dance. He looked to the edges of the forest, to the darkness beyond the sun-lit field. For a heartbeat, she imagined that his eyes could penetrate to the thicket where Jalina lived, to the northern woman and her hidden son. What exactly did Tovin know about them? Why did he care?

She forced herself to snort in indignation. "Fine, then. Let the children play all day long. I have work to do, at least. I have potions to brew, if I'm to hold off the cold of a long winter's night."

Tovin said nothing as she crossed the clearing, making her way back to her cottage. She resisted the urge to turn about, to see if he was following her. He would come to her soon enough. He would return to her cottage, drawn by the power that he sensed in her, pulled to the lessons she might teach him. And then she would get him to tell her his dreams. She would learn the power in him, the power of the players that she had seen in the children's silken dance.

3

Halaravilli ben-Jair looked down the forest path and choked back the urge to bellow in frustration. This was not how he had planned things. This was not how he had imagined his life would be. He was supposed to be home in Moren, looking out at his groves of riberry trees, counting the riches of his octolaris spider venture. He was supposed to be standing beside his wife, gazing fondly at his children as they romped about the royal garden. He was supposed to reign in peace and prosperity, leading his people to riches they had never imagined in the days of his most worthy ancestors.

But Hal's dreams had shattered long ago—even before the loss of his heirs, even before soldiers had driven him from his homeland. His dreams had been destroyed when an arrow took his older brother, when he was required to set aside his tin soldiers and command real men of flesh and blood. Flesh that could be torn. Blood that could flow.

Blood that had flowed within the very House of the Thousand Gods.

Blood flow. Body blow. Bitter foe.

Once again, Hal's mind was assaulted by the frantic confusion of those dark moments in the secret passage beneath the altar. He could recall the sound of his men fighting on the cathedral floor above him, the stench of smoke and blood and ruin as they paid their lives to protect him. He had huddled with his advisors for endless heartbeats before someone—Farso? Mair? even now it wasn't clear—began to lead them through the darkness, down the hidden passage, beneath the city streets, out to the abandoned First Port on the edge of the city's oldest section.

Hal had fought against his advisors, then. He had argued that he could not flee Moren, could not abandon his city when rampaging armies roamed her streets. He had vowed to massacre the Briantans, promised to destroy the Liantines.

His loyal men would hear nothing of it, though. They hurried him onto a low-slung boat and threw a cape over his shoulders to deceive a harbor master who proved to be absent from his duty post. All of them ignored him—Puladarati, Farso, even Rani Trader.

Only when they were out of the harbor, bobbing on the open sea, could Hal look back at the horror behind him, at the rising smoke. The black clouds saturated his senses as completely as they blotted out the sky. He could not look at his loyal followers; he could not listen to them. He scarcely heard Farso muttering oaths of revenge. He barely made out Father Siritalanu tolling the names of the Thousand, asking for their mercy and their guidance. He was barely aware of Puladarati roaring defiance, bellowing like an injured lion as he watched Briantans swarm the streets.

The loudest sound, though, the clearest voice, was Mair's—Mair's mad chatter as she narrated events to the square of black silk around her wrist. So many lives gone, so much traded for so little . . .

In the end, only Rani had been able to persuade him to leave the railing. She had turned his head away forcibly, guiding him down the steep, narrow stairs to the hold. She had handed him over to his squire and told him that he must shed his royal robes, that he must burn those clothes, now, before they could incriminate him. She had told him to be strong.

And he had listened to her. He had begun to plan, even before the sun had set on that first dark day of banishment. He had gathered up the ship's charts and its maps. He had led his puny army in long strategy sessions as the boat rocked back and forth, as he forbade himself from imagining the ruins of his capital.

Hal had balanced safety and speed, calculated security and strength. Ultimately, he convinced them that they should head for Sarmonia, for the southern kingdom that had so far stayed uninvolved in Moren's brutal politics.

Sarmonia was a risk, of course. It was no accident that King Hamid had removed himself from the fights among his northern neighbors. He plied trade with Liantine, but he had almost no connections to the distant Briantans. In the past few years, he had begun to purchase spidersilk from Hal, gladly undermining his own costly bonds to the original spiderguild. But would he take up arms against Liantine's bellicose house of Thunderspear? Would he set his own kingdom on the line?

Amid the uncertainty, Hal convinced his followers that they could not approach Hamid directly. They should avoid the great Sarmonian coastal cities altogether, put in at some village on the shore, or better yet, an unprotected natural port. They should make their way across the land slowly, carefully, sending out their own messengers to gather information, to sense Hamid's will before they forced his hand.

And so it had been done. The soldiers who had rescued Hal in the Morenian cathedral proved competent seamen, purposely beaching their shallow boat along a stretch of deserted coastline. Reluctantly, Hal had helped to stave in the bottom, had watched water seep up between the well-caulked planks. Retreat by sea became impossible.

Hal had led his men into the great forest that spread across the northern third of Sarmonia. He tried to make a game of it, keeping up his followers' spirits by acting as if they were on an extended hunt, making merry in the woods as a sort of late-summer play. He used his maps to measure out paths through the forest, to trace the ancient roads that passed beneath the wooded canopy.

All the time, he maneuvered his men closer to his true destination, knowing that he was creating a new danger even as he sought to ease the fear deepest in his heart. Mareka hid inside the Sarmonian woods. His wife and son were safe within the forest. That much Hal knew from a lone messenger who had made his way back to Morenia during brighter days, in a more hopeful time.

If Hal's men wondered at his familiarity with the maps, if they questioned how he knew the woodland paths, they did not speak of their suspicions. Instead, they followed his lead, acting for all the world as if they were celebrating a prolonged feast day of the gods. They managed to ignore the fact that they set a guard at night, that Mair prowled about the camp like a mad ghost, that Rani Trader watched and waited, silently assessing their progress.

And Hal listened to the voices growing inside his mind, the despairing voices that he thought he had silenced, once in Amanthia, then again in Liantine. He knew the seductive power of their rhymes, understood the singsong power of their chants. They pulled him deeper into himself, into his sorrow, into his fear. They made him less a king and more a mortal man. They cut him off and left him lonely and afraid.

Afraid for his life. Afraid for his wife. Afraid of a knife.

A knife, or a sword, or a vial of poison. The Fellowship could find him here, or Briantans could, or Liantines, even the good loyal men of King Hamid. All could bear death.

Hal ran his palms down the rough clothes that he had donned on the ship, that he had worn every day since arriving in Sarmonia. The doeskin was well tanned, for which he was grateful. The breeches were neatly cut, as if the hunter who had worn them before him had been his twin. The jerkin was loose enough that he could move with ease, and yet it felt protective. It had not saved the deer that gave it, of course, but it might keep him secure a while longer.

"Sire!"

Hal knew the voice before he even turned around. "Rani."

"The men are gathered for their midday meal, Sire."

"Have them eat, then."

"They will not. Not until you join them."

It was some blasted conspiracy, he knew, some plot to save him from the whispering creatures inside his own mind. Whether the cabal was led by Rani or by Farso, or most likely of all, by Puladarati, it had worked so far. He was responsible for his men. They demanded leadership of him; they dragged him out from the dark places deep in his own thoughts. After all, how could a good king let his loyal men go hungry?

I'm not a good king, Hal wanted to say. I can't be that leader. I can't be that man.

Instead, he turned to Rani and forced a smile, hoping that she would understand if it was somewhat wan. "Let us go, then."

The men were gathered in the center of the small clearing. They had built rough sheds on the edges of the woods, using fallen limbs for walls and woven leaves for ceilings. The shelters would never suffice in the winter, but for the summer, they were good enough.

Immediately upon arriving in Sarmonia, Father Siritalanu had assumed responsibility for cooking for the party—on their first day in the clearing, he had pulled the grass free from a circle in the precise center of the field. He tended his fire with the devotion of a fanatic, managing a pair of tripods and their matching cauldrons. The man was a fair hand at stews, and he had managed to grill a string of river trout the night before without losing a single one to the flames.

"My lord!" called out one of his soldiers. The men were not calling him "Sire" here, and certainly not "Your Majesty," not while they were assuming the guise of mere hunting companions. Nevertheless, the informality reminded Hal of all that he had lost, all that he had left behind. Not that he had ever craved being called king, not that he had ever wished for the title . . .

He started to grimace a reply, but Rani stepped closer to him. She spoke in a low voice: "They need you, my lord. Be their leader."

She was right. He knew that. He must be the man that they could respect. He must be the one that they could look up to, that they could honor with their lives. Only if he remained worthy were the deaths of their comrades justified. Only if he were a great king did the lost Morenian lives have meaning.

Hal forced a smile and gestured about the clearing, making sure that his motion was expansive enough to include all the men. "What have we here? Some sort of broth, by the smell of it. There looks to be enough for me, but what will the rest of you eat?"

The feeble jest was appreciated. Puladarati nodded once from across the clearing, and Hal felt a rebellious flare of pleasure. Of course he knew how to lead his men. Of course he knew what was right.

He filled his wooden bowl from the cauldron, consciously striking a jaunty pose in his doeskin breeches. "Thank you, Father," he said. "This smells as good as any fare I've eaten from the royal kitchens." Siritalanu's face was flushed from the fire, and his color deepened at the compliment.

As had become his custom during their stay, Hal stalked across the clearing and settled on a fallen log. The unusually smooth trunk did double duty as both table and chair. He was not surprised when Puladarati came to join him, balancing his own bowl in his three-fingered hand. "The men were worried about you, my lord."

"I was not far. I went down the path to find some quiet, some space to think. They could have heard me, if I'd called for help."

"They're more comfortable if they can see you."

"They're afraid I might disappear, stolen away by wood sprites? That would make this entire adventure unnecessary, wouldn't it? They'd all be free to return home."

Puladarati did not laugh at the grim joke. Instead, he set

down his bowl and leaned closer to his king. "They don't want to go home, my lord. Not without you. Not without a crown upon your head and an army at your back."

Hal tried to look away from the old general's commanding gaze. "I know that."

"I don't think you do. I don't think you realize what you mean to these men. They chose to do this. Back in Moren, when things grew grim, they came to me. They volunteered for service, based only on the growing rumor of threats against you. When we first learned that the Liantines and Briantans planned to attack together, those men purchased a boat. They obtained the charts. They paid off the harbor master to escape Morenia. They love you, Halaravilli ben-Jair, and they will fight to see you returned to your rightful home. With them. Not without."

"I know that!" Hal said again, and he looked away in hope that Puladarati would not see what the admission cost him. Of course he knew that men would die for him. He also knew that he was not worthy of that sacrifice. He was not worthy of that price, not worthy of the lives that had already been spilled out on the cathedral floor, in the Moren streets, at the city gates and in the waters of its harbor.

"Then act as if you know it!" Puladarati insisted, sounding for all the world as if he were once again Hal's regent, once again a strict disciplinarian bent on bringing his rebellious young charge into line. "Talk to them! Guide them! Give them some assurance that you have a plan, that all will be well in the end!"

"And if I don't? If I don't have the least idea of how I'm going to get us out of this forest and back home?"

Puladarati gazed at him steadily. "Act as if you do, Sire."

Sire. Father. Leader of all these men, all of Moren, all of Morenia. "Act as if you do. You might begin now."

With that, Puladarati glanced up, seeming to discover by chance a newcomer on the edge of their conversation. "Ah! Davin! Come and join us!"

Hal did not have an opportunity to gainsay his advisor, did not have the chance to escape from Davin. Instead, the old man hobbled over to the trunk. Hal stood instinctively, reaching out to steady the ancient retainer's arm, to ease him down to sit. As always, Hal was captivated by the wrinkles on Davin's face, by the gulleys etched deep beside his eyes, flowing into his long, tangled beard.

There was a tattoo carved high upon his cheekbone, a mark that had been given him when he was born in the distant kingdom of Amanthia. No one could read that symbol now, could decipher it from the deep lines of age. Not for the first time, Hal wondered if Davin had been marked as a worker—a sun—or if he had been labeled a thinker—an owl. He might have been a soldier—a lion—or even a leader—a swan. Status and history were long lost on the ancient man's face, in the years and years and nearly endless years of his life.

"Come, Davin. Eat with us and tell us what you've learned today in strange Sarmonia."

"I've learned that an old man's food will grow cold if he shares all his knowledge with the young."

Well, thought Hal. *Here's another man who does not hold me in awe.* "Drink your broth, then. Drink, and listen to me while you chew whatever roots our good father has added to the pot."

Davin grunted and raised a spoon to his lips.

Hal said, "Here's the problem, as I see it. You've spent

the past six years strengthening my capital, securing Moren's walls, protecting her against invasion. You forged a chain to block her port, and you belted her gates with iron. You increased the guards upon her walls, and the stations where they could shelter. You had my soldiers dig a moat on the landward plain, and you diverted seawater to fill it. You created stone spikes and sank them in the harbor, and you crafted the machinery to raise them up again, to pen enemy ships at will."

Davin shoved a partly chewed bit of food into his cheek and nodded. His eyes were midnight dark, but a shadow of pride lurked in the downward curve of his lips as he said, "Aye, I've done all that."

"And now you must undo it. Now you must devise a way for us to break past those defenses and regain our homeland."

"Your enemies now hold all that I built."

Hal fought against his immediate angry reply—those enemies would not have succeeded if Davin had done his job well enough. "*Our* enemies"—he gave strong emphasis to the first word—"have broken through some of those strengths. Now we must defeat the others. Now we must find our way back to fair Moren, liberate her."

Davin downed another spoonful of broth, acting for all the world as if he had not heard his king. He stared across the clearing, blinking hard. He grimaced at two of the younger soldiers, snorting at their horseplay as they fought for extra rations.

"Did you hear your king, man?" Puladarati prompted at last.

"Aye, I heard him." Davin swallowed. "I heard him, but

he has no idea what he's saying. I built those defenses to keep all men out."

"Then you failed!" Hal said, before Puladarati could stop him. "Or maybe you did not notice the Briantans who stormed our gate? Maybe you forgot about the Liantines who blockaded our harbor?"

"No defenses are perfect. I told you at the time that men enough and time enough would break the iron gates."

"The city was taken by soldier-priests from Brianta! Not hardened warriors! Not trained fighting men!"

Davin pinned Hal with shadowed eyes, with a gaze so dark that Hal could not distinguish pupil from iris. "The city was conquered by traitors, and you know it. The city was conquered by your Holy Father Dartulamino, who opened the gates, or had them opened. The city was conquered by fools."

Conquered by fools. Treacherous tools. Blood stood in pools.

Hal's anger crashed against his self-condemnation, against the nagging echoes of his own failure that had chased him ever since he left Morenia. Like a blind man familiar with a smooth path, he repeated the litany of his mistakes: He should have realized the danger before it struck. He should have determined that the Fellowship would move against him. He should have known that Holy Father Dartulamino would rise up, would sell him out to the Briantans, the Liantines, to anyone!

As if Puladarati could read the raging accusations inside Hal's mind, the leonine councilor gave him a stern glance before saying, "Very well, then, Davin. The city was taken by fools. We're all wise men here. We're all brave. Tell us how we can take it back. Fashion a solution for us."

"Wise!" Davin snorted.

Hal felt a stout stick break across the rigid back of his control, a flash of anger and frustration sharper than he had felt since before the aborted War Rites in the cathedral. "Silence, old man!" He sprang to his feet and pointed a shaking finger at Davin, barely aware that Puladarati was jumping up to match his stance. "Loyal men died for me back there! They were not fools. They were not cowards. They were victims of a circumstance they did not choose, one they could not have predicted! They were men who were true to me, true to the house of ben-Jair, true to Moren and what she has stood for throughout all history."

The words rushed into Hal's head, tumbled out of his mouth. They were hotter than the broth that Davin drank, hotter than the raging tears that Hal had smothered since his escape, hotter than the doubts that whispered behind his every thought. "Years ago, you came to us in shame, old man, having aided one of our greatest enemies. We took you in because we are merciful, and we fed you and we clothed you. We gave you a room to work in and supplies and assistants, all so that your old age would be comfortable. We looked to you as a confidant, as a companion, as a vassal."

Hal's anger annealed into something new, something rigid, something stronger than all his years of self-doubt. He filled his lungs and braced himself against that rage, steady, firm, confident for the first time since he had fled to Sarmonia. "We expected great things from you, Davin of Amanthia. We expected you to serve us until the end of your days. You may not now walk away like a child who is tired of a game. You may not abandon us like a craven, a coward. You *will* find a way for us to return home. You *will* find a way for us to enter Moren. You *will* find a way for us to liberate our city and free our people and regain the crown and throne that are rightfully ours."

A hot breeze whipped across the clearing, carrying the smell of a wood fire. Suddenly, Hal realized that his entire company was staring at him. Every voice was silent, every mouth open.

Embarrassed, Hal returned his attention to Davin. The old man gazed at him as well, a curious light in his bottomless eyes. Hal expected anger. He expected rebellion. He expected a sullen refusal to cooperate.

Instead, he found respect.

For a heartbeat, anyway, and then that emotion was replaced by Davin's usual hint of a smile, by the sardonic attitude he affected when he wanted most to annoy his liege. "As you command, my lord."

Hal nodded once, accepting the agreement as if it were the most natural thing in the world. Then he turned his attention to Puladarati. "Tell the men to finish their meals. We'll organize a hunting party for the afternoon, give them something to do."

"Aye, my lord." Hal heard the emotion, even though he could not see it on his retainer's face. He heard scarce-smothered laughter, and he knew that Puladarati was pleased with him. With him? Or with Davin? What did it matter? The old man had agreed to explore options to regain Moren, and the company would bring them fresh meat. More than that, no one could ask of a banished, endangered king.

Hal waited until the moon had risen before he ducked outside his tent. A guard ghosted up to him immediately, whispering, "My lord?"

"Nothing, Litanalo." He gestured to the forest with a matter-of-fact wave of his hand. "I'll be back in a moment."

"I'll come with you, my lord."

"No need. Keep watch over the camp here." Hal put enough steel into his voice that the suggestion became a command. The soldier was clearly reluctant, but he yielded.

Hal disappeared into the fringe of the forest, but he did not pause to tug down his doeskin breeches. Instead, he cast his head from side to side, checking for the faint path that led away from the clearing. By daylight, the earth showed, but at night, he needed to rely on the shadows of tree branches, the memory of having passed this way three times before in the fortnight that his men had hidden in the southern forest.

Three times . . . Hal had treasured those stolen moments more than anything he had enjoyed back at court. They had almost made his flight and hiding in the woods worthwhile. They had almost redeemed the betrayal of Dartulamino, of his troops at his own city's gates. Such was the power of an infant, the power of an heir.

There—the two oak trees that grew together, like twins joined in the womb. Hal ducked behind them and found the shadow of the last trail through the woods. There was a whiff of stagnant water from a pond that had overflowed its banks. His feet caught in mud for an instant, but he was close to running now, eager, desperate to be at his destination.

A fallen tree rested across a fast-running stream, already looking as if it had lain there for decades, even though Hal knew it had been set in place less than a year before. He eased across it, aware that the bark would be slippery with dew. He passed the large stand of ferns and then the crumbling stone remains of some ancient gamekeeper's hut. Under a falling arch, around a bend in the trail, back to another loop of the stream, the water moving even faster here, cutting deeper into the forest floor. A few steps forward. A few more, and—

"Halt!" The command was barked into the air, loud and fearless. Hal splayed his hands by his sides, resisting the urge to reach for his sword, to slip his fingers into his boot for the dagger hidden there. "Who dares disturb the sleep of Lady Jalina?"

"Her lord and husband," Hal said wryly, taking a step back so that the moon would better light his face.

"Si— My lord!"

The guard fumbled with his greeting, and Hal could read the man's intention to drop to one knee. With a regal wave of his hand, he dismissed the formality and asked, "Is my lady still awake?"

"Of course, my lord." The voice came from beyond the guard, a woman's voice, husky in the night. Hal doubted that Mareka had been awake before her guard had shouted out his alarm, but she was now.

The guard disappeared into the darkness, and Hal stepped toward his queen. He brushed a kiss against her cheek, oddly discomfited by the thought that others must be watching them; soldiers must be observing their every move by moonlight. Mareka merely cocked her head to one side, and then she took him by the hand, leading him into the hut that was built into the riverbank.

It never failed to surprise him when she touched him. He could still remember the moment in Liantine when she had first come to his chamber, when she had taken off her shawl and overwhelmed him with the power of her octolaris nectar. The antidote to spider poison was strong, a danger in its own right, and Hal had been swiftly snared.

Not that Mareka wasn't attractive without such means. The Liantine woman was slight, dark, apparently as vulnerable as a child. Hal knew, though, that she was stronger than he had ever been. She had manipulated him to her own ends, first in her homeland of Liantine, then in her adopted land of Morenia. She had found the strength to cremate four infant corpses. She had stood unyielding when an entire kingdom demanded that he set her aside, when all his people cried out against her guildsman birthright and her flawed womb.

Mareka was no child. She was born to the spiderguild and accustomed to identifying the needs of the wealthy—identifying those needs and filling them, no matter what the cost.

Hal nearly shook his head, surprised that he still thought of his wife in such mercenary terms. Mercenary? Or merely accurate? Surely she had manipulated him when first they met. Surely she had played him falsely. But that was three years past, nearly four. Now she was the mother of his son. The mother of his heir.

"Marekanoran?" he asked, as breathless as the naif who had once succumbed to Mareka's octolaris-enhanced charms.

"Here." Mareka closed the rounded door behind them and took up the rushlight she had set in an alcove. She moved across the room with confidence; this was her home for now, her refuge, and she moved as if she were in her apartments in the royal palace.

Hal followed, his heart beating faster. He wondered if Mareka was playing with nectar even here, but then he saw the cradle, and he knew that there was no evil here, no manipulative potion. He was merely excited to see his only living child, the son who would carry his name down through the ages.

"He's grown!"

"Aye." Mareka bent down and lifted the boy, oblivious to his fussing as she folded his swaddling around him. She touched a fingertip to his nose, brushed imaginary fluff from his brow. "He eats and sleeps—that's a recipe for growth."

"He's sleeping well, then? You said that he was restless when last I visited."

"I found a potion to help with that. It's making him stronger, too."

A warning pricked behind Hal's ears. "A potion?"

"It's nothing, really. An old wive's cure. You needn't worry."

Old wives. Those would be the herb-witches that Mareka had consulted, the women who had conspired to help her bear this son. Disdain brought hot words to his lips, sneers that any Morenian noble would cast upon such superstitious creatures.

But what right did he have to suspect them? How could he challenge the herb-witches when they had done what his own medics could not, what his own priests had failed to do? The witches had given him a living heir, and he would forever be in their debt.

Nevertheless, he feared whatever brew Mareka was feeding Marekanoran, worried that the draft might carry some subtle poison.

As if to forestall argument, Mareka offered him the bundle of cloth. Automatically, he stepped back. His hands suddenly seemed too large, too awkward, and he knew that he would trip over his own toes if he took a single step. The cloth would slip away from him, the child would squirm when he least expected it.

A tiny smile quirked Mareka's lips. She understood him. She understood his fears, and yet she would not ridicule him, not when he merely thought to protect his child, *their* child. She gestured for him to sit in the chair beside her fire, a sturdy three-legged stool with a stark frame back. He complied and held out his hands.

The child weighed more than he had before—what was it, five days past? Or did Hal misremember his own son? The boy squirmed as Hal took him, sleepily stretching amid his soft swaddling. Hal quickly lowered the baby to his own joined knees, intent on balancing the precious burden, protecting him, keeping him safe from harm.

Marekanoran's eyes flew open, as if he were surprised by the strange touch. Hal's gaze met his son's, and he felt a shock of recognition, a rush of power. This was his heir. This was the child who would carry the ben-Jair blood into the future. This was the son who would cap the meaning of his life, the meaning of his father's life, and all his fathers before him. Pride swelled inside Hal's throat, crushing tears against his eyes. Pride, and love, and a great, glorious sense of righteous power.

"He's doing well, Mareka."

"Aye." He heard the smile in her voice. "Ah! There! He's awake now!"

Her announcement was accompanied by the infant opening his mouth, gathering in air as if he were determined to live on breath alone. Then he began to squall, the sound echoing off the earthen ceiling in the close room.

Frantic, Hal tried to gather up the baby, but his motions were awkward, and the boy began to slip from his knees.

Hal started to speak to the child, trying to calm him, but he knew the boy would not understand any words. He was an infant, after all, a helpless, senseless creature.

The sound grew louder, more forceful, and Hal cast a nervous look to the ceiling above them. It was plastered, and it looked secure, but it might crumble at the assault.

"Mareka!" he started to cry, but she was already moving forward, already lifting the baby, already clicking with her maternal tongue, cooing in a soft voice that Hal had never heard her use before.

As soon as the child was taken from him, Hal sprang to his feet. "Is he all right? Did I do something wrong? Did I hurt him?"

"He's fine," Mareka said, taking the stool that Hal had vacated. She balanced the baby with one hand as she reached for the carefully draped neck of her gown. "He's only hungry."

Hal could feel the blood rising in his face as his wife bared her breast to their child. He knew that her actions were only natural, that mothers throughout Sarmonia, throughout Morenia, throughout all the known world, fed their children. All babes suckled. And yet, he wanted to open up the argument again; he wanted to demand that Mareka have a wet nurse.

And she would have, if they were back in Moren. She would have, if he had made his kingdom safe for her. She would have, if the Fellowship were not howling for her death, for Marekanoran's murder, if war were not whistling about them. His blush of embarrassment turned to one of anger—raw fury at himself.

Before he could vent that rage, before he could offer up

yet another round of promises, of apologies, the door to the cottage glided open. "Sire!" called a familiar voice.

A familiar voice, but the title was unfamiliar, here in these foreign woods. Hal stepped forward automatically, blocking the newcomer's view of the hearth, of Mareka. "Yes, Farso?" He did not even try to keep his puzzlement from his voice. How had the nobleman known that he was here? How had he been permitted into the protected sphere of Mareka's camp?

"You are needed back in the clearing, Your Majesty."

"Farso, we've agreed that no titles—"

"Aye. And as soon as we set foot outside this refuge, I'll call you naught but 'my lord.' For now, though, you must come with me."

"What's wrong?" Hal cast his thoughts ahead, wondering what had happened, despairing of how he would react.

"King Hamid's men. They've found us."

Hal cursed. He had thought he might have a little more time to get settled, a little more time to structure a plan. He was not yet ready to bring his case before Hamid of Sarmonia, not yet ready to plead his hopeless cause. *Alas,* he thought, *a beggar cannot choose the time of his meals.* "Very well, Farso. I'll join you in a moment."

The nobleman bowed like the courtier he'd trained to be, and he whispered the door closed. Hal turned back to his wife and son. "I must leave, then."

"Aye."

"You'll be safe enough. Once I can get Hamid alone, I'll explain to him, tell him why we're here, tell him about you."

"Say nothing about me for now. Marekanoran and I, we're safer with no one knowing that we're here."

"No one but the herb witches, you mean?" The question

was more bitter than he intended, and anger sparked immediately in Mareka's eyes. "No," he said quickly. "No need to explain. No need to justify. I'll see what Hamid knows. I'll tell him only if I must."

"He might be a member of your Fellowship."

Hal's jaw tightened involuntarily. "Aye, he might, at that."

"I won't trust that lot with our son."

Hal thought of the grieving man who waited for him outside the door, of the child that Farso had lost to the Fellowship's machinations. "Neither will I, my lady."

"Go safely, then. May Arn watch over you."

Courage, she bade him. She knew him well, for all that they had started as strangers to each other, four years before in Liantine. "Be well," he said. "I'll come to see you when I may. May Nome protect you."

He wanted to take his son again, wanted to hold that tiny body one last time. He knew the child would fuss, though, would start to wail again. If danger did walk the woods that night, silence was Marekanoran's greatest ally. Hal settled for leaning toward his wife, for brushing a kiss in the air above her head. He forced himself to meet her eyes, to register the strange mixture of her pity and sorrow and raging frustrated helplessness. "Be well," he repeated, and then he ducked outside.

He waited until they were back to the twinned oaks before he spoke to Farso. "How did you know that I was here?"

"I followed you." The answer was stated simply, as if it were the most natural of replies in the world. "Tonight, and the other times that you've visited."

"I told the guard that I'd be back."

"And if you'd taken this long just to relieve yourself, the guard would do us all a favor by setting a knife in your back. Rid Morenia of a king well aged before his time." Hal cast a quick glance at his former squire, who gave a toothy grin as if his words were jokes. There was a wildness about his expression, though, a gleam in his eyes that reminded Hal of a warhorse crazed on the edge of battle. The old Farso would never have jested about murdering a king, would never have imagined the words, much less spoken them aloud.

"Who else knows that my lady is there?"

"No one," Farso said quickly. "No one knows of her or . . . her companion." Even as the man swallowed the baby's name, Hal saw rage tighten a muscle in his cheek. Farso had not forgiven the animals who had executed his son. His fury burned hotter now than when he first had learned the bitter news; the passing months had served only to teach him the full weight of his loss. The nobleman must have felt Hal's eyes upon his face, for he stopped his crashing progress along the path and faced his liege lord full on. "No one knows of them, and they'll not find out from me. I swear that on the memory of Laranifarso."

There were no more binding words in Farso's vocabulary. Hal sighed. Time enough, after the immediate crisis, to learn when Farso had first followed him through the woods. First things first. "Tell me, then. How many of Hamid's men have found us?"

"Our outer guard reported in and said there were a dozen of them. They seem to be riding standard patrol through the woods. We don't think they were looking for us in particular."

Hal's heart sank, though. "They'll have gathered up the others, by now. My men will be paying for my absence."

"Give them more credit than that, my lord." Farso's teeth flashed in the moonlight. "When we first learned that the soldiers approached, we scattered. Hamid's men will have to track each of us separately through the woods; they might not even start until daylight. You and I will be brought in with the others, as if we'd been in the camp when the warning came."

"A good plan, Farso. Yours?"

"No, my lord. Rani Trader's." Farso tossed his head to the side, his silvered hair glinting. "You know that I can make no plans. I am crazed by my grief, after all, scarcely able to serve my liege lord."

Hal tumbled over a half-dozen responses, all the time thinking of his son's weight in his arms, of the overwhelming emotion that had welled up in him as he looked inside the babe's eyes. How had Farso borne it? How had he stood learning that his child had been sacrificed on the Fellowship's unholy altar?

"Let us join the pack, then, Farso. Let us face King Hamid and explain that we are worthy trespassers in his forest. And then we'll start to build the road back to Moren."

"To Moren," Farso repeated. "And to the bloody death of every one of her enemies." The nobleman licked his lips in the moonlight, savoring his vow like a wolf lapping up a lamb's fresh blood.

4

Rani Trader shifted her weight from her right foot to her left, trying to shrug her shoulders into a more comfortable position. The soldiers who had lashed her hands behind her back had been grimly professional, and the ropes had had plenty of time to cut into the flesh at her wrists. That stinging was only compounded by the burning of overstretched muscles at her shoulders.

Nevertheless, she told herself to forget her discomfort and focus on the room around her. Located at the center of the city of Riadelle, King Hamid's receiving hall was a vast cavern, long and low, with few windows to relieve the gloom. Rani had walked the length of it, trying to keep her face impassive. She refused to be impressed by the throne room of a southern monarch. She refused to be overwhelmed by a gathering of his retainers.

Apparently, this was the day when King Hamid held court—there were numerous noblemen scattered about the hall, swathed in fine robes of satin and velvet. There were others present as well, a group of merchants by the look of them, a handful of farmers, and a clutch of guildsmen whispering heatedly in a knot at the edge of the room.

At least the great hall was cool in the heat of the midday

sun. That might have been what King Hamid's ancestors had counted on when they constructed the cavernous chamber. The walls were obviously thick; the late-summer heat was banished to the sunny outdoors. The weather would already be autumn cool back in Morenia. Rani shook her head, wishing that she could rub at the crust of sweat salt on her brow.

The motion let her get a good glimpse of her fellow prisoners. Mair stood beside her, also cruelly lashed. The woman had fought like a wild beast when the soldiers pulled her arms back; she had struck out with her fists and landed a few solid kicks. Rani knew that Mair's desperation was centered on her square of black silk; if the cloth were taken from her line of sight she would go mad. Mercifully, one of the soldiers came to understand Mair's obsession; he slipped the ragged square into her belt and was ribbed by his fellows for taming the northern she-beast.

The other Morenians had submitted more gently; they knew that they had violated the law by prowling in the forest, and they trusted to their liege lord to make all right. Hal had been one of the last men rounded up. Rani wondered how he had managed to get so far from the camp, whether he had thought to elude the Sarmonians altogether, or if he had some other plan. He acted strangely once he was brought back to his men, and he refused to meet her eyes. Farso was no help; he had clearly been brought in with Hal, but he remained silent as he looked out at his captors, merely running his tongue over his lips like a great panting dog.

Very well, Rani thought, glancing about King Hamid's chamber. First things first. Tally up the resources. Like any good merchant, she set about calculating the goods she had at her disposal.

First, Halaravilli was a king; he could argue that he was present as an ambassador from Morenia, and that he should be accorded all the perquisites of that position.

Second, the men with him were nobles, and they had not actually hunted stag or swan while they camped in the woods. They had not technically violated the Sarmonian laws.

Third . . . Rani stretched her mind around the facts, struggling to name a third advantage. There was nothing she could think of, nothing more that she could offer up to argue for mercy and kindness from the Sarmonian court.

Rani swallowed a sigh. Well, perhaps Hal had a plan where she had none. Perhaps he had calculated some other escape. That might be the meaning of his strange silence, his apparent refusal to step forward and demand Hamid's appearance, demand like a king to present his cause to a peer.

Any further speculation was cut short by a flurry of activity at the far end of the hall. A pair of young pages entered the room, resplendent in royal blue tunics trimmed in gold. Behind them came an honor guard of a dozen soldiers, men clearly chosen for their size and strength. In fact, the guards looked as if they might all be brothers, so similar was their coloring, their stance, their grim pomp.

A clutch of noblemen followed the guards, five men wearing robes encrusted with jewels. Rani saw that two of them wore their coats of arms quartered with the king's stag; they were married into the royal house then. All of the arms were charged with a strange device, a scroll overlaid with a swan's plume.

Another page entered the audience hall before Rani could

parse the meaning, a child carrying a pillow larger than his head. On the cushion rested a crown, an ornate circlet of gilded leaves and entwined golden branches that glinted balefully across the room. A second page carried a similar pillow, but his burden was a lead-framed glass orb.

Under other circumstances, Rani might have wondered about the globe. She might have questioned its provenance and the workmanship that had gone into its construction. She might have studied the lines of lead, learned from their placement, calculated how to better them. Now, though, the blatant statement of worldly power merely annoyed Rani. She wanted to see the man who possessed such a treasure, the man who had kept the Morenians waiting like common prisoners.

And she was not disappointed. King Hamid of Sarmonia ended the procession, sweeping into the room with the confidence of a man who knows he owns a kingdom. He was younger than she expected—perhaps only ten years older than Hal. Tall and lean, he was so slender that Rani sensed a master seamstress's hand at work in his robes, garments that conspired to make him appear majestic. His short hair was jet-black with only a whisper of grey at his temples, and he had groomed his sable beard into a cruel point. His mustache was perfectly trimmed to accent his lips; his stark cheekbones were sharp as a hawk's wings. His eyes squinted at the assembled crowd as if he were taking the measure of all those present.

Rani nodded to herself. She knew men like King Hamid, men who were accustomed to bargaining for what they wanted, negotiating for all that they desired. She had bested such men in the past, in the Morenian marketplace, in the world of royal politics. She could do so again.

The youngest page stepped forward and announced to the crowd: "All bow before King Hamid, elected ruler of Sarmonia! Let those who have business before him seek His Majesty's counsel, and may all the Thousand Gods watch over the happenings here today."

Elected ruler of Sarmonia . . . Rani had heard rumors of this kingdom's strange customs, of how the nobles all gathered together and selected a man to rule over them for the duration of his life, unless the nobility demanded another vote. How could a kingdom function with such instability? How could it survive the passage from one king to another without knowing who the heir might be?

Even as she questioned the strange Sarmonian custom, a niggling thought tickled Rani's mind. Hal might have been a stronger king if he had not needed to secure his dynasty with a son. He could have devoted his attention to his kingdom, to its needs, rather than struggling to quiet the outcries against Mareka, the voices that demanded he set his childless queen aside. Perhaps the Sarmonians were not as odd as Rani had first imagined. . . .

She had no further chance to speculate, for King Hamid ascended to the platform at the end of the room. He took his throne with a flourish, spreading his robes so that they framed him, adding to the impression of his bulk. Once again, Rani was struck by a man who understood how to work with the resources that he had, how to structure positive results from apparent shortcomings.

"At ease, electors, honored lords, my guests," King Hamid said. His voice was higher than Rani had expected, a sweet tenor that floated across the room with a musical lilt. He did not back up his cushioned command with any physical threat, and yet Rani could imagine his tone turning razor sharp, leveling against his assembled nobles, against those who sued in his court. "We understand that there is a matter to be dealt with before our petty court today, a matter of intruders in the northern forest."

"Aye, Your Majesty." The leader of the guards who had surrounded the Morenians stepped forward and bowed to his king, touching his forehead to his knee in his apparent eagerness to flatter.

"And you are?"

"Baliman, Your Majesty. Baliman of the northern watch, and a landed man."

Rani watched King Hamid acknowledge the name; he seemed to sit a little straighter at the final claim. A landed man? What difference could that make?

"Very well, good Baliman. Tell me what you have found."

"These intruders were encamped in the northern forest, in an unnamed clearing just east of the Oaken Trail. They cleared a fire circle in the center of the grass, and they built shelters. We found evidence that they were fishing in your streams, Your Majesty, and that they scavenged in the forest."

"And did you find that they hunted?"

"Not for stag, Your Majesty."

"And did they disturb the lakes?"

"Not that we could tell, Your Majesty. We found no evidence of swans in their midst—not feather nor egg nor bone of any sort."

King Hamid nodded slowly. Surely he was not surprised by the accusations; his advisors must have given him the main facts before he ever entered the audience chamber. Rani's impatience began to boil inside her; she wanted to set things straight, to finish with this playacting. Nevertheless, she saw the pointed look that Hal flashed to Puladarati, the clear instruction for the lesser noble to step forward and speak. Very well, then. The duke was to serve as Morenian ambassador. Rani fought back to silence, reminding herself that Puladarati had served Hal for decades, served as a nobleman should.

King Hamid addressed his comments to the group at large. "What do you have to say for yourselves? Were you roaming in the northern forest?"

Puladarati stepped forward, inclining his head in a salute that stayed a mere hairbreadth on the side of politeness. His words were frosty, as if he resented being challenged before Hamid's court. "We entered the forest, and we camped there, my lord. But we were not roaming, not if you mean wreaking havoc along the woodland paths. Not if you mean causing any harm to your people or your kingdom."

If King Hamid were surprised by the leonine councilor's tone, he managed to disguise that emotion. "Nevertheless, you did light a fire in the woods."

"A carefully tended cooking fire, only so large as we needed to prepare our food."

"A fire," King Hamid repeated, leaning forward slightly.

"A fire," Puladarati conceded.

"And you made shelters from the trees in the woods."

"Only from deadfall, my lord. We did not cut down a single branch."

"You used the wood in our forest?"

"Yes, my lord." Puladarati appeared disconcerted to make a second admission. King Hamid's soldiers were unsettled as well; they moved closer to the prisoners, and they settled their hands ostentatiously on their weapons. As if the

Morenians needed further warnings, Rani thought. Their own weapons had been taken from them when they were rounded up in the forest. Besides, every northern man present was bound as tightly as Rani, tighter for those who had offered resistance to their captors.

How could Hal fail to make a statement? How could he submit to whatever King Hamid was going to say?

The southern king continued. "I see little reason to continue this charade. You have violated the King's Peace in the northern forest. You have strayed from the path. You have built fires in the forest. You have used wood to build shelters. The penalty is clear. From this day forward—"

"If I might be permitted to speak, Your Majesty."

King Hamid seemed surprised by the interruption. Rani realized, though, that he was not as astonished as a northern king would be; he somehow expected his retainers to have the right to stop him in midsentence.

Some of his retainers, at least. The man who stepped forward was not one of the Sarmonian electors, not one of the jewel-encrusted men who had entered before the king. He was not one of the noblemen, honoring his lord's court day, not one of the suitors, intent on bringing his own case before his king.

He was Tovin Player.

Rani thought that her heart had forgotten how to beat. It froze within her chest, stopped its mundane pulse as if a hand had clenched around it. Then it remembered its mission with all the vigor of a soldier awakened on the day of battle, squeezing so painfully that she thought she would cry out.

Tovin Player, who had fled Morenia nearly ten months before . . . Tovin Player, who had nearly refused to speak with her before his departure. Tovin Player, who had blamed her for his own decision, who had insisted that *she* was the one who had driven *him* away, who had forced him to abandon peace and prosperity in Moren . . .

Tovin Player, who had loved her once, and whom she had loved.

King Hamid turned to the player with a practiced look of patience. "Player, you have no standing in this court. You are neither an elector nor a landed man."

Tovin bowed fluidly, as if the mild rebuke were praise. "Nay, my lord. But I still would speak with you, if you will. In private, if I have no license to speak before your court."

"You and I have no dealings that must be hidden from my people." King Hamid sounded angry at the suggestion; he looked to his gathered lords, as if he feared they might be troubled by Tovin's words. What strange patterns this king drew in his court; what odd ties he created . . . Rani glanced around, beginning to understand a little more about how things worked in Sarmonia.

King Hamid had gained his throne upon the approval of his lords, and he kept that position only so long as they were content. For that reason alone, he was beholden to them, but not with the good, powerful bonds of a liege and his vassal. Rather, he was tied to his lords with darker bonds, with tighter ties.

Where Hal might have agreed to speak with Tovin in private—*had* agreed to do so many times in the past—King Hamid could not afford the appearance of any impropriety. He could not have his lords even imagine that anything clandestine might transpire with the player. If those lords felt threatened, they might summon up a new election; they might banish Hamid from his post.

And Tovin Player understood that. The man was as good at spotting patterns as Rani was; he understood bonds between those who watched his players' creations, between those who might sponsor his troop. Tovin knew that King Hamid could not agree to a private consultation. Therefore, the player must actually want his words to be heard by all in the chamber. He wanted his words to be heard by Rani.

If there could be any doubt, it was dispersed when Tovin met her gaze directly. "Your Majesty," he said to King Hamid, "there has been a misunderstanding here. Your men thought that they stopped common intruders in your forest. Instead, they have caught important people from the north."

No! Hal had chosen not to reveal his true identity. That much was evident from his decision to have Puladarati press his case. If Hal admitted who he was, if he said that he was king, then he would have to recount why he was in Sarmonia. He would have to admit to the invading army back in Morenia, the blockading navy. He would leave the Sarmonian monarch with no choice but to declare his intentions in the battle that had broken out back at home. King Hamid would be forced to declare himself for or against Morenia, for or against the spiritual center of Brianta, the wealthy land of Liantine.

And Rani realized that the danger was even more complicated than that. If Tovin spoke Hal's name, he might alert the Fellowship to the Morenians' presence. Who knew how many members of the cabal lurked in the great hall's shadows? Who could tell which Sarmonians wore dark hoods at night, traveling to secret meetings and promising private loyalties? The Fellowship had vowed to destroy Hal; naming him in public might be tantamount to securing his assassination.

"Tovin!" Rani heard the name torn from her throat, ripped out of her like entrails from a slaughtered beast.

Before the player could respond, King Hamid leaped to his feet, thundering questions at Tovin. "You know this woman? You know these criminals?"

The player glanced at Rani before taking a confident step toward King Hamid. "Aye, Your Majesty. I know this woman well. She is the patron of my troop, my sponsor back in my homeland. I humbly ask that you grant her the same license that you have granted to me and to my troop, the same safe passage through the northern woods."

Rani stared at Tovin, conflicting emotions roiling within her. At first, she was relieved that he would intervene on her behalf; given their bitter parting, she had not expected ever to speak with him again. She did not want to owe him, though; she could not bear the thought of being indebted to him.

Obviously unaware of her turmoil, King Hamid asked the player, "And her name?"

There. Tovin would answer the question, and the Fellowship would be put on notice. They would know to find her here in Sarmonia; they would know that Hal must be nearby. Their assassin blades and poisons would find homes soon enough—and all because Tovin had sought to aid her . . .

Rani closed her eyes, taking a centering breath, trying to regroup, trying to adjust to the knowledge that her end was fast approaching. She almost failed to hear Tovin's reply: "Varna Tinker, Your Majesty."

What? Varna Tinker had been lost to Rani for nearly a decade, gone in the chaos that had followed the destruction of the glasswrights' guildhall. Even now, Rani could remember heartbreak as her best friend betrayed her to the

King's Men, calling out for their assistance as Rani sought help, sought order in the midst of sudden, complete confusion. Now, in Sarmonia, she cast a frantic glance toward Mair, toward the friend that had emerged from that betrayal.

Mair, though, was not able to offer any assistance. The Touched woman was drawn into her private suffering, contorted by her bound wrists, eyeing her square of black silk as if it held her private key to the Heavenly Gates. She would be of no assistance.

Had Rani told Tovin about Varna? Had she unveiled the pain that she had suffered so long ago?

She must have. There was no way that he chose the name by coincidence. And yet Rani could not remember having spoken of her childhood playmate, could not remember telling the tall player man about that passage in her youth.

Even as she wondered at his knowledge, she realized the answer. She had Spoken with him about growing up in the city; she had shared numerous stories of her past. She must have mentioned Varna once when she was under the strange spell that Tovin wove. She must have said something in passing, and he had remembered it. What other secrets had he cataloged to use against her? What else did he know, could he use at his will, whenever he felt the need?

And what did it matter, here in Sarmonia, with another crisis at hand?

"Varna Tinker," King Hamid mused, as if he were trying out the syllables prior to purchasing them. "A merchant, then, by your northern method of naming. That explains how she has the funds to sponsor your troop. It hardly tells me what she's doing here, though, Tovin Player. Or what she was doing in my forest."

Tovin smiled easily. "We were to meet—"

"Silence, Player." The king's command was mild, but there was no mistaking the royal command. "I'd like to hear the explanation from Varna herself."

Rani stepped forward and cleared her throat, wishing that her hands were free, that her shoulders were eased so that she could speak without the distraction of that burning pain. "We were to meet, Your Majesty. My caravan and the players." She warmed to her story when she was not cut off immediately. "I am a tinker by trade, and I'd hoped to discover new riches to offer in the Morenian marketplace. Tovin Player had already come south to work with his troop. I hoped that he would make contacts for me, discover sources for goods that I could bring up to Morenia and sell at a profit in the marketplace."

"The men who travel with you hardly look like merchants."

Rani nodded agreement. "They're not, Your Majesty. It's a long road between here and Morenia. I hoped to protect my riches against any who would attack me on the road."

"My men found no trade goods with you. We found no evidence of your . . . caravan."

"No, Your Majesty. We've made no purchases yet. We only just arrived in Sarmonia, two days, no, three days past. We were waiting to make contact with Tovin Player."

"Then you should have wealth with you. What did you expect to trade for Sarmonian goods?"

What indeed. Rani's story was unraveling like a lie told to a parent. She had no wares with her. She had no trinkets. She did not even have a stash of coins. Before she could weave another chapter from thin, desperate air, Puladarati stepped forward. "We travel with drafts from King Halaravilli ben-Jair, Your Majesty."

King Hamid narrowed his eyes even more than his customary squint. "Is this true, Madam Tinker? You bear scrip from the king of Moren?"

Rani forbade herself to look at that king, even to look at Tovin Player. She must answer earnestly; her future depended on her ability to play her role. "Aye, Your Majesty. We have the honor of providing cooking wares to the royal kitchens. We left Moren just before the summer silk auction, and the king gave us signed drafts to cover our debts here in Sarmonia."

"Show me one of these drafts."

Rani gave Puladarati a tight nod. The duke, in turn, shrugged his massive shoulders expressively. "Your Majesty?" he said to King Hamid.

"Untie him," the Sarmonian King commanded. "But keep a close watch."

The guard complied, and Rani read volumes into the man's motions. He might have been proud of capturing his prisoners out in the woods. He might have believed that he served his lord well, gathering up intruders. But now he was disarmed by Rani's explanations; he had clearly decided that the ragtag group of northerners was innocent, safe, no threat at all to Sarmonia.

As if to foster that belief, Puladarati made a show of moving slowly after his hands were freed. He reached for his saddlebags as if he were an ancient man, taking time to uncinch the buckle, open the flap, shift his possessions with care.

The old retainer's game worked. His guards relaxed even more when they saw nothing to alarm them in the satchel. Rather, Puladarati produced a handful of scrolls, each sealed with Hal's crimson wax.

King Hamid broke the sigil on the first one himself, and he scanned the words with casual negligence. Whatever was written there clearly matched Rani's story; she appeared to have royal drafts to underwrite her supposed merchant trip. "Very well, Madam Tinker. These papers support your words. Nevertheless, you had no royal charter to be in the woods."

"I did not know—" Rani started to plead, but she was interrupted by Tovin.

"Please, Your Majesty. Varna did not know the laws in Sarmonia. She is a simple tinker, not a diplomat wise in the ways of foreign courts. She did not think to challenge your authority. How could she, with a serving girl"—he gestured toward Mair—"and an aged accounts man?" Tovin's hand included Davin, deprecating the so-called merchant caravan with a shrug. "They are hardly an invading enemy force."

"And yet they are. She and her companions had no business in the clearing."

Tovin smiled easily; he might have been discussing sweetmeats at a feast. "Your Majesty, their business was to be with me. Perhaps they were confused about our meeting place. After all, Sire, you gave permission to all my players to use the Great Clearing. Certainly, one small merchant party could not cause more disruption at a lesser place in the woods."

Rani heard the camaraderie in Tovin's voice, the casual manner in which he addressed the king. She had seen this side of the player before; she had watched him melt into courts as readily as if he were noble born. He could play a Touched man as well, she knew, or a merchant, a guildsman. Rani did not trust Tovin for one instant, not when he smiled that easy smile, not when he tossed his chestnut curls back from his face.

"Tovin Player, you would make me break my own rules."

"Your Majesty, I would merely have you stretch them. You have granted a charter to me and my players. Surely it is only logical to extend that charter to my sponsor."

King Hamid stared at the player for a long minute, then cast his eyes over Rani's companions. He counted out the soldiers, but his attention merely brushed over those he considered too old or too unimportant to recognize—Davin, Mair, Hal himself. At last, the Sarmonian sighed. "Very well, Tovin Player. You plead your case well. Your charter covers your sponsor."

Tovin bowed his head and muttered thanks. King Hamid ignored the words, saying, "You have inconvenienced me, though. For that, I should be recompensed. I will expect your players to attend my supper this evening, in my private apartments. A short piece, a comedy, I believe. That will help me to forget all this bother."

"Of course, Your Majesty. I know just the selection. In fact, if you have time after you hear the other matters of your court, we could Speak of it before you retire for the afternoon."

"Speak of it . . ." King Hamid repeated the words, and Rani read the thirst in his narrow eyes. The king had already had occasion to meet with Tovin, then; he had already been lured into the quiet depths of the players' Speaking. Rani could not blame King Hamid for the gleam in his eyes; she herself craved the power of the secret places where Tovin could lead her. Even now, even here, in the dangerous southern receiving hall, Rani could recall the strange power that the player held over her, his awesome ability to take her deep into her own thoughts, into her own pasts, into memories so distant that she could not consciously remember them. She remembered the peace that she had found in the Speaking, and the power and the strength. "Yes," the king said, as if he were shaking himself awake from a dream. "We will Speak later this afternoon. Until then, take your sponsor and leave us to our work."

The king waved his hand in a dismissive gesture, and Rani found herself being rushed from the hall. Only when they were back in the courtyard under the late-summer sun, did the guards see fit to loosen their prisoners' bonds. Rani bit back tart words as the blood began to flow into her fingertips.

Hal's men did not bother to smother their comments; most of them swore at the discomfort. None was so foolish, though, as to comment on the charade they had just witnessed. Tovin merely glanced at the Morenians as if he were accustomed to their companionship, and then he said, "Varna, I have taken a room at the Golden Bee. Shall we go there, so that I can tell you about our bookings here in Sarmonia?"

The assumed name still sounded odd in her ear, but she agreed for the sake of the Sarmonian soldiers who still stood within earshot. "Aye. My men would do well with a pint in the common room."

It was a testament to the training of Hal's Morenian troops that they did not hesitate to group around her, acting as her escort when they left King Hamid's palace. They even turned toward her with the slight deference that trained fighting men owed their employers. Rani could not help but notice that Hal stayed close to her side—that made the job easier for his men, no doubt.

They held the formation out into the city streets, permitting Tovin to guide them through the warren of Riadelle.

"Very good, men," she said, on the threshhold of the Golden Bee. "Tovin Player and I will take our cups in the far corner. We'll be safe enough in the common room. Order supper—first ale for each of you will come from my purse." She tried to sound as if she had directed caravan guards for her entire life, lest any observers run back to the king.

The men allowed some honest pleasure to crease their faces, and then they commandeered three long tables. Rani was not surprised to see that Hal ended up in the middle of the crowd, protected, made invisible by his loyal men. Mair huddled in the shadows, apparently doing her best to look like a merchant's serving girl, although she held her black square of cloth in nervous fingers.

Rani forcibly set aside her worry and followed Tovin to a small table in the corner. The seats were close to the fire, and everyone else in the common room had the good sense to avoid the heat. Rani found herself thinking of fires back in Moren, of a welcome glow against autumn's growing chill. The first harvests would be coming in: fresh grain, strong new wine. . . .

She recognized the pattern of thoughts in her own mind. She was attempting to avoid the fact that she sat across the table from Tovin, that they were alone together for the first time since their ragged parting. She had dreamed of the things that she would say to him; she had imagined the apologies that he might make. She had despaired that she would see him ever again.

Trying to set aside the cloud of quite unmerchant-like thoughts that besieged her, she said, "Varna Tinker?"

"If I'd given your real name, the Fellowship would be

upon us in a heartbeat. You know they must be searching for you. You and your king."

She appreciated his restraint, his failure to indicate that Rani's king was in the very room, even as she wished that he was yet more discreet. Even as she wished that they were discussing something else. Even as she wished that he would take her hand, place his fingers against her cheek, against the flesh at the V of her neck. She cleared her throat. "What do you know about that? You weren't even *in* Morenia."

"I have my sources. My players are still there, of course. They have ways of conveying messages faster than Hamid's intelligence."

She must not look at his copper eyes. She must not think about the feel of his curls beneath her fingertips. She roughened her voice and asked, "If your troop remains in Moren, who are you working with here? Who will perform for King Hamid?"

"My new company hails directly from Liantine. They arrived in Riadelle just as I did. We've been together now for seven months. They had some good basic players, and I've been able to teach them a thing or two."

"From Liantine?" Rani asked. "Then they are sworn against Morenia in the northern battle?" She could not keep condemnation from her tone, even though she knew her question put herself and her companions at risk, even though she knew her words might tell too much to anyone who overheard.

"They are players, Tovin said, shrugging "They have no loyalties to kings, to boundaries on a map. They honor their sponsor, their plays, and cold, hard coin."

"So you feel nothing for the land you left to come to Sarmonia? For the people in the home you built away from Liantine?"

She knew that her voice sounded hurt; she was not speaking merely of players.

He knew as well. "What is that to you?"

She struggled to stake out a claim of righteousness, of moral high ground for the battle that she wanted to wage. "Do you know how much your mother has missed you? Have you even thought about the players you left behind? They need you—your glasswork and your guidance and your skills."

"My mother always misses me. She knows that I've been gone for longer trips in the past, buying silk, trading for glass. She always survives. As for the other players, they hardly remember I'm in the troop until I come back bearing riches."

Rani could not gainsay him; she knew that the others *were* accustomed to his strange comings and goings. Far more accustomed than she had ever become, in any case. She looked away, suddenly fascinated by the hem of her sleeve.

She should not have let Tovin speak for the Morenians in King Hamid's reception hall. She should have figured out some other way to escape. She should have worked out some other solution, found some path that did not include debt to Tovin.

For this way was simply too hard. She longed to tell him all that he had done wrong, all the ways that he had hurt her, and yet she feared to hear his bill of woes filed against her. She knew that he could manipulate her; she had given him license to do so many times in the past. She knew that he could make her feel guilt, and pity, and responsibility. . . .

As Rani took a steadying breath, Tovin accepted two tankards of ale from a serving girl, and he ordered a plate of roasted capon. Rani drank deeply as soon as he placed her cup on the table. She had not realized the thirst she'd built as she was hauled before the king. Tovin waited until she had finished, and then he passed her his own cup, offering it with a crooked smile. She dispensed with politeness and swallowed half of it as well.

"Tovin," she said, fortified enough that she could meet his eyes. "I've missed you."

"You say that now. I doubt that you took the time to notice your feelings while you were still in the north."

"How can you say that? You *know* that I did not want you to leave."

"I know that you wanted me to stay. And you wanted to be alone. You wanted to pursue your guildwork and your courtly life. You wanted to keep me as some sort of hound, a devoted beast who would stay beside you until you sent him to the kennels."

"Or the mews," she said, without thinking first. Tovin was no dog, no devoted, slavish follower. Rather, he was a falcon, a scarce-tamed raptor who would flee from her if she gave him half a chance. Who *had* fled from her . . .

She caught her breath, aware that her words might be construed as an insult, knowing that she now owed him, no matter what she might otherwise have wished.

"Or the mews," he repeated, and he grinned. Her body responded to that open smile. She relaxed and leaned toward him, as if she would harvest more of his good nature. He sighed and said, "Shall we dispense with tales, my merchant girl? You say that you miss me, and yet you never sought me out. I say that no one in Morenia mourns my absence, and yet I've avoided sending messages to my mother, to my troop, to my sponsor. Peace?"

She wanted to argue. She wanted to tell him that he was wrong, that he was selfish, that he was stubborn and foolish and vain. Instead, she nodded. "Peace," she said, but she had to lick her lips and repeat the word so that he could hear her.

"So," he said, his voice full of brio. "Are you going to tell me what you're doing in Sarmonia?"

"Not here. Not now."

"But the stories are true? Halaravilli is a hunted man?"

He phrased the question in the abstract, as if the subject of the question was not sitting a dozen paces away. Her face flushed, and she could not say if it was from the lie they presented to the tavern patrons, or the fire beside her, or the rush of ale to her head. "Aye. He's hunted. Rumor says that he's fled Moren. That he's hoping to regroup where it's safe. Once he's had a chance to plot a course, he hopes to find allies."

Tovin nodded, as if she were discussing the unseasonably warm weather. "He'll do well to avoid Sarmonia, then. No allies to be had here. King Hamid has loyalties no Morenian will ever understand, between the electorate and the landed men."

"What exactly does that mean?" Rani asked, her curiosity getting the better of her. "The landed men?"

Tovin shrugged. "Here in Sarmonia, each man who owns ten hectares is allowed to cast a vote. He names an elector, a sort of regional liege lord. The elector takes his region's concerns to the king. When an old king dies, the electors gather together and choose the successor."

"How secure is the king, then, if he has to answer to all these men?"

"An elector can call for a vote at any time. But if he calls too often, or if the challenge goes against him, then he's not likely to stay elector for long."

Rani nodded, trying to make sense of the strange pattern. Electors to keep fulfilled. Landed men to satisfy. A king who ruled at their pleasure, with the goal of keeping them happy, but advancing himself as well. A king who already traded with Liantine, who already embraced a player's troop from that distant land.

And spinning out from the tangled web were strands that Rani could not even see. "The Fellowship?" She risked the open question, more desperate for information than for perfect safety. "Have you made contact with them here?"

"They haven't sought me out, and I haven't identified any members. I'm almost certain that Hamid is not one. They'll be in among the electors, though, and the landed men. The servants, too, in the palace, and merchants."

Rani did not want to ask her next question; she was afraid of the response. Nevertheless, she had to know what she was up against; she had to know just what she was fighting in Sarmonia. "And Crestman? Is he here?" Tovin eyed her steadily, and she knew that he was countering her question with one of his own. She had told Tovin too much over the years, shared with him as her lover, shared with him in the Speaking. She forced her voice to level before she added, "I ask for my liege lord, Tovin. Not for myself. Crestman has tracked us down before, and he's the greatest danger we are likely to find."

Crestman had been responsible for the kidnapping of Mair's son. He had ordered Rani to kill Queen Mareka or risk her own life in exchange. He hated Rani with a passion as great as he had once loved her, and he used the Fellowship to further his own bitter goal of revenge.

Tovin paused before saying, "I have not seen him nor heard tale of him. He'll likely be keeping quiet, though. He's too easy to spot, too easy to describe. If he even still lives. From all you've said, his injuries were great enough that he might have died since Brianta."

"Oh, no," Rani said. "He still lives. He's too bitter to die."

Tovin might have replied to that, but the serving girl arrived with their food, setting a trencher on the table between them. Rani had not realized how hungry she was until she felt the bones beneath her fingers; the first bite of well-cooked meat made her head swim. Tovin grinned and pushed the bird closer to her. "Eat," he said as she started to protest, started to offer up some semblance of polite hesitation. "After all, it's your coin that's paying for my meal. You're my sponsor, Varna Tinker, and I expect to get my due from you."

Rani looked across the room at Hal, saw him watching her from amid his covert guard. She wondered who expected what from whom, who owed precisely what to whom. She wondered what aid Sarmonia could possibly bring to them, and if she had the strength to assist her king. She wondered if she could make full peace with the player across from her, and if she could bring the pattern of their lives back into balance. She wondered what the future held.

Nevertheless, she set aside her questions. She set aside her questions and her fears and her worries. And she ate.

5

Kella watched Tovin Player stride into the woods, carrying himself with complete confidence. She expected nothing less of him; in the months since he had first come to her cottage, he had never admitted being wrong about anything.

Kella smiled. Well, in reality he *wasn't* wrong about much. She was willing to grant him that. How much of his success was due to his easy smile, and how much was due to his striving to be at the correct place at the correct time, well, she wasn't going to speculate on that. Not now. Not when she had her own business to tend to.

Glancing at the edge of the clearing, she saw that the day was getting on. She stepped back into the hut, expecting handsels to arrive shortly. No reason not to get some of her own work done before they came, though. No reason to let these travelers crisscrossing her forest leave her behind in her herb work.

Kella lifted down her medium-sized cauldron and began to count out the herbs that she needed to boil for her strongest liniment. She measured out handfuls of mint—the cooling scent would bring relief to anyone who paid. Then she added a healthy dose of fireleaf; its peppery heat would draw out a variety of injuries. She included a thimble's worth of ground nettle, because the irritant would work wonders on sore muscles. Grumbling to herself, she realized that the last herbs she needed, the very binding elements to the working, sat in the back corner of her loft.

She grunted as she pulled herself to her feet. She might benefit from the concoction herself once she had finished boiling it down. She grimaced at the slow ache in her thighs. Those muscles might have gone untested for years, but Tovin Player's games forced her to push her body. She smiled and shook her head, closing her eyes as she remembered the words that he had whispered during the night. A young man's words . . . A foolish boy's words . . .

She heard the blow an instant before she felt it. An arm moved through the air, creating its own wind. If she had still been a young woman, she could have pivoted on her knee, could have ducked away from her assailant. Now, she had only an instant to brace herself against the certain pain.

And there *was* pain. The blow came from a cupped hand, slammed hard against the side of her head. For an instant, she could only blink her eyes, stunned, and then she heard the echoes in her ear, the muffled rumble of thunder made distant by the blow. Tears sparked down her cheeks without waiting for her permission, and she bellowed a curse that would have made her mother blush.

She turned to confront her assailant, stretching sideways so that she could grasp the poker that nestled on the edge of her fire. He—it must be a man, given the force of that blow—he predicted her movement and cut her off, knocked her to the ground and placed one booted foot on top of her wrist.

She did not doubt that he could follow through on his

threat, lowering his weight and grinding all her small bones to dust. Her imagination flashed on the pain, on the stunning agony. More than the pain, though, would be the loss of her hand. How could she brew her potions? How could she harvest her herbs? She might know more herb lore than any of her Sisters, but even she did not know enough to regenerate a ruined hand.

She splayed her fingers on the hearth, pressing her palm against the stone. *I'm no threat,* she thought. *I'll not hurt you. Leave me be. I'm no threat.*

The invader's breath was harsh in the small cabin. It caught in his throat, as if he were arguing with himself. She suspected that he had not exerted himself overmuch; she sensed the strength that trembled in the foot poised above her wrist. Rather, his breath caught on the excitement of the chase.

How long had he watched her? How long had he waited for Tovin Player to leave? Had he heard them chatting by the fire when the sun rose? Had he heard the player's gentle words as he lured her back to the pallet for one more toss before the day began? Had he heard the player's attempts to charm her into Speaking, heard her remonstrations, her throaty laugh as she distracted the traveling man?

"What?" she grunted. "What do you want?"

He lowered his boot, putting weight onto his foot. The nerves in her hand protested, squeaking against the pressure, and she longed to buck up, to throw off this domineering ox. She had done that once before—fought off a man who was determined to harm her, to mock her and ridicule her after she had foolishly agreed to let him stay for the winter.

Kella had had her revenge against that one. She had mixed ladyleaf in his stew, in his bread, over the grilled meats that she had prepared through the long winter's quiet. He had been suspicious, of course; he had made her eat before he would taste anything that she prepared. The herb had done nothing for her, nothing but make her hair shine a bit brighter in the daylight.

Ladyleaf was less kind to men, though. The last time that she had seen him, he had worn a loose jerkin, trying to hide the soft breasts that he had grown. All his clothes were loose, in fact; his breeches hung empty at his crotch, for his stones had shriveled with every bite he swallowed.

Revenge. Kella might have it, if she lived long enough. If she found what her intruder wanted. She tried again. "I'll give you what you need. Take it; it's yours. My summer harvest is nearly done."

"I don't need your weeds, old woman."

She knew the voice. The horseman who had come to her before, the soldier who had offered money to learn Jalina's whereabouts. She contemplated pretending not to know him, but she decided she'd gain more by admitting the truth. "You know that I barter more than weeds, soldier. I trade information as well."

For the first time, he eased the pressure on her hand. The release let blood surge into her fingertips, and she gritted her teeth to keep from crying out as pain flowed, too. How long would her fingers ache? How many potions would this cursed man keep her from brewing? She began to grow angry.

His gruff voice cut across her emotion. "Information? Who says that's what I need?"

"Why else would you come back here?"

He grunted, as if accepting the fact that she had placed him, that she knew his identity. "Well enough. Are you ready to tell me what you know? Are you ready to answer the questions you couldn't bother with before?"

"Get off my hand." She placed all of her authority into the command, summoning up all the strength of her mother, and all the mothers who had lived before her. They had faced challenges, all of them. They had confronted deranged men in the woods. They had stood fast against invaders who had threatened their lives, their chastity, the safety of their herbs. "Get off, or I'll tell you nothing."

Apparently angered by her stubbornness, the soldier grabbed her hair. He pulled her head back against his chest, using the motion to raise his other hand. The knife that he held against her throat was very sharp, and she forced herself to breathe shallowly.

She was not a fool. She knew that one word from her, any word, would shatter his balance. Anything she said would push him over the crumbling edge of his rage. She wondered if tears would appease him, if he would be softened by a sobbing old woman. Something about him warned that tears were not the right approach, though. He had surely bullied other old women. He had confronted them somewhere far in his past, somewhere in the darkness that had shaped his twisted soul.

His twisted soul and his twisted body. She remembered the tortured way that he had pulled himself onto his saddle after his first visit. His right leg was withered. His right leg and his right forearm, the hand that held the knife.

Kella could hear her mother's cool tones, calm and quiet, speaking years ago in their peaceful cottage. "Some day a man might come here. A man who is bigger than you, stronger than you. A man who wants nothing of your herbs.

There are ways to defend yourself, though. There are ways to keep yourself safe."

And Kella remembered how her mother had taught her to turn her head into the angle of a captor's arm, to duck her chin toward his elbow. Her mother had said to stomp on the inside of his foot, on the stretched flesh of the arch. Her mother had said to put all her energy into one attempt, one exploding effort to be free.

Breathing a grateful prayer to the memory of her mother, Kella twisted her head and ducked her chin, lifting her right foot to pound her captor's arch. She ignored the rip of her hair, ignored the pounding of her heart, ignored the fear that suddenly threatened to fill her throat, her lungs, her soul.

The soldier swore and let her go, stumbling as his weak leg crumpled under her onslaught. Kella leaped for the door, slamming her hand against the iron latch. She tore the door open, gasping to fill her lungs with clean, cool air. She managed one step, then another, and she hitched up her skirts to run down the path toward the Great Clearing.

And then he fell upon her. His full weight slammed against her back, toppled her forward. His good forearm pressed against the nape of her neck, forcing her chin into the ground. His knee planted in her kidney, sending explosions of white light behind her closed eyes. "Tell me, Witch! Tell me where she is! Tell me where Mareka hides!"

Mareka. That must be the true name of the handsel he had already asked her about, Jalina's true name. Kella had paused too long to translate, though. The soldier's knife pricked at her neck, and she knew that his blade was poised to plunge into her skull. "I do not know!" she gasped. "I would tell you if I could, but I do not know! I swear on my mother's books of herblore, I do not know where she hides!"

His muscles tensed, and she knew that he was ready to move the dagger, to force it past her flesh, through her bones, into the meat of her brain. "I will help you, though!"

He paused. She continued in a quieter voice. "I will help you. She trusts me. She comes to me often. I'll find out where she lives. I'll find out for you. I'll tell you, and you can find her." With each phrase, Kella felt the soldier relax a little more. She babbled words, spilling out reassurances as if she spoke to a fussy infant. "Her babe is young. He came early. He's weak. He needs herbs early, often. She'll come for them. I've helped her. She'll come to me." The knife whispered back; only the point nudged her neck. "I'll help you. You'll get her. You needn't worry anymore."

He removed the knife, but he fumbled at his waist, and it took her a moment to realize that he was collecting a length of rough rope. He pulled her arms behind her, lashing her wrists so tightly that she bit her tongue to keep from crying out. When he was through, he climbed to his feet, standing over her and panting like a well-run dog.

"You'll help me," he said.

"Aye." She swallowed hard, trying to slow her racing heart. "As soon as she comes back to me."

"You'll find out where she hides, and you'll tell me."

"Aye."

"And you'll tell no one else."

"No one." She was promising to break the handsel, to break the sacred contract that bound her to one who had sought her for herb lore. The Sisters brooked no dissent on that—she must protect those who came to her for cures. That was the way that witches secured their future, guaranteed their value to new generations of seekers.

The soldier seemed unaware of her concession. He growled, "If you lie to me, then you will die."

"I do not lie." If she kept the handsel, she would die. She would never be able to help another person. She would never aid another anxious mother, never save another weakling babe. Never earn another copper coin. By violating one confidence, she could save countless lives. Including her own.

"Swear it, then. Swear it in the name of Jair."

Jair. Not the Thousand Gods that the northerners usually invoked. Not a king, or a nobleman, or some other powerful force. First Pilgrim Jair . . .

Even as Kella took the oath, "I swear it in the name of Jair," her mind raced. She had heard rumors, when was it? Years ago? A decade or more in the past . . .

She had left the forest and traveled to Riadelle, selling her potions in the marketplace, thinking to make enough money for fine silk and velvet, until she realized the costs of living in the city.

In Riadelle, though, she had met the Sisters, dozens of other herb-witches, trained even more thoroughly than Kella, for they shared their knowledge. They shared their gossip. She had laughed at tales from the king's court, the rumors about electors and landed men who found themselves in the wrong beds. She had rolled her eyes over the tales of ladies who bore children that looked nothing like their sires, ladies who could have been helped by any herb-witch, any one at all, if only they had signed the handsel early in their nine-month passage.

But there were other stories. Darker stories. One Sister had whispered about a secret cadre, a cabal that moved behind the electors, behind the landed men. Kella had listened to stories about meetings held on the darkest nights, meetings where conspirators swathed themselves in midnight cloaks and determined the fate of a kingdom.

What was that Sister's name? Kella fumbled for it, her mind skittering as if it chased after a dropped pebble. Dania. Yes, Dania had joined the secret organization, had been sworn into the heart of their hidden meetings. . . .

Yet Dania understood that her first loyalty would always rest with the Sisters. She had attended hidden meetings, sworn to secrecy, and then she had violated that oath, in light of prior ones. . . . "The Fellowship of Jair . . ." Kella whispered, remembering the tales that Dania had carried back to her sisters.

The soldier's eyes narrowed for a fraction of a heartbeat, and then he snapped, "What?"

"You speak for the Fellowship, don't you? They're the ones who want to find the woman."

"I speak for myself," he said gruffly. "That's all you need to know. My knife will be the one you'll answer to."

Kella's mind reeled. She had agreed to break her handsel, to betray a woman who had come to her in need. And yet if she acted to better the Sisters . . . The other herb-witches could not hold her in disgrace for long if she provided them with information, information about the Fellowship that might very well save their lives. The soldier had murder on his mind, of that Kella was certain. If he killed her, then Jalina would seek out another Sister. She would sign another handsel, and another herb-witch would be threatened.

Kella must protect her Sisters. She must collect information for them, divine the extent of the threat from this northern soldier and his Fellowship. She could see the balance as clearly as if she weighed bitterroot against deergrass on her scales. One handsel, for saving all the Sisters . . .

"I know your people," Kella said. "I know their goals. I know that they meet in Riadelle's alleys, and I know that they control the future of my land."

"I have no people."

Kella reached back into her memories, stretched for the words that Dania had told her years before. "You do not search for the Royal Pilgrim, then?" He grunted, and she knew that she had hit her mark. She resisted the urge to smile as she asked, "You do not think that the Royal Pilgrim will reign over all lands in the future?"

"You are one of us, then?"

"One of you?" She started to mock, "How could I be one of you? You do not exist." She stopped, though, and contemplated a more useful elaboration, one that would not be an utter lie. "It has been many a year since I first heard of the Royal Pilgrim."

The soldier glared at her for a long moment, obviously debating whether he should challenge her directly. Before he could make the wrong decision, she said, "I can help you, soldier-man. I can help the Fellowship."

"How?" He did not waste time with more words.

"I can locate the one you seek. I can tell you about the others who seek for her."

"Others?"

"You know that many travel through the woods these days."

"The players." He made a rude noise as he shrugged.

"The players. And others. Northerners."

"Who?"

Kella had seen a gleam like that before, in the eyes of the

old men who came to her for mandrake, in the most desperate of the girls who sought love potions. Hunger. Pure and unalloyed. "I'll tell you. After you bring me to one of your meetings."

"I could beat the information out of you now."

"You could beat me, but I would not tell you."

"You can say that, after the way I bested you?"

She made herself laugh, as if she weren't afraid. "You tricked me, soldier-man. You caught me unawares." She read the indecision in his eyes, and she lowered her voice, dropped it to the register that she reserved for telling her customers the most dire news—about deaths, and stillborn babes, and plots of murder. "If you set a finger on me, you'll never eat an easy meal again. You'll never know when my Sisters will appear, when they'll seek you out. We have fast poisons and slow. We have drafts that will make you as forgetful as your grandfather's grandfather. We have herbs that you'll never smell, never taste, but they will make your good arm shrivel worse than your bad one. Bring me to a meeting! Let me see your Fellowship."

Let her see the Fellowship. Let her see the power base in Sarmonia. Let her see who to approach, who to confront, who to pamper. Let her see her future.

He stared at her for long enough that she began to question her own gamble. She had no doubt that he could kill her in cold blood, that he could reach out and slash her throat as easily as grant her request. This one had killed before, killed both to save himself and for the pure pleasure of it. At last, he nodded. "I'll take you to the Fellowship. Tomorrow night. After moonrise. Wear a dark cloak." Almost as an afterthought, he added, "You can ride a horse?"

"I will." Well, how could she answer his question? She couldn't know until she'd tried.

"Good enough." He glanced toward the door of her cottage, and she knew that he was wondering what herbs were hidden there, what power hung dusty and untested in the rafters. He swallowed uneasily, tightening the scar high on his cheekbone. His knife flashed out, and he cut the rope that bound her wrists, sawing it free in one even slice. "Until tomorrow," he said.

"Until tomorrow." She watched as he left her clearing, limping heavily. She imagined the herbs that she could mix to ease his hurts. She imagined the herbs that would kill him.

The following afternoon, Kella was basking in the last of the afternoon sunlight. She had a sharp knife in one hand and twine in the other. It was well past time to harvest the last of the garden by her door.

She hummed to herself as she worked, an old song that her mother had taught her when she was a young girl. It felt good to stretch her muscles—she was stiff after her fight with the soldier the day before.

She shook her head in irritation; she still could not believe that she had failed to get his name. She had been so surprised by his attack. . . . She was getting old, older than she'd dare admit to anyone but one of the Sisters. Old enough that she had driven off Tovin the night before, scarcely admitting to herself that she was too sore to enjoy his sort of attention.

Even as she shifted to get a better angle for one stubborn clump of herbs, she heard footsteps behind her. She whirled quickly and was only a little relieved to find a newcomer standing there. Not the soldier. Not Tovin, who might require another lie.

This man was clothed all in green, his robes the color of spring's first leaves. He was a priest, then. Not likely to be well disposed to her profession. He puffed slightly from his exertion; he must be unaccustomed to walking through the forest. His round face was flushed; the color made him look like a boy. She suspected he was older than he first appeared, a conclusion that was bolstered by her realization that his hair was thinning.

"Good dame," he said, and he bowed a little from his waist. At least he was making an effort to be polite. That was more than she could say for many of her visitors. Ruefully, she resisted the urge to rub at the bruise that spread across her back, above her poor kidneys.

"Sir." She kept her voice on the narrow edge of politeness. This might be a handsel, after all, a man in search of a potion. Scarce chance of that, though. The priests all acted as if her herbs were sacrilege.

"Tovin Player sent me here, good dame. He said that I might learn from you. If you have time, that is. If you aren't busy. If—"

Tovin, sending her a priest? The notion was difficult to imagine, as if all the birds in the sky had chosen to fly upside down for the day. Surprise made her voice sharp. "What do you want to learn?"

"About your . . . skills."

"My skills?"

"Your knowledge," he amended.

"My knowledge?" She laughed, letting a little of her fatigue sharpen her tone. "Here's something I know: The day is getting old, and I have a great deal of work left to finish."

His gaze was drawn to the leaves, to the small green arrows that cascaded across the ground before her. "What do you use those for?" He swallowed hard, and forced out a second question. "Could it make a man go mad? Could it kill?"

She stared at him, surprised by the awe and horror mingled in his voice. She was accustomed to people who scorned her arts, handsels who acted brave in the face of her potions and incantations. She had never before seen such fear, though, such blatant terror, even if it was washed with respect. Her first inclination—to toy with the man and create imagined properties of the herb—fled. "It's sorrel. I place it in soup."

"Sorrel." He breathed a sigh of relief, and she thought that he might collapse on her very doorstep.

"Good sir, perhaps you were led astray by Tovin Player. Perhaps you do not truly wish to speak with an herb-witch such as myself." She saw him flinch at the word "witch," shying like a child who remembers a beating. His fingers twisted in a strange gesture, an automatic motion that seemed to bring him peace. Against her better judgment, Kella nodded toward his hands. "That twist you just made. What is it good for?"

"Twist?" He looked confused. "Oh, the gesture of warding."

"Warding?" Perhaps the man was crazed. Perhaps he was some sort of fool who Tovin had come across in his travels, a rogue who might amuse her. "How do you think that waving your fingers will protect you here?"

"Not here," he said, shaking his head. He sighed. "Far away from here."

Kella was growing tired of the game. "Where, then?"

"Brianta. Where they torture witches. Where they pile stones upon them until they confess their evil and then bury the corpses in the middle of the road." The man began to weep, great, silent tears rolling down his cheeks as if he were unaware of the emotion.

"Someone you loved was named a witch?"

His face set, as if he would deny the accusation twisted into her question. "Princess Berylina Thunderspear. I was sent to protect her. I failed."

"And your princess died in Brianta?"

"She was not a witch! They accused her falsely! She fell because she was too good for them, because they could not understand! She was not a filthy witch!"

He stopped in midtirade, remembering his audience with a nearly comical gasp. He started to mumble a retreat, to explain away his anger, but she waved his words away. "Come inside, Father. . . ."

"Siritalanu."

"Come inside, Father Siritalanu. Let me brew you a cup of tea." She watched the fear blossom on his face. "No, father. Mint tea. You can pick the leaves yourself—they are there by your feet."

He let himself be mollified by her gesture, yet he did bend down to pick his own herbs. He stooped as he entered the cottage, and he watched intently as she filled a kettle with fresh stream water from the bucket on the hearth. As she moved the iron kettle over the flames, he looked about the room, taking in the festooned rafters, the clay pots on shelves, the glass jars that glistened on the windowsill.

"Relax, Father," Kella said, and she gave him a bowl to hold his crushed leaves. The aroma of the herb filled the cottage, and she wished that she dared to slip something extra into his tea, a drop or two of heartsease to calm him. "Why don't you tell me of your princess while we wait for the water to boil."

She thought that he would not respond. He swallowed, and he raised his hands to his face, as if he were surprised to find the remnants of the tears that he had shed outside. "She was blessed by all the Thousand." He paused, as if to confirm that she understood that he meant the gods. She nodded, and he continued. "She prayed to them with purity in her heart. She was making her pilgrimage, dedicating her life to their service."

"But the Briantans did not trust her?"

"The Briantans did not understand. She *knew* the gods in ways they'd never seen before."

The water began to boil, and Kella scowled as she found a mug. She made a show of upending it, proving to the priest that nothing would be added to his mint. She filled the mug with hot water, and she let him drop his own herbs into the cup. He moved mechanically, as if he were an exhausted child. Kella could see that he had lost more than a member of his congregation. The man before her was bound up in grief, as stricken as any widower.

"Knew the gods?" Kella asked, keeping each word perfectly neutral.

"She heard them. Saw them. Not their voices, not their bodies—sensations that no person has a right to know. She tasted them, by all the Thousand, she smelled them! She felt them touch her flesh!"

Kella reached out to steady his hand, to keep the steaming water from splashing over the edge of the mug. He flinched at her touch, as she said, "And for that the Briantans called her witch?"

"They did not understand."

Well they might not, Kella thought. "But what brings you to me, Father? Why have you come to my cottage?"

"I thought that if I could meet a true witch, if I could learn the true scope of your powers, then I might understand what they accused her of being. I thought that I might understand the threat. I might understand why she had to die."

"You want to hate me, then?" She kept her voice neutral. "You want to find me so terrible that I deserve death myself?"

"Yes," he whispered, and she could see that he longed to flee from the room, to be far away from her.

"And?"

For answer, he set the mug upon her table and placed his face in his hands. His sobs were violent cloudbursts, breaking from his chest like a wild storm crashing through the woods. This was not the quiet emotion that she had witnessed outside; this was a man tearing himself apart, destroying himself in a final, desperate attempt to build meaning in his world.

"Tarn," he wailed, and the word was meaningless until Kella remembered the name for the god of death. "Tarn! And Mip! Zil, and Ile, and Nim!"

He repeated the names, his chant growing more frantic, his breath coming harsher and harsher. Kella feared for his mind, feared that he would rip what little of it remained. He was not a true handsel, and she had promised that she would not dose him with her herbs, but she was afraid to do nothing. Her hands darted out without her planning to move; she reached for pots that ranged about the hearth. She crumbled a leaf of henbane into his mint tea, added a pinch of thorn apple. He had not seen her; his eyes remained closed as he chanted the gods' names in agony.

"Father," she said, trying to break his concentration. "Father!" She pushed the cup into his hands, held it there as she raised it to his lips. "Drink, Father. Drink your tea. Swallow, Father. Your princess would have wanted you to drink this. Another sip, Father. Another . . ."

The herbs acted quickly, as she had known they would. It was pure luck that made mint enhance their properties, simple good fortune that the priest's herb masked the flavors of her own. The henbane made him docile; he let her lead him to the low stool beside her fire. The thorn apple opened his mind to her suggestion, and she leaned close to him, whispering, "Ease your heart, Father. You did not cause your princess to die." She repeated the words three more times, and he took them up on his own, forming his lips around them like a child discovering a new flavor.

Kella dared to step back, summoned the nerve to look to her cottage door. What was happening here in the woods? How had her quiet corner of the world become so busy? Why were so many people coming to her, bothering her?

As if to mock her question, a shadow fell across the threshold. Kella did not even pretend to welcome the newcomer as a potential handsel; instead, she grimaced and said, "Yes?"

The woman who stood there blinked as her eyes adjusted to the cottage, and then she rushed to the priest. "Father!" she exclaimed, trying to capture his attention. "Father, it's me. Rani Trader."

The man continued to mouth his silent words of comfort. The newcomer turned accusing eyes on Kella. "What have you done to him?"

"Rani Trader," Kella said, taking possession of her visitor's name. "He'll be ready to travel in a moment."

The woman swallowed hard, her skin paling beneath her blond hair. "How have you dosed him?"

"In no way that will cause him harm. He became agitated, and I gave him a tea to . . . assist his calming himself. He's working on the words now. Once he has recognized them, he'll be fine."

"Words? You cast a spell on him, then?"

Kella laughed grimly. "No spell." At least not in the way that Rani Trader meant. "By the Jair you northerners hold in such esteem, no spell. The Sisters would not permit that."

"The Sisters?"

"Other herb-witches. The ones in Riadelle who dictate what we may and may not do. They would not permit my casting a spell on an unknowing guest who did not sign a contract, a handsel. I merely gave him something that will help him find the paths he wants to travel inside his own mind."

"He wants to go back to Brianta."

She knew, then. "He wants to save your princess. What was her name? Berylina?"

"Yes," Rani Trader said, and her own face was grave. "Berylina. He loved her."

Of course he loved her. That much was obvious from his behavior. He loved her, but he was one of those priests who swore off acting on such love. Well, no wonder the man was stricken, then. No wonder he had grown mad at the mention of the dead woman.

Rani Trader braved another few steps into the cottage, until she could see the priest's moving lips. "What is he saying?" she asked.

"That he did not cause the princess to die. That's correct, isn't it?"

"Aye," the woman said, her own brow creasing. She clearly had her own memories of the princess's death.

Kella decided to probe a little more—purely as a matter of professional curiosity, she assured herself. She should know what was being done to herb-witches in distant lands, or to those identified as such. She should learn so that she could tell the Sisters. She might even use the information when she met with the Fellowship—that very evening, if the soldier-man kept his promise.

"Your priest mentioned Tarn."

Rani Trader reeled under the name, as if the herb-witch had struck her. Before she recovered, she looked behind herself, hunching her shoulders as if she would ward off a physical blow. Odder and odder, Kella thought. These northerners had strange relationships with their gods.

"I'm sorry," Rani Trader said. "I was not expecting to hear the god of death's name here."

Kella stepped closer to her visitor, reminded herself to watch closely. "He mentioned others as well: Mip and Zil. Ile and Nim."

Yes. She definitely reacted. Each name made Rani Trader flinch: She shook her head as if she heard a distant sound, and she swallowed hard. Kella had spent a lifetime watching people process tastes and smells. Kella would stake her collection of dried mushrooms on her belief that Rani Trader tasted a flavor that she liked when she heard the last god's name. A flavor that she liked, but that she feared. Like a child sneaking boiled sweets when a parent has denied the treats.

Before Kella could devise a method of measuring out the

oddity, the other woman shook her head and turned to the priest. "Father Siritalanu?" she asked, and then she glanced at the herb-witch. "Can he hear me?"

"Aye. He's almost through with his thoughts. He'll respond when he's ready."

"Father?" she asked again. The priest took a long time to look at her, and his blink was very slow. Nevertheless, his eyes were focused when he opened them, and he seemed to recognize the woman.

"Ranita?"

"Yes, Father."

Yet another oddity. Strangers roaming the forest who communed with their gods in mysterious ways and who answered to multiple names.

"Ranita, I came to learn of herb lore. I wanted to know what cost my Berylina her life."

"Herbs had nothing to do with it, Father." Rani Trader's voice was firm, as if she were explaining a difficult truth to a child. "They thought she was a witch. Not an herb-witch. A darker sort. A sorceress."

"I had to learn. I had to see what I could know about Berylina."

"I understand, Father. Come with me, now. We'll go back to the Great Clearing."

"Great Clearing!" Kella interrupted, remembering again that Tovin had sent the priest to her, that Tovin must know this Rani Trader.

"Aye." The woman was working her arm under the priest's, helping the man to his feet.

"Then you are with the players?"

"What do you know of the players?" Her question was

sharp, and Kella could not fail to hear the possessive note in her words.

"Nothing, my dear." Kella shrugged elaborately, showing her empty hands in a gesture that she knew indicated goodwill. "Only that they have a license from the king. I have come across them when I've been walking through the woods. I've spoken with their leader."

"With Tovin?"

"Is that his name? The young one." Kella shook her head slightly, dismissing the man, and she saw Rani Trader relax. "You travel with the players, then?"

"Not with them, precisely. I'm with a group of . . . merchants; we're from the north. We know Tovin Player from Moren. We're staying with him in the clearing."

A girl of noble bearing, with a northerner's merchant name and a guildish one, and a familiarity with players. A priest near mad from grieving. Kella would not buy the story lightly. Nevertheless, she shrugged. "Your priest should be fine for walking now. He'll be tired when you get to the clearing. Let him sleep through the night. He'll wake rested, with his mind at greater peace than it has been."

"For that I thank you, good dame. Did the father pay you for your troubles?"

"He did not have the chance." Even if he had, Kella would have denied receiving her due.

The other woman reached into a pouch hidden at her waist, and she extracted some copper coins. "Thank you. It was a mercy to ease his pain."

Kella took the money, not bothering to note that it was three times the price of her herbs. "It pleases me to help others," she said with a humble bow. She stepped forward and helped the man climb to his feet. "Easy, Father. Take a few deep breaths."

He looked at her with guileless eyes, his round cheeks still flushed pink. "Did I sleep here?"

"Not exactly," Kella said, as she assisted him toward the doorway. "Come now. Rani Trader has come to see you back to the Great Clearing."

"The Clearing? Very well." The priest was still enrobed in the herbs' peace.

"Thank you," Rani Trader said as she came to the man's side.

"My pleasure." Kella nodded her head and gestured to set them on their way. Only when the pair of northerners had reached the edge of the forest did Kella call out, "Rani Trader!" The woman stopped. "When you return to the clearing, give my best regards to Tovin Player. Tell him that Kella is brewing the black willow that he likes."

"Black willow?" Her voice was puzzled.

"He'll understand."

Kella turned her back and entered her cottage before the other woman could ask further questions. The player man would recognize the name of the herb. After all, he had drunk it in her cottage many times before. He had felt its heat spread through his chest. He had felt the awakening in his loins, and he had stayed awake for long hours exploring the strength of the dingy green plant.

Tovin Player would understand the message, and he would come to her. If she were already gone for her meeting with the soldier's Fellowship, then that would be the player's loss. He would wait for her. He would wait for black willow.

6

Hidden in a copse of trees, Hal realized that he might have laughed at the scene before him if the circumstances had been less dire. After all, the old woman was so obviously discomfited by the mare, she might have been performing one of the players' comic pieces. She had walked around the animal, gazing at it from all sides. She was startled when the horse snorted; she leaped back with a gasp of astonishment. Extending a tentative hand to stroke the mane, she had jerked her fingers back when the horse twitched at the ticklish contact.

And then her struggle to mount the animal . . . Admittedly, the old woman had eased her foot into the stirrup with more flexibility than he had thought possible, given her age. As if she'd learned the danger of her earlier hesitancy, she'd planted her hand firmly at the base of the horse's mane, grabbing onto the saddle with her other hand and pulling herself up, even as she pushed off the ground with her stable leg.

The mare, though, would have nothing of the odd weight on her right side. The animal had snorted a warning, and when the old woman persisted, the mare had tried to sidestep away. The woman's scolding scratched the night, and the animal pasted back her ears, clearly thinking her own condemning thoughts. The woman's shout forced those ears forward then, and it was entirely unfortunate that the witch chose to pull the reins at *that* precise angle.

Certainly, if the stakes had been lower, Hal would have been amused. Instead, he swore under his breath as Crestman shouted a warning. The soldier lurched forward, muttering his own curses. Hal was surprised to see the gentle pressure Crestman summoned into his hands as he helped the old woman; the calming manner was unexpected.

Crestman soothed the horse before turning his attention to the herb-witch. By working in that order, he spared the woman a fall. In almost no time, he had the mare settled and ready to move, with the old woman cradled gingerly in her saddle. Nevertheless, the sliver of moon had climbed noticeably higher in the sky by the time the entire operation was complete.

Only after the witch was settled did Hal fully realize his own predicament. He was ill prepared for this spying mission. He had no horse of his own. His flight from Moren had been so precipitous that none had been taken. Since arriving in Sarmonia, there had been no opportunity to acquire good horseflesh; Hal and his men had yielded to other priorities. If Hal decided to follow Crestman and the witch, he'd be traveling by foot.

He should have planned better. He should have mustered his meager strengths. But there had been no time.

Only the afternoon before, he had strolled through the woods, purposely seeking out the old woman's cottage. He had wanted to learn more about the herb-witch, to gain a better understanding of why Mareka took such comfort from her. He wanted to understand his wife's confidence in the woman, what a queen could gain from an herb-witch's potions. He wanted to know why his own son had been subjected to the old woman's brews.

Sheer luck had brought Hal to the herb-witch's doorstep just as Crestman was attacking her. Hal had ducked back into the thick brush on the edge of the clearing, forcing himself to keep silent even as the rampaging soldier beat the defenseless witch, even as he threatened to end her life then and there. Hal had wrestled with his conscience, enraged panic flaring in his veins.

Had Crestman been here before? Had he forced Kella to add something to the draft that Hal's son had consumed? The soldier had tried to poison Hal's family once before; what would make him hesitate here in Sarmonia's lawless forest?

A part of his mind warned that revealing himself would be foolish. Even wasted by his hideous scars, Crestman was more than a match for Hal. The soldier had always been a hard man, conditioned by his years with the Little Army. He could defeat Hal at swordplay, even with one withered arm, even with a dragging leg.

By staying hidden, Hal could learn what Crestman planned. After all, whatever harm had been worked on Marekanoran was done, complete, and Hal could measure out vengeance only as a reply. For now, he listened.

He discovered that the Fellowship was indeed established in Sarmonia. He discovered that Kella knew something of the secret organization, that she was familiar with its secret teachings. He learned that he could follow the mismatched pair the following night, that he could track them and learn still more of his enemy.

For a fleeting moment, Hal had thought to bring Farso

with him on his reconnaissance. That would have been foolish, though. The nobleman had suffered too much at the hands of the Fellowship; he had lost his treasured son. Farso could not be depended upon to stay quiet, to be shrewd.

Rani was an even worse choice. Her past was too tangled with Crestman's. Whatever her words of denial, Hal knew that she had once loved the man, that she had planned a life with him. She might have discarded that dream, for she knew that she had been used harshly. Nevertheless, Hal could not trust her to mind her anger, her own bitter brew of revenge.

And so Hal hid alone in the woods and watched the woman's comic horsemanship. He watched Crestman's unexpected calm. And he watched the pair begin to ride down a forest path.

Well, the old woman would not win any awards handling her mount. In fact, she would delay the pair, especially given the dim moonlight. Hal swore to himself and set off down the path they had chosen.

It actually felt good to run, good to stretch his legs along the pounded earth track. The horses required one of the larger trails in the woods, so that Hal was not very concerned about twisted roots blocking his path, about overhanging branches. Occasionally, he caught a glimpse of the pair he chased. They were making bad time; the herb-witch must be having even more difficulty than he had predicted.

Hal grimaced to himself. Crestman would be displeased. The man had no patience. His anger would flare.

Anger would flare. How much to dare? Must chase the pair.

Where were they going? Where would Crestman take an herb-witch, take a woman who clearly had never traveled by horse anywhere in her life? Hal had been a fool to set out after them. They might be going leagues. He had acted out of frustration, out of concern for his wife and son. What did he think he was going to do, run all the way to Morenia?

He was a fool.

Oh what a fool. Call Crestman to duel. Fate could be cruel.

Grimacing, Hal thrust down the chittering voices. He could not say how long he ran. When he glanced through the tangled branches, he could make out the moon sliver, higher than he'd expected. He checked the lateness of the hour against the breathlessness in his lungs, against the ache in his legs, and he was surprised—his body seemed to accept its punishment, to embrace the chase. He was determined to succeed.

Several times, the forest path branched, but Hal was always certain of his quarry; the pair of horses left clear marks in the damp earth. Once he found a scrap of grey cloth on a snagging branch, and he grinned grimly—the herb-witch had likely fought to keep her balance against the tree's prying fingers. The trail narrowed, spread out again, found a woodland stream to wander beside.

Then, without warning, the path debouched into a clearing. A grassy field spread out before him, grey in the moonlight. Horses snorted in the darkness, several steaming as if their owners had run them hard and arrived late. Hal ducked back into the shelter of the woods, forcing himself to take quiet breaths, to calm his pounding heart. He closed his eyes and offered up a quick prayer to Arn, adding another to Gar for good measure. Courage and vengeance—they made good companions in the moonlight.

Then, when he thought that he could make his way

around the edge of the clearing without drawing unwelcome attention, he began to explore. He worked in the shadows, testing each step with careful feet, verifying that there were no traitor branches before him, no trailing vines to snag his tunic or briars to catch his leggings.

There were more horses than he had thought at first, perhaps three dozen shuffling beneath the autumn sky. Hal identified three guards posted around the cottage, all men by their size. Each was cloaked in black, anonymous and nearly invisible in the darkness.

Hal imagined striding up to them. He could make up a password, insist that he had the proper hidden words. He could invoke Jair, demand that the First Pilgrim's fellowship accept one of its own.

He had no cloak, though. No hood. Not a single friend in the Sarmonian enclave. His ruse would fail.

His ruse would fail. His heart must quail. He should turn tail—

No!

Before Hal could succumb to the songs in his mind, he gave himself over to another noise, a dim thunder that grew as it approached. Horsemen. Two by the sound of them. Yes. There they were, bursting into the clearing from the far side. From the east. From the direction of Riadelle.

The men took a moment to drop blankets over their mounts before they shrugged their black cloaks into place. Even in the dim light, Hal could make out the plumes on the blankets, the single white feather that was blazoned across each man's arms. These were electors, then, men who controlled King Hamid. These were men who proved that the Fellowship had its claws deep into Sarmonia.

Crestman used the Fellowship. The Fellowship used the electors. The electors used Hamid.

Hal must place himself at the head of that chain. He must defeat Crestman to guarantee that Hamid was a free man, free to aid Morenia. But how was he to best a soldier who was stronger than he, wilier, more inclined to use any means, fair or foul?

There was another way, Hal thought as a deceptive silence settled over the clearing. He could grab the other end of the chain. He could step over Crestman and the electors, go directly to Hamid.

It was time to reveal himself. Time to make his true birthright known in Sarmonia, to talk to Hamid as one king to another. Hal would gain nothing more by lurking in the dark, from chasing after conspirators on foot like some hero in a folktale.

He must return to his own camp. He would gather his own advisors and tell them of his decision. He would listen to their complaints, their fears, their certainty that he was endangering himself and others. And then he would act; he would go to the king of Sarmonia.

Hal crept away from the edge of the clearing, stepping around a handful of dried branches. His chest ached from his long run, and his legs trembled like leaves in a breeze. Nevertheless, he straightened as he struck the main path, and he forced himself into a rough trot.

He was the king of Morenia, and he would fight to save his land.

Kella swallowed hard as the opening prayer faded into the silence of the rundown hut. Her thoughts chased after inconsequential details, desperate to avoid focusing on her frightening surroundings.

What was the name of the old man who had lived here? He had been ancient when she was a child; he must have been dead for three score years. And, from the smell of mildew emanating from the walls around her, no one had paid any great attention to this croft since his passing.

Well, someone must have, or the walls would have fallen well before this. Someone must have trimmed the grass back from the doorway, kept the woods from reclaiming the structure. Someone had kept the clearing from yielding to the forest, from giving itself back to the encroaching darkness of trees.

Kella shuddered as she thought of those trees grasping her cloak. She'd spent her entire life walking through the forest; she was well accustomed to the feel of branches catching at her clothes, tangling in her hair. In a strong wind, they could whip by her face with a frightening speed. But she had never felt the forest assault her with the energy it had mustered as she sat upon the horse's back. She had never been subjected to the forest's prying fingers with so much vehemence.

Riding on horseback might be fine for some, but she saw no reason to repeat the experience after this strange night ended. There was no place that she needed to reach in such a hurry, no reason to rush about so. After all, when she was mounted up on a horse, she couldn't see the herbs growing by the path. She couldn't interpret the scents of the night flowers unfolding in the darkness. She might have missed any number of perfect herbs as the soldier led them pell-mell through the woods.

No. Once the soldier-man got her home, she'd be through with horses.

As Kella shook her head, determination hardened her jaw, and her hood started to slip backwards. The soldier had given it to her when they dismounted in front of the cottage—the hood and a mask. He had waited in silence as she sorted out the silk garments, nodding in blunt approval when her face was completely hidden. Then he had set a firm hand upon her arm, pulling her forward with an urgency that brooked no protest.

She knew that if she could see his face, she would recognize the same determination that had planted his knee in her kidney the day before. He was a soldier on a mission, and he was not about to be put off by any details of decency or common politeness. "Stone," he said, and she barely heard the word against the forest night. "Bone. Moonlight."

What? Had he been driven mad by their nighttime flight among the trees? Was he babbling random words? A dose of feverfew might cure him, but what was she to do here?

As they approached the cottage, two hooded figures materialized from the darkness. Kella caught a glint of sharpened steel, and her breath snagged as the soldier pushed her forward.

She staggered to a stop in front of the cloaked pair. "Speak, Fellow," one of them whispered, and Kella wondered what she should say. She started to turn back to the soldier, started to demand that he negotiate for her, but then she thought of his whisper. "Stone," she said, and her voice sounded strange in her own ears. "Bone. Moonlight."

She could imagine eyes upon her, glaring through the midnight hoods. She pictured steel flashing in the darkness, brilliant white beneath the moon, then shimmering red with her blood. She started to turn, gathered her breath to run, but then the shorter of the pair gestured with one hand, summoning her forward.

The soldier pushed behind her as he said to the pair, "Stones bleach pale as bone in the moonlight." The passwords worked more easily for him. The shadowed watchers eased back a breath. Kella was not certain that she was relieved to step inside the rotting cottage.

Certainly she was no safer with the mad soldier by her side. She was no more likely to survive the night surrounded by his colleagues. Nevertheless, she felt a little thrill of victory that she had passed some test, that she had been cleared for the secret convocation.

And convocation it was. A cloaked person stepped forward, an old man by his gait. His voice confirmed Kella's suspicion as it quavered a greeting. "Let us be joined in the name of Jair."

"Let us be joined in the name of Jair," the group repeated, and Kella was surprised by the volume of the assembly. They might hide in the woods. They might wear disguises in the night. But they were not afraid to state their unity, to proclaim their bonds in the night. She shivered and wondered about the identity of her secret neighbors.

"I will not waste your time, Fellows," the old man said. Kella heard his voice and realized that he did not live in the forest. Of that she was certain. She would have known him, if he did. She would have known his querulous voice, recognized the fragile set of his shoulders. "We are gathered this evening because of a visitor, one of our number who has ridden far, with momentous news. He was the one who demanded our coming together. He was the one who asked to speak to all of you tonight."

Kella heard the old man's irritation. He wanted to be the one to make decisions for this group. He wanted to be the one to say when they would ride their horses through the forest, when they would make their journeys beneath the moonlit sky. He had been used by this mysterious visitor, forced to call a meeting, and he did not like it one jot.

Neither did the soldier beside her, Kella realized, as the young man's grip tightened on her arm. She started to pull away from him, to ease the pressure as his fingers bit almost to her bone, but her resistance only heightened his control. His breath came short and sharp; if they'd been back at her cottage, she would have suggested a tisane of heartsease.

They were not in her cottage, though. She was at a secret gathering in an abandoned croft, meeting the Fellowship of Jair under the light of a freshening moon. Others stepped aside to let a hooded stranger walk to the front of the room. "Greetings, in the name of Jair," the newcomer said, and his words were thick with a northern accent.

"Greetings, in the name of Jair," the assembly responded, but Kella did not join in, even when the soldier pulled her closer to his side.

"I come to you from the north," the stranger said. "From Morenia. I come to report upon our progress as we search for the Royal Pilgrim, as we seek the one who will join together all the lands and give us power to rule them all as one."

Kella's own breath quickened. The Royal Pilgrim. Just as the Sisters had reported years ago. Who might join together people as diverse as all those around the world? Who might pull together northerners with folk from across the sea? Who could bring the prayerful Briantans into a group of godless Liantines?

Kella could well remember the gatherings of her own little coven, the endless nights when the Sisters had discussed the Fellowship, even as they worried about the best poultices and teas and healing herbs. The Sisters had decided that the Royal Pilgrim was only a dream, a wish, the Fellowship's fantasy.

If so, though, the fantasy had lasted for long years. The Sisters had tired of the Fellowship long ago, but the cabal's obsession clearly continued.

The northerner continued in a cultured, well-educated tone. "The kingdom of Morenia is in chaos. The gates of its capital are broken, and its king is fled. Its king, of course, was one of us."

Kella felt the soldier beside her grow even tenser at that statement. There was some bond, then, between him and the northern king. Was he a loyal fighting man, sworn to protect his liege lord against murderous attackers? Kella could not believe that. She could not believe that the brute who had assaulted her belonged by any king's side.

What, then? Why did his heartbeat pound down his arm and into his gripping fingers? Why did his blood boil at mention of the Morenian monarch?

"Tell us, then," the soldier said, and he might have been involved in a private conversation with the northerner. "What steps have been taken to bring Morenia under our control?"

The visitor looked about the room, pinning the soldier with a gaze that managed to be steely despite the intervening silk. "Morenia's army has been broken. Its men have been tamed by public execution—one out of every ten soldiers was selected by lot and staked out on the high road leading from the city gates to the palace. Any citizen caught aiding such a soldier was executed on the spot as a traitor. Traitors were then drawn and quartered, and their heads were placed on pikes beside the public wells. Legs, arms, those were posted at the intersections of the city's greater roads. So far, only seven wells have been marked. Fewer than thirty roads are posted."

Kella's belly turned at the grim recitation. She was not so disturbed by the words; she knew that men were harsh in times of war. Rather, she rebelled against the northerner's cold tone, his utter dismissiveness for the people his accent proclaimed to be his own. Did he not care that his countrymen had been routed? Did he not care that his homeland was crushed?

"And the Liantines?" a woman called from the group. "Have they taken back their spiders?"

"They liberated the Morenian octolaris, at least the ones within the palace. Some nobles had spiders in their own courts; we work to regain those. The Liantine silk monopoly has not regained its perfection, but it is stronger than it was before the breaking of Moren."

Again, Kella was appalled by the man's tone. Did he not realize that he spoke of men and women and children, suffering in times of war? Did he not recognize that a city was more than stone and wood, more than trade goods, that it was the people who lived within it?

And yet Kella could sense the assembly's overwhelming satisfaction with his response; she heard approval in their sighs and muttered prayers. They were pleased that this northern city, this Moren, was broken. They clearly desired it to be destroyed, no matter what the cost to any individual people.

Then Kella realized the true import of the story she was

hearing. The northerner was willing to break his own homeland; he was willing to murder soldiers, to execute citizens, to put into danger the lives of innocent children and women. For his own goals, for the goals of the Fellowship, he was willing to hand over an entire kingdom to the invading Liantines.

And if he would aid them, there was nothing to keep him from helping the Briantans, the fervent worshipers who—at least according to the green-robed priest who had come to her cottage the day before—put witches to death.

Witches like Kella. Witches like all the Sisters.

Kella must do something. She must keep the northern conflict from spilling over into the Sarmonian forest. She must do anything in her power to keep the Fellowship from opening the gates to Sarmonia, from letting Briantans come to her. Briantans who would kill her, kill her Sisters. She must save the herb-witches, whatever the cost.

She scarcely remembered to shutter her own excitement. The soldier beside her must not realize that she now had a plan, that she had recognized at last the full threat that he represented, him and his assembly. If he detected that she was more interested in the Fellowship than she had been, that she cared more, then he would cut her down on the spot.

Kella forced herself to draw three calming breaths, exhaling her tension as she emptied her lungs. She would listen to the Fellowship with new ears. She would learn all that she could, and then she would share her knowledge with the Sisters. Together the herb-witches would figure out a way to protect themselves, to keep Sarmonia clean of the Briantan scourge.

Listening sharply now, Kella heard how the Sarmonian fellows deferred to the northerner, how they asked tentative questions, how they nodded obsequiously at his answers. All of the discussion centered around the Royal Pilgrim. The entire assembly agreed that the time for the Royal Pilgrim was drawing nigh; each had a vision of who that person might be, of what they might discover.

Kella could not care one root or petal about the Royal Pilgrim. She must speak with the northerner, collect other information. She must learn what the Briantans planned, if they intended to move south. She must ingratiate herself with the Fellowship to secure her safety and the safety of those she loved and honored.

Her teeth were grating by the time the Fellowship bowed its head in a final prayer. She barely made herself whisper with the congregation as First Pilgrim Jair was invoked. She waited, silent, as the group began to disperse, as first one, then groups of two or three drifted out the door. Kella heard their horses whinny in the night; she knew that all too soon she must mount the mare that the soldier had brought for her.

And, sure enough, the cottage emptied out until there was only the soldier and the northerner standing with her, listening to the last of their colleagues ride away. Kella was surprised as the soldier limped a step closer to his companion and then raised a hand to tug away his own dark hood.

"Ah, Crestman." Crestman! The soldier had a name at last! In fact, he—*Crestman*—turned to glare at her, as if *she* had somehow disclosed his identity. The northerner glanced quickly in her direction; she could see hawk's eyes darting behind his black mask. He declined to reveal himself, though.

"Well met, Dartulamino." Crestman delivered the name coldly, precisely. He knew full well that he was endangering his fellow, that he was violating a confidence. Well, then. Crestman would risk angering his companion, if only to even the score. Kella nearly shook her head. Like blackbirds squabbling over territory, they were. Likely to damage their own plumage, just to save a spot of earth they thought their own.

Dartulamino sighed and cast back his own hood, peeling his mask from his face. The man's hair was rumpled, as if he had just risen from bed. His skin was sallow; if Kella had not heard the strength of his voice, she might have recommended a healthy dose of ginger tea as a tonic. His lips were steady, though, thin and dry within his sparse black beard. She could make out the hint of a green robe about the neck of his black outer garment, and it reminded her of the other priest she had met, the fragile man who had come to her the day before. The woods were full of mysterious newcomers, and she was losing her capacity to be surprised.

Crestman was speaking. She'd best pay attention if she was going to turn anything about this situation to her own advantage, to hers and her Sisters. "I tell you, Dartulamino, we can trust her. She knew about us already. She knew about the Fellowship before I said anything."

"Aye, good lord," Kella said, dipping into as much of a curtsey as her tired legs and Crestman's clutching hand would allow.

The visiting priest pinned her with a gaze that seemed too dark, too intense for his face. "And how do you know of us?"

"I have many ways of learning, good lord." The soldier's fingers dug deep, and she realized that she must elaborate. Elaborate, or risk her muscle being pulled from her bone. "I serve many people in the forest. My handsels are grateful for what I give them. They pay me with coin when they can, with goods when they must. And always, they pay me with news of what goes on in this land of Sarmonia."

There. She would not reveal the Sisters' existence. She would let the men believe that some desperate soul had divulged the existence of their cabal, trading it for herbal cures.

Dartulamino's eyes were shrewd, as if he were accustomed to prying apart men's souls and studying the dark spaces inside their thoughts. "So. One of your . . . handsels decided to tell you about the Fellowship."

"Aye. The Fellowship of Jair." She paused before deciding to cast her last die. "And the Royal Pilgrim that you wait for, the one who will rule over all the kingdoms and place the Fellowship in true power."

"You know too much, woman!" The northerner's anger was immediate.

"He came to trust me, my handsel did," Kella said, working hard to make her voice seem simple, to make herself appear as trustworthy as the ever-rising sun. "He came to me for many months, and he was grateful for the treatments I provided. His lumbago was cured, and he walked like a young man. Walked and rode and indulged in . . . other mannish sport." She smiled crookedly, shrugging her shoulders as if she were not truly aware of such worldly things.

"And where is this man now?" The northerner's liver-colored lips pursed into a suspicious pout.

"I cannot say."

Dartulamino gazed at her for several heartbeats before he nodded. "Very well, then. You come to us with knowledge of the Fellowship. You speak of the Royal Pilgrim. You can be permitted to live with this knowledge."

Kella's relief was swallowed by her astonishment. She had not realized the terms of the test she had just passed; she had not known that she bargained for her life. A great weight descended upon her shoulders, a burden that she had not imagined only a moment before. She thought again of the people who had been executed in the north, of brave soldiers staked out on cold city streets, merely because they had fought for their king. What was she doing here? Why was she playing with fire?

Because fire brews the strongest tinctures. Because fire warms the blood against the winter's ice. Because fire is strength in the woods.

Kella needed the Fellowship. She needed to work with these men to guarantee that she and her Sisters would be free for the future, to guarantee that Briantan fanatics would never march through Sarmonia. She cleared her throat and spoke with a young woman's confidence. "I can serve you."

Dartulamino nodded as if she had completed some traditional formula. "Oh, that you will. Our fellows all share their knowledge, pouring it into a common pool. You have observed our meeting, and we expect nothing less than your complete devotion."

She forbade herself to swallow hard, knowing that these men would see that reaction as a sign of weakness. "Aye."

"Then it is time for you to offer your knowledge. All of it."

"Now?"

"Now."

Kella thought of the dista bark drying on her rafters. She remembered the sweetvine that she had harvested only a few days before. She thought of her calamus root, and catmint, and sweet euphrasia. But she knew that these men were not interested in her herb knowledge. They did not care about potions and tinctures, poultices and tisanes, no matter the strength of the herb-witch who brewed them.

These men wanted to know about Jalina.

After all, that was why the soldier—why Crestman—had come riding through the forest. That was why he had stopped her originally.

Kella could remember her decision that first day, as clearly as if she were making it again. She had determined to lie to the soldier so that he would increase his offer, so that she could gain more from him.

That was before she had felt the fury in his wiry fingers. That was before he had dug his knee into her back. The soldier had no good reason to find Jalina, probably less of a cause to lay eyes upon the boy child. No, Kella had worked hard enough to bring that boy into the world; she wasn't going to yield him up to the first man with a sword and a temper who came along looking for him.

Besides, Jalina and Mite were protected by the handsel.

"Witch!" She had taken too long to respond. Crestman's face darkened, his rage transparent in the glimmering scar that stood out in the dim cottage. Dartulamino's eyes flickered toward the other man, but the northerner did nothing to calm his colleague. Kella must act. She must give them something, anything, or she might not return to her own home.

"I can tell you where a woman hides in the woods."

"A woman?" Crestman's greed suffused his features, and he raised the claw of his left hand, as if he would pluck the information from her then and there.

"Aye. A woman."

"Queen Mareka? The one that I asked you about before?"

"Queen?" She let a little puzzlement seep into her tone, even as the information slipped into place. Jalina. The woman who ordered about her attendants with an air of confident superiority. Queen . . . Well, that was a taller bush than Kella had thought to grow.

"Don't play games with me, old woman! I described her to you. I told you she would be with child, or newly delivered."

"I don't know a Mareka," Kella said. That much was true. The woman that she knew, the woman who had signed the handsel, had a different name. She doubted that the soldier would appreciate the split of words, but she was required to work with the few tools at her disposal.

"Who, then?" Dartulamino asked, and Kella blinked, for she had almost forgotten the threat that he represented. Almost forgotten, but not quite.

"This one calls herself Rani Trader."

"Rani?" Crestman's entire body froze as he whispered her name, as if the words were dusted with crimson-kissed mordana petals.

"Aye," she said, almost sorry to have mentioned the girl who came to guide the forlorn priest home.

"She is here? In the forest?"

"She is."

"Is she alone?" Dartulamino interrupted, edging in his question before the soldier could react.

"I have seen her with one other. With a priest."

Dartulamino nodded, as if all the petals of a coneflower suddenly aligned within his mind. "Of course. Mareka is hidden away here, and so Halaravilli fled south. He brought that merchant brat with him and Siritalanu as well. They must have come straight from the cathedral, directly from the Rites . . ."

"Where?" Crestman's question was louder than necessary in the lonely cottage, and Kella jumped at the jagged edge of his tone. "Where is she?"

"I cannot say for certain," Kella hedged. "I have not actually seen her camp."

"But you suspect! You know these woods!" Kella would not have bargained with the merchant's name if she had known Crestman would become so enraged. The herb-witch in her wanted to ease him over to the deserted hearth, wanted to soothe him while she brewed a posset of comfortleaf.

"She has come to me, that is all. She came to my cottage."

"When?"

She thought quickly. "Most recently, yesterday." That was true, even if it led him down the wrong trail. Kella could see him calculating, measuring, determining just how far away the girl might be.

"Will she return?"

"I cannot know. If she needs me, she knows where to find me."

Crestman began to pace, a hideous action that only drew attention to his crippled leg. One firm stride, one dragging step, another stride, another drag . . . Kella wanted to ask him to stop, to stand still, to let her think, but she dared not say a word.

"When you return," he said at last, "you will find her. Get her to your cottage and bind her fast. Leave a white cloth wrapped around the triple oak at the bend in the stream. You know the one that I mean?"

Kella nodded. She could get the merchant girl. Tovin would help with that. In fact, Rani Trader was almost definitely staying in the Great Clearing, with the players and the other northerners who plagued the forest.

Crestman continued. "Leave the white cloth, and I will come. I will collect Rani Trader and settle my long-kept debts." The light in the soldier's eyes kept Kella from responding aloud. There was no good reason for a man to speak of a woman in that tone. There was no good reason for him to long for her, to pine for her.

Kella was no fool. She could read people's faces. She knew when a man wanted a woman's love, when he offered up his own heart hopelessly, desperate for a soft bed to rest it on. She knew when a man hated an enemy, when he wanted poison to execute a rival. She read both in this man, in this angry, bitter soldier.

Dartulamino nodded as Crestman paced. The sallow man captured Kella with his shrewd gaze. "You'll do that. You'll catch Rani Trader for us. Only then will we know that you are a true friend of the Fellowship. Only then will we be certain that you need not pay for what you've seen tonight."

Kella permitted herself to swallow hard at those words. She could not prevent herself, could not hide her fear of the northern man.

Why should she worry, though? After all, the merchant girl was not a handsel. Kella violated no oaths by speaking of her. Rani Trader had no way to bind Kella, no way to harm the herb-witch. Kella had greater concerns than one transplanted northern girl in all the forest. Kella was trying to save all the Sisters, trying to keep the Briantans at bay.

She looked at the still-pacing Crestman, saw the rage that measured out his twisted steps. She turned her gaze to Dartulamino and confirmed, "Aye. I'll bring you Rani Trader. You have nothing to fear from me. Not you. And not the Fellowship."

"So be it," Dartulamino said, and Kella fought the chill that walked along her spine. "So be it in the name of Jair."

7

Rani muttered to herself as she walked along the forest path. She was tired of life in Sarmonia, tired of wandering through the woods. She wanted to feel a real mattress beneath her, rather than a pallet stuffed with grass. She wanted to eat bread baked in an oven, instead of the charred stuff that Father Siritalanu managed beside a campfire. She wanted to bathe with heated, scented water, rather than splashing her face clean in a stream.

She wanted to return to Moren.

And yet she had only herself to blame. Nearly a year ago, when she had stood in Morenia holding a vial of poison meant for her queen, she had thought that she made all the correct decisions. Discarding the poison, replacing it with water . . . She had warned off Mareka, informed Hal of the danger that he faced.

But she had not done enough. She had not managed to save her city, to protect Moren against the combined forces of Brianta and Liantine. A dull rumble of thunder rolled across the back of her mind—Shad whispering that there was nothing she could have done differently. She grimaced at the god of truth. She might have become more accustomed to the Thousand prowling through her mind, but she would never *like* the prickling sensations that they brought.

She turned her mind back to her mission: finding Mair. The Touched woman had wandered off from camp. Again. Hal had been truly angry this time; he had been as restless as a molting octolaris ever since he discovered the Fellowship in the forest. Rani's heart beat faster as she thought of her sworn enemies, here, beneath the peaceful canopy of trees.

Why was she surprised that Hal had observed them in Sarmonia? They were everywhere, after all, melting into cracks of power and authority throughout all the known lands. The Fellowship was determined to find its way into her life, into whatever peace and prosperity she attempted to build.

No, Rani was not truly concerned about the cabal. Oh, she had pledged to fight them to the death, to destroy them for the evil that they had wrought upon her and those she loved. But her greatest worry now was Hal's announcement that Crestman was loose in the forest.

A chill walked down her spine, despite her flushed face. She had first encountered Crestman in a forest. That was in the north, though, in the kingdom of Amanthia. She had watched the young soldier managing his troops, and she had been taken with the power of him, with his certainty, with his commanding charm.

Here in Sarmonia she knew the rest of the story. She knew that Crestman was dangerous. Deadly.

And she suspected that he was looking for Mair, to finish the job that he had begun in Brianta. If he had killed a child to get at Rani, would he hesitate at murdering a grown woman? "Mair!" Rani cried out again, letting some of her desperation spill into her voice. Without fully realizing her actions, she found herself counting massive tree trunks as she walked along the path. Even in her distress, she could not help but smile as she heard the numbers grow in her mind. This was what Mair had taught her so long ago, back in Moren, back in the days when Rani was a lost and frightened child, abandoned by her guildhall, orphaned and alone.

Count the buildings in the Nobles' Quarter. Count the houses as you creep the alleys. That was how you found the back gates of the richest houses. That was how you measured out the treasures. Find the house that presented the finest face to all the City.

Despite her exhaustion and anger, Rani grinned at the memory. The City. That was how she had thought of her home for the first thirteen years of her life. As if there could be no *other* city at all, no other lands. As if there could be no other home.

Well, *that* had all changed. At least she had learned something in the course of all her travels. There were other lands, to be sure. Northern Amanthia, where she had met Crestman, where she had been sold into slavery. Eastern Liantine, where she had bargained for the riches of a lifetime, breaking the spiderguild's monopoly and bringing home a fortune in octolaris and riberry trees. Western Brianta, where she had journeyed on pilgrimage, struggling to find her way back into the guild that had betrayed her.

And now, Sarmonia. The southern kingdom must have something more than trees, something more than endless forest that confounded her best efforts to find her way in the clear afternoon. Something more than the sorrow and the madness that Rani stalked.

Shad's thunder rumbled again, a note of warning deep inside the hidden message.

"Mair!" she cried again, and then she stopped walking, drawing a deeper breath to force aside the god's voice. Was this what Berylina had done? Was this how she had communed with the Thousand? What had kept the princess sane, then? How had she managed not to be driven mad by their constant voices, their constant touches and sights and sounds creeping across her mind?

Rani edged to the side of the path instinctively, wanting to crouch in the trees' dark shadows as she opened up her mind to the god of truth, completing her communion with the god and silencing him for long enough that she could continue on her quest. Before she could address the thunderous rumble, though, her eyes were drawn to a shaft of sunlight knifing through the forest, falling to the loamy earth a dozen strides off the forest path.

In the sunlight, centered as if it were a stage in one of the players' pieces, was a stony outcropping. The giant boulder was smooth across the top, as if some ancient peoples had used it as an altar. But Rani was not struck by the rock. She was not startled by the sunlight. She stopped because she had found Mair.

Rani watched her friend, and the glasswright was frozen by the scene that she had interrupted. Mair's head was thrown back, her neck arched as if she were a hind whose blood was being drained after the hunt. One hand stretched toward the heavens, clenched into a fist as tight as stone. The other hand pushed down, fingers jagged.

Rani blinked, and she could make out steel in that rigid hand, a blade that glinted in the sunlight like new-polished glass. The reflection was all the brighter because it lay against flesh, against the pale, unflinching stretch of Mair's thigh.

As Rani watched, the Touched woman drew the knife across her leg. There was a heartbeat's pause, and then a thin line of red began to weep from the cut, a delicate tracery that flowed behind the knife like rainwater down a pane. Rani caught her breath, but she did not have a chance to exclaim before Mair lifted the knife, saluting the streaming sun, then lowering it to her leg and cutting again.

"Mair!"

The touched woman looked at her, unsurprised, as if she had known that Rani would find her here in the woods. "Rai." Her tone was matter-of-fact, as though it were the most natural thing in the world for her to be sitting on a rock in the forest sunlight, watching blood seep from two long wounds on her leg.

"What are you doing?" Rani dove through the underbrush, frightening off some ground-nesting creature in her rush to her friend's side.

"Makin' it right. Feelin' the pain o' me puir lost bairn." Mair's voice was far away, her Touched brogue thick on her tongue. " 'E'd love th' woods 'ere. 'E'd chase th' squirrels 'n' listen t' th' chatter. Much better than th' rats o' Moren, ye ken."

Rani's hands shook as she reached out for Mair's. She was surprised that the Touched woman yielded her blade easily, but then Rani did not know what to do with the implement. She settled for wiping it clean on a patch of moss, then thrusting it into her own belt.

"Aye, you were thinking on your son." Rani tried to make her voice gentle, tried to remember not to shout out the anger in her chest. Anger at Mair. At herself. At Crestman, may all the Thousand curse his shriveled limbs. "You were thinking of Laranifarso. But what were you doing to yourself?"

Even as she kept her voice calm, Rani glanced about, frantic for a cloth to wipe away the seeping blood. Mair's square of black silk rested on the ground in front of her, deep as a midnight shadow against the emerald moss. Rani knew, though, that she could not use it, that she could not bring herself to touch the emblem of the lost child. The frustration made her voice harsh. "Mair, you could kill yourself! If your hand slipped, you could cut a vein!"

"I 'avena cut no veins yet, Rai." Mair's smile was sad.

Rani scrambled for her flask of water, pouring some onto the edge of her skirt. Thank Lote she was dressed for the woods and not for court, she thought grimly. Her quick prayer was greeted with the forest god's sweet scent of apples. She bit back a curse as she knelt beside Mair, ministering to the cut with a trembling touch. She caught her tongue between her teeth as she saw how deep the wound was at the center. "Mair, how could you have done this?"

"I gi' meself t' th' power, Rai."

"Power?" Rani could barely say the word without shouting. She heard the raw emotion in her voice, fought to muster her calm. She must get Mair back to camp. It was not safe for them here, not in the open forest. When they had fled from Morenia, they had imagined Sarmonia a reprieve, but now that Crestman stalked the woods . . . Rani glanced into the shadows, chewing on her lip as she realized the sun was sinking lower in the sky. Night came quickly beneath the trees. "Sit still, Mair," she said, letting fear make her voice harsh. "Let me wash this. I can't believe you'd do this to yourself."

"I did, Rai. Me. No one else. Not you, 'r yer king, 'r th'

noble Farsobalinti." Mair's eyes were haunted as she made her brave declaration.

"I'd never dream . . ." Rani let her words trail off as the cut continued to bleed. She contemplated grabbing for the silk square anyway, even though she knew the battle such a move would precipitate. No, Mair should not move her leg, not like that. Rani settled for raising her own hem to her teeth. She bit through the thread that held the garment neatly tucked, and then she strained her jaws until she'd started a long tear. She ripped away a wide strip.

"Ye should put more strength in yer dreams, then, Rai." Mair spoke as if she hadn't heard the cloth tear, as if she did not see Rani pour water over the makeshift bandage. "Ye should think o' th' power o' pain."

"Power of pain," Rani snorted as she sponged the wounds clean. She made herself ignore Mair's automatic twitch, the involuntary wince.

"Aye, Rai. *I* choose 'ow deep t' cut. *I* decide 'ow much t' pay. We Touched take our strength where we find it. Mind yer caste, ye know."

Mind your caste. Rani had learned that lesson a lifetime ago, when she fought for survival in Morenia, fought for her life after her guildhall had been destroyed. The Fellowship had been her teachers then, her benefactors. Back when she had thought that they battled for good and justice and right.

"You're no longer a Touched urchin living in the City streets, Mair. You don't need to prove yourself with bloody knives."

"I dinna need t' prove m'self t' *ye,* p'r'aps." Dreamily, the Touched woman looked beyond Rani, casting a smile toward the square of black silk as if she were engaged in a private conversation with the cloth. "But fer me son, Rai . . . I failed 'im once, but 'e's learnin' I mean t' be true fer th' rest o' time."

"True? What do you mean?" If possible, Rani was more discomfited by Mair's lack of response, by the fact that the bleeding woman did not flinch again as Rani cleaned her wound. Rani knew that she would have jumped, herself, that the touch of cloth on raw flesh could not have been gentle. She repeated, "What do you mean?"

"I swore t' remind m'self o' all I did wrong, o' all I fergot. I use th' knife t' force th' thoughts into me 'ead. I canna be as smart as I used t' be, when I was a girl, 'n' runnin' i' th' city streets. I canna remember all I used t' know."

"You don't need a reminder like this." Rani clicked her tongue against her teeth as she pressed her cloth against the wound. She held it for a count of ten, then peeled it away slowly. "You'll never forget. None of us will ever forget."

"Lar's afraid, Rai. 'E thinks we'll be a'runnin' fro' 'im. I'm 'is dam. I'm th' one t' let 'im know we're 'ere, 'n' always will be."

Tears sparked at the back of Rani's eyes, and she swallowed viciously. "Nome watches over him, Mair." Merely mentioning the god of children brought the sound of pipers skirling through the air. Rani nearly reeled at the volume of the music.

"What?"

"Nothing. Nothing important." The pipes rose in volume, as if Nome would not be denied, but Rani knew that she could not spare the time to acknowledge him properly. She would never have the courage to reach for the gods purposely. She'd never have the strength.

Mair's eyes narrowed to slits, becoming the wise friend,

the shrewd one, the one who had accompanied Rani on her many journeys. "I dinna believe ye."

"I wouldn't lie." Rani pressed once more at the deeper of the two wounds, then breathed a sigh of relief when she discovered that the blood had stopped seeping. "We don't have time to waste, though."

"I've time," Mair said, her voice flat. "I've all th' time i' th' world."

"Mair! Crestman is in the forest!" Rani said it without thinking, without measuring out what the words would mean to Mair, to the mother who had lost her child to the soldier-madman. "He's here, and the Fellowship is here, and it isn't safe for us to be alone!"

Rani heard her shout echo off the trees around them, and she stopped. What was she saying? Her friend was mad enough to *cut* herself over what Crestman had done, and now Rani was saying that they were in danger. What would Mair do? How would she react?

The Touched woman laughed. She threw back her shaggy head and bellowed guffaws. Peals of amusement bounced off the trees. Mair leaned forward, reaching out to Rani as if she were trying to stop herself, as if she were trying to rein in her gales of laughter, but she could not stop.

"Mair!" Rani reached out for her friend, trying to get her arms around the grieving woman's shoulders. Desperation was thick in the laughter, notes that hovered on the jagged edge of despair. Rani tried to fit her fingers over Mair's mouth, tried to press in the noise, to cut it off, to save them, to save herself. "Mair! Stop it! Stop laughing! Stop it! You're going to make your leg open again! Mair!"

At last, Mair's hysteria quieted, or else she needed to breathe. She gulped in great lungfuls of air, shuddering and threatening to collapse into a fit again. Rani could not smother her anger, drown out her fear. "In the name of Fen, what was that?" Even the god of mercy's aroma of fresh-baked bread was not enough to distract Rani. "Do you want to get us killed?"

"If 'e wanted t' kill us, 'e can. 'E's been movin' closer since we came t' th' forest, Rai. We werena certain, though, Lar 'n' me. Not till yesterday."

"Yesterday? What happened yesterday?"

Rani thought that Mair would not answer. The Touched woman stared into the forest, her gaze distracted, and Rani felt a prickle of apprehension march down her spine. Was Crestman watching them even now? Did he have an arrow pointed at her heart? Was he waiting for her to take a step forward, to turn her face toward that deepest pocket of shadow?

Or maybe he was moving closer to where she now stood. Maybe she placed herself in greater danger by *not* moving. Maybe all he needed was for her to stand still another heart-beat, another, another . . .

Rani slicked her palms against her skirt, forcing her tone to remain even as she repeated to Mair, "What happened yesterday?"

"Lar ran off, ye know. I told 'im t' be a good boy, but 'e couldna keep back fro' th' shadows a' th' edge o' th' forest. I 'ad t' look for 'im, I did, 'n' i' was trickier than I thought, gettin' past the King's Guard."

Well, Rani thought, thank the gods for that small favor. If Hal's men could keep people *in* the camp, there was a shadow of a chance that they could keep others out. At least that was how she tried to reassure herself, how she tried to argue reasonably. She did not let herself think that her relief was based on the story of a madwoman, on the tale of a mother who believed her son was embodied in a scrap of silk. "But you got past them, did you?" she prompted, when it seemed that Mair had forgotten to continue her story.

"Aye. I' th' end, I walked past Farso. 'E tries not t' see me most o' th' time, 'n' 'e looked t' th' clearin', as I thought 'e would." Rani heard the hurt behind the words, raw as the seeping cut on Mair's leg. She longed for words to salve that pain, but she could think of nothing, nothing that she had not already said a hundred times.

"Tell me that you won't do that again, Mair. It isn't safe to go wandering about the woods alone. Even if Cr—even if enemies weren't out here, there are animals. You might spook a boar, find yourself slashed by a tusk before you knew it."

"Aye, Rai. 'N' then I might bleed." Mair managed to make the admonition serious, as if she weren't mocking her friend. She waited to see what sort of reaction she might get, but Rani muttered a quick prayer to Plad and was promptly distracted by the god of patience's vinegar tang across the back of her tongue. "I left th' camp, Rai. I left, 'n' I followed Lar, fer I could 'ear 'im callin' fer me i' th' woods. 'E led me t' th' man 'oo murdered 'im. 'E took me t' Crestman."

So that was the way her mind worked now, Rani thought, with all the dispassion of a battle chirurgeon. Mair must have seen things that guided her along the way. She must have applied her woodcraft.

Who was Rani fooling? Mair did not have any woodcraft. She was a Touched woman, born in the City streets, raised in the shadow of stony palace walls. She could not have tracked a man through the Sarmonian woods, not a soldier who wished to stay hidden.

But what was the alternative? Was Rani turning mad herself? Was she ready to believe that a scrap of cloth spoke secrets? Was she ready to believe that Lar lived on?

"You met with Crestman," she said, her voice full of misgivings.

"Do ye think I've turned fool, Rai?" Rani bit back the obvious answer and settled for shaking her head. "I found th' man's camp. 'E wasna there."

"How do you know it was Crestman's? How do you know it wasn't some Sarmonian holding?"

"Would a Sarmonian 'ave that among 'is things?"

Mair pointed at the blade that Rani had taken from her, the short knife that she had used to mutilate her leg. Rani's belly twisted as she pulled it from her own leather belt, as she studied it closely.

The pommel was fashioned like a spider's body, attached to the blade with eight legs of iron, legs that twisted about the hilt. Rani had seen work like it before, in Queen Mareka's personal belongings, in her remnant possessions from Liantine. The knife was a product of the spiderguild, of the ruthless silk merchants who had held Crestman enslaved.

No wonder Mair had cut herself with the blade. Her anger and shock at finding evidence of the man who had slain her own son must have driven her into a frenzy. She must have sliced at her own flesh without thinking, trying to exact revenge, trying to balance the hurt in her heart with hurt in her flesh. Nevertheless, Rani protested, more for herself than for Mair. "It could have come from elsewhere."

"Aye. But would it lie next t' these?" Mair thrust her hand into a deep pocket hidden in her skirts. As she closed her fingers around her stolen treasure, a look of revulsion crossed her face, but she managed to extract whatever she had taken.

Rani took it from her friend slowly, turning it about twice before she realized which end was up and which was down. Her fingers smoothed the midnight silk without her conscious thought, moving the garment so that eyeholes emerged out of the tangle, so that a mouth could breathe through the bottom. A mask and a hood. Simple garments, not threatening in some other time and place.

But here, in Sarmonia, in the woods where Hal had witnessed the Fellowship's meeting . . . "Mair! Why did you take Crestman's mask? He'll know we've found him! He'll know that we've figured out that he's about!"

"Will 'e, now?" Mair eyed her steadily. "Will 'e, Rai? 'N' that would be so terrible because?"

"Because we aren't ready to face him! Because we have not yet met and decided how to handle this new threat?"

"New threat? Th' threat is th' same one its always been, Rai. Th' same one that killed me bairn."

Rani wanted to argue. She wanted to tell Mair that the Touched woman was all wrong, that her rash theft had brought about a new danger. And yet Rani was not certain. Was she going to spend the rest of her life running from Crestman? Was she going to spend all of her remaining days hiding from the Fellowship?

Perhaps Mair was right. Maybe it *was* best to take a stand, to confront the evil that was known. After all, Rani had confronted the old Brotherhood of Justice, back in Moren. She had stood against the agents who had killed Hal's brother, who had assassinated the lawful Defender of the Faith. She had placed her hands upon the Inquisitor's Orb and had faced its burning questions. She had felt the flesh of her palms burn, but she had stood fast, and she had emerged unscathed.

"Where is he, Mair?"

"P'raps I shouldna tell ye. Ye dinna seem t' think we can do nawt wi' 'im."

"You have to tell me, Mair. We have to know. We have to keep ourselves safe, if nothing else."

Mair turned her head to the side, eyeing her friend like a suspicious hawk. Rani thought back to the birds that she had hunted with in Morenia, to a disastrous outing with a kestrel that had escaped her hold. Rani had been responsible for the bird but had failed to tame it properly, had failed to protect it against the attack of a larger hawk, a crueler beast. In the encroaching forest gloom, Rani shuddered. She had failed to protect Mair as well. Failed to protect her friend and her friend's son.

"Come along, Mair," she forced herself to say. "Let's get back to camp. We'll talk to Hal, tell him what you've learned. We'll figure out what to do from here. Besides, you'll want a bandage on that leg, to keep a fever from settling in it."

"There willna be fever, Rai. Dinna ye care."

"Mair, it's a deep cut. You've done yourself some real harm here."

"I've cut meself deeper, Rai. Th' bleedin' takes th' fever out o' it. None o' me cuts 'ave turned."

"None of your cuts." Rani's heart clenched in her chest. "What do you mean, Mair?"

Mair looked past Rani again, tossing a smile toward the black silk square. She turned a rising laugh into a humming sound, and then she began to croon a lullaby. "Hush, sweet son, and rest you well, beside the river, deep the dell. Rest my boy, and don't you cry, sleep you well, come by and by." The sweet notes were soft in the air, gentle in the afternoon light. Rani shuddered at the melody, knowing that it was one sung by royal nurses, by noblewomen comforting their sons. No Touched woman would sing so. No Touched child would be soothed by those words. The song was as much a lie as the life that Mair had eked out in the palace.

"Mair," Rani insisted. "What do you mean by 'none of your cuts?' "

Still humming to herself, Mair turned a beatific smile on Rani. She shook her head and shifted her weight on the stone outcropping. The motion pulled her rough skirts to one side, and Rani saw a line of angry scabs marching up her friend's leg.

"Mair!"

"Rai." The Touched woman turned the single syllable into a note of warning.

"What have you done to yourself?" Rani's belly twisted as she looked at the wounds. The oldest ones had healed to pale pink lines, narrow scars that started just above the knee. The damage progressed though, from pink to angry red, and then to irritated scabs that looked as if they had bled only recently. "Mair, what have you done?"

"Sweet Lar bled fer me, Rai. I told 'im 'e'd be safe 'n' I lied. I bleed fer 'im now. I bind 'im t' me. I keep 'im in me thoughts."

"Oh, Mair . . ." Rani fought back tears of anger and frustration. "He does not need you to cut yourself. He knew that you loved him."

" 'Ow could 'e know that? 'E was a babe, too young t' understand my words. 'E could 'ear 'em, but 'e couldna know what they meant." Slowly, deliberately, Mair reached down to the most recent cut on her leg, to the one that Rani had cleansed, had finally stanched. Catching her tongue between her teeth, Mair stretched at her flesh, pulling it open so that the cut began to bleed again.

"Mair! Stop it!"

"I can bear th' pain, Rai. A little pain t' remember th' son I let die."

"You didn't let him die!"

"I left 'im when 'e most needed me."

"You left him with a nursemaid! You thought that he was safe! You did nothing wrong. He still *could* have been safe if—" Rani caught her words at the back of her throat, but she knew that her eyes had widened in horror. No. Not that secret. Not those words that she had vowed she would never say.

"If?" Mair asked, and her eyes were suddenly locked on Rani's.

"I don't know, Mair," she whispered, wishing fervently, desperately, that she could steal back her words.

"If what, Rai? Laranifarso could have been safe if what had happened?"

Rani did not miss the fact that Mair had lapsed into her courtly speech. The Touched woman had drawn herself up straight on her stone seat; she had raised her chin imperiously, applying all the tricks of command that she had learned at court. Rani swallowed hard. "It won't change anything. No matter what I tell you, your son will still be gone."

"You must tell me what you know, Rai. I have the right."

How could she argue with that? Didn't she believe that Mair had the right? Wasn't that why Rani had spent the better part of the past ten months avoiding her friend? Wasn't that why the bloody cuts on Mair's thighs ached on Rani's own flesh?

Rani collapsed onto the stone outcropping. A part of her mind registered that the rocks still radiated heat from the height of the noonday sun. The air was cooler now. There would be fog in the glade that night. Fog might obscure the sliver of moonlight.

"Rai."

She was delaying. She had delayed this moment for months.

"Rai."

It was time. Mair deserved as much. Laranifarso deserved as much.

"When—" She had to stop. She had to swallow hard, and then she licked her lips, trying desperately to moisten them enough to speak. Her heart pounded inside her chest, pushing against her lungs and making her take short gasps. "When we were in Brianta, I went to see Princess Berylina. When she was in prison. Before she was brought before the Curia."

Mair stared at her, not interrupting, not breathing, not betraying her thoughts with a single movement.

"I left Berylina, Father Siritalanu and I did. As we returned to the inn, to you and to Tovin, we were stopped. Attacked." She waited for Mair to ask a question, to clear some sort of path. The Touched woman offered no such assistance. "By Crestman," she managed to choke out. "He forced a vial into my hand, told me that I must kill Queen Mareka."

At last, Mair spoke. "And he said your test was held in the balance, that you would not make master if you did not comply." The story was familiar, of course. Rani had told as much before.

"He made another demand." Rani's voice had shrunk, shriveled to a dry whisper that required Mair to lean closer. "He said that he had taken Laranifarso. He said your son would die if I did not act."

"Act." Mair repeated the word as if she had never heard it before. "But you did not kill the queen. You spilled the poison and left water in its stead."

"Aye."

"And you failed your master's test."

"Aye." Rani watched Mair measure out the betrayal, weigh the full offense.

"And you killed Laranifarso."

"I did not kill him!"

"You set the wheels in motion. You acted in a way that was certain to cause his death!"

"Not certain! Mair, do you think I would have switched the poison if I'd known I would fail? Do you think that I would have forfeited my rights within my guildhall?"

"Your guildhall, aye . . ." Mair repeated the words as if she were discovering them for the first time, as if she were seeing Rani all anew. "You wanted a position of power and prestige. How foolish of me to think about my poor, defenseless babe."

"Mair, it wasn't like that! It wasn't choosing one and ignoring the other! I was trying to do the best that I could. I was exhausted, and I was starving. I had that trembling sickness, and my hair was falling out—"

"My son died because you lost your hair?"

"Mair, that isn't fair!"

"Don't tell me what is and isn't fair, Rai. Don't tell me

what your actions cost you. Don't tell me what price you paid the day that *you* thought out your course of action, that *you* chose to save Mareka. You chose to defy the Fellowship and Crestman. Don't speak to me of fairness!"

Mair's shout ended as she grabbed the spiderguild knife from Rani's unsuspecting fingers. The Touched woman was fast, faster than Rani had imagined. She set the blade against her forearm, cutting quickly, smoothly, moving the blade perpendicular to her arm.

"Mair, no! Stop it!" Rani leaped for the knife, toppling them both from the rock. The fall knocked the air from her lungs, but then she scrambled to her feet, fumbled for the weapon, for Mair's arm. Her breath came out in a sob, and her fingers came away sticky with her friend's blood. "Mair, this isn't your fault! You can't cut yourself again. You were not responsible for Laranifarso's death! You had no way to stop it!"

Mair scrambled backwards until her spine rested against the rock. She was panting like a wild thing, but she made her words absolutely clear. "I *did* have a way to stop it. I should have stopped you."

"You did not know, Mair. I told no one. I could not think. I could not stop to ask for help. I could not figure any other way, and I thought that it would all work out. I thought that all would be well."

Mair pulled herself to her feet. She stared down, a look of disgust twisting her lips into the ugliest sneer that Rani had ever seen. "You thought wrong. You, Ranita Glasswright. You, Rani Trader. You used your guild knowledge and your merchant ken, but you thought wrong. A little of the Touched, and you might have been saved. A little turning to your troop, and we all might have come through this. Alive."

Mair took one step forward, the spiderguild knife flashing in her hand. Rani bit back a cry, but Mair only laughed, a bitter sound as chill as the fog that had begun to breathe from the earth. She stooped down, and Rani had to blink to identify the object that she held. The silk square, of course. The remnant of Lar.

The Touched woman held the cloth against her wrist, pressing it hard as she worked to stop the bleeding. Without lifting the fabric, she turned on her heel and started to walk away, into the forest, away from the path.

"Mair! Wait!" But Mair continued walking. "It isn't safe! You should not be alone in the woods!" The Touched woman's skirts melted into the shadows of the trees. "Mair, come back! Mair, please!"

But no amount of calling made the grieving mother return.

8

Hal watched from the shadows as Tovin Player came forward on the stage. Hal and Tovin had debated long into the previous night about which play the troop should present. Hal had argued for one of the tragedies, a dark tale of secret mystery, of ominous instruction that would serve as a reminder of all the obligations of the crown.

Tovin, though, had said that he should present a comedy, a froth of amusement and humor. He had argued that such a production would lighten Hamid's mood, make the Sarmonian monarch receptive to demands that would be difficult for him to meet, even under the best of circumstances.

At last Hal had given in, stifling a yawn against the back of his teeth. What difference did the players make, in any case? What were the chances that Hamid would pay them any mind, no matter how telling the production proved to be, no matter how crafty the players?

Hal had to admit that if the tables had been turned, he would not be inclined to help out another royal. Not one who had been driven into exile by *two* enemy armies. Not one who had hidden in his forest under false pretenses. Not one who had lied before his very court.

Lied to the king. Long to take wing. What will fate bring?

Hal grimaced at the dark rhymes in his head and thrust a quick glance at Puladarati, hoping that the duke had not noticed his momentary distraction. Fortunately, the nobleman was focused on Tovin, fixed on the player's singsong proclamation: "We hope you liked our ballads; we hope you liked our show. We'll please you well the next time; for now our troop must go."

The player swept his cape behind him as he bowed, the flourish nearly as thrilling as the play had been amusing. As he stepped back into the shadows, three machines rolled onto the stage. Earlier in the evening, Hal had watched the players consulting with Davin. The ancient engineer had been instrumental in pushing the troop to use his toys, to experiment with their possibilities.

Each engine rolled forward on a nest of interlocking gears, rounds, and pegs that Davin had fashioned from deadwood in the forest. A shield set atop each creation, sheltering the workings and disguising the motive power—a crankshaft that had been wound tightly by teams of players just off the stage.

The watching Sarmonian nobles fell silent as the engines crept forward, their wooden parts rattling in the hall. As one, the shields slid back, revealing carved pegs striped with bright colors. Hal heard a few exclamations, a number of whispered questions, and then each crankshaft finished its unwinding. The machines stopped, frozen on the edge of the stage.

Hal glanced at Davin, saw the old man's lips moving inside his long, grey beard. One. Two. Three.

And then the machines sprang to attention. The ribbon-wrapped pegs flew from their horizontal position to an upright stance, and the energy carried lengths of silk forward, streaming across the audience. The nobles cried out with surprise, and then they laughed as soft silk billowed to the floor—brilliant lengths of cobalt and crimson and topaz. The audience erupted into applause, stamping their feet against the floor and roaring their pleasure.

Hal did not think that the trick had been as good as all that, but it was more memorable than the play. Thinking back, he could not recall a single word of the performance. There had been a shepherd boy and a dog—Hal remembered that much. The sun had been a character as well, and a maiden, and a fat, pompous mayor from a silly mountain village.

The Morenians lent their applause as well, but without the Sarmonian enthusiasm. There were too many worried watchers, too many northerners who knew precisely what was to follow the production. Puladarati surveyed the assembly of Sarmonians, nodding occasionally as he counted out worthy allies. Farso was less obvious in his calculation, but he remained tense by Hal's side.

Only Rani seemed to measure out the crowd's approval for its own reward, noting who stooped to gather up the silk banners, who edged forward to view Davin's wondrous machines. Perhaps she was counting her potential wealth from sponsoring such fine players. Her merchant mind must function even here, even now, when the moment of confrontation drew near.

Had Tovin chosen his play well? Or might Hamid see himself mocked as the fat mayor? Might he take exception to the depiction of political might?

Political might. Traditional right. Soldierly fight.

No! Hal must focus. His mind must not wander. Too much depended on what was said next, on the alliances that he might forge on the heels of the players' tale. His ears buzzed as if he had consumed a deep draft of Mareka's spider nectar, but he managed to force his rhyming schemes into a small corner of his mind. He made himself turn a mental key, locking away the distraction of despair.

Silence. He was ready, then. He was prepared.

On the stage, Tovin had sunk to one knee and bowed his head to Hamid in unaccustomed humility. "Your Majesty," he said, "if our piece pleased you, I would beg a boon."

"A boon?" Hamid pounced on the request like an eagle snatching a fish from a mountain lake. "Beyond the right to settle in my forest, you mean? Beyond the right to make your camp in the middle of my Great Clearing?"

For all the anxiety Tovin showed, he might have been cajoling his mother for a bauble or an extra portion of pie. Hal envied the man. The player grinned and shrugged. "Aye, Your Majesty. Those gifts have served us well, of course, and we have been honored to return your hospitality upon this stage tonight. There is more, though, that I would ask."

Hamid's nobles looked to their king expectantly, clearly curious as to how he would handle such an unaccustomed request. After all, what reason did Hamid have to cater to the players? The traveling troop was not likely to curry him favor with his electors.

As if to protect their own rights, several noblemen edged forward, taking up bellicose stances. Hal watched three of the nearest electors expand their chests with pride, forcing attention to the symbols blazoned there, to the scrolls of parchment and plumed pens. These were the men who had made King Hamid, they seemed to say, and they could unmake him if he showed undue favor to an outsider.

Tovin appeared oblivious to Sarmonian politics. "Come

now, Your Majesty!" he gestured toward the stage. "The lesson of our little play was clear! The shepherd was asked for three things, and his riches grew each time he gave of himself."

"Your piece was meant to prepare me, then? You will request three favors?" Hamid's tone was dry, and he clearly hoped to shrug off the player's request.

"Nay, Your Majesty." Tovin laughed infectiously, letting his copper curls catch the torchlight. "A king is mightier than all the shepherds in the world. One favor from a king is worth infinitely more than any three from a shepherd."

"One." Hamid set the word between them with the wariness of a forest beast expecting a trap.

"Aye. And this is something easily within your ability to grant, Your Majesty. Perhaps by the granting you will grow, like the shepherd in our play. You will grow, and I will grow, and then I can beg more indulgence in the future."

The assembled nobles, even the electors, waited for Hamid to smile before they laughed at Tovin's impertinence. As if he had been outwitted, the king waved one bejeweled hand. "You'll keep at me, if I do not give in. I learned that much when you asked for rights to the Clearing, and again when you insisted that your sponsor be permitted to join you. Go ahead, Tovin Player. Ask your favor."

Tovin took a single step forward, and his eyes grew sharp. Suddenly, Hal wondered if he could trust the man. Might Tovin turn against him? Might Tovin actually work for the Fellowship, work against Hal and Morenia and all that hung in the balance?

Then the dangerous moment was past. The player gestured expansively, directing Hamid's attention to Hal's dark corner. "All I ask is this, Your Majesty. Speak with my friend. He has some questions to ask of you."

"Questions?" Hamid peered into the shadows, apparently taken aback by the request. "He can wait until I hold court in a fortnight."

"His questions are more urgent than that, Your Majesty. He needs you now." With a player's touch, Tovin placed a low rumble of urgency behind his words. "This only do I ask, Your Majesty. Speak with my friend, and then my players will be at your command—to play for you or leave your court, whatever you desire."

Hamid measured Tovin carefully, his narrow eyes ignoring his nobles, ignoring their questioning looks. "Very well, Player," he said at last. "Whatever I command."

Tovin bowed deeply. "You are most generous, Your Majesty."

Hal caught the pointed glance that Tovin cast his way, the certain proclamation that debts were changing hands upon the players' stage. Hal nodded once, accepting the new bargain. Yes. He would pay Tovin later, pay with coin, if he could devise nothing else that the player wanted from him. With coin, that was, if this gambit was successful, if he managed to find his way back to Morenia, and his throne, and his treasury. Otherwise, all debts would be cleared with Hal's annihilation.

Tovin's arm swept toward the shadows, toward Hal. "Then I present my friend to you, Your Majesty."

Hal made sure that he had removed his hand from the pouch at his belt before all eyes turned in his direction. It would not do for the Sarmonians to assume he fumbled for some weapon. He emphasized his innocence by shrugging, by turning his palms outward and displaying their pale flesh like a treaty flag upon a battlefield. He forced himself to stand straight, to throw his shoulders back.

And then he stepped toward Hamid and bowed the short courteous salute from one man to an equal. "King Hamid," he said, carefully avoiding any superlative title, even as Puladarati and Farso flowed into place behind him like an honor escort.

Hal raised his eyes in time to see anger flit across the Sarmonian's face. From the southern king's perspective, he had just been tendered a grave insult. He was slighted, embarrassed in front of all his court. Hal did not have long to clarify his stance, did not have many heartbeats to explain what was happening.

"We are honored by your welcoming us into your court, brother." Hal made the words hearty, boisterous, as if he had just returned to the Sarmonian hall after a good day's hunting.

Hamid cast a quick glance toward one of his retainers, the court herald who stood against the wall. The man resorted to shrugging. He clearly did not recognize Hal's face or the guise of his companions. "We?" Hamid said before the pause became embarrassing. His voice was dry, skeptical.

"We hope that you will not think ill of our loyal retainer Tovin," Hal soldiered on, brushing a hand to bring the player into the circle of his power, even as he attempted to absolve his vassal. "The player acted solely at our command."

"Command? What power do you think to hold in my court?"

"The power of embassy, I hope," Hal said, and he thrust his hands forward, turning his wrist so that the large signet on his finger caught the light: J for Jair, for the ancestor of his house.

The herald recognized the symbol. The old man eased to his king's side, leaned close to whisper in Hamid's ear. Hal waited, feeling tension expand in the crowd behind him. Whispers started to roll; sharp eyes penetrated between his shoulder blades.

"Halaravilli ben-Jair," Hamid said, and the name sounded almost like a curse. "You come to my hall, Morenia, when half the known kingdoms search for you."

"More than half, I suspect," Hal said, forcing a grim smile across his lips. "Certainly my own land and my enemies of Liantine and Brianta."

"And your retainers in Amanthia as well, no doubt," Hamid said, for the herald had whispered more information. "Duke Puladarati. Baron Farsobalinti." Hamid nodded greeting, clearly measuring, calculating. "We should be honored that you chose Sarmonia for your sojourn, Halaravilli ben-Jair. We trust that you found our Great Clearing to your liking?"

"It met our needs," Hal said smoothly. He could see Hamid's anger; the king resented being pulled into the politics of surrounding kingdoms. "Those needs were great, my lord, and our mission secret."

Hal forced himself to keep his attention on Hamid. There was no time to wonder who among the Fellowship was watching. He must not speculate on who might have slipped from the hall already, who might be carrying messages to Dartulamino or Crestman, or any of the Fellowship's other hidden forces.

First God Ait started at the beginning, Hal reminded himself, taking cold comfort in the familiar nursery saying. "We would speak with you, my lord," he said. "With more privacy than this hall can provide."

Hamid eyed him steadily, weighing the request as if it might cost him his life. "You've lied to us once already," he said at last. "We'll not meet with you alone. We'll bring our men." He pointed rapidly toward three of his retainers, electors who stiffened to prompt attention.

"And, with your kind permission, we will bring ours."

Hamid weighed the request, obviously balancing Hal's appearance of respect with the need to continue commanding the situation. "Not that one," he said, pointing toward Tovin. If the player were offended, he gave no sign. Hal merely added to his mental tally; the player would surely demand additional payment for the insult. Fine.

"Not Tovin Player," Hal agreed. "Duke Puladarati, if it pleases my lord. And Baron Farsobalinti. And Rani Trader."

"Who is this Trader?"

"You met her as Varna Tinker. She is a loyal retainer of mine, so true that she risked all to disguise her name before you." Hal gestured toward Rani, who completed a perfect bow, well practiced from her years of service in his court. Hamid measured out the obeisance, and then his eyes pinned Tovin once more. It was the player who had hidden Rani's name, who had purposely misled Sarmonia. The lie would cost Hal still more gold coins. It had seemed a better bargain at the time.

At last Hamid shrugged his acceptance. "Let us retire to my study," he said, and a page led the way from the Great Hall, apparently oblivious to the hum of curious courtiers behind them.

As they made their way through the long corridors, Hal wondered again what he might say to convince Hamid to form an alliance with him. After all, Morenia could not offer wealth or prestige or meaningful alliances, not at present.

No path, his feet scratched out against the stone floor. *No path. King's wrath. Blood—*

No! He would not yield to the voices. He would not give in to their hopeless suggestions. This was what Hal had bargained for. This was why he had traded his safety and his security, the anonymity that had sheltered him, his men, his wife. His son. He was risking all so that he could end his charade, so that he could return to the sort of life that he and his family and his devoted followers deserved.

When they arrived at one particularly well-carved portal, Rani stepped up to his side, almost as if she intended to enter before him. The movement was awkward, but she succeeded in capturing his attention. "I will speak," she said, the words so soft that he might almost have imagined them.

Was he a coward, then, to hide behind a retainer?

No, he made himself answer in the silence of his mind. Not a coward. Rather, he was a shrewd general, mustering his forces. He relied on a loyal soldier, a warrior who had a specific skill destined to win the day. Rani Trader's negotiations were her strength, her very identity. They formed the core of her being, for all that she had masqueraded through other lives within Morenia and without.

Hamid stalked across his study, drawing up near a carved wooden desk. From the far side of the room, Hal could make out a tangle of writing implements—scrolls, quills, ink, and sand. A gnarled knot of wax rocked as Hamid set his hands upon the desk. The Sarmonian king cleared his throat peremptorily, and Hal's attention was drawn to the men that came to flank their king.

The electors' own symbolic scrolls and quills were embroidered on their chests. Fleetingly, Hal thought that the men looked like prison guards, that they seemed to corral Hamid and subdue him.

Was Hal any less controlled by his own retainers, though? Puladarati stepped closer, his three-fingered hand smoothing his forest leathers as if he'd been born to the disguise. Farso shifted from foot to foot, a sheen of perspiration brightening his features as he measured out the room, no doubt calculating approaches and escapes. Like Hamid, Hal had a past with his lords; they bound him to certain futures.

And yet Hal *was* permitted to make his own decisions. Even if every member of his council disagreed, Hal held his throne by the divine choice of First God Ait and by all the Thousand. Hal ruled because First Pilgrim Jair had ruled; he could not be voted from his throne. Strange Sarmonia, where Hamid was bound directly to his electors, bound to please them and all their landed men! How could any king rule for longer than a season when he must answer to so many?

Hamid nodded once to his electors and then narrowed his eyes toward Hal. "Very well. We have left my Hall that we might speak honestly with each other, without the need to pose and preen for the folk who assemble there. What would you say to me, Halaravilli ben-Jair?"

Hal nodded once toward Rani. He could read her nervousness in the set of her jaw, but her voice was steady as she answered for him. "I, Rani Trader, speak for my king. We come as ambassadors to Sarmonia, Your Majesty. We offer riches that your kingdom cannot refuse."

If Hamid were surprised that a woman spoke for a king, he managed to hide the emotion. Instead, he spun a sardonic grin across his thin lips. "Riches? From a group of northerners hiding in my forest? Offered by a woman who assumed a false name the first time she dared to speak in my court?"

"Wealth, Your Majesty, from an embassy of noblemen who took the time to measure out the extent that you might help them." Rani paused for a heartbeat and then added, "And they you."

The electors flinched at that, and Hal bit back a wince. Now was not the time to imply that Hamid needed the northerners. They stood in the study as supplicants, not as equal parties to a fair bargain. Hamid laughed, the rumble rising from his narrow chest. "*They* help *me*? Perhaps you took ill in my forest, Varna, er, Rani Trader. Your brain seems soft, if you believe I need any assistance from lurkers in my forest."

"I took no illness in your woods. But I have used my time in your forest. I have listened to the tales of your kingdom, Your Majesty, to the rumors of power."

"Power?" Hamid actually seemed intrigued by Rani's words, even as the electors shifted in discomfort. Where was Rani taking this negotiation? Why hadn't they worked out her words the night before? Hal had spent all his time arguing with Tovin, fighting over how he would gain an audience with Hamid. He had not focused adequately on what he would say once the dialogue began. He had not spent enough time with Rani.

Of course, he thought honestly, it would hardly have made any difference. When was the last time that Rani had listened to him? When was the last time that she had done what *he* desired in any instance, regarding anything?

"Aye," Rani said. "Power, Your Majesty. Those who stay in your forest learn many secrets, by Jair." Hal understood what Rani was doing, knew that she was trying to draw a reaction from one of the electors. Her bid failed, though. None of the three men started at the name of the First Pilgrim. She continued with scarcely a pause. "We hear rumors of those who would move against you. We watch meetings in the night, secret gatherings beneath the full moon."

Hamid's eyes narrowed further; Hal wondered if the man could actually see through the tight slits. The Sarmonian glanced at his electors before he barked, "If you have knowledge of traitors in our midst, you must share it with us immediately. We will not tolerate games of words."

Rani raised her chin. "I do not play games, Your Majesty. I promise you that."

The king of all Sarmonia took the full measure of the insolent woman before him. Rani's fingers moved once across her robes, clenching the silk as if she gained strength from the fibers there. Perhaps the cloth reminded her of other battles she had fought, of the spiders that she had stolen from Liantine, of the clever negotiations she had once fashioned to the east.

Maybe, in some strange way, Hamid could sense all that Rani had won, all the decisions that she had made, all the paths that she had wandered in the years that she had lived at court. Maybe the Sarmonian king was swayed by the knowing look that one of his electors cast to the others, a look that spoke of power and secrets behind the throne, even if it did not betray the Fellowship. Maybe Hamid had his own secret reason for wanting an alliance with Morenia—land routes perhaps, or ports, or grain markets, or a source for more silk. For whatever reason, the Sarmonian inclined his head. "Speak, then. Tell me what you know, and I will weigh the value."

"Nay, Your Majesty." Rani's insistence surprised every Sarmonian in the room. "You speak first. Tell us you will support us. Tell us you will stand beside us, as Morenia's sworn ally."

No! Hal wanted to cry. She went too far. Rani acted precisely like a merchant in the marketplace; she was forgetting the strictures of noble life. It was not meet to demand Sarmonia's support without first making some showing of good faith.

"Ally!" Hamid's voice was hot; he did not need to glance at his electors for that reply. "How am I to make an alliance when I do not know what issues are in play? What dangers do you face at home that you would rather take your chance jousting here in my private study, than fighting for liberation with a strong right arm and loyal soldiers at your back?"

Rani! Hal longed to say. *Yield to the man. Give him something. Tell him what he asks.*

What he asks. End these tasks. Shed our masks.

Of course, Rani did not yield. Instead, she took a step closer to Hamid, looking for all the world like an ale merchant closing a deal in the marketplace. "Certainly, you've heard rumors, Your Majesty. You've heard that Liantines have taken our harbor, that Briantans hold our castle. You know that the king of all Morenia is exiled from his land. But you know older tales than that, Your Majesty. You know that Morenia is a longtime friend of Sarmonia. We have been a market for your goods, as you have been for ours. We sold you spidersilk for half of what the Liantine guild once commanded. Pledge your support, and Morenia's undying friendship is yours. Pledge your support, and Halaravilli ben-Jair will be your trusting ally, your endless friend, in the marketplace, on the battlefield, wherever you find yourself wanting."

"My ally," Hamid said, clearly sampling the flavor of the word. Perhaps Rani had not mismeasured. Perhaps this matter truly was as simple as a marketplace bid. Hal read the hope in Hamid's tone, the possibilities, and he tried to hold himself tall, seeming worthy of Sarmonian investment.

"Yes, Your Majesty!" Rani urged. "If you stand with Morenia now, we will stand with you through all the future. Our fighting men will be your fighting men, our soldiers yours."

Hal saw the instant that the electors identified the threat. Their anger was transparent, their determination to silence Rani so swift that he momentarily feared for her life. One man glided forward, placing his arm on Hamid's and making the king step forward for counsel. The motion disclosed the Sarmonian's slight frame, revealed just how slender Hamid was.

The elector's words were unclear, mere hisses in the otherwise silent room, but the direction was plain. Hamid was to ignore Rani. He was to set aside her offers, her arguments, her inducement to alliance. He was to ignore her offer of freedom—independence from the electors—once and for all.

As if he were buying time, Hamid reached for one of the pens on his table, fingering it as if it were a talisman. His fingers were lean and wiry, calloused from weapon play. The elector ignored the distraction of the pen; rather, he stepped even closer to his lord, moving his hand in a chopping motion, speaking even more emphatically. The other two electors flanked their king, standing just a shade too close for comfort.

Hal read Hamid's decision even before Rani did. He felt no surprise as Hamid shook his head, no relief as the electors stepped back. He could not even muster pity when he saw the flash of anger in Hamid's eyes, anger quickly stowed away.

The Sarmonian king shook his head, and his words were bitter. "We gave you a chance, Rani Trader of Morenia. We asked for you to show your value, to lay some guarantee of the intelligence you bring before us. Your words are naught but bluster, promises like a nursemaid's whispering to her charge. We are busy here with our court, and we have no more time to play. You will leave us now."

"Your Majesty—" Rani began.

"Now." Hamid set the word down firmly, not even bothering to glance at his retainers.

"Your Majesty—" Rani tried one more time.

"Rani," Hal said, for he could see that Hamid would never yield. Not with the electors at his side. Not with his crown held in the balance.

Rani heard the note in Hal's voice, clearly understood that she must not brook his command, even if she longed to deny the explicit order of another monarch. Swallowing hard, she managed to sketch a bow toward the Sarmonian king, and then she faded back to Hal's side.

"We will stay here," Hamid said, gesturing at the table's parchment rolls. "We will review these accounts and do what must be done to manage our kingdom. We have wasted enough of our time with players' fancies."

Hal made his own smooth bow. He curled his tongue around proper words, words that accepted his defeat. He set his arm on Rani's elbow and guided her toward the doorway, leaving Puladarati and Farso to make their own retreat. Only as they made their way down the long corridor did he realize that he had no idea where they might turn next. He had no idea how he could work to save Morenia, to save his people, to save himself. He had no idea how to defeat the Fellowship of Jair.

9

Hal listened to Rani sigh again and say, "I don't know how I misjudged him so badly."

He barely kept his irritation from smothering a reassuring tone. "You've spent a lifetime bargaining with merchants, and you struck the wrong balance with a nobleman. Eat your pie." He blew on a steaming bit of kidney to make his point, refusing to speak more until Rani had placed a bite in her own mouth. "The man is not free to act. If he could, your arguments would have swayed him."

"He did not listen at all."

Hal raised a pottery mug to his lips and swallowed some surprisingly good ale. "You might as well have made your arguments to a father whose son was held at knifepoint. His decisions are not his own."

"I'm a *trader,* though." Hal raised an eyebrow at her elevated tone, and she hissed, "I am supposed to be better than that! I should have found a way to offer a deal that he could accept."

"That *he* could accept? Or that his electors could?" Hal darted a glance about the tavern common room. They were alone now; no one could overhear his using the word 'electors.' Nevertheless, he lowered his voice to a bare whisper.

"Rani, you could not structure a deal to meet everyone's needs—not his, not . . . the nobles', not our own, all bound together."

"I might have—"

"You might have done nothing! There was no way to bring him to our side!" He forced himself to calm down, to swallow more ale. Why was he so angry with Rani? She had only tried to build an alliance with Sarmonia. How could they have guessed that the electors held Hamid on such a short lead?

Short lead. Men bleed. Crows feed.

Hal pushed aside the whispers of defeat, smothering them with false bravado. "Rani, you're no use to me if you lose faith in yourself."

"I'm not losing faith!" She slammed her hand down on the table. Together they glanced toward the motherly woman who stood at the far end of the room. The proprietress of the tavern had looked up from her task of trimming tallow candles with a short, sharp knife. Rani lowered her voice and repeated, "I'm not losing faith. I'm the one who thought to come *here*, didn't I?"

"Aye," he agreed, hoping that she could not discern how much the admission cost him. Even as they had left Hamid's palace, she had devised yet another plan to save him. She had figured out where they might find one last ally in Sarmonia, where they might forge a final bulwark against their rising tide of enemies. "But are we sure that you were told the truth?"

"They'll be here," Rani said, easily abandoning her guilty irritation to comfort him. "This is the fourth day after the full moon."

"Full moon," he muttered. "Superstitious, trust-in-magic

claptrap. Why a group of—" But he never completed his tirade. The Sisters arrived before he could finish his rant.

Rani had argued that the Morenians must stave off the Fellowship, first and foremost. Now that Hal's identity was revealed, the shadowy group must immediately be located and penetrated. Only by direct confrontation could Hal avoid assassination.

They had precious few tools to find the enemy. They could attempt to use one of the electors that Hal had seen in the forest, but only if they could identify the specific men who had journeyed to the cottage. Identify them, find them, calculate a lever to use against them. All possible, but only with time and knowledge—two commodities in pitifully short supply.

They could comb the forest for Crestman or Dartulamino. Those enemies, though, were heavily armed, and known to be deadly in a fight.

There was one other, however, one last person who could take them to the Fellowship. Kella. The herb-witch in the forest. If they could challenge Kella, she might break. She might bring them access to the Fellowship if they could find the proper . . . motivation.

Once Rani thought of the herb-witch, Hal warmed to the idea. Of course, they could not threaten the woman directly. She was Hamid's vassal; the Sarmonian king would hardly tolerate one of his people being terrorized in her own cottage.

Hal had proposed that they use Tovin to manipulate Kella. After all, the player had sent Rani to the witch's cottage weeks before, to retrieve Father Siritalanu. Rani had dismissed the idea flatly. When he had pressed her for a reason, she had merely said, "Black willow. That is reason enough, no?"

Black willow? That meant nothing to him, but Rani refused to elaborate. Refused to elaborate and refused to be swayed. Well, who was he to comment on the player? He certainly did not trust himself to measure the man fairly. Not when he saw the troubled memories that skated across Rani's brow. Not when he imagined the . . . conversations that had passed between Tovin and Rani, here in Morenia and before.

Rani had paced the narrow streets outside Hamid's palace gate, muttering to herself as she considered options, measured out ways to make the herb-witch help them. Hal had stared at her with concern, with growing certainty that she had turned as mad as he. "Wait!" Rani exclaimed as the sun darted behind a fluffy autumn cloud. "The Sisters!"

Kella had delivered the possibility herself. She had told Rani about the Sisters, about the conclave that controlled all herb-witches. Kella must obey the Sisters. If Rani and Hal could reach them, the Sisters could motivate Kella.

Once they hit upon the plan, it took Rani little enough time to find the circle of herb-witches. The Sisters were more discreet than secret; their existence was known throughout Riadelle. Rani had taken Hal's leave to wander through the city's Merchants' Quarter, to ask a series of careful questions. She was pointed first toward one merchant and then another, and a last kind soul directed her to the Blue Rose Tavern, to the proprietress whose name was Zama. The directions had been easy enough—take the second street from the market square, enter the first inn past the apothecary.

In fact, it had proven easier to locate the coven than it had to slip away from Hal's retainers. Puladarati and Farso had argued for an immediate return to the Great Clearing, to the comfort of Hal's meager troops, now that his name was known in Sarmonia. Ultimately, Hal had pleaded exhaustion, insisting that they pass the night in a city inn. He had said that he would steal a nap, in hopes that he might make fresh plans later that night. He and Rani had barely succeeded in sneaking down the servants' stairs, escaping Farso's nervous patrol of the common room.

Upon entering the Blue Rose, Hal and Rani were treated like any other tavern patrons. Zama herself had served them, pridefully setting down plates of kidney pie. The tavern was tidy, the floor strewn with fresh rushes, the tables scrubbed. A small fire burned on the hearth—enough to chew the edge off the autumn's chill, but not so much to make the room uncomfortable. And so they ate and drank and waited for the coven to gather.

Coven to gather. Mind in a lather. Anything, rather.

Hal shook his head. The chittering words were constant now, a ceaseless muttering that distracted him if he gave it half a chance. He could not risk frayed attention, not now, not with Zama approaching from behind her long wooden bar. "Good lady. Good sir," she said, wiping her cracked hands on her apron and nodding her head in a casual approximation of a bow. "Is there aught else that I can get for you this evening?"

Hal sensed her expectation, her desire to close the door behind them. Swallowing his nervousness, he managed an easy smile. "Nay, good dame. My companion and I, we'll just sit beside the fire a bit longer."

The woman was clearly accustomed to having her way, even with difficult patrons. "I'd love to accommodate you, but that won't be possible this evening. I'll give you each a pasty, now, a nice meat pie to take into the night. But I'll need to close the door after you both."

"Close the door?" Rani laughed, as if she did not understand. "But you have new customers who have just arrived!"

Zama looked up as a half-dozen women shrugged out of their cloaks. She nodded a greeting to the newcomers, but she was not to be deterred. "Aye. Those are my sisters. We've a bit of family business to discuss."

Hal pointedly scanned the collection of women. One stood taller than he, with broad shoulders and a waist-length braid of shimmering blond hair. Another was so small that she might have been a child, a dark-haired woman with skin to match who barely came to his belly. "Your family is a mixed one."

"A close one, rather. Get on with you, then. We haven't much time, and we have a great deal to discuss about our poor, aged parents." The door opened and four more women entered.

Rani lowered her voice so that Zama had to lean closer. "We have a message about one of your sisters. We come from the forest. From Kella."

Zama's eyes darted toward the door and a half-dozen more newcomers, and her face lost some of its professional good humor. "Kella has not joined us for more moons than I can recall."

"Aye," Rani agreed. "She spoke of you with fear."

"What do you know of Kella?"

"She uses your family's knowledge. She takes actions that will affect all of you directly. She leaves you vulnerable to one outside the circle of your family."

Under other circumstances, Hal might have wondered

aloud. How did Rani do it? How did she make her paltry handful of facts sound like a valuable commodity? How did she manipulate the wise old woman so smoothly?

Zama made a decision. "Very well, then. You may stay. But he leaves." She nodded toward Hal as if he had no ears of his own, no eyes to see the insult of his dismissal. "This is a business of women."

Rani's response was steady, as if she were negotiating a good price for eggs. "This is a business beyond your usual terms. He stays, for he's the one who knows the true dimension of Kella's threat to you all."

More studying, this time with the eyes of other women upon them. Hal resisted the urge to scrutinize them one by one. What good would it do? He must convince Zama, first and foremost. If he failed that, there would be no need to try the other sisters, no need for anything but retreat to the forest and his doomed men and their misplaced trust.

Misplaced trust. Fall to dust. Yield, he—

"I've seen her!" he said loudly, drowning out the whispers. "I've seen Kella meet with dangerous folk. I've seen her follow them into the night, through the woods. She's made plans, plans that endanger herself, her craft. Her Sisters."

Zama scowled as if he'd told a tasteless joke. She flicked a quick hand gesture, and the woman standing closest to the door set a heavy wooden bar into place. There would be no more custom at the tavern that night. Hal and Rani had infiltrated the Sisters' meeting.

For a hidden society, the Sisters subscribed to none of the mystery and danger that Hal had learned to expect. There were no hoods, no cloaks, no morbid passwords. There were no incantations to bring the meeting to order, no promises of vengeance and wrath.

These women all seemed relaxed, easy, comfortable with each other and with their secret organization. Small groups chattered together, one pair discussing the cost of cork, a trio debating the relative merits of flaxseed oil or pressed almonds as a binder for poultices.

As they spoke, the women worked. In short order, they had pushed the tavern's clean tables back to the walls. They brought the benches into a rough circle, cooperating to lift the heavy wooden seats. While one young sister added a log to the fire, several of the older women disappeared into the kitchen. They returned carrying smooth wooden trays, laughing as they passed among the assembled group, handing out tumblers of some drink.

When the sisters came near Hal and Rani, they offered up the trays, as if guests were common in these meetings. Hal hesitated, but then he took the proffered beverage. Wary as he was, he could fathom no harm in the drink. After all, there was no way that the sisters could have predicted which cup he would choose, which would be Rani's.

He sniffed the stuff and was pleasantly surprised by the fragrance—apple blossoms, a hint of honey, and something that smelled like fresh-cut grass.

When everyone held a cup, Zama stepped into the center of the circle of benches. "Sisters!" she called, and her voice cut through the chatter easily. Three or four of the women finished quick stories, and then all were silent. "Sisters!" the tavern mistress repeated. "We are gathered for our moonmeet. Let all who would join with us sit within our circle."

There was a general shifting of place, and each woman settled on a bench. Hal found himself guided to a specific place, opposite from Rani. Zama raised her cup and said, "We have guests among us, and we welcome them with refreshing drink and open words. Hail, honored guests!"

"Hail, honored guests," repeated the Sisters, and they toasted both Hal and Rani before draining their cups. Hal found himself flushing at so much female attention. One woman looked like the twin of the nurse who had nurtured him in his childhood. Another reminded him of his mother's favorite lady-in-waiting. That laughing redhead resembled one of the more annoying ladies that his councilors had tried to choose as wife for him.

Rani did not seem troubled by the distaff attention, though. She merely glanced at Hal across the circle. In for a raindrop, in for a storm, her expression seemed to say. She raised her glass and shrugged before she tossed back the draft.

Hal touched his tongue to the liquid. The flavor was more complex than the aroma. Was the drink based on pressed apples? Pears? He could not place the sweetness. Aware that the women were watching him, he fought down another blush and swallowed deeply. Well, there was no alcohol, but surely there was *something* in the stuff. He felt it tingle on its path to his belly.

Before he could dwell further on the libation, he forced his attention back to the meeting. At first, it was difficult to follow the conversation because he knew little of herbs and less of their application to treat various ailments. He quickly realized that each substance went by many names; it appeared that the women switched easily between formal appellations for plants and more casual ones. A cure for fever might be called melisias felidora by one woman but feverfew by the next.

Not that Hal actually cared about cures for fever. Or about a new harvest of greenwort. Or about a method for storing tinctures in glass that kept them as fresh as the day they were brewed.

His mind began to wander. He knew that his need was urgent, that he must speak with the Sisters, convince them to join with Rani and him, to work against the Fellowship. And yet he found himself smothering a yawn, tightening his throat and popping his ears against an unseemly show of disinterest. He should pay attention. There was no telling what he might observe among the witches.

Among the witches. Run for the ditches. Dance among riches.

He almost smiled at the rhymes. For the first time in months, there was no darkness in the words, no grim prediction of his fate. Rather, the sounds became a child's playful song. He was carried by the easy rhythm; he followed the laughter without fear. Only with great reluctance did he force his attention back to the meeting.

Two women were engaged in a heated debate about the cost of flaxseed oil in the marketplace, insisting that all the Sisters should refuse to purchase it until the vendors saw reason. Hal cast a quick glance at Rani. She understood trade. She understood enforcing a market cost for goods. She had helped him price his silk. *Price the silk. Drink some milk. Silk milk. Milk silk.*

He smiled at the silly words. The Sisters' autumn drink must have tamed the voices. The herb-witches could not be all bad, he wanted to tell Rani. They had stopped his madness, replaced his endless chants of doom with funny little poems. The witches made his head sing. *Head sing. Heart ring. Joy bring. Sing ring. Ring bring. Bring sing.*

When he glanced at Rani, she shook her head, and the lines of a frown cut beside her lips, between her eyes. She turned back to the sisters with a fierce look of concentration, and Hal followed suit, drawing himself up straight and forcing himself to pay attention to the woman who was talking.

"We're agreed, then," she said. She had a kind face, wrinkles folded in the comfort of age. She reminded Hal of the kindly old woman who had assisted Cook years before in the Morenian kitchen. That woman had always had a curl of apple peel for a naughty prince, a kind word for a boy who should have been out on the practice field with his sword and shield.

Apple peel. Courtly meal. Dance a reel. Peel meal. Peel reel.

This time, Hal did not look at Rani. He did not want her disapproval to squash the happy song inside his head. Instead, he let the words carry him to his feet; he staggered to the center of the herb-witches' circle.

The conversation died as soon as he stood. He glanced around and saw that every woman in the room watched him. Rani, too. She stared at him with eyes that were dark with concern. Concern, and something else. He realized that she was trying to join him, trying to get her feet under her, but there was something odd about her legs, something strange about the way she placed her hands upon the bench. Her body refused to obey her, refused to come to his aid.

To his aid. (*Blade,* his mind said, but laughter pushed the dark word away.) *In the glade. Hair abraid. Feast well-laid.*

Zama stepped forward. "You would speak to us, good sir?"

"What—" His voice was strange in his ears, too high.

"What have you done to me?" The words were too fast, too breathy.

"Nothing, good sir. You are not harmed." Zama's voice was determined and bright, but he heard the steel beneath her words. *Not harmed. Quite charmed.* His own mind would have reached for "deadly armed", would have threatened him with a dark rhyme. What had the herb-witches done? What had he drunk? And why had it not affected the Sisters?

"Give me back my thoughts!"

"I swear by Yor, we have not taken your thoughts," Zama replied calmly. Rani cried out when the herb-witch called upon the god of healing, and she started rubbing her arms with sudden vehemence, sucking in her breath and catching her lip between her teeth.

Zama looked up in surprise. Hal tried to move toward Rani, but he could not make his feet take the steps. The harder he tried, the faster his heart pounded, and his breath began to come in frantic pants.

"What have you done to us?"

"Nothing that we have not done to ourselves," Zama said. "You saw us drink."

"But you don't feel it!"

"Calm yourself, good sir." Zama spoke like a woman accustomed to soothing frantic children. "Tell us why you came here. Tell us what brought you to the Sisters."

Rani was clawing at her skin, her nails leaving streaks on her flesh. Blood welled up, fresh, red. *Red. Bread. Fed. Fed bread. Bread head.*

He wanted to shut the foolish voices out, drown them and replace them with the dark thoughts he knew and understood. Now every word he thought was echoed, chimed.

Each syllable broke into a prism, and the sounds threatened to drown him.

Rai. Gay. May. Bay. Day.

Nee. Lee. She. Bee. Free.

"Speak," Zama said. *(Speak. Creak. Beak. Leak.)* She had come to stand before him. He could not keep his eyes on her as she leaned close and felt his brow, as if she were diagnosing some ailment. He managed to glimpse her hand *(tanned, brand, land, sand),* and he made out a new cup, a cup filled with drink *(think, sink, clink, brink.)* "Speak," she said again. "Tell us why you came here. Give us your message, and I'll give you this cup. It will still the other that you drank. It will return you to yourself."

"You," he managed to say, ignoring the resulting cascade of sounds. "You . . . drank."

"Aye," Zama agreed. "I did, and all my sisters. But we take the antidote before every meeting. There's no telling who might try to join us, who might insist on staying with the Sisters when we meet." *Meet. Feet. Fleet. Heat. Heat. Heat.*

His mind stuck on the word; he could not move his thoughts forward. His heartbeat was loud in his ears now, and his lungs began to ache with the effort of drawing such rapid breaths.

Rani. Where was she? What had happened to her? He turned his head, ignoring the sound of the bones moving in his neck. Rani had slipped from her bench. Her head thumped against the pounded earth floor, rhythmic as the one word sparking in his mind, over and over again. Her hands still tore at her flesh, but they were weaker now, leaving only an occasional angry stripe.

He could see the rapid rise and fall of her chest, hear the

rattle as she tried to fill her lungs. She must be smothering as he was. She must feel the panic filling her body, drowning her mind. . . .

"Help. Her," he made himself say. "Dose. Her."

"You must speak to us first," Zama said easily.

"Help. First."

"You'll lose your ability to see in a few moments." Zama spoke as if she were counting out sausages in the marketplace. "Your vision will fade from the edges, narrow toward the center. If you wait until it disappears altogether, it will be too late. Even this cup won't help you then."

He tried to move his head, testing the edges of his sight. There! Was that it? Was that a blur of darkness?

"Speak to us, man. You said you had news of Kella. Tell us what she's doing. Tell us how she puts her Sisters at risk."

He had no choice. "Fellowship," he forced out, and the three syllables cost him most of his remaining strength. "Jair. Kella. Gone. To. Jair."

The last word proved too much for him. His knees buckled, and he crashed to the floor. Rushes pricked his face, and he tried to close his eyes, to protect them from the sharp plants. He could not manage the feat, though, could not force himself through the motion. He could see almost nothing now, only a tiny patch of fire before him, the edge of the hearth's well-trimmed blaze.

And then he felt a hand upon his neck. His head was raised from the ground. The edge of a cup pressed against his lip. Liquid trickled into his mouth, but he could not move his throat; he could not make himself swallow.

The hands tilted his head back to an expert angle, and the trail of liquid cut like an ice blade down his sternum. The frozen path woke him, dragged his body back from a shadowed precipice. He concentrated and moved his throat muscles, managed a single swallow on his own, then another and another.

Zama held him upright, cradled his head against her soft bosom. He knew when she poured more of the antidote into his mouth; he felt more of his body thaw from the icy draft. She nodded with a practiced move, and then she took a step back. "More for you when you've spoken. Tell us the rest, then. Kella. What is she doing with the Fellowship?"

He would not tell them yet, though. He needed to bargain for one more thing. He managed to flick his tongue over his stone-carved lips, forced a breath into his lungs and whispered, "Rani."

"What?" Zama's placid face creased into a frown.

"Rani. Dose her." At first, he thought the witch would refuse. He saw the woman glance at Rani, saw the disinterest as she worried about the safety of her Sisters. He put all his meager strength into a vow. "Rani first. Or no Kella."

Zama clicked her tongue and started to shake her head, but then she turned the motion into a nod, directing one of her sisters to administer the antidote to Rani. Hal watched as his companion's shoulders were supported; he measured the careful angle of the cup. Some of the antidote dribbled down her chin, leaving a meandering brown stain. More, though, managed to get past her lips. He watched Rani's supreme effort as she swallowed, and then the conquest as she opened her eyes.

He forced the most minute of nods, and then he created a complete sentence. "Kella has joined the Fellowship."

"The Fellowship?" Zama sounded dismissive. "What group is that?"

"The Fellowship of Jair." The antidote had iced its way

along his arms, his legs. He found himself thinking more clearly, as if he stood on a parapet in the middle of a frozen winter night.

Zama shrugged. "We knew them once, this Fellowship. But they have long kept clear of Sarmonia. The electors run the king. There is no room for Jair."

"They are here. I have seen them. Kella works with them now."

"We would know if they were back. There are some among us who are members." Hal saw Zama's quick eyes flick about the circle, but he could not tell which Sisters she branded.

"They are here!" Hal repeated. "They met in the forest. And your Kella attended them! Guided by a northern traitor, she met with the Fellowship. She'll sell your secrets and leave you all alone."

"How do you know Kella?"

"I watched her. She has brewed potions for my wife, my son. I fear that she will harm them at the Fellowship's command."

"What?" That last phrase gained Zama's attention, focused her like a goshawk on a coney. "What do you fear?"

"I fear that Kella will harm my wife and son. The Fellowship desires their deaths." And then Hal heard his voice break, heard a terrifying sob rip at his throat. Words boiled out of him, thawed by the ice draft. He told the Sisters how Mareka had sought refuge in the forest, how she had sought out Kella to keep her unborn son and then for help in delivery. Hal explained how much Mareka had come to rely on the herb-witch, how much she trusted the wily woman. He spoke of Crestman, trying to convey that twisted man's desperation, his fury, his thirst for revenge. He told how the madman had attacked Kella, how he'd taken her to a Fellowship meeting. And he told of the Fellowship's hatred of Mareka, of Marekanoran, of Hal himself. He spoke of battles and betrayals, of pledges all gone wrong. "They've already beaten Kella. She'll break. She'll tell my family's secrets."

Twice, he needed to stop, waiting in frustration while Zama administered more of the antidote. Both times, he plotted out a little more of the truth that he would tell the Sisters. Both times, he glanced at Rani for confirmation that he was spinning the tale properly. Both times, he saw that she sat a little straighter, that her cheeks had more color, that her scratches had stopped bleeding.

Zama drew herself up as he spoke; each phrase stiffened the witch's spine. The Sisters in the circle had come close; their tension was like the charge before a summer storm. "Kella will not betray your wife," Zama said when he was through. "She will not yield up a handsel."

Hal did not know the word, but he understood enough to protest. "She will, though! She will yield to the Fellowship! You must help us find them! Only if we reach them first, only if we confront them and defeat them can we guarantee the safety of my wife and child!"

"Kella would be cast out from the Sisters if she harms a handsel."

"She'll have no choice!"

"All Sisters have a choice."

There was a long silence while Hal stared at the woman. Wordlessly, painfully, he pulled himself upright. He forced himself to take a step, and another, and another. He moved across to Rani, reached out a hand, pulled her to her feet. He took as much strength as he gave, and they leaned upon each other as they gazed about the circle. His voice was ragged when he spoke, torn by his exhausted lungs, by his weary frustration. "Not Kella. Kella has no choice against the Fellowship. She is lost, and my wife will be, too. My wife. My son. Me. Rani. And you. All of you will be lost to the Fellowship."

Zama held his gaze for so long that he thought he would collapse. Then, when he believed that he truly could not draw another breath, that he could not listen to another hammered heartbeat, she spoke. "We will investigate your claims. Those of us with access will return to your Fellowship. We will see what they intend, and we will monitor our sister. We will watch Kella and see that she minds her handsel, that she keeps her promise to the Sisters."

"But—"

"Enough. You are not fit for further talk tonight. Tori?" A young woman stepped forward, brushing mousy brown hair from her eyes. "Take these two abovestairs. Place them in the front room, and leave them bread and water. We'll continue with our meeting and work out details of what must be done."

Hal started to protest, to demand that he hear the rest of the discussion. Even as he shook his head, though, a wave of fatigue crashed over him. Rani was suddenly a dead weight at his side, a burden rather than any sort of aid. The pounding behind his eyes expanded into a midnight cloud, and only the deepest of breaths kept him from collapsing in the middle of the tavern. "Go with Tori," Zama said. "We'll speak in the morning. All will be well. Never fear."

Never fear, Hal thought, as his leaden feet found the stairs. Tori bolstered him with one hand even as she turned to assist Rani.

Never fear. Shed a tear. Lose all dear.

There, he thought. At least the voices were back to normal. He fell asleep on a thyme-scented pallet with grim rhymes circling through his nightmares, wondering if he had gained anything at all by coming to the Sisters.

10

What do you want me to do?" Rani asked Tovin. "Should I throw myself at your feet and thank you for your everlasting kindness?"

The player shook his head. "Ranita, I'm not being unreasonable. I merely suggested that you should not spend too much time with Kella. Not alone. She's not reliable, that one."

"What? Her black willow is not always brewed to perfection?"

"I've told you," Tovin said, keeping his tone even, "black willow was a joke between us. She mentioned it to you only to disturb me."

"Not likely," Rani muttered, resisting the urge to scratch at the scabs on her arms. None of the herb-witches was to be trusted. Her flesh was finally beginning to heal from her encounter with the Sisters. Even now, two weeks after she had been bespelled on the Blue Rose's rush-covered floor, she wondered what exactly had happened that night, what had driven her to hurt herself.

She blinked hard, remembering the circle of benches. She had met Hal's eyes across the room, agreed that they should both drink the coven's draft. After all, she had reasoned, each of the other women was downing the stuff without hesitation.

The sounds had begun almost immediately—the whispers of the gods around her. That noise was followed by flashes of light and by ghosts of sensation across her skin. She had swallowed hard and tasted a myriad of flavors on the back of her tongue, and when she'd opened her mouth to speak, her nose was filled with scents—pleasant and unpleasant, strong and mild.

The Thousand Gods had surrounded her. They had filled each of her senses, threatened to overwhelm her. They had made her body heavy with their presence, and Rani had scarcely been able to lift her arms, to raise her head, to look out at the Sisters.

And then Zama had invoked Yor, the god of healing. Yor, whose wizened face and gnarled fingers were symbolized in Rani's mind with the stinging touch of a nettle.

Rani had met him once before. She had felt the mild irritation of his touch. In fact, she had wondered if that god's presence was tied to his function; Rani's own mother had sung the praises of brushing nettles across flesh to draw out fever.

Whatever comfort Yor might have brought with his prickles, though, was outweighed by the sheer force of the god's presence in Rani's mind. Aided by the Sisters' drink, Yor was so strong, so powerful . . . Even now, in the safety of the Great Clearing, Rani could remember how her flesh had burned. She had truly thought that she was dying, that she was being flayed upon the tavern floor. The pain was so precise, so overwhelming. . . . She would have done anything to stop it. She had *tried* to do anything, to strip off her skin, to beat herself into unconsciousness, anything at all to free herself from Yor and from all the other gods whispering about her thoughts.

"There!" Tovin exclaimed. "You've done it again. Where do you go when you leave me? Where are your thoughts?"

"My thoughts are right here," she said wearily, knowing that she could never explain the hold that the Thousand had taken over her. "My thoughts are with you, Tovin."

"Easy to say. I see no proof in your actions, though."

His petulance reminded her of all the reasons they had parted, of all the reasons that he had traveled to Sarmonia in the first place. "What do you want from me?" Her anger burned so hot that it frightened her. "You were the one who left me! Have you forgotten that? Have you forgotten that you left me all alone in Moren?"

"I forget nothing, honored sponsor." His sarcasm dripped heavily. "I am merely a humble player who watches over the woman who supports his troop."

"You haven't been humble a day in your life. And that's not fair, Tovin. You were the one who insisted on my sponsorship. Whatever passed between us, I never harmed your players. I never stood between them and a commission."

She saw him weigh his response, and she wondered which lines he was considering. He had thousands at his disposal, short couplets that captured the perfect invective, solemn quatrains that left her feeling ignorant and ashamed. He had not been like this when they shared apartments in Moren. Then he had often been Tovin the man, not always Tovin the player. He had spoken to her directly, without the constant burden of hurt and anger. When had they stepped onto this endless, angry road? And where was the path to lead her away to a new and peaceful place?

But no, this time he did not quote a player's piece for her.

Instead, he shook his head, and she could imagine the glint of tears in his copper eyes. "Why do we do this, Ranita Glasswright? Why do we fight this way?"

"I'm not fighting," she said immediately, but she heard the very lie in her tone. She sighed. "I'm sorry, Tovin. I'll sponsor your troop, now and forever, as much as I can. But that still won't make me the woman you want me to be." She turned to leave the tent.

"You're going to Kella, then."

"Yes. We misjudged the Sisters. They have not come to Kella, have not pressured her about the Fellowship. There has been no sign of them since we left Riadelle. I have no choice but to work with Kella, convince her to bring me directly to Crestman and the others."

"Ranita—"

She turned back at the urgency in his voice, moved quickly enough to see the conflict spread out across his features. "Yes?"

He paused for a long moment, and then he said, "Nothing." She waited for him to change his mind, but he only shook his head and repeated, "Nothing."

As she walked along the forest path, she wondered what he had been about to say. What would he tell her about the herb-witch? What had he observed in the long months before she and Hal had arrived in the forest? Tovin had an unerring sense of power; he would have gravitated toward Kella if he thought that she could serve him. After all, that was what the player had done to her, to Rani. He had come to her because he sensed her power, her strength, the riches that she held as one of Hal's favored retainers.

A whisper at the back of her mind told her that she was being unfair, that Tovin had stayed with her for more than her influence in Morenia. She set the nagging voice aside, turning her energy to watching the forest.

Hal would have her whipped if he knew that she was walking the pathways alone. He feared that Crestman was waiting behind every tree, that Dartulamino lurked at every forked path.

Rani had seen other patterns, though. The Fellowship would not waste time skulking in the forest. Since they had not struck in the first few days after Hal had been revealed, they were clearly gathering strength for their last great offensive. They were preparing to wipe out Hal and his line once and for all. They would not be content with dispatching him, alone, beneath the trees. They wanted total victory—complete and unalloyed—Hal, his wife, his heir. They wanted total warfare. Rani was safe. For a while.

There was another who might be hiding in the forest, though. Mair.

Rani had not seen her friend since their encounter in the glade, since Rani had confessed to her role in Laranifarso's death. The guards about the camp reported nothing, no sign of the Touched woman. Rani was surprised; she could not believe that Mair would abandon her entirely, not after all their years together, not after all the battles they had fought. Nevertheless, she felt a thrill of fear as she imagined Mair watching over her at night. Surely the Touched woman would not harm her as she slept. Mair would not seek direct revenge for Lar's death.

And yet Rani had to admit that she could not be completely certain. She did not know the woman that Mair had become, the madwoman, the crazed mother. And so, with every step down the path, Rani tried to convince herself that she could see her friend stepping from the shadows into the light, ready to leave off lurking in the forest, ready to rejoin the civilized world.

But Mair was nowhere to be found.

Arriving at Kella's clearing, Rani felt relief. She emerged from the gloom of the forest canopy and turned her face toward a brilliant noon sun. The cottage sparkled in the light. Its thatched roof looked comfortable and hearty, like an overstuffed pallet. The mullioned windows glinted, as if they concealed some amusing tale. A pathway led to the door, each round stone brushed clean of dirt. Along the way, herbs perfumed the air, their heads grown heavy with flowers of late summer. Lavender and rosemary baked in the sun.

Rani stopped short and filled her lungs, letting the beauty soothe her. She moved to the door only when a crow's murderous screech cut through the cheery sunlight.

Still, she hesitated on the threshold. What if Kella had learned that she was sought by the Sisters? What if the coven *had* come to her, secretly, without sharing their actions with the Morenian camp? What if, even now, Kella knew that the Morenians intended to use her, knew that they meant to reach the Fellowship through her?

Nonsense. The Sisters had been outraged by Kella's behavior. Rani and Hal had compared their memories after their strange night in the Blue Rose. While their drugged perceptions had been completely different, they had both known that the herb-witches were furious with Kella, enraged that one of their own would threaten a handsel.

A handsel. One bound by contract. Rani's merchant heart understood that bond, understood the outrage that an herb-witch might harm a customer after swearing otherwise. Wondering again why the Sisters had stayed their hand, Rani knocked on Kella's door.

Silence.

She rapped again, surprised at how hard the wood was beneath her knuckles. There was a curious rustle inside the cottage, and then nothing else. Rani waited several breaths, and then she knocked a third time. Before her hand fell back to her side, the door was flung open. "What?" Kella demanded bluntly.

Rani leaped into her masquerade, determined not to let the witch gain the upper hand from the beginning. "Do you remember me? I'm Rani Trader. I came here when you were helping Father Siritalanu."

"I remember you." The herb-witch squinted in suspicion, edging forward half a step as if she wanted to keep Rani from looking into her cottage. Rani thought she glimpsed a quick emotion beneath the suspicion. Fear? Guilt? Something quick and furtive, anyway.

"I've come to learn from you," Rani said, as if demanding instruction from herb-witches were the most natural thing in the world. "I'm here for you to teach me all your herb lore."

At first, Rani thought that the old woman would laugh out loud. The witch's surprise was quickly replaced by a closed expression, though, a grim tightness about her lips. Her fingers clenched on the edge of her door, and she cast a furtive glance toward the woods.

Who did she look for? Did the Fellowship watch them even now?

Before Rani could reconsider her rash plan, Kella seemed to remember something, or at least she appeared to settle on some decision. She took a step back and turned her head to one side, looking for all the world like a crow studying a shiny treasure. "And why should I teach you?"

"Because I'll pay you." Rani jangled the purse at her waist.

Rani feared that Kella would refuse. Caution twitched across the witch's face, as if she were a coney scenting danger on the wind. The witch must not back away. She must not retreat into her cottage. Rani must get inside, must get Kella talking. Rani must negotiate the bargain of a lifetime, learn about the Fellowship, about Kella's contacts. The witch was the last bridge to Crestman and the others, and Rani would do whatever was necessary to gain the knowledge she required.

"What will you pay me?" Kella asked at last, and Rani almost smiled. She recognized the tone of a bargain begun, a negotiation that would have a mutually satisfying conclusion.

"One copper penny for every herb you explain to me."

"Twenty. Every herb is its own reward."

"Seven. With a silver flower to teach me techniques for drying, and grinding, and the other work you do."

"Fifteen for each herb. And a silver for every skill, separately."

Rani shook her head. "Do you think that I'm the queen of all Morenia?" She peered at the herb-witch as she made her protest, saw the faint smile that curved the woman's lips. No. Kella had learned the identity of Morenia's queen. Kella knew Mareka's power, her prestige. The knowledge was perfectly clear on her face.

"Queen or no, I must support myself." Kella shrugged. "I'm an old woman, and all alone. Winter comes soon, and I must buy a new blanket against the cold."

"Ten coppers for every herb, then. And three flowers for all the skills combined."

Kella studied Rani's face, then let her eyes dart to the leather pouch at the glasswright's waist. "The silver paid now."

"The silver paid now," Rani agreed, and out of habit, she half-turned away as she dug in her pouch. She let the coins clank against each other, though, not minding if she sparked more greed in the witch. Let Kella have incentive to teach her. Let the old woman fight to keep Rani in the cottage, talking, listening, learning more.

The three flowers glinted in the afternoon sunlight for only a heartbeat before the herb-witch stored them away, deep in the pocket of her apron. "Come along, then. I was grinding up alton bark. You might as well learn about that."

Rani took a deep breath before she entered the cottage. It was dark inside. There was a pallet in the corner, stretched so that it took advantage of heat emanating from the hearth. Rani's nose twitched; herbs scented the air like heavy fog. "Lavender?" she asked, speculating on the first that she could identify.

"Ten coppers."

Rani grimaced, but she counted out the coins. Kella nodded over each one, studying the edge of the last piece closely, as if she suspected Rani of shaving off a bit for her own advantage. When she had the coins safely in her own apron pocket, Kella shrugged and said, "Lavender. It smells nice."

Rani's anger was immediate. She wanted to snatch back her coins, to rip them from the selfish old woman's pocket. Instead, she reminded herself to think of the coppers as an investment, as a payment made toward future knowledge. She would remember Kella's craftiness, though. She would apply the lessons learned here for all her days to come.

"Very well, goodwife." She chose the Amanthian title of respect. Kella reminded her of another old woman she had met years ago in the soldiers' camps of the north. Rani did not have time to concentrate on the past, though. Not with so many problems in the present. "Very well," she repeated. "Show me the alton bark."

Kella held out her hands for more coins, and Rani bit back angry words. She settled for a more tradesman-like, "Let us run an account. Here." She dug in her leather pouch, pulled out a handful of coins. "You can see that I am good for my debt. Let us keep a tally. Those sticks of kindling. Set one on the edge of the table. It will count for the bark."

She thought that Kella would protest, that she would demand money across her palm before she would share anything with Rani. In the end, though, the old woman only nodded, her eyes narrow. Certainly she was plotting her lessons, planning all that she could milk from this willing customer.

"Alton bark," she said at last. "I scrape it from the sapling trees at sunrise on the first morning after the moon is full. It comes off in sheets, flexible, like parchment."

"And if you do it any other time?" Rani asked the question without thinking. Her main purpose might be to reach the Fellowship, but she could not let herself miss the opportunity to gain a bit of herb lore. There was no telling when she might need it in another trade.

"Then the bark's power is lost." Kella's words were short, as if the question were offensive. "Listen to me, girl. All the things I do, I do for a reason. It would be easiest for me to stroll through the forest, gathering flowers and roots as the fancy takes me. That would never work, though. That would never seal the power. There are rules for all these things. If you think you'll learn my herb craft, you'll listen to the details."

Rani let the old woman's rant wash over her. She had suffered through enough angry instructors to last a lifetime. First her mother, intent on teaching her how best to display trade goods in the family's tidy shop. Then the glasswright masters, who had shown her the basics of her craft. Mair, who had taught her the ways of the Touched; Shea, who had guided her through life as a child soldier . . . Even Berylina, who had modeled her lessons with grace and patience, teaching Rani how to walk among the Thousand Gods.

Without thinking, Rani brushed her fingertips against the scabs on her arms. Yor. As she expected, she felt the prickle of nettles. This touch was a gentle reminder, though, not the overwhelming pain that she had felt in Riadelle. She looked up to see Kella eyeing her strangely. "All right," Rani said. "I'll listen to the details."

And details she heard. Alton bark was gathered at sunrise after the first full moon. The wood was pressed flat between smooth rocks. After four days of drying, the bark was crumbled into a reed basket, and the container was suspended in the smoke from a fire layered with willow, ash, and rowan. The bark took on the color and aroma of the smoke, turning completely black. Then it was allowed to cool beside running water. Only when it had been stirred by noontime breezes on three consecutive days was it ready to be ground.

"A mortar," Kella explained, raising the tool, "and a pestle."

Rani nodded at the familiar implements. She had mastered grinding out pigments—first in Morenia's glasswrights' hall, then in Brianta's. She looked more closely at the tools that Kella showed her. "What are those?" She pointed with a steady finger.

"Ah . . . Your eyes are sharp, then." The herb-witch ran her palm over the edge of her grinding bowl. "Those are symbols of the gods. We southerners don't hold much with the Thousand, but there are some who watch over the preparation of our herbs."

"Who?" Rani asked, and she braced herself for the responses.

"Mart." The god of earth. Rani was surprised by the sound of clucking chickens filling her ears, but she knew better than to look around the cottage for the source. "Mip." The god of water drowned out the chickens with his nightingale song. "Gir." The god of fire flashed across Rani's vision, his gold-and-white raiment brilliant in the cottage. "And Ralt." The god of air coated Rani's tongue with the flavor of new-pressed olive oil.

Kella appeared not to notice her pupil's reactions; she settled her hand on the edge of the mortar. "This tool is very old. Many hands have gripped its edges and worn down the signs, but they still offer their protection and their blessing."

Rani nodded. "And when the alton bark is ground?"

"Then it can be sprinkled onto food. It tastes mostly of the smoke in its preparation, so it is hidden best on meats."

"And its effect?"

"If a woman takes it every day, swallowing a portion the size of the nail on her little finger, she'll conceive a boy child by the next moon."

Rani wondered if Mareka had heard of alton bark. Was that how Marekanoran had been conceived? Was that how Hal's living heir had finally made his way into the world? "And what do you charge for the bark?"

Kella's eyes glinted, and she might have been any shrewd merchant in Moren's marketplace. "One gold coin. The price is not negotiable." The herb-witch turned her head to the side. "Are you hoping for a boy, then? Are you trying to give your man a son?"

Rani blushed, and then she cursed herself for the reaction. "No. No son. I trade in knowledge, not in children."

Rani knew that she must begin to drive this negotiation toward her own destination. After all, as fascinating as she found the herb craft, she'd come to the cottage for another reason. She must find the way to the Fellowship. Attempting to keep her voice casual, Rani said, "There are many men afoot in the forest. An unsuspecting maid could find herself surprised by one of them."

Kella raised an eyebrow. "But there are no unsuspecting maids here, are there?"

Rani shook her head. "No," she said firmly. "None at all." She waited for Kella to elaborate on the strangers in her forest. When the herb-witch was not forthcoming, Rani thrust down an inner grimace and said, "Tell me about another element of your craft, then. What are those roots over there?"

Kella peered into the corner, squinting at the earth-crusted balls. She nodded to herself as she stood, and Rani could hear her counting out the coins in her own mind. The witch took a stick of kindling and added it to the one already on the table. Twenty copper pennies. A fair enough price to reach the Fellowship. "You have a sharp eye," Kella said at last. "Those are demons' teeth."

"Demons' teeth?" Rani had never heard of them.

"Aye. They grow deep in the forest, beside running water where a rowan tree has rotted into the river-bank." The old woman returned to the table, holding three of the dirty globes by their withered stalks. She set them in front of Rani with a small grunt and pulled up a bench to sit on.

As Rani looked at the roots, she thought that they were moving, as if the plants were still alive. Leaning closer, she realized that the motion was caused by tiny worms, the largest no greater than an eyelash. "That's disgusting!" she said, and her stomach turned as she thought of weevils spoiling good wheat, of maggots eating flesh.

"That's the power of the teeth," Kella said with a grim smile. "The worms eat the roots and leave behind a black powder. Here," she said, pointing to the fine dust that spread across the scrubbed table. "See?"

"And what do you do with that?"

Kella must have heard the revulsion in her voice, for the herb-witch shook her head and clicked her tongue. "This is the power of nature, girl. You shouldn't look askance at it."

"I don't," Rani protested automatically. She swallowed and said, "I just can't imagine what you would do with the worms and their waste."

"We take the worms one at a time," Kella matched actions to words, plucking up a grub with a two-pronged wooden tool. "Four of them, placed in an iron cup filled with water from a clear-running spring. At midnight, the cup is set in the embers of a fire that has burned for four days and four nights. By dawn, the worms are ready. You pluck them from the water, and you cut them into an equal amount of their own black dirt. White with black, wet with dry, it's all about the balance."

"You cut them?"

"Aye, with a knife. It has to be a special knife, though. One without a metal blade." Kella pushed herself up from the table and crossed to the low table beside her pallet. She returned with something in her hand. "Like this."

For just a moment, Rani was not surprised by the diamond knife in Kella's hand. After all, she had held one hundreds of times herself, used it to cut glass for her guild, used it to create panels for the players. Even as she registered the item, though, she realized how odd it was to see one here in Sarmonia, in an herb-witch's home.

Keeping her voice even, she extended her hand. "May I?" Kella passed the knife to her. "Where did you find this tool? What is that blade?"

"It's a diamond knife," Kella said, and Rani heard the pride in her voice. The witch stood a little taller as she identified the tool, and a soft smile curved her lips. She glanced toward the pallet, and Rani knew more than she had ever wanted to hear. More than black willow. More than Tovin's touchy temper.

The blade spoke all the tale. Tovin Player had been here. He had shared Kella's bed. He had left behind his diamond knife. That was why the player had tried so hard to talk Rani out of coming to the cottage.

Rani knew that her jealousy was wholly unfounded. She and Tovin had parted months before; they had decided to follow their own paths. She could hear him berating her, accusing her of faithlessness with Hal, with Crestman, with any man in pants. (Unfair, that last one. Mean and angry and simply unfair.) And yet, it still cut her to know beyond doubt that he had come to Kella.

The herb-witch was an old woman, after all. How much time had he spent fondling her sagging flesh? Had he kissed the wrinkles on her cheeks? Had he turned her head to the side and whispered against her crepey neck. . . ?

Rani flushed, and she forced her mind away from the image. Tovin was his own man. He always had been. He always would be. She could not control him. She did not *want* to control him. She made herself ask, "And what use are the demons' teeth? What do the grubs do?"

"The poultice will heal venomous bites—snakes, bee stings."

Venomous bites, Rani thought, intent on ignoring the diamond knife. Bites like those from an octolaris spider, from the beasts that she and Hal had successfully brought to Moren years before. Thinking about Hal reminded Rani once again of her true mission here in the cottage. She forced her thoughts away from Tovin, made her voice drop back into its casual register. "There must be plenty of poisonous creatures here in the woods. Do you ever get frightened here, living alone?"

"I've lived alone for a long time."

Not so alone, Rani wanted to cry out. Not recently! Tell me about the Fellowship!

She was getting nowhere. Crestman might as well be a figment of her raw imagination. She pressed harder, desperation making her clumsy. "I've seen strange folk coming and going throughout the forest. Three days ago, I was in another clearing, closer to the road to Riadelle. There was another cottage there, one that looked like it might belong to a woman of your calling."

"There used to be many herb-witches in the forest."

"But not now?" Rani's voice ratcheted up a little as she spun out her story. "There had been many people at that cottage, and not long before. The grass was trampled, and horses had passed by. Their droppings were still fresh."

"You should not look too hard in the forest." Kella's

voice was as sharp as the diamond blade. Once again, fear darkened her eyes, fear overlaid by something suspiciously close to greed. "Not if you have no special knowledge, girl. The forest can be a dangerous place."

Rani heard the warning, as blatant as her own questions. The Fellowship hung between them, as heavy as the iron cauldron sitting on the hearth, as merciless as the diamond blade in Kella's claw.

The herb-witch broke the silence first, nodding her head once, as if she had made some decision. "If you would truly learn about herbs, your study is not complete without maiden's veil. I do not think that it grows in your northern forests."

"Maiden's veil? I've never heard of it."

"Here," the witch said, and she added a stick of kindling to the accounting on the table before she shuffled to the far corner of her home. She lifted a stick up to the rafters, a sturdy branch that had a natural hook at the end of its length. With more agility than Rani would have expected, the herb-witch plucked a close-necked sack from a high peg.

Kella brought her treasure to the table. "Let me open it." Before she untied the sack, though, she crossed the cottage to a row of wooden pegs that marched beside the door. She selected a long white cloth that hung like one of Father Siritalanu's priestly vestments and shook her head as she returned to Rani's side. "Maiden's veil. *You* needn't worry about it. You're a young woman. If I were to breathe the dust, though . . ."

She did not finish the ominous thought. Instead, she knotted the cloth around her face, wrapping it several times so that it covered her nose and her mouth. The effect was unsettling; Rani could not see Kella's lips as she talked, could not measure the tiny motions of sarcasm and truth. "Maiden's veil has no power when it's fresh. The flowers are a common white, with a flash of crimson at their throat. They've graced many a table, I suppose, but they have no fragrance, and the leaves don't give flavor to any tea."

As she talked, Kella worked at the tight knot that closed the neck of her silk bag. Her fingers were strong and wiry; her hands belonged to a much younger woman. Was that what had drawn Tovin? Was that what had lured him into the witch's cottage, into her bed?

When the knot was finally loose, Kella eased open the mouth of the bag. She reached inside, gingerly extracting a length of clean muslin. "Extra care," she said, "for one as old as I."

"And what does maiden's veil do when it's dried?" Rani asked, trying to breathe shallowly despite the witch's assertion that she would not be harmed. Kella rolled the silk bag back on itself, revealing the dusty grey of a dried plant. Its leaves were long and shaped like swords. Between them, balanced on fragile stalks, were chains of flowers. As Kella had promised, each little cone shimmered white, and each was brushed with crimson at the bottom, as if a single drop of blood had melted down the flower's throat.

Firelight caught on the closest flower, the flames reflecting in a prism from the flowers' dust. Rani stepped forward, fascinated by the rainbow effect. Kella raised the dried flower, rotating it a bit, so that the fire touched the crimson spot. "It's the fragrance," she said. "As a dried plant, maiden's veil sends out a scent equaled by nothing in the woods. It's elusive, but you'll never forget it once you've had the chance to smell it."

Nodding, Rani leaned closer. She still smelled nothing.

There were so many competing aromas in the cottage—the fire on the hearth, the lavender wafting from the pallet. She took another step so that she stood directly in front of Kella, and then she doubled over the flower. She put her nose directly against the crimson spot and inhaled as deeply as she could.

And Kella smashed the dried blossom against her face. Rani leaped back in startlement, but the herb-witch gripped her head with a strong hand. The dried plant scraped against her nose, crumbling against her upper lip. Reflexively, she opened her mouth to scream, and Kella pressed her advantage, crushing the flower past Rani's lips, grinding it against her teeth, her tongue. The taste was terrible—bitter and acid, so strong that Rani's stomach lurched.

She thrashed like a fish on a line, twisting her head from side to side, trying to slip free from Kella's grip. She raised a foot to stomp on the old woman's instep, but the witch proved too fast. The bitter taste spread across her tongue, down her throat, leaving behind a sparking tingle. For the second time in as many weeks, Rani's heart was pounding; her lungs ached. She remembered falling upon the floor of the Blue Rose Tavern, and she thought of the harm she had done herself there, the jagged scratches she had made upon her flesh as she tried to flee Yor's nettles.

She needed the gods now. She needed them to help her escape. Arn, she thought, don't fail me now. Amazingly, the god of courage reached through her struggle; she heard the sound of a baby suckling.

The sound gave her strength. After all, the Thousand Gods were on her side. They were gathered around her, watching over her. She had proof of their presence, as no other living person had.

She screamed as she opened her mouth. "Stote!" she cried, calling upon the god of mountains. As she had hoped, as she had prayed, the sensation of water poured down her throat. She had met Stote before, discovered him as she tested her newfound powers. She knew that he brought water, brought refreshment, brought life. "Stote," she called again, and the god surged through her once more, slaking her desperate thirst. "Stote!" she cried a third time, and the bitter edge of the maiden's veil blunted under the force of the water. "Stote!"

As Rani washed away the maiden's veil, Kella gave up the fight. The herb-witch staggered back a few steps, dropping the remnants of her white and crimson flowers onto the cottage floor. She stared at Rani in astonishment, as if she had never heard the name of the god of mountains.

"What was that?" Rani demanded. "What were you trying to force on me?"

"You should not be speaking!" Kella panted. "You should not be able to stand."

"I have the power of the Thousand, herb-witch. By Jair, I'll know what you tried to dose me with!"

Before Kella could craft another lie, before she could spin out another story, there was a terrific crash. The door lurched on its leather hinges, and the room flooded with women, young and old, tall and short, fat and lean. They rushed in, ten, fifteen, twenty. . . . Rani lost count as she backed against the scrubbed table.

The last woman stepped over the doorway with the calm of a queen. She waited until her sisters had seized their own, until Kella was forced to her knees, her hands tied before her with rough rope. Rani waited while Kella's cloth mask was removed, while her nose and her mouth were exposed. She waited while three of the women approached the white and crimson flowers that lay upon the floor, covered them with their silk sack and then with the lavender-scented pallet that they dragged across the floor.

Only when all eyes turned back to her in expectation did the woman on the threshold speak. "Kella Herb-Witch, what evil do you work here in the forest?"

"Zama!" Kella exclaimed, and Rani's heart flooded with mixed emotions. Zama, too, had poisoned her. Poisoned her, made promises, and then betrayed her by not coming to Kella sooner.

"Kella, what purpose could you have, trafficking in mordana? You know that it is forbidden. One dried petal on the tongue is enough to paralyze a man."

"I had no choice, Zama!" Kella's voice cracked, and she repeated her protest. "I acted to save the Sisters."

"Save the Sisters? And has Rani Trader threatened us in some way?"

Kella did not waste time showing surprise that Zama knew Rani's name. Instead, she began to speak, words spinning so rapidly that Rani could scarcely make them out. Rani dashed through the cavalcade of the gods, wondering if there were one who could clear her ears, sharpen her hearing. She settled for a quick prayer to Glane and was rewarded with the heart-calming whisper of a lullaby. The god of salt eased her pounding pulse, let her focus on Kella's frantic tale.

"There are strangers in the forest," the witch was saying. "We knew them once, long ago, the Fellowship of Jair. They've come to me, bound me with ties tighter than any handsel."

"There are no ties tighter than the handsel," Zama said.

"There are! We Sisters are stronger than all the handsels in the world! We Sisters must stand together!"

"And the Fellowship would threaten us?" Zama shook her head. "We have known this Fellowship in the past. They never caused us grief before."

"They came to me, and they demanded access to my handsel, to a woman called Jalina!" Kella's voice grew shrill as Zama started to interrupt. "I refused! I did not break our witches' bond. I did not give up my handsel." She gulped a deep breath and said, "I offered them this one instead. One not bound to me, to any of us."

Zama's gaze was hot enough that she could have roasted alton bark. "You offered another to save yourself."

"To save all of us! The Fellowship will destroy us, Sisters! They will let Briantan priests roam our land. Briantan priests hate all witches—they would gladly see every one of us killed! But if I give this one over, they would leave us all alone forever. They will take her, and all the witches would be safe!"

"They said that? And you believed them?" Zama's voice stung with scorn sharper than Yor's nettles. "What would keep them from demanding another of your handsels? What would keep them from coming back and forcing you to deliver the northerner called Mareka? Mareka and her son Marekanoran?"

"I thought to help us all. We must be safe if we are to practice our craft. We must be secure."

"You thought to trade their lives for the hard touch of gold."

"That's a lie! If I had wanted to give them up to the Fellowship, I could have done so long ago. The soldier-man came to me at the height of summer."

Zama's eyes narrowed. "Aye. You waited. You spared your handsels' lives in hopes that the bounty would grow."

Rani could see that Zama had struck the truth. Kella's blood drained from her face. "No," she started to protest, but there was no vehemence behind the word.

Zama went on as if the old woman had not spoken. "You waited, and you watched. You knew the price would rise if the Fellowship did not find its prey. You knew that your 'soldier-man' would be back, and he would carry with him more gold. You worked for your own good, not for the good of any handsel. Not for the good of the Sisters."

Zama stepped forward until she stood so close to the kneeling woman that Rani thought Kella would topple backwards. "Mareka Octolaris ben-Jair. Marekanoran ben-Jair. Rani Trader. You would have paid them all over to the Fellowship. Three innocent people. Three people who would be safe if you did nothing, who would remain invisible to the Fellowship. Three people who would be unharmed, if you simply stood by your vows as an herb-witch. As a Sister."

And then Rani realized that she needed to act. The Sisters would banish Kella. They would strip her of her rank, cast her from their midst. They would send her out into the woods, alone, with no money, no herbs, nothing to support her. Or they would banish her from all of Sarmonia. Or they would make her brew her own bitter herbs, drink some deadly tea. Whatever they did, they would remove Kella from the forest. They would sever the one fragile link that still connected Rani to the Fellowship, that gave her access to Crestman and Dartulamino and all the evil that they planned to work.

"No!" Rani cried, and she was startled to find every

witch staring at her. "Kella must not be punished. Not yet." Even the old woman looked surprised.

Zama's lips tightened. "You must not understand, Rani Trader. Mordana would have frozen all your limbs. It would have left you helpless if Kella had succeeded in getting it in your mouth. This woman meant to poison you."

Rani's response was hot on her lips, as if Gol, the god of liars, were warming her with his sunny rays. "Poison seems the favorite trick of herb-witches."

Zama scarcely acknowledged the jibe. "Kella had no antidote sitting at the ready."

"And yet I stand here. Safe. Unharmed." Rani took a deep breath, and the smell of lilacs washed over her. Hin. The god of rhetoric. What did he want with her here? Why did the Thousand want her to speak? Compelled in ways that she did not fully understand, Rani said, "Whatever you think you interrupted, Kella did *not* paralyze me, and I know why."

"Why?" Zama's voice was cold.

The answer was starkly apparent, laid out in Rani's mind like words on parchment. "The Thousand Gods are with me. The Thousand Gods wanted me to live."

"That is all well and good," Zama began.

Rani cut her off. "The Thousand Gods wanted me to live so that I can follow through on Kella's plan." Shad rolled thunder through her mind. Rani raised her voice, making her words sound strong, making the god of truth proud. "The Thousand Gods want me to submit to the Fellowship." Shad thundered approval. "They want Kella to offer me up to the Fellowship. They want my mission to be completed!" Shad crashed against her ears, so loud that she was certain the Sisters must hear; they must acknowledge the truth.

However, Zama could not hear Shad. She merely looked at Rani as if the glasswright had taken leave of her senses. "This one plotted to bind you over to your sworn enemies, and you agree with what she planned?"

"I recognize the necessity of what she did." Sorn, the god of obedience, coated Rani's tongue with honey, filled her with strength. "I submit to her intention. I give myself to the Fellowship."

Zama shook her head. "Once you are in their hands, we cannot aid you in any way. Our Sisters have been unable to rejoin the Fellowship. We have tried for a fortnight, but those meetings are now closed to us."

"I understand," Rani said. The rustle of the gods let her know that she was making the correct decision. "I understand and I accept. By all the Thousand, I absolve you from any wrong."

Zama looked around the room, clearly asking her Sisters for guidance. Rani could not read the looks that passed between the herb-witches, but she had no trouble translating the resignation on the leader's face. "Very well, then," Zama said. "You will do what you must do."

"There is one more thing," Rani said, and she braced herself for a final protest. "You must not seize Kella. Not yet. She must go to them. She must tell them that I am taken prisoner, that I am here for them to find. Give me time to do my work, and then you may do whatever you must to your sister."

Shaking her head, Zama took another silent poll of her sisters. When she finished, she pursed her lips and met Rani's eyes. "Very well, Rani Trader. This too we grant you. We will let Kella go for now. But she must present herself at the Blue Rose by no later than noon tomorrow."

"Noon tomorrow." Rani shrugged. She would be with the Fellowship then. Even if Kella fled Sarmonia, even if she escaped the Sisters forever, it would make no difference to Rani. "Done."

Zama turned to Kella. "Do you understand, then? Do you agree to come to the Blue Rose, without pretext or deceit?"

Rani could see the old woman thinking, twisting her mind around her momentary reprieve. Surely Zama knew that Kella might run away. But such flight might even further the Sisters' goals. Disobedience would give them a pretext for drumming Kella from their corps. Kella could never endanger another soul in the name of the Sisters.

"Aye," Kella said, and it sounded as if she sucked on lemon rind. "I will come to the Blue Rose as you demand."

Rani was grateful for the Sisters' protective presence as Kella was freed, as she gathered up her bonds and turned to the glasswright. Rani submitted to the rope with as much grace as she could muster, reminding herself that the Thousand had commanded her submission, that they had singled her out for their mission and their goals.

It was time to see the Fellowship. It was time to confront Crestman and Dartulamino and all the others who had worked to bring her down. It was time to face her enemies, once and for all.

11

It wasn't fair.

This was Kella's forest. She had lived in the woods all her life. She knew all the pathways, all the secret glades. She knew where to find the finest herbs, the shiest flowers. She had planted and cultivated thousands of plants throughout the forest, groomed and harvested them.

And all that would end now. All because of the cursed northerners. Kella's life was ruined, all because she had agreed to tie a white cloth to the triple oak, all because she had agreed to send a signal to the soldier-man.

Crestman.

The witch spat. She wished that she had never learned his name, had never thought to spy on his Fellowship meeting, to try to save the Sisters from Briantan fanatics.

Ungrateful Sisters. They had not even listened to her, had never realized their danger. The Briantans could massacre every last one of them, and Kella would shed no tears. Let them all die.

And Rani Trader, too.

Kella pictured the woman lying in her cottage, trussed up like a suckling pig on the lavender-stuffed pallet. Had Crestman reached her already?

It had taken Kella little enough time to gather her white silk banner. She had made her way through the woods quickly, and she'd wasted no time with neat knots as she tied the cloth to the triple oak.

The signal turned out to be unnecessary. Crestman had been waiting in the underbrush. He had rushed Kella and knocked her to the ground. His arm had chafed across her windpipe, and his knee had dug into her belly as he bellowed about the weeks that had passed since he'd commanded her to deliver Rani Trader.

She told him that the woman waited for him in her cottage, helpless and alone. She'd thought that news would calm the beast, but it only excited him more. He'd drawn his knife and held it against poor Kella's throat.

She had listened to his ranting then. She had agreed to all of his demands. She had promised anything, everything, just to make him leave her alone.

Let the Sisters curse her. Kella was as good as banished anyway.

Why had Rani Trader even come back to Kella's cottage? Why had she knocked on the door, come inside, *asked* to smell the mordana? No one could truly be foolish enough to smell a flower they'd never seen before, could they?

As if she might truly be protected as a "maiden." Kella remembered the girl's expression when she recognized Tovin's diamond knife. Something had passed between the traveling man and the girl.

Tovin would not be pleased when he learned that Rani lay in Kella's cottage, bound and waiting for the Fellowship's attention.

All the more reason for Kella to move quickly. She must reach the player before Crestman got the girl, before the Fellowship made its victory known. And there was no faster way to reach the traveling man than to stride into his camp.

"Halt!" The witch jumped. She had not expected a soldier at the edge of the clearing. After all, this was King Hamid's forest. However jealously the Sarmonian might guard his hunting, he had never shown love enough for the Clearing to post a permanent guard.

She blinked and realized that the man who stood before her was no Sarmonian. He had the leaner look of a northern soldier; his leather leggings were far more primitive than anything worn in Riadelle. Kella raised her hands, showing her empty palms like a flag of surrender. "Lower your weapon, boy." She lapsed easily into her role of an angry old woman. "You wouldn't want to stick your grandmother."

"My grandmother sleeps in a fine feather bed, many leagues north of here," the youth said. Nevertheless, he lowered his pike a little. "Speak your name and your business in the camp of Halaravilli ben-Jair."

"I need to talk to one of the players, to one who was here before you soldiers took over the Great Clearing."

"Name the one you seek."

"Tovin. Tovin Player."

The youth blinked, as if he had not expected her actually to know a name. "Very well." He crooked his pike in his arm and raised both hands to his lips, twisting his fingers in an awkward pose. When he whistled, the sound was a perfect match for the first evening owl. Even watching him make the noise, Kella could not keep from glancing at the tree line, from eyeing the setting sun.

She must hurry, if she were to succeed. If she were to escape Sarmonia with her life.

Another soldier ran across the Clearing. This one was

younger yet—he would be nothing but a page in a true king's court. "Yes, sir?" asked the child as he slipped to a halt on the early autumn grass.

"Check this woman to make sure she carries no weapons."

"Yes, sir!" The boy took his duty seriously, not waiting for Kella's acquiescence. His young hands were steady on her arms as he searched for hidden blades. He swallowed hard as he felt through her skirts, though, and she wondered if he were biting back an apology. She sighed and held her body steady. If she challenged him, she would only waste more time.

"Sir!" the boy said when he was through. "I found only these!" He held four packets of parchment, the contents carefully protected by heavy wax seals.

"What are they?" the youth asked her.

"Herbs for my evening tea. Shall I brew you a cup?" The young soldier scowled, and she remembered that she must not make herself suspicious. She must not seem anything more than a tired old woman. "They're harmless," she made herself say. "They'd be very fine with a toothsome biscuit."

The younger boy started to grin, and she knew that he was remembering biscuits from his past. Kella matched his smile with one of her own. She must convert these children, and quickly, too. "I'd make you some tea, if I had the time." She would do that, too. She'd watch both boys swallow the dara bark, watch them drift into the deepest sleep of all. . . .

"Very well," the youth spluttered, as if his authority were threatened by memories of peaceful times. He ordered his companion, "Take this woman to the players' camp. Release her to Tovin Player and no other."

"Yes, sir!" The boy handed back her herbs, failing to

mask a longing frown. He was silent as he marched Kella across the Great Clearing.

She could see many changes in the grassy field since her last visit. The northern soldiers had put up ramshackle shelters close to the center of the field, circling them around a large firepit in apparent disregard for King Hamid's restrictions. Torches fanned out from the edges of the blaze, ready to kindle against the night.

Kella's eyes traveled across the field to the players' enclave. Nothing had changed there, at least. The solid stage still stood on the edge of the field. Children ran beneath the structure, playing some game that led them into the shadows on the edge of the woods. Men and women lounged about their brightly colored tents, calling to each other in the growing twilight.

Fools. They should learn from the soldiers around them. They should realize there were dark forces afoot. There was danger in the forest, danger that could silence their easy laughter forever.

Kella strode across the clearing, lengthening her stride so that her young guard needed to trot to keep up with her. When she reached the players, she marched to the largest, most gaudy tent. She did not clap a warning, did not call out any greeting. Instead, she ducked inside as if she had every right to be there.

"My lady," the page gasped, comically lifting the flap and peering after her.

"That's not a lady," Tovin said, looking up from his worktable. "That's an herb-witch." He smiled lazily as the boy's eyes goggled. "Go ahead, Calindramino. You may leave us."

The page looked uncertain, but he complied with Tovin's

easy command. As the tent flap fell into place, Tovin stood and walked around his worktable. "And I suppose you're here to complain about Rani?"

"Rani?" Kella had planned her answer to the question, and she managed to sound as if she'd never met the interfering little merchant in her life.

"Aye." Tovin sounded a shade uncertain. "She said that she was going to see you this afternoon."

"No one has come to my cottage." She forced herself to meet his eyes, to drop the words with casual ease.

He started to protest but turned the words into a shrug. "To what do I owe this pleasure, then?"

"I've come to try your Speaking."

If he were surprised, he did not betray the emotion. "Now? You want to Speak?"

"Aye. I think that I did not apply myself before. I've taken some euphrasia, to heighten my memories."

"Speaking does not require herbs, Kella. You should be able to do it by focusing your thoughts alone."

"And you should be able to remember your dreams, traveling man! Are you going to help me in this?"

Tovin shrugged and smiled easily. "I'll help you. But you know the players charge for their services."

"I've three silver flowers. They're yours. Let's do this now!"

The first flicker of concern crossed his brow. "Kella, I can help you to Speak, but first tell me what is wrong. Why are you in such a hurry?"

"I cannot tell you." She read the concern on his face, wondered how his expression would change if he knew that Rani Trader was bound inside her cottage. "Traveling man, you do not want to hear my tale, I assure you." She put all of her energy into the lie, harnessed every lesson she had ever learned about human nature.

He must help her. Now. Here. Without asking more questions, without pressuring her to say what had happened that afternoon. Without alerting the northern troops around them.

And by whatever miracle, he yielded. He nodded toward the low camp chair in the center of the tent, beside his well-tended fire. "Sit, then, Kella. Sit and stare into the flames. Tell me where you wish to go with your Speaking, and I will try to lead you there."

She had thought hard about how to phrase her search. "There is a handsel that came to me at the height of spring. She promised payment if I would help her, but she has not yielded up her gold. I need to remember what she said, determine where she lives. I need the gold she owes me."

Tovin's lips crooked in a smile that did not quite reach his copper eyes. "You'll fight for the Speaking, then, when your purse is on the line. It was not enough that I wanted to bring you there myself?"

"I'm too old for your games, traveling man," Kella said, and anxiety sharpened her voice. "I need this! I thought that you would help me!"

"I'll help," he soothed. "We players collect our tales where we can. I'll listen to the story of your handsel, and I'll be content."

"I can't tell you that!" Panic tightened her chest. "I can't share information about her!"

Tovin shook his head. "I do not Speak for free. Not even for you. You must pay for the Speaking."

"Three silver flowers."

"Coins alone never pay for Speaking. The telling is part of the bargain."

"No!" Her desperation honed her voice until it was as sharp as the blade that Crestman had traced across her throat. "I cannot tell. Not if I expect to remain an herb-witch one more day of my life."

For a moment, they merely stood there, gazing at each other without compromise. Kella read more strength in the traveling man than she had ever seen in her cottage, more determination than he had ever let on. She pleaded, "Let me do this, traveling man. Let me work the Speaking. If I can find this tale in my own mind, I'll Speak another for you tomorrow night."

He paused, and she wondered if he were remembering other nights with her. Did he recall lying on her pallet? Did he think of the pleasures she had shown him, the lessons that she'd taught after a lifetime of enhancing senses with her herbs?

"Very well," he said at last. "I'll lead you in the Speaking tonight, and you will return tomorrow night. You'll share another tale as payment."

She forced her voice to be even, forced herself to believe in tomorrow, if only for a broken heartbeat. "I'll share another tale."

He gestured again toward the chair, and she seated herself, grateful for the support as relief rushed over her. He said, "You remember how to begin?" He brushed his hands over her shoulders, and she let his touch carry away some of her tension. He must have realized the calming effect the contact had, for he returned his hands, settled them lightly so that she was just aware of his physical presence behind her. "All right, then," he said. "Breathe deeply. Inhale. Exhale. Again. Again."

She forced herself to listen to him, to lean back against

his chest. He was a traveling man, a young man, a man who could never be trusted with a foolish old woman's heart. But he had never lied to her, not in all the time that he had come to her cottage. He had never harmed her. She could trust him, trust him to stand behind her, trust him to guide her along his mysterious Speaking path.

"Picture a stream that wanders through the woods. You are walking beside the stream, watching the water. Watch the water, Kella. Let it flow. Let it go by you. Let it take your thoughts. Let it take your worries."

She could see the stream; she had wandered through the forest countless times. She gave herself over to his words, let them wash over her like the flow of water over silt and sand.

As if he saw the images in her mind, he said, "There are stones in the river, stepping stones. You can reach the first by stepping out from shore. Your footing is sure. You are steady and confident. The water flows around your feet easily, gently. As you step to the first stone, count out loud. One," he prompted.

"One," she whispered. And she *could* feel the stone beneath her foot. She could feel the water. This was different from all the other times that she had tried the Speaking. She was not trying this for him. She was Speaking for herself, for her own need, her own growing, demanding—

"Easy," he said, and his voice soothed her back toward the river. "Breathe easily. Stay at the stream. Stay at the stones. You're on the first one. Picture the second. Picture the second, and when you're ready, take the step. When you're ready, count the stone. Count two."

"Two," she breathed, and she felt the second stone.

"And when you're ready, take the next. You can count them. You don't need me to count them for you."

"Three," she said, and the third stone was there. "Four." Surprise welled up inside her, but she offered it to the stream, let it wash downriver before it could topple her from the stepping stone. "Five."

She thought about counting the other stones, thought about saying their numbers out loud, but that was not necessary. Tovin would understand. He would stay behind her; he would continue to guide her. She felt his voice more than heard it, felt the words whisper inside her mind. "Very good, Kella. The next stone is a large one. You can move to it now. Take the step. Very good. You can sit on this stone. You can let the water flow around you. You can stretch out on the stone, lie flat upon its surface. Let the water flow past. Feel it in your hair. Feel it against your body. Let the water take you farther away. Farther. Farther."

With a part of her mind, she knew that she was leaning against his chest, sitting upright on a stool in the middle of the northerners' camp. She could open her eyes whenever she wished, come back to the camp and its dangers and its threats.

With more of her mind, though, she was suspended in the river of her memory, deep within her own recollections. She was safe there. She was secure. Tovin spun out more words. "You can see the water flow beside you. Shapes form in the water. You can see them without opening your eyes. You can watch the shapes, watch them like a dream playing out before your eyes. One of the shapes is your handsel. Do you see her?"

Jalina materialized from the water, appeared before Kella as if she had stepped from a bank of fog. Tovin was waiting for an answer, waiting patiently, and she took her time replying. "Yes."

"You can hear your handsel speak. She is saying the words that she said on the night that you first met. You have greeted her at your cottage, and she is responding to your greeting. Do you hear her?"

Jalina made a curious bow, far too formal for a rustic woman. The strange greeting was made more bizarre by the careful hand she held over her just-swollen belly. "Greetings, madam," Jalina said. "I have asked along the road, and they tell me that you are a wisewoman with herbs."

Again, Tovin was waiting. Kella pulled away from the memory just enough to say, "Yes."

"Look through the water, then," Tovin said. "Look at your handsel and listen to her. Remember what she told you—with her words and her actions and her very appearance. Remember all that you need to recall, so that you can settle your debts."

Kella heard the words as a suggestion, realized that she had the power to do whatever she wished. If she desired, she could end the Speaking then and there, open her eyes, stand straight on her feet, leave the player, leave the tent, leave the Great Clearing. But she chose to stay. She chose to linger in the stream, to contemplate her vision of Jalina.

The woman had clearly walked to Kella's cottage. She was flushed, and perspiration dampened her brow, but she was not exhausted. She could not have come very far, then. Not in her delicate condition.

Kella looked at Jalina more closely, checking for more evidence of her hiding place. There was fresh earth upon the hem of her gown, a deep red clay that glinted almost black in the moonlight. Kella recognized the stuff; beds lay all along the Greenbank Creek.

There. On the sleeve of Jalina's robe. Bright yellow pollen stood out in the moonlight, glinting like the gold that the woman promised to pay her. Pollen from the otria plant; Kella knew it well. It grew up the Greenbank's left fork, just beyond a giant clump of ferns.

And there. Sap glistened in sticky beads against Jalina's hair. She had brushed against a tree. Kella took a deep breath. A spruce tree. Spruce grew above the crook in the left branch, the tiny tributary of the Greenbank that flowed back to the north.

And then Tovin was speaking to her again. "When you are ready, let the images flow down the stream. Let your handsel leave you." Kella closed her mind's eye, let Jalina spread out over the surface of the water. "When you are ready, you can sit up on the stone. You can stand and turn back toward the riverbank. You can walk back to shore, where you will awaken from our Speaking, feeling rested and at peace. You will remember all that you learned about your handsel. You can cross back over the stones whenever you choose. Count them as you go. Five. Four. Three. Two. One."

Kella's eyes flew open. Speaking. She had done it. She had reached inside her memory . . . She stood up, astonished by the energy that beat through her veins. Her first step, though, left her swaying.

"Easy!" Tovin said, and his voice hid a laugh. "Take a moment to center yourself. Tell me what you saw."

"I can't!" She heard the power in her voice, remembered all of her reasons for rushing, for hurrying. "I mean, I will. But I have to go now. I'll talk to you tomorrow night."

She wouldn't, though. She could hear the knowledge in her own voice, she could hear her acceptance. If by some miracle she were alive tomorrow night, she would be far from the Great Clearing. Far from the Sisters, and the Fellowship, and the forest she had known all her life.

"Kella—"

"I have to go. I'll come back to the camp, though. I promise. As soon as I am able."

He let her go, of course. There wasn't anything else that he could do. There wasn't any way to keep her, short of tying her to his camp stool, and she knew that he would not do that.

He was a young man. He would forget her soon enough. She smothered the pang of loss that shot through her chest. She had never harvested his dreams. She had never learned the strange things that drifted through his mind while he slept.

And now she never would.

It was dusk outside the tent. Shadows melted into dim evening light, and Kella would have missed the page if he had not asked, "Will you come to the cooking fires, then?"

"No. Just back to the path." She drew her cloak high over her shoulders, settling the hood so that it hid her face. It would not do to encounter anyone she knew in the camp. Not now. Not when she had a solid path beneath her feet for the first time in weeks.

And, for once, her luck held. She left the Great Clearing and made her way along the wide forest path. She found the narrower trail she needed. She arrived at the Greenbank, and she followed the stream until full darkness had settled over the forest.

Her own hem became stained with red clay. Twice she

slipped, and only the strength in her hands, her strength and her speed at reaching out for strong grasses and spindly trees, kept her from splashing into the stream.

She reached the fork in the waterway, and she chose the left branch. She could smell the sharp otria beside her. The riverbed turned to the north, and she followed it easily. The moon had risen now, high enough that she could make her way without difficulty. She could smell the spruce trees around her.

There! That fallen tree was new since the last time she had walked beside the Greenbank. Something about it seemed wrong, out of place. She crossed it quickly and made her way past the stony tumble of an abandoned huntsman's cottage.

She should be almost there now. . . . She should be able to see something, something indicating that a northern woman was camping beside the waterway. . . . She should—

"Halt!" The command was quiet in the night-time, but sharp enough that there could be no doubt of its serious intent. Kella blinked, and she made out glinting steel in a soldier's hand. "Who disturbs the forest's sleep?"

"It is I," Kella said, casting back her hood. "Kella Herb-Witch. I come to see Jalina and Mite." She swallowed and added their true names. "Mareka and Marekanoran."

There was a whispered consultation between two guards, and one slipped through the underbrush that grew down to the river. It was not supposed to be like this, Kella thought. She was supposed to have saved much money from her labors. She was supposed to have turned the northern soldiers in the Great Clearing, used them to her own advantage.

Kella was the one who had been turned, though. She was

the one who had been changed by her encounters with all the strangers in her world.

Once it had been simple. She had known how to use her herbs. She had known the rights of a handsel, and she had known her own obligations, and she had lived by both. Crestman had destroyed all that, though, with his wicked hands and his long, sharp blade.

Maybe things would be different when Kella was through. The northerners would leave. The Fellowship would leave. They would take the gift that she had left for them, take Rani Trader, and all would be as before. All would be peaceful, and quiet, and the same.

In the time that Kella had been thinking, Jalina's guards had come to some decision. The first one, the one who had challenged her, held his post. The other led her up the riverbank, took her behind a massive clump of tree roots. He knocked once on a carefully concealed door, and then he stepped back.

Jalina answered the door herself, as if she were a common woman, as if she were no queen. "Kella!"

She held a candle in her hand, a fine beeswax taper, and its golden light softened her dark hair. She was tiny, Kella thought. No wonder she'd had such trouble bearing a child, bearing a living son.

"Good even," Kella said, and her voice was as gruff as ever.

"What brings you here? How did you find me?"

"I'm an herb-witch, aren't I? I know my forest." If Jalina was surprised, she managed to hide it. "I've come to check on the little one. How is Mite?"

"He's fine," Jalina said, her surprise melting into puzzlement. "Why wouldn't he be?"

"He's sleeping well?" Kella asked, momentarily dodging the question.

"Yes. The moonbane works. That is, he's not sleeping through the night yet, but he's still so young." A note of concern shimmered through Jalina's pride. "Is something wrong?"

"Nothing serious." Kella heard the lie in the back of her head, spoke it without hesitation. "Sometimes, though, the benefits of moonbane pass. Some children grow more restless than before they drank the herb. The problem can be especially acute with early boys. If they do not sleep, they fail to grow properly. They start to fuss during the day, and they stop taking milk. . . ." She trailed off suggestively.

"Well, he has been difficult the past few days. I thought that was just a phase."

Kella nodded grimly at the young mother's blossoming concern. A phase. Every baby had them. If Mite had not been fussy, then Kella would have suggested something else—that he was fixing his eyes on one moving point, or he was failing to clap his hands together. She would have snared Jalina. She would have gotten to Mite somehow.

She needed to. Her life depended on it.

She shook her head. She hadn't much time, but she must not push the young mother too hard. "I've brought something for him. It's a gentle tisane. Actually, truth be told, it's mostly mint, but it has a little something more. It will settle him down, put him right to sleep."

Jalina looked to the blanket before her hearth, to the child who was holding on to his own feet and cooing. "If you think it's necessary," she said doubtfully. "I'll give it to him tonight."

"As long as I'm here, I can brew it myself." Kella produced the four packets from her skirts. "There's a bit of a trick to the mixing. Order is important, you know."

"I— Well . . ." Kella could see the indecision; she knew that Jalina's common sense told her to ignore the witch, to protect her baby. Kella also knew that the young mother would still be childless if not for the herb-witch's potions.

And Jalina seemed to remember that last point on her own. "Go ahead," she said. "Mix the potion."

Kella nodded, doing all she could to make her old eyes sympathetic. "Come sit with me by the fire. Talk to me while I work."

Jalina came to the fireside, pulling up a low stool while she watched the witch work. "What is that?" she asked, as Kella opened the first of the herb packets.

"Powdered dara bark."

"What does it do?"

"It brings deep sleep," Kella said. And she wasn't completely lying.

"And that?" Jalina watched as Kella measured out the second powder, stirring it into the first with a quartet of fast whipping strokes.

"Pollen from the ataline flower."

Jalina shook her head, as if Kella were muttering gibberish. "And what will it add?"

"It regulates the heart. Makes for sounder sleep." Again, that was the literal truth.

Jalina did not ask about the last two elements, mint and something else. Instead, she watched Kella's mixing in silence, observing as the herb-witch poured the combination from one cup to another, once, twice, three times, four. Jalina's attention was half snagged by the child who played on her hearth; she crossed to the blanket and gathered up her son.

When Kella had finished preparing the potion, Jalina stared at her with dark, earnest eyes. "Explain again why this is necessary."

Kella thought about the true answer. She might explain about the soldier-man, about the murder that she had seen in Crestman's eyes when he caught her beneath her white banner, about the demands that he had made, about how he had threatened Kella's own life if she did not do as he instructed. She might tell how she had realized that she could never stay in Sarmonia, how the Sisters would never trust her, never let her bind another handsel for all the rest of her days. She might say how she was tired, so tired, how she had never intended for everything to spin so far out of control.

But she had not created all the webs of deceit on her own. Jalina was responsible for her own actions. The young mother had sought aid from Kella under false pretenses. Jalina had come to the forest pretending to be someone she was not, masquerading as a common woman, an ordinary mother hoping to bear a healthy son.

Kella might have refused to help Jalina if she'd known the truth! She might have refused to be drawn into the tangle of northerners, into their conflicting alliances. It was all well and good for Kella to have passed time with her traveling man, but she had never bargained on Crestman, on the sobbing Father Siritalanu, on Rani Trader.

Jalina should have told the truth. The lies invalidated the handsel! Jalina was responsible for what was about to happen. Jalina had made it come to pass.

Kella raised her eyes, met the mother's troubled gaze. "It will help your son to sleep," she said. "It will complement the moonbane that we gave him before. Here. You give him a swallow. Place it on his lips. Let him lick it. The mint tastes good. The potion is sweet."

Jalina still hung back. "I'm just not sure. . . . He hasn't truly had any problems sleeping, no more than any boy his age."

"But is his sleep deep? Is it what he needs to grow into a strong and healthy man?"

"I —"

"This is truly a mild physic," Kella said, lapsing into her scolding voice. "If you fear so much for your son, then you should drink some first. Here. Leave a swallow or two for the boy, but test it, if you will."

Kella held out the cup. Inside, she rejoiced that Jalina had made it easier for her. Kella would not have to find a ruse to make the mother drink after the child. "Go ahead. You'll see how harmless it is."

Jalina took the cup. She sniffed it, and then she touched it delicately with the tip of her tongue. "It doesn't burn," she said, as she swirled the liquid.

"Why should it?"

"I was taught that poisons burn. Long ago, in the guildhall where I was raised."

Kella smiled tightly. "And why would I poison you? You must not be sleeping well yourself, if those are the sorts of tales you're telling. Go ahead. Drink. Just save a swallow for the boy."

Jalina raised the cup to her lips.

Kella knew that she could stop the young mother. She could knock the cup from Jalina's hands. She could send it flying across the room, let the deadly drink seep into the earthen floor. She could cry out and startle Jalina, make the liquid spill down the front of her dress.

But Kella said nothing. She watched Jalina lift the cup. She watched the woman's throat bob, once, twice, three times, four. She watched Jalina cross to the hearth, pick up her son. She watched Jalina poison Mite.

Only when the cup was empty did Kella permit herself a smile. "You'll feel tired soon enough. The herbs will make your limbs grow heavy." Jalina nodded, and her eyes were slow to raise from blinking. So soon? Well, Kella had permitted herself an extra portion of dara bark, confident that the sharp flavor would be masked by mint. "Why don't you lie down by the fire? I'll watch over you until you're sound asleep."

"I—" Jalina said, shaking her head in apparent confusion. "The guards . . ."

"I'll talk to the guards when I leave. I'll tell them not to disturb you."

"I am . . . sleepy." So fast, Kella thought. She would not have believed the herbs could work so fast. But then Jalina was a very small woman. A very small woman who had been under a great deal of stress. And Mite likely had *not* let her sleep well, many of these past nights.

Kella flicked her gaze to the boy where he lay cradled in his mother's arm. His mouth was still pursed, as if he hoped for more of the sweet, minty tea. Already, his breathing had slowed. Already, Kella had to blink hard to see his swaddling clothes rise at all.

The witch leaned over and took the child from Jalina. "Lie down, now, Jalina. Lie down and rest."

"Mmmm," Jalina said, and her forehead creased into a frown. "Give me back my baby."

"Certainly," Kella said, leaning forward to tuck the boy beside his mother. She could not see him breathing now, could see no sign of life.

"Marekanoran!" Jalina whispered, but she seemed unable to raise a hand to her son's face, unable to move the child in any way.

"Sleep," Kella crooned. "Sleep and all will be well."

For Kella, in any case. She heard the scuffle before she had a chance to gather up her herb packets.

"My lady!" A man called, nerves tightening his voice.

So soon! The Fellowship must have sent its notice to the northerners, let them know that Rani Trader was captured. The news had naturally heightened concern for the Morenian queen.

Kella glanced around the earthen room, knowing there would be no means of escape. Why hadn't she made her way through the forest with more speed? Why hadn't she pushed to arrive at Jalina's earlier? Cursed Speaking! Why had Tovin's games taken so long?

"Your Majesty!" another man called. The door crashed open. "My lady!" a soldier cried, one of the leather-clad ones, one who was staying in the Great Clearing. He took the scene in immediately, bellowing his rage as he saw his still queen, the lifeless child.

He whirled on Kella, and his sword clattered from its sheath. She fought to still her gasping breaths, to keep her breastbone from the point of his weapon. Even as he threatened her, he wailed, "What have you done?"

"Peace," she said. "I'm nothing but an herb-witch."

What had she done? The only thing she could. She had acted to save herself. She had followed Crestman's orders, hoped that he would honor his promise, that he would spare her life, let her live in peace. Peace . . . She spoke to the soldier in a voice that was meant to calm. "They are at peace now."

"You've murdered them!"

"I've eased them on their journey. They felt no pain. They are in no danger now."

"You'll die for this, Witch! The king of all Morenia will see you drawn and quartered."

"I've done what I needed to do," Kella said, holding fast to the words.

She was not surprised when other soldiers streamed into the room. She was not surprised when they felt for Jalina's pulse, when they touched the babe. She was not surprised when they pushed her to her knees, when they pulled her hands behind her back, when they lashed her wrists together.

But she was surprised—for just an instant—when she saw the knife rise high. She was startled by the firelight flashing on the metal. She was cowed by the sharpness of the edge, reflecting in the room. And she was overwhelmed by the brilliant burst of stars that spread behind her eyes as the pommel struck hard behind her ear.

12

Rani lay on the floor in Kella's cottage, trying to count the hours that had passed. Eight, had it been? Nine? Long enough for the sun to set and for deep night to envelop the room.

Perhaps she had made a mistake. The Fellowship might not come for her. Certainly, they had bargained with Kella, but who knew the terms of their deal? Maybe they would not retrieve Rani, not that night, not the next day, or the next.

Once the Sisters had agreed to Rani's mad plan, Kella had embraced her role with enthusiasm. She had pulled each rope tight, double-checked every knot. Rani had endured the rough treatment and reminded herself that she had a plan. She had a goal.

But she would not last long tied up as she was. Even now, thirst blazed across her tongue. Her belly rumbled with a hunger as deep as any that she had experienced when she was an apprentice glasswright.

At least, she thought wryly, she was learning a new trade. She was perfecting her woodcraft, identifying the sounds of the forest, interpreting more signals than she had ever thought existed. At first, she had listened to every movement outside the cottage with an alertness born of desperation.

There was a surprising amount of noise in the twilight—birdsong, and the bark of a nearby fox, and trees soughing in the wind.

As the evening wore on, though, she could no longer listen to the forest. Her blood beat too loudly in her veins; her breath rasped too harshly in her lungs. Her mind fed her terrifying stories, the sorts of tales that she had first whispered to herself when she joined the Glasswrights' Guild, when she was a lonely apprentice sobbing on a lumpy pallet.

No one cared if she lived or died. The Sisters had left the cottage; they would never return. The Fellowship would not search her out, even if they had once clamored for her blood. Hal would never search for her; his life was simpler with her gone. Mair might come—but only to laugh over her bones.

Rani was entirely alone, without family or friend.

And perhaps, she thought as her belly cramped with hunger, that was fair and just. After all, she had let Laranifarso and Berylina die. She had watched Crestman be enslaved by the spiderguild. She had lifted her own knife against the soldier Dalarati, a handsome young man who had done her no harm, no matter what she had believed at the time. She had let dozens of glasswrights be maimed. She had summoned Prince Tuvashanoran ben-Jair to his death.

So much blood had been shed by her and for her. She must pay for her past. She must do what she could to balance the scales. And that payment could be made only to the Fellowship, could be made only to the secret brothers who plotted even now to control all the known world.

She was through with running. She was through with seeking escape. She was ready to face the Fellowship, to confront them, and to be done with their threat forever. She was ready to take back her life, even if that life was forfeit in the process.

The cottage was very dark. Its windows were nestled too deep in the walls for starlight to penetrate. Rani let her eyes close, allowed her neck to relax so that her head touched the floor. She had long since lost sensation in her fingers and toes. She could no longer feel the edges of the ropes that bit into her flesh.

She had mortified her body in the past, and she had survived. Upon arriving in the glasswrights' guildhall, she had broken more rules than she knew existed. She had been summoned to the Hall of Discipline more times than any apprentice in the guild's long history, ordered to kneel before altars erected to the strictest of the Thousand Gods.

Sorn, the god of obedience, had become her friend and nearly constant companion.

Sorn. As she thought the god's name, the taste of honey coated her throat. Honey. Sweet. Soothing. Nurturing, even as it soothed flesh grown raw from her harsh breathing.

Reviving at the god's sustenance, Rani tried to remember who else had lived in the Hall of Discipline. There was Lene, of course. As if he had never been more than a single step away, the god of humility sparked against her flesh, his icy touch cold enough to burn. The sensation was not calming, could never be comforting, but Rani found herself more alert.

After all, she must stay awake. She must not slip off in the furry darkness. She must . . . she must . . .

Lene stepped closer, chilling her back to wakefulness. Yes! She must be alert when the Fellowship arrived. She must be conscious when she joined the final confrontation with the secret society that had used her since they first made her acquaintance.

So many years had passed since Mair had brought her under the Fellowship's protection. Mair . . . Poor Mair, still wandering, still searching the forest for the peace she once had known. Had Rani been right to tell her friend the truth? Had she been right to force Mair to give up hope, to give up any possibility of peace and happiness?

With one single breath, Rani was back in the glade where she'd last seen Mair. She could feel the sun beating down on her shoulders; she could smell the grass that she had crushed as she ran to the boulder where her friend sat. It had seemed right to tell Mair the truth then. It had seemed fair.

But what if Rani had acted only for herself? What if she had confessed only because she wanted to rid herself of guilt? What if, what if, what if. . . ?

In the quiet of the darkened cottage, her thoughts spun around themselves like the ribbons of player children as they shouted out their patterned games. She felt herself drifting high above her trussed-up body. The pain in her shoulders was gone now, nothing but a memory stretched tight across her chest. The loss of her fingers, her toes—what did she care? She was floating. She was separate. She was alone. . . .

And still, a corner of her mind worked on the question she had set herself minutes ago, hours ago, a lifetime ago. Who were the gods in the Hall of Discipline? Whom had she served when she was a wayward apprentice? Honeyed Sorn. Icy Lene.

Plad. A splash of acid vinegar woke her up. The flavor was acrid, sharp, and she forced herself to swallow. Patience? What god of patience would rouse her from her sleep so cruelly? How could Plad take such bitter exception to her wandering thoughts?

She started to curse his name, but she choked on another sour splash across her tongue. She spluttered and spat, trying to rid herself of the flavor. The motion pulled her shoulders back, stretched them against her bonds, but it was worth the pain to be free of the taste.

Only as she started to relax her shoulders did she hear the feet on the walk. Bold steps. Boot-shod feet clapping down on the stone path with grim authority.

Rani had only enough time to turn her face toward the threshold, to set her features into a grimace of defiance, and then the heavy oak door flew open.

Five men stormed into the cottage. Two bore torches, flickering flames that threatened to catch Kella's dried herbs, to kindle all the knotted plants that hung in the rafters. Two other men carried knives—long blades that caught the torchlight and glinted like burning tongues. The leader was not encumbered by fire or weapon; he merely stood inside the doorway and commanded his men with a single curt hand gesture and one barked word.

She had expected the newcomers to be rough. She had expected them to be angry. She had braced herself for harsh words as they demanded her compliance, as they issued their sharp orders to stretch, to stand, to face them in her shame.

But she had not completely prepared herself for the pain.

She watched the knife in the soldier's hand. Its honed edge slipped beneath her bonds, sawed away at the rope around her ankles. The other armed man moved behind her, and she was shoved from side to side, nearly unbalanced by the force as a knife cut through the loops at her wrists.

For one glorious moment her shoulders were unpinned. Reflexively, she took a breath so deep she nearly choked. Her lungs came close to freezing in the night air, freezing as if Lene kissed her. Filling her lungs again, Rani ordered her fists to unlock, her fingers to uncurl.

Then the nearest soldier jerked her to her feet. Her knees buckled immediately, and only the man's quick grasp kept her from plummeting back to the floor. She could not feel his fingers on her arm, though, could not feel the pressure as he supported her, swearing all the while.

She could not feel his fingers, but she knew her blood was running back into her arms, into her hands, into her own fingers. First like ice, and then like fire, then like a million stinging wasps. . . . Rani drew a breath to cry out, but her lungs were overwhelmed by the freezing air. She turned toward the man who held her, gasping, choking, desperate for anything to help her breathe.

She knew that she should call upon the Thousand. She knew that one of the gods could help her, could pump sustenance into her chest, into her body. She should go through the cavalcade, count the gods in their decades until she found one who could save her.

But as she looked at her captors, words tumbled from her mind. The names of gods, prayers for mercy, petitions for assistance, all were driven from her thoughts. Instead, all that she could do was watch the grim face of the soldier-man before her, the soldier who had suffered for her, fought for her, nearly died for her.

Crestman.

His face was drawn, the skin grown tight over the sharp bones of his cheeks. His hair was cropped short, ready for a soldier's helmet. His eyes darted about the cottage, keeping watch over the door and the windows, the fireplace and the pallet, any place where danger might lurk.

It was his scar that held her attention, though. The smooth flesh tensed beneath his eye, glinting in the torchlight. Even now, even with her arms burning, her legs quivering, her lungs pulsing to expand, she could not help but wonder what he would have looked like if his lion tattoo had never been removed. What would have happened if he had stayed in Amanthia, if he had led the soldier's life for which he had been bred, for which he had trained?

She took a single step toward him, watching the flicker of torchlight carve his face. She remembered other flames that she had watched with him, other soldiers who had answered his commands. She raised a hand, as if she would touch his scar, as if she would summon back the boy who had lived beneath the tattoo, who had loved her in the clumsy way that boys love. "Crestman," she said, pouring her returning strength into the two syllables, even though she knew that her mission was hopeless.

"Silence!" His voice cracked against the cottage rafters.

But she could not be silent. She could not forget the boy who had reached out for her so many years ago. "Crestman," she said again, and she stumbled as she moved toward him.

His hand rose faster than she could follow, his fingers curled into a fist. She realized that he was using his left hand. She reached out toward his right side, and then she saw that his entire arm was withered, his fingers curled into a tight claw. Quicker now, she glanced at his leg, and she recognized the full extent of the damage that she had only glimpsed once before, in a darkened alley in Brianta.

He had been crushed by the spiderguild. He had been destroyed by the poisonous octolaris. His strength and his power had been leached from him, sucked away by the vicious creatures that he had been forced to tend.

"Crestman," she said one more time, and she heard tears at the back of her throat.

"I said 'silence!'" he roared, and then his fingers tightened, his fist moved, his arm sailed through the air, across the space that separated them. She heard the impact before she felt it; she heard the smack against her flesh, the snap of her jaw sliding to the side. Her head lashed back, and her neck stretched, and she whirled around and down and down and down. The floor of the cottage was harder than she remembered, hard enough that it felt like wood as her head slammed against it, and she slipped away to darkness.

She dreamed. She dreamed that she was back in the Glasswrights' Guild, wandering the stone hallways. Her hands were filled with the implements of her craft; she carried a grozing iron and a length of lead stripping.

She wanted a diamond blade. It was important for her to be ready, to be armed. The grozing iron could hit someone over the head. It might even knock someone unconscious if she could get enough room for her swing.

But she needed to protect her life at closer quarters. She needed a diamond knife, a sharp edge, a thin blade.

She fled down a corridor, barely making the turn that led to the hidden staircase. She and Larinda had hidden in the stairwell often, sheltering in the shadows as they gnawed on crusts of bread, laughing at the masters' unbelievable demands.

Now there was no laughter. Now Rani did not pause. She leaped up the stairs, taking them two at a time with legs that were longer, stronger than her legs had ever been when she lived at the guildhall.

She emerged on a narrow balcony overlooking the refectory. She could see the full room beneath her, the mingling crowd. She recognized masters and journeymen and apprentices.

She barely managed to stop herself as the balustrade caught across her waist. She was so startled by the stonework that her hands opened. The grozing iron clattered on the ground below her, followed by the duller thud of the lead stripping.

The sound drew the attention of all the guildsmen in the hall. Every face turned to look at the tools; every eye turned to the balcony, to Rani.

Blood pounded in her ears. Her lungs burned in her chest, ached with her panicked flight. Her skin stank with sweat, rank with pungent terror.

She tried to step away from the balcony, tried to escape, but she was pinned there, drawn forward by the haunted faces below.

And then, as one, every glasswright lifted his hands. Every glasswright pointed toward the balcony, toward Rani, toward the traitor who had destroyed the guild.

Rani choked in horror as she saw those hands, as she made out the bleeding stumps where skilled thumbs once had been attached. Blood dripped from every glasswright—thick crimson rivers that flowed to the floor, that covered the tile.

The room began to fill with blood, and the glasswrights' robes were stained. Rani cried out for them to lower their hands, to stop their wounds.

No one moved, though. No one spoke. They only stared

at her in silent condemnation, watching as their lives drained from their hands, again, and again, and impossibly again.

The smallest of the apprentices drowned in the blood, and still it flowed. The journeymen and masters gurgled wordless curses as they died. The tide rose, higher and higher, and Rani's toes were stained. Her feet were soaked. Her legs, her knees, her waist, her chest.

She turned her face upward and closed her eyes. The blood washed across her lips. Her eyelids glowed with its warmth, its pulsing scarlet light. She took a last deep breath and held it, waiting for the end. Waiting. Waiting. Waiting . . .

"Dammit, boy! I told you to lash her hands to the saddle!" A rough hand reached out and grabbed her, pulling her upright.

"I didn't think she could slip," whined a young voice. Younger than the guild's apprentices. Younger than the children who had drowned in her misdeeds.

Rani took a deep breath, startled by the feel of cool air around her. Her eyes fluttered, but she squinted them closed almost immediately, blinded by brilliant sunlight. Sunlight, through her eyelids. That was what she had seen. Not blood. Not the retribution of hundreds of glasswrights.

Swallowing, she found that her jaw ached. Pain spidered down her neck, radiated across the back of her skull. She tried to push it back, tried to tame it with the power of her thoughts, but she could not order herself to stand against its force.

The Thousand. They should be there for her. They should help her.

She struggled to think of the gods, to think a name that could help her. One single syllable. One single word.

Mair.

No. Mair was not a god. Mair was a Touched woman who hated her. Mair was an enemy who thought that Rani had killed her son. Mair would not help her now, would not assist Rani in any way.

Rani could count on no one but herself. Herself and the gods who were too distant through her crimson haze of pain.

She fought to raise her fingers to her jaw, to measure the extent of her injury. She could not lift her hands, though. They were so heavy, so awkward. She thought about the strangeness of the weight, tried to figure out what kept her from moving.

Of course! she finally realized. Her wrists were bound together. The boy—whoever he was—might not have lashed her to her saddle, but she was still bound tight enough that escape was impossible.

As the horse jogged on, she gradually remembered that she did not want to get away. She swallowed hard and tried to concentrate, tried to remember past the hideous ache in her face. She did not want to escape. She had wanted the Fellowship to come to Kella's cottage. She had wanted to confront them one last time, wanted to attend one final meeting.

Once more, she braced herself against the pain of swallowing, and she forced herself to take stock of her surroundings. She was on a horse, traveling at a bone-jarring trot. Her jaw pulsed with every step, and a tendril of queasiness explored her throat. She pushed back the nausea, not permitting herself to imagine the level of resulting pain if she failed to master her body.

Back to measuring up her world . . . There was earth underfoot, hard-packed earth. She could smell pine needles. A stiff wind rustled tree branches. The sun was warm on her face; the road must cut a wide swath through the forest.

"Stop pretending. We know that you're awake."

Crestman.

Rani's heart clenched in panic even as she squelched her pity. She had created the twisted man inside Kella's cottage. She had broken a fine soldier, changed him into a bitter, hateful killing engine.

But he could not mean to kill her. Not now. If he had intended her death, he could have finished the job, left her to starve on Kella's cottage floor, even stabbed her, let her life pour onto the witch's hearth. She was safe here. At least for a while.

She forced her eyes open.

He seemed older than she remembered, older than he had appeared in the Briantan alley when he had offered her a soulless bargain. Then, she could still remember the tormented boy he had been, the child soldier who had been pushed beyond his reason by cruel circumstances.

Now, lines of bitterness had etched his face into something entirely new. No child remained in his body, not even a memory of the boy he once had been. She tested his name in her mind before she said it, making sure that the two syllables would stay level. "Crestman." She spoke despite the agony that shot across her jaw.

"Rani." He matched her, sound for sound. No warmth. No recognition of the past that they had shared. His ice was dangerous. A man could kill if his heart was frozen.

She tried to make her voice sound young, like the sixteen-year-old girl he had met in the Amanthian forest. "Untie me."

His laughter was a harsh bark. He once had loved a puppy. He once had killed the pet.

She steeled herself for the argument she needed to make. Again, she thought to reach out to the Thousand, to find comfort in their strength, but they muttered around her, undefined, indeterminate. Perhaps it was the blow to her jaw, perhaps it was the hunger that raged in her belly, the thirst that swelled her tongue. The gods were beyond her reach for now.

She was alone and making the most important bargain of her life. She must let Crestman believe that he was making the decisions, that he was directing the trade. He must believe that he was forcing her to yield, that she was giving in with only the greatest reluctance. He must never know that she had gone to Kella's cottage willingly. He must never know that she had decided to end her game with the Fellowship, that she was orchestrating this final confrontation.

"Crestman." She forced herself to swallow and then to enunciate past the throbbing pain. "Crestman, where are you taking me?"

He answered too quickly, as if he had long ago anticipated the question. She knew the tone of guilt, even if it was coated with snide superiority. "You can't tell? You, the honored glasswright? You, the expert in all patterns?"

She choked back an angry retort, settling for the easier course of a single word. "Where?"

"When you were in the Little Army, you learned that much fieldcraft at least."

The Little Army were nothing more than slaves, she wanted to say. Children, who were sold into lives of desperate service. She swallowed her anger and glanced at the lowering sun to her left. Had she slept an entire day, jolted on this horse? No wonder she was so dazed. Dazed and hungry and thirsty. She made herself speak. "North, then." Crestman said nothing. "Morenia?"

Before he could answer, another horseman edged beside him. A thick-chested bay stallion tossed its head, as if to protest a restrained pace. Rani glanced at the new rider, and the ache in her jaw grew sharper, even as she reminded herself of her plan. "Dartulamino."

"Ranita." The priest's eyes narrowed as he looked at her. She recognized the expression of a predator; she knew that he was merely calculating how best her death could serve him. She had never trusted the man, not when he served the old Holy Father, not when he first revealed himself to be a key player in the Fellowship. She had never trusted him, but she would use him now. Use him to redeem herself, to redeem her past.

"What are you doing with me?" she forced herself to ask defiantly. Her jaw tolerated the angry question better than she had feared. "Where are you taking me?"

"You'll know soon enough. You never were one to resign yourself to those in power, Ranita." The Holy Father laughed. "You should have learned your lesson by now. Mind your caste."

Mind your caste. She hated the words, hated the lesson that she had mastered as a frightened glasswrights' apprentice. The phrase had served her well enough when her world was simple, when she could navigate right and wrong by remembering the teachings of her merchant youth, the core of her trading family.

Nothing was so simple anymore, though. Nothing was simple when the Fellowship perverted all castes, when the secret organization twisted the meaning of nobility and soldierly service, of trade and craft.

Mind your caste.

Rani had tried that, and she had lost friends, lost those she loved. She'd be cursed a thousand times before she lost herself in the Fellowship's simple platitudes again.

For now, though, she must remember the tricky game she played. She must make Dartulamino think that she dreaded a return to Moren, that she feared being taken before the Fellowship more than anything else she had faced. "Please, Holy Father. Whatever you do, don't take me to the Fellowship. I know their power. I know what they can do. Hal and I, we came to Sarmonia to escape the Fellowship. We yield. We concede the Fellowship's power."

The priest cast a quick glance at Crestman. "I've always thought this one had more fight in her."

Rani let some of the ache from her jaw siphon tears into her words. "I did, once. That was before Laranifarso died. Before I failed my guild test."

The words were acid on her tongue, sharper even than Plad's vinegar had been. She sensed the gods grow nearer, stirred by her recollection of betrayal in holy Brianta. She could reach for them now. She could stretch out to the Thousand and draw in all their power. . . . She could—

"Failed your test." The priest threw back his head, his thin lips pressed into a mirthless smile. "I must say that I took personal pleasure in that, Ranita Glasswright." He sneered her guildish name. "Time and time again you thought to thwart the Fellowship, but you've never truly understood the extent of our power. You've never truly believed all that we can do."

She tried to still her hatred, tried to keep from spitting out her reply. She failed. "What? What can you do? Your Fellowship is rotten to the core, Dartulamino!"

The priest's sallow cheeks shook as he pulled up on his stallion's reins. "Enough!" Dartulamino's voice snapped louder than any whip, and his horse hopped forward a few steps. "Silence her, Crestman. Dose her, or I'll see that she does not speak again." Dartulamino spurred his horse and pounded down the road before them.

Rani's heart was thundering. She should have curbed her anger. She should have held her tongue. After all that she had suffered, all that she had done, to come so close to losing, so close to speaking out her plan. . . .

As Crestman watched the priest ride off, Rani could see a spark of resentment in his eyes, a flicker of loathing across his scarred face. It was there for only a moment, and then Crestman raised his good hand, signaling two of the other riders. "Take her down."

Before Rani was prepared, the men had lifted her from her horse. She could not quite figure how they cleared her feet from her stirrups, how they caught her horse's reins. She was cowed between them, breathlessly aware of their grim height, their stolid bodies. Each took hold of an arm, forcing her to look directly at Crestman as he limped to stand before her.

The glass vial in his hand was familiar. Rani had held its twin months ago; she had taken it from Crestman in the alleys of Brianta. Then, the vial had held poison.

Panic surged inside her. How closely was Crestman leashed to Dartulamino? Would his own quest for revenge be tamed by the priest for now? Her entire body longed to fight for freedom. Her mind screamed that she should twist away from her captors, struggle to reach the shadowy margins of the forest.

No. This was the only way that she could get to her

enemy's heart. This was the only way that she could strike a deadly blow.

Crestman used his good hand on her clenched teeth, but she gave way almost immediately, desperate to save her bruised jaw from further abuse. Still, he was harsher than he needed to be. He poured the liquid quickly, nearly drowning her with the burning stuff.

Kella might have known what she drank. The herb-witch might have been able to identify the compounds that made up the stinging liquid. She might have explained the brewing process, the stirring, the fermenting.

But Rani did not care. She knew only that Crestman's drink scalded. It singed her lungs, enflamed her heart. It ate away at her belly, kindled her torso, her arms, her legs, her fingers, her toes. She tried to speak past the fire, tried to speak past the flame, but she could do nothing.

The smallest corner of her mind remained aware that she was lifted back onto her horse. It knew that they rode late into the night, that she finally slept upon the ground, staked out like a beast of burden beneath the night sky.

It knew that someone came to her while she slept, a woman, lithe and silent. It recognized the danger of a knife against her throat, the flash of yet another weapon. It heard the whispered oath, and then the soft brogue. "Not yet. It inna yet yer time."

That spark of awareness knew when Crestman came to her in the morning, when he poured more poison down her throat. It felt him lean close to her, felt him brush back a sweat-darkened lock of hair from her face. It heard the whisper of his voice as he leaned closer, as he formed words so soft that she might have dreamed them.

"I would have had it otherwise, Ranita. I would have

saved you from the Fellowship. I only ever wanted to serve you, but you would not have me. You sold me out in Liantine. I wanted once to save you, but now I know that you will die."

And Rani could only listen and hope and try to remember that she had fought for this. She had fought for one last chance to see the Fellowship.

13

Hal rolled over on the feather mattress, flinging an arm across his face to shelter his eyes from a piercing beam of light. His head pounded as if it were a military drum, and he tried to raise enough spit in his mouth to rid himself of the foul taste that coated his tongue. "Leave me alone," he groaned, and the words sliced through his skull.

For several blessed heartbeats, that was all that he could remember, that he had ordered everyone to leave, to let him rest in peace. Forcing one eye open, he looked across the strange room. Had he thrown that flagon at the door? A waste of fine wine, that.

Hamid's electors, Hal remembered fuzzily. They had shown him to this room. But how had he gotten to Riadelle?

Hal took a deep breath to still the pounding in his head. He could recall standing in his tent, in the center of the Great Clearing. He had been talking with Farso, trying as ever to cheer the man, to restore him to the carefree youth he once had been. He had wished that he could find a way to remind Farso that an entire kingdom needed the knight, that *Hal* needed him.

And then, all in a blink, Hal remembered what had happened. The full force rushed in on him, punching his belly and forcing the breath from his lungs. He was blind; he was deaf; he was struck mute by what he remembered.

And somehow, he managed to groan. Old Thait must have laughed himself silly, beyond the Heavenly Gates. The god of irony had always enjoyed a vicious sense of humor, but had he ever been so cruel? Had he ever worked such ruin on a man?

Pushing through the fog that filled his skull where his brain should be, Hal could recall the soldiers who had stormed into his tent, the captain who had fallen before him, prostrate even before he delivered his report. Hal could see the bound and gagged herb-witch, the old woman shoved to her knees in front of him. There had been a single endless moment when he had known what his man was going to say, when all of the blood had drained from his face.

And then the words. The terrible words.

Mareka. Dead. Marekanoran. Dead.

Hal had forgotten himself entirely. He had thrown himself at the herb-witch. He pummeled her bruised face, kicked her, scrambled for a weapon, anything to inflict one thousandth of the pain that split his heart. Only Farso had dared to stop him, had dared to restrain him and order the woman taken away.

Farso had held him as he bellowed out his rage, as he tore at his clothes, his face, at anything that would yield to his blind, desperate fury.

He had been so cursed foolish! He had thought that he protected his wife, that he protected his only son and heir! He had thought that he kept them safe, hidden in the forest. He had believed that they would be more secure in their hiding place than with him in the Great Clearing, that they might yet avoid the Fellowship that surely knew where to find him.

What a fool he had been. Tarn could seek out people anywhere. The Heavenly Gates groaned open when people least expected. There was nothing Hal could do to stave off death, nothing he could do to protect his innocent family. The Fellowship had targeted him, and he was cursed, cursed, cursed.

At last, Farso had said that he must compose himself. He must ride into Riadelle, demand an audience with the king. Hal must extract his due immediately, before anyone had a chance to whisper rumors, lies. Kella Herb-Witch, a vassal of King Hamid, had murdered Morenia's queen and only heir, and Hal must demand compensation. He must demand an army, so that he could fight the Fellowship, once and for all.

This was his sole chance to build the alliance he so desperately needed. Now. Bidding over the still, cold bodies of his wife and his son.

Hal had let himself be dressed in his finest robes. He'd been curried and combed like some fine beast, guided through the forest, down the road to Riadelle.

It had been after midnight when they arrived at the city gates. The captain of the guard was finally persuaded to let them pass, but there was no lever that could be applied to Hamid's chamberlain, no argument that would get them to the king in the wee hours of the morning. The servant had only sniffed down his thin nose and reluctantly agreed to place the visitors in state apartments. He would arrange for them to see Hamid after first daylight.

He would summon the night guard if Hal persisted in his impossible request. Electors backed up the threat.

So Hal had conceded. As soon as he was locked into his finely appointed cell, he had stalked to the mantel, poured a glass of Hamid's finest red. Farso had asked some foolish question, pointed out some stupid detail, and Hal had flung the flagon.

Farso had not taken offense, though. Instead, he had shrugged and found another flagon, one that was wonderfully, gloriously full. He had poured for his king, and again, and again. He had listened to Hal's raging, to the royal insistence that all the Thousand Gods were liars and cheats, that the world was all unfair. He had smoothed back the hair from Hal's face as the king collapsed onto his feather bed, as his rage melted into tears. Farso had murmured like a child's nurse as his king sobbed, weeping like the boy he once had been, decades ago in distant Morenia.

And now, in the light of day, Farso stood over him, shaking out a simple tunic and leggings. The black fabric hung as limp as Hal's hair. "Come, Sire," Farso said. "It is time for you to dress for your audience with Hamid."

Hal's belly turned as he saw the funereal clothes, and he scarcely managed to scramble from the bed, to find the chamber pot before bile burned his throat. His retching lasted longer than he would have thought possible, leaving his sides aching and his throat raw.

Farso waited for him a few steps away. Ever the mindful servant, the baron had a basin of water at hand and clean strips of linen. When Hal finally managed to stand, Farso eased him to the edge of the bed. The man was more comfort than any nurse could have been, silent and watchful as he sponged his king's face, as he offered up a cup of pure water and a simple clay basin to spit into.

Hal accepted the attention woodenly. This was impossible, he thought. Impossible that he should once again don the black of mourning. Impossible that he should once again contemplate a pyre. Another son lost—this one, who had been born alive, who had thrived.

And Mareka. Gone. The spiderguild journeyman who had snared him with a poison. The wife who had worked beside him to build an empire. The woman who had trusted him to keep her safe, to keep her alive, even as she fled from her house, from her adopted land.

Adopted land. Murderous hand. All unmanned.

The rhymes swirled through his thoughts, louder than they had been for days, for weeks. Hal nearly lost himself in the echoes, stumbling down dark corridors, through reeking hallways where there was nothing but madness and sorrow and hopeless, hapless memories.

Somehow, he became aware that Farso was offering him a crust of plain white bread. "It would be best, Sire. You have a difficult meeting ahead of you."

"I cannot eat, Farso." Hal was surprised that his voice could sound so even, that his words could be so measured, so calm, even as they tamped down the voices.

Of course, Farso understood. He bowed and set aside the bread.

Hal let his friend dress him then. He allowed Farso to slip a black tunic over his head. He waited while the bands of satin were straightened, while the hem was tugged into place. He permitted Farso to adjust the silk leggings, to pull them into alignment over Hal's knees. He forced his heel into one black boot, and then another, forbidding himself to wonder where the grim clothing had been found and on such short notice.

Only when he was fully dressed did he speak, and then

the words were pulled out of him, sharp and painful, like a blade from a wound. "Who waits out there?"

Who waits. Heavenly Gates. Tarn sates.

The voices were a physical burden that pulled down his spine, and Hal's knees nearly buckled.

Farso said, "Puladarati, of course. Father Siritalanu. The electors who escorted us here last night."

"Rani?" He asked the question as a hedge against further thought, already certain that she was there, even though he could not remember her on the late-night march through the woods, could not recall her face staring at him in helpless concern.

Farso shifted from one foot to the other. He scrutinized Hal's shoulder, picking at a bit of lint. "Farso," Hal said more pointedly. "Rani will be there, won't she? I need her to bargain for me. I need her to present our case to Hamid."

Present our case. Enemies face. Win the race.

The voices chattered faster now, more eagerly, as if they knew Hal was on the edge of a precipice, at the end of his resources.

"Sire . . ." Farso's voice was strained.

"Where is she?" Hal flashed on an image of a woman's throat, slashed and bleeding. "What has happened to Rani?"

"Sire, the herb-witch—"

"No!" Not another death. Not another soul counted out against his own. "I'll poison her myself! My wife and son were not enough? She has killed Rani, too?"

"No!" Farso shouted, and then he lowered his voice. "No, Sire. The herb-witch did not kill Rani." Hal heard the words, forced himself to take a breath, to listen. "She did not kill Rani. But she left the glasswright in her cottage. Left her bound."

"Bound?" Hal might never have heard the word before.

"Bound. For . . . the Fellowship." Farso winced at Hal's wordless cry. "Sire!" he managed, when Hal had to pause, had to take a breath. "Sire, she still lives."

"How can you know that?" Rani was dead. *Dead, dead, dead.* No rhymes, only the single word, repeated over and over again in his mind. *Dead. Dead. Dead.*

"Would the Fellowship be stealthy in something like this? They long to see you defeated. They long to see you ruined. If they had killed Rani Trader, they would have left her body for you to find."

"Then where is she?" *Dead. Dead. Dead.*

"We believe that she returns to Moren. Hamid's men saw a large company on the road, riding north in the darkest hours of the night."

"We will go after her." *Dead. Dead. Dead.*

"Aye, Sire."

"We will go after her, and we will get the Fellowship, and they will pay for all that they have done." *Dead.*

"Aye, Sire. But for that you must speak to Hamid."

"Aye." Hal must garner support. Not for him—he was lost forever; he would never find the path away from the whispering voices in his mind. Not for dead Mareka, for dead Marekanoran. For Rani. Rani, who had fought for him. Rani, who had worked to build his kingdom. Rani . . .

Hal knew that he should notice more as he walked through the corridors. He should be more aware of the Sarmonians who hovered in doorways. He should listen to the rumors whispered behind raised hands. He should see the pitying stares, the shaking heads. He should acknowledge the condolences of his lords, of Puladarati and Father Siritalanu, of the soldiers who formed an honor guard behind him.

But Hal could see only the dreams inside his head. He could see Mareka, her sly face smoothed into the contented mask of motherhood. He could see his son, his own Marekanoran, sleeping by the fireside.

And Rani. He could see Rani a hundred different ways—as merchant and glasswright, as soldier who had stood beside him in the battle against their staunchest enemy.

Dead. For even if the Fellowship had not killed her yet, it would soon enough. It would murder her when he least could stand the blow. It would cut off the last of his great supporters, the last of his true allies. Rani would pay with her life so that he might be controlled. Her name would be added to the lists, along with Mareka, Marekanoran, with all the loyal men and women who had died in his service.

Somehow, they reached Hamid's Great Hall. Somehow Hal was announced, was ushered into the king's presence. Somehow, he made his appropriate bows, gracefully, fluidly, as if he were not wearing borrowed clothing and the weight of death, as if his belly were not roiled by too much wine and too little sleep.

"My lord," Hamid said, and his sharp voice was solicitous. His narrow frame was swathed in midnight-colored silk. "I grieve with you at your loss. I wish that our stories might have been different, that I might have known the forces that sought you out. I would have offered you all the protections of my house, for all we kings are brothers."

Fine words, but scarcely the truth. Hamid had not wanted to borrow grief, not from Hal, not from any of the Morenians. Hal glanced at the assembled electors, thinking that Hamid had known trouble enough, even before the Fellowship made their presence known in Sarmonia.

Unaware of Hal's scrutiny, Hamid continued. "If there is

anything that I can do for you, Halaravilli ben-Jair, if there is any comfort that my house can offer yours . . ."

Hal inclined his head in acceptance of the sentiment, ignoring the flurry of death whispers that the movement evoked in his skull. He was supposed to demand support now. He was supposed to say that Kella had belonged to Hamid and that the Sarmonian must pay for the herb-witch's wrongs.

Looking at Hamid, though, Hal knew that the argument would fail. Oh, Hamid would likely execute Kella. That was easy enough. But he would never agree to raising an army against the Fellowship. Not here. Not in front of his electors.

Perhaps Rani Trader would have had the skill to persuade Hamid. But Hal did not. Hal would need a different approach. He would need his own subterfuge. He glanced at Puladarati and Farso, knowing that his councilors would not approve of the step he was about to take. He flicked his gaze toward Father Siritalanu. Would the priest be swift enough to follow what Hal would say?

These were desperate days. It was time for desperate measures.

"There is one thing, my lord." Hamid merely quirked an eyebrow, waiting for Hal to continue. Swallowing hard, Hal spun out his lie. After all, what was one more story? What was one more tale in the face of all that had transpired in Sarmonia? "In my kingdom, it is customary for brothers to drink together over a loss. The Thousand Gods expect us to raise a cup as family, in salute to those who have reached the Heavenly Gates. The gods intend for us royals to grieve without restraint, in private and away from the eyes of all our retainers, all our people."

To foster credibility, Hal gestured at Father Siritalanu.

Fortunately, the priest had learned something in his time at court—he merely inclined his head and looked for all the world as if he were familiar with the custom Hal described.

Farso appeared surprised, but he stayed silent. Puladarati, alas, was less accepting. The old advisor stepped forward, reaching out with his three-fingered hand as if he would interrupt the delicate balance that Hal was creating.

"Please, my lord," Hal said to Hamid, rushing his words a bit so that he would not be interrupted. "Is there a chamber where we could raise a glass? Where I could tell you of the kin that I have lost and you could grieve with me like the brother you pledge yourself to be?"

Hamid glanced at his electors, and Hal sensed the quick debate that flashed between them. Of course the retainers did not want their king to act alone. Of course, they did not want to lose any shred of the power that they had gathered over Sarmonia. But they were wise enough not to try to correct their leader in public, wise enough to recognize the power of death rites and rituals.

"Very well, brother," Hamid said, when he had confirmed permission to speak. "Let us drink, that we may share your loss."

Hamid led the way from the dais. Hal remembered the hallways that led to the study, the stone walls that had seemed to eavesdrop on him the last time that he passed this way. Like Hamid, he allowed his retainers to come with him this far, to follow carefully behind.

The entire procession was silent, as if each man counted out his own sorrow, his own loss on this bitter morning. Hal suspected that his own people attempted to think their warnings loudly enough that he could hear them through his pounding skull. He swallowed with his dry mouth, unable to imagine any convincing arguments above the tattoo of his boot heels, above the single repeated syllable: *Dead, dead, dead.*

When they arrived at the study, Hamid ordered his men to wait. One of the electors challenged propriety enough to step forward, to make a bow in Hal's general direction, and to say to his own lord, "Your Majesty, we electors would add our grief to yours. We would speak for all the people of Sarmonia as we join together to mourn our northern brother's loss."

Hal thought that he heard a slight emphasis on the word "together." He waited while Hamid formulated an answer, counting out his own heartbeats. If the electors came, all would be lost. If the electors entered the study, Hal's fledgling plan would be shredded like a cobweb in a gale.

"Thank you, my lord," Hamid said at last. Hal could hear the ripple of tension beneath his courteous words. "I must yield to Morenia in this. We support him in his loss, and we honor all his customs, however different they might be from our own. Wait here, and we will all return to the Great Hall together."

Hal's relief was so intense that he felt faint. As wings of blackness swept in from the sides of his vision, Farso slipped a supporting hand beneath his elbow. Hal permitted himself only a moment of leaning on his friend, on his true, heartfelt brother. Any longer, and Farso might think himself bound to enter the study. Any longer, and Hamid's retainers would follow suit.

A single deep breath steeled him enough to cross the threshold, to watch Hamid close the door. He thrust down the whispers in his head, banished them with a strength that he did not know he possessed. He waited only for the Sarmonian to come close enough to hear him, and then he whispered, "Fast now. We have much to discuss, and not enough time to do it."

"What?"

"Quiet! Do not let them hear you. Quick. Pour a glass, that we might leave behind what they expect to see." Hamid hesitated, uncertainty moving his hand toward the jeweled dagger at his waist. Hal saw the edge glint in the brilliant morning light, imagined the sharp blade against his own throat, cutting his wrists, plunging into his chest.

Pain, yes. But not a pain as deep as he already suffered. Not a pain as endless as the one he now faced . . .

He sharpened his voice, reminding himself not to yield. Not now. Not yet. "Will you let your electors call you a liar after we leave this room? Pour the wine, and listen to me!"

Hamid crossed to his writing desk. A pitcher was set close to hand, covered with a slip of parchment, as if he were particular about dust settling on his wine. "There is only one cup," he said, and Hal noted that he projected his voice, as if he wanted the assembled nobles on the other side of the door to hear.

"That is well," Hal said in a similar tone. "In my land, brothers share the same cup, as they share the burden of their loss."

Hamid shrugged and poured, and Hal closed the distance between them with a few quick steps. "Listen to me," he whispered. "You have no reason to believe me, I know, no reason to trust me. I will tell you only what I know, and then you must make your decision.

"My wife and son were killed by the Fellowship of Jair, by a secret band that seeks to gain power in all the kingdoms in the world."

"Your family was poisoned by an herb-witch!"

"Upon the Fellowship's orders. The Fellowship has long sought to destroy my line and gain all power in Morenia. It is behind the Briantan invasion. It supports the Liantines who barricade my harbor."

Hamid stared at him as if he were insane, and Hal nearly laughed aloud. Of course Hamid thought him mad. Why wouldn't he?

At least Hamid ventured a question. "Who is this Fellowship? How could anyone hold such power over a king?"

"They work beneath the surface of a kingdom. They select their members from all the castes. The draw their strength because no one expects them where they are, no one thinks to look for them."

"How have you learned of them, then?"

"I was one of them." The words were bitter on Hal's tongue. "For more than a decade, I was welcomed in their meetings. I, and members of my closest circle." Rani. If only she were here. Her words could convince Hamid; she could sway the king.

She was dead, though—now or soon enough. Dead, as he would be. As he and all his kingdom, if he could not convince Hamid, if he could not bring Sarmonia to his side . . .

Hamid was confused. "And you have left it now, left this . . . Fellowship of Jair?"

"Aye. I left once I was certain that they worked for my downfall. They already have Brianta and Liantine. If they take Morenia, they get not only my kingdom, but Amanthia as well. After that, Sarmonia could be plucked at leisure, like a ripened fruit."

Hamid shook his head in protest, his pointed beard emphasizing his disagreement. "That's absurd! If these people lurk beneath the surface of society, how can they gain such power? How can they control so much?"

"You can ask that?" Hal's frustration flashed through his hands; he pounded Hamid's table and scarcely remembered to lower his voice. "You? Who lives on the leash of your electors? How do *they* control *you*? How do they dictate what happens in Sarmonia?"

He had pushed too hard. Hamid's face darkened like a thunderhead, and he flashed a look at the door of his chamber.

"Yes!" Hal said, knowing that he had to give a focus to that rage. He stepped closer so that his harsh whisper could be heard. "Power rises when we least expect it. When was the last time that you sat alone in this room, my lord? When was the last time you made a decision without them? The electors control your every move. They might appear to stand aside; they might permit you to be seen in public. They let your people think that you act as a free man, but they control every rein."

Hamid bristled. "You know nothing of how we do things here in Sarmonia. And even if your worst accusations were true, even if every one of my electors were corrupt, my land is stable. We could never fall to some lawless cabal. We could never be controlled by your Fellowship."

"You already are." Hal gripped Hamid's arm, closed his fingers around the satin and velvet until he felt the hard muscle beneath. "A fortnight ago, I watched the Fellowship gather in your forest. I watched three riders come down the path from Riadelle. Three riders with the badge of electors on their chests. You have lost your throne as surely as have Brianta and Liantine. As surely as I will now if you do not help me."

Hamid tugged his arm away, swearing harshly. "There is a balance in my land! We Sarmonians are enlightened. We share power among our people, among all the landed men. I would not expect you to understand how the system works. I would not expect you to comprehend what a kingdom *can* be when wise men wear the crown."

Wise men, Hamid meant, instead of some blood-bound son. Hal pulled himself to his full height, not hesitating to take advantage of Hamid's slight build. Consciously setting aside all the voices, all the whispers, Hal said: "I know you think your system is better. I know you think your elections are fair and your methods just. Nevertheless, the Fellowship moves against you. It's stolen your electors, and the rest of your kingdom is next."

Hamid shook his head. "For your Fellowship to steal my throne, it must corrupt a majority of the electors. The only way to manipulate electors is to manipulate all landed men. No secret society could be that strong."

"They need not build the system from the ground. They need only to grab you now. Grab you now and change the rules." Hamid started to protest, but Hal overrode him. "Do you have a queen, my lord?" Mareka. Hal felt tears rise hot behind his eyes, let them hover on his lashes, splash down his face. "Do you have a son and heir?" Marekanoran. "Who do you hold dearest in all the world?"

Hamid brushed Hal's hand from his sleeve, as if Morenian tears might be contagious. He crossed to the window and studied the cloudless sky, apparently seeking answers there. He stared out over Riadelle, over the surrounding countryside, out to the forest that smudged the horizon. He twisted the golden band around his wrist, the symbol of his marriage.

Hal pitched his voice low. "Dead, brother. All of them. Dead. The Fellowship can do it. These mourning rags are proof." He tugged at his own forlorn tunic.

Hamid's jaw was set as he finally said, "What would you have me do, ben-Jair?"

"Raise your army." Hal rushed through the words before he could lose the foothold. "Take the men that you trust, the ones that are loyal to you directly. Ride with me to Moren, and help me deliver my homeland from our common enemy. Liberate Morenia and crush the Fellowship, and make yourself secure."

"The electors would never permit that. Not in autumn. Not when they must return to their own halls and attend to the landed men, to their own local courts."

"You must defy your electors, Hamid. If you do not, you will have no kingdom left to rule."

"If I defy them, they will cast me from my throne."

"Let them try! Even if they choose to replace you, the voting will take time! Time that you can spend strengthening your bonds with your loyal men! Time that you can spend consolidating your own base of power, your own means of support."

Hamid glared at him, but his fingers still twisted his golden armband. When he spoke, his words were sharp. "And do we have a single chance against your Fellowship?"

"All I know is this. We have *no* chance with them."

"So you would drag my wife and heirs into your battles?"

"I drag no one. All I can promise, Hamid, is that you will lose your family if you do nothing. Maybe not this winter. Maybe not the next. But when the Fellowship rules Sarmonia and has need of your compliance, your family will pay the price."

"And if I ride with you? How can I keep them safe while I am gone?"

Hal swallowed acid sorrow. "Hiding will not work, no matter how secure you think the place. Bring your lady with you, your lady and your heirs. Keep them in your sight, and hope our battle will be fast."

Hamid shook his head, and Hal sensed that the man longed for the easy days, for the times when he could look to his electors and know what he should do. "If I stand with you, you can defeat the armies that hold your land?"

"How many men can you bring?"

"I cannot be certain. Five score, perhaps, if we send word now. Five score by the time we reach Moren's gates."

An entire kingdom at his disposal, and Hamid could promise no more than one hundred men.

Something was better than nothing, though. Something was better than the ragtag group that had fled the cathedral with Hal so many weeks before. "Five score can win," Hal said, marveling inside that he could pretend such confidence. "I know Moren's defenses. I have the man who designed her ramparts with me here in Sarmonia."

"But so few . . ." Hamid seemed to shrink within his magnificent robes.

"Enough." Hal nodded, the tang of imagined revenge giving him strength. "Enough to win. For I have everything to gain by fighting and nothing left to lose."

Hamid shook his head again, but he extended his hand. "I will join you then, brother. I will join you in your fight against the Fellowship, Halaravilli ben-Jair."

"Against the Fellowship," Hal echoed. He raised the pounded goblet to his lips and drank, and then he passed it to Hamid. "Against the Fellowship," he said once more, and then both men turned quickly to the table, and their plans, and their goals to liberate Morenia.

Hal bit back an exasperated sigh as Hamid leaned back in the small boat and squinted into the moonless night. "This cannot work," Hamid said.

Hal did not bother to fashion a reply; he had already tired of comforting the man. He had fought down enough of his own questions, banished enough of his own doubts. Even now, he rallied his spirits with a bold—if silent—retort. *Can not work! Who was Hamid to say what could and could not work! Had he ever seen Davin's miracles? Had he ever seen the marvels that the old man could craft?*

Hal tried to remind himself that he must be patient with the Sarmonian. After all, Hamid had broken against all tradition in his southern land. He had fled his own capital, leaving behind his palace, his throne. He had traveled north with only a handful of loyal companions, men who had marched because they were faithful to him and not his electors.

Hamid had a right to be pessimistic. Whatever the outcome in the north, the electors would be furious that their power had been challenged. Hamid would not rule in Sarmonia again.

And yet, he had come with Hal. He had brought loyal knights and their vassals. He had left behind comfort and familiarity and certain power to fight with Hal against known evil. It was no wonder that the man questioned their ultimate success.

Hal nodded to Davin who crouched near them in the boat, huddled next to Tovin Player in the prow. "Are we ready, then?"

"Aye." The old man was disapproving as ever. Hal had

never seen Davin smile, and he certainly did not expect that to change as they crouched in a coracle on a glass-smooth autumn sea, just off the Morenian coast. "Better to do it now. The players' muscles will cool down, and they'll become less flexible."

"Very well." Hal gestured to the two soldiers who held oars. The men bowed their heads and stroked forward. Once. Twice. A dozen times.

The boat glided into a pod of similar craft, a dozen vessels all, bobbing on the glassy water. If the moon had been out, they might have been visible on the ocean, clear to any sailor who looked out from the ships that barricaded the Morenian harbor. In the darkness, though, they were practically invisible.

Hal looked at the faces in each small craft. They had rowed all the way from shore, launching from a sheltered cove well after sunset and laboring hard to reach this spot outside the Morenian harbor. The players were accustomed to hard work, but the necessity for silence had weighed heavily on them. They were ready for their performance to begin.

Hal looked to Tovin one last time. "You are certain?" he asked in a low voice.

"Aye. It is all that we can do." The player had volunteered his men as soon as Hal and Hamid began to plan their attack. At first, Hal had laughed away the prospect—it was hardly likely that they could defeat their enemies with rhyming comedies, with woeful tragedies, all performed on a well-lit stage.

But then, Davin had mentioned an old plan that he had sketched in his endless notebooks. He needed strong men for it to work, but men who were short and light. As soon as

Tovin heard the plan, he volunteered his players, and the troop leaped into their rapid training with an infectious enthusiasm. Hal had reluctantly conceded that the players had the precise skills that Davin's desperate ploy demanded, even as he wondered what payment Tovin would require. Hal was scarcely in a position to haggle, though. He would pay the players, pay them richly, if ever he saw his treasury and his throne.

Each member of the troop was tested, to be certain that he did not fear the water. Each had been trained, quickly, in the rudiments of swimming, in case Davin's invention failed. Each had been reminded that he need not volunteer for a mission that might well mean death, that he need not agree to Davin's outrageous plan.

And each had proclaimed, in a loud, clear player's voice that he would undertake the task for his sponsor. Each had agreed to fight in honor of Rani Trader.

Hal had looked away when he saw the glint of tears in Tovin's eyes. Hal had never understood the player, but he had no problem comprehending loss. Loss and aching sorrow. Perhaps the player would not demand gold after all. Perhaps love had extracted its own toll.

Now, as Hal's boat bobbed on the ocean surface, he heard Mareka's voice, whispering in the deepest part of his brain. *There is no sorrow here, my lord. No sorrow beyond the Heavenly Gates. You can come with me, you know. Just lean against the edge of the boat. It is not so far. Not so far to the water . . .*

He had heard Mareka for days now, for the fortnight that his men had been marching north. At first, she had come to him in his dreams, her voice soft, comforting, saying that she and Marekanoran felt no pain.

Then she had whispered to him as he scraped away the bristles of his beard, telling him that the edge of his blade was sharp. He could come to her with one quick slash, one painless cut. He had cried out, and she had slipped away.

But not for long.

He had heard Mareka when he sat beside a well-built fire—she had whispered of the power and the beauty of the flames, reminded him how quickly they could consume a man. He had heard her when the road passed beside a swift-running river. She had spoken to him when they camped under sturdy tree branches, limbs that were strong enough to support a man and a length of clean-knotted rope.

Each time, he set her aside. Each time, she cried out as if he wounded her, as if he assaulted her with whatever mayhem she was suggesting. Each time, he heard her sobbing, desperate, frightened, alone.

He was still king. He must not yield to her ghost. He must not yield to death, no matter how strong the attraction.

He shook his head, looking out at the expectant faces, at the taut players' bodies in their stretched-leather boats. He hoped that they would think his voice shook because he was trying to keep it quiet in the night. "Men," he said. "You are the first link in a chain. Tonight, the work that you do will allow us to enter our harbor, to reclaim the port that is rightfully ours. You go forth with a power never seen by man before. May all the Thousand watch over you."

Hal leaned back, permitting Hamid to say a few words of his own. He thought that the Sarmonian king might only repeat his negative motto, might remind them all that their scheme could not work. The man was made of sterner stuff, though. He threw back his thin shoulders and said, "Morenians, my Sarmonian soldiers stand with you, ready on the shore. We rise up together in a battle that will change our lives forever. Our children's children will speak of our glory for all the years to come."

And then both kings leaned back. They allowed Davin to look about the players, to check the hastily crafted handiwork that would support such spirited lives. The old man had bullied the troops on the long march north, grumbling over great bone needles and lengths of leather thread. Davin had shown the players how to cut shapes out of the well-tanned leather that Hamid had produced from his treasury before they left Sarmonia. Davin had shown how to join the edges with a quick whiplash stitch. Children had been set to dripping wax over the seams, to oiling the finished products.

If Hal had seen Davin's creations in another context, he would have laughed. Even now, as hefty soldiers manned fragile bellows, he felt wholly inappropriate amusement rising in his throat. The players looked as if they played with toys, as if they bobbled in a summer fountain.

But this was no game. Lives were at stake. Brave men and women went forth to reclaim the harbor.

Hal watched as the volunteers strapped on Davin's leather contraptions, sealing the pods tightly around each foot. Oiled laces were rigged around each player's calves, laces that fit into holes sewed into leggings. The leather sacks were secured, oiled again, waxed closed.

And then each player sat in Davin's specially designed rope harness, dangled over the open sea. Each spun back toward his boat, leaning in the suspended chair so that the soldiers' bellows could find the small access holes, could pump the leather full of air.

In the dim night, the pods looked like nightmare feet, like bolsters attached to the players' legs. The strangeness was only accentuated by the final piece of Davin's handiwork—matched poles made of the lightest wood, each ending with an inflated bladder.

Even though Hal had heard the tools described, even though he had learned never to doubt Davin's creativity, he was amazed when he saw the first man walk across the water. The player's gait was awkward, and he fumbled with his poles, but he was walking on the ocean like a clumsy man on land.

"Slide, you fool! Slide!" Davin's instruction hissed down from Hal's boat. The player stiffened and seemed as if he would turn about to respond, but then he flexed his knees and kicked off for a longer glide on the water's surface.

Under other circumstances, Hal might have laughed. He might have marveled at a mind that had imagined men walking on water—imagined and then made that vision a reality. He might have sighed at the wonder of the poles—tools to help with balance, but weapons in their own right. Weapons who would reveal a poisoned spike swaddled inside the bladder. Weapons that would be wielded against the Liantines that slept on ships in the harbor. Weapons that would gain back access to the port even as they sowed confusion.

You could take one of those poles, Hal heard Mareka say. *You could remove the bladder and plunge the spike into your chest. You could lean your full weight against it. It would hurt for a moment, but then you would be safe. You would be here, beyond the Heavenly Gates.*

Hal tossed his head, pushing out Mareka's suggestion. Another coracle bumped against his, and Hal found himself looking into Farso's earnest eyes. "Come, Sire." The baron nodded his head to include Hamid. "My lords, we must go meet the landward army. While we have tarried, they have moved into position outside the city."

Army. That was hardly the word for it. One hundred men that Hamid had gathered—every last soul who owed loyalty directly to him and not to one of the electors. One hundred men who had never seen Moren, who had never walked the city streets that they hoped to conquer before the next nightfall.

Hal set aside his doubts. One hundred men must be enough. One hundred warriors relying on Davin's tricks. One hundred soldiers well fed and already rested from their march north. If there had been more than five score, they could not have eaten from the tithing barns along the road. If there had been more than five score, Hal and Hamid might have already lost the war, before the first battle was begun.

The boat returned to shore without adventure. Along the way, Mareka whispered to him, assuring him that the water would close over his head quickly, that his lungs would only burn for a few minutes as he drowned.

He thrust away his wife and made himself think about Rani Trader. She had feared the sea. He had watched her face that fear, watched her try to conquer a rebellious stomach besides. She had been a brave woman, braver than he. He tried to convince himself that the moisture he wiped from his face was innocent sea spray.

The short march inland was easy enough. The roads were clear, and when the light breeze blew from the north, Hal could make out the sound of the Pilgrims' Bell, tolling across the hills. It would guide him now, he vowed. He would embrace its solemn tones like the holiest of pilgrims reaching out for the Thousand Gods. For the gods, for the Heavenly Gates . . .

Hal sighed and pushed away yet another of Mareka's invitations, this one to grab the short sword from his bodyguard, to plunge the blade into his heart.

He was tired. More tired than he had ever thought he could be. How had his father lived to be such an old man? How had King Shanoranvilli stirred himself to rise from his bed every morning, no matter what chaos he faced?

Chaos he faced. Ever he raced. Sometimes he paced. Paced. Paced.

Hal let the rhyme carry him down the road, ignoring the mutter of the men beside him, forcing down the constant expectation of a cry from some Briantan guard. Surely the invaders had left sentries upon the approach to the city. . . . Surely they knew that someone would come to oust them. . . .

Perhaps they did not, though. Perhaps they believed themselves completely invulnerable—and that thought was even more distressing. If the Briantans believed themselves so secure, who was Hal to challenge them? Perhaps he should call a halt, stop the soldiers, try to save a few lives before the carnage of the battle.

Hal looked to his right, to Farso's grim face, barely visible in the moonless night. How could Hal stop now? He had been bereaved for a handful of weeks. Farso, though, had lost his child more than a year ago, had watched his wife succumb to a madness worse than any clean battle death. How could Hal say that he was unable to go on?

And so he found himself on the edge of the great plain that stretched before Moren's gates.

The soldiers moved swiftly. They had practiced their maneuvers on the long march north; their captains had drilled them, over and over, so that they could assemble Davin's engines with speed and accuracy.

Hal was still surprised by the creations. He had watched the players use them on their stage, but he had never seen the potential of the tools, never seen that they could be rebuilt as instruments of war. Certainly, the streams of silken ribbons had been beautiful, but they were so far removed from a hail of burning bolts that Hal had not imagined Davin's true genius.

Now, though, the men assembled their creations with brutal efficiency. Hastily smoothed wooden beams were lowered into carved cradles. Gears fashioned of sturdy southern trees were meshed together, set on one side and then on the other, so that the engines could gain more power with every circuit they made, rolling forward.

Davin had *tsked* at the necessity of using wood. The engines would not last the day, he had exclaimed. The gears should be fashioned of metal, hammered out by the finest smiths.

Puladarati was the one who had convinced the old man to stop his fussing. The engines would work or they would not. Hal and his Sarmonian army would gain the gate, or they would be repulsed. There would be no long battle. One day, with wooden gears, would suffice. Or it would not.

Davin had grumbled, but he had conceded the point, supervising the men who carved the engines as they traveled northward. The best of the soldier craftsmen were carried in litters, allowed to carve all day, without the fatigue of walking.

Withdrawing behind the last of the sheltering hills, Hal turned to Hamid. "We are met, then. Till dawn."

The Sarmonian nodded, the gesture scarcely visible in

the dim light. "I'll see to my men. A word from their king will do them well as they face this battle."

Hal watched the southerner disappear into the inky night. He should talk to his own men, try to raise their spirits. There were few enough of them—the handful that had fled the cathedral with him months past, supplemented by a dozen players who had agreed to ride Davin's engines on their destructive path.

Destructive path. Army's wrath. True bloodbath.

Hal was startled from the voices by Puladarati coming up beside him. The leonine man looked out at Moren's walls, his shaking head just visible in the darkness.

"It's come to this, then."

This? Hal wanted to ask. *What? That I attack my own city? That I rely on an army of strangers? That I am doomed to failure, even if I succeed, for I have no wife, no heir?*

I have no heir. Burden to bear. Why should I care?

When Hal stayed silent, Puladarati stepped closer. "By this time tomorrow, all will be ended. You will be back on your throne, with the Briantans and Liantines fled."

"You don't truly believe that, do you?" Hal heard the words come out of his throat, but they might have been spoken by another man.

"I believe because I must, Sire," Puladarati said. "I have served the house of ben-Jair all my life, and I'm not going to stop now."

Hal thought of a dozen replies, each more saturated with doom and death. He settled for a question. "We can't win this, can we?"

"We have Davin's engines. We have the finest men the Sarmonian king could gather."

"We can't win," Hal repeated.

"The players will cause a diversion in the port. They'll keep the occupier busy on two fronts."

"We can't."

Puladarati sighed gustily, running a three-fingered hand through his hair. "It's not likely, Sire. Not unless there's an uprising within the city. Not unless something disrupts the occupiers from within."

Hal nodded, content at least to hear the end of the lies. He turned back to the city walls to watch the final preparations, dim as they were under the moonless sky. To watch, and to wait, and to wonder if death would ever be quiet inside his clamorous skull.

14

A disinterested part of Rani's mind knew that she had never been this frightened in her life. No, she told herself. Her mind was not disinterested. She was very much interested in the outcome of this confrontation.

Not whether she lived or died. Like one of the players that she had sponsored for the past four years, she had worked through the script of what was likely to happen. She was held captive by the Fellowship. Her hands were bound behind her back. She was clothed in white robes, garments that wrapped around her several times, as if she were a swaddled newborn child. A newborn child, or a corpse ready for the pyre.

No. She could not see any way that she might live. Her future truly was with the Thousand Gods. She had learned that they were in her, they were of her, they *were* her, in a way that she had never dreamed before. The Thousand had a plan for all the world, and she was merely an instrument in that plan. She was merely a tool. And Rani knew all too well the fate of tools.

How many times had she left her own grozing irons on her glasswrights' table, the tips dirtied with lead solder? How many times had she ground an edge of glass with a diamond blade, only to toss the knife aside with casual disregard for its edge? How many times had she left lampblack on the bottom of her pestle, soiling the next color that she settled down to grind?

Tools were not given an easy course in this world.

But tools could create beauty. They could create strength. They could create new entities where none had stood before. Tools changed the world, in ways that were ultimately positive and beautiful and good.

So Rani told herself as she stood on a dais at the center of a great chamber, an underground room that she had never seen before, never dreamed of before. So Rani told herself as she stood in the center of the great Meeting Hall of the Fellowship of Jair.

Dartulamino tugged at her bonds, making sure that the knots had not slipped loose as he led her from her holding cell to this chamber. The man had done his work well, though, not trusting to one of the lesser lights in the Fellowship's sky. Each knot was exquisitely tight; each cut into her flesh in such a way that even the tension of her muscles tightened her bonds.

Rani glared her anger, and the priest laughed. "Aye, Ranita Glasswright. You never knew we had this chamber. You never knew the full strength of the Fellowship you served."

"The very secrecy of this chamber shows that the Fellowship is corrupt. If you cannot trust your members with knowledge of a *room,* how can you trust them with your mission in the world?"

Dartulamino laughed, and the sound echoed off the high ceiling. As near as Rani could tell, they were deep beneath the cathedral, in a chamber that must have been hollowed out by Hal's most distant ancestors, when they first staked claim to Morenia. The room was a perfect circle. The paving stones in the floor traced out a labyrinth, a secret path that led to the dais where Rani stood with the priest. She could make out the twists of black stones on white, see the intricate mosaic that had cost untold craftsmen their vision, their lives.

For who would have permitted workers to live once they had seen the secret chamber? Who would have let the iron workers survive once they had set brackets into the walls for the score of torches on the perimeter? Who would have let the stone carvers return to their ordinary lives after they had decorated the room with the ornate grill that traced the perimeter of the circle?

The Heavenly Gates, Rani realized. The grill was supposed to represent the Heavenly Gates. As she looked around the chamber, she could see that symbols for the Thousand were woven into the stonework, standard iconography made ominous by flickering torches.

There, directly ahead of her, almost mocking with its clarity: a grozing iron. Clain, the glasswrights' god, was recognized. Rani nearly laughed aloud at the familiar sigil, even as a flash of cobalt light momentarily blinded her.

To the right of the grozing iron was a candle. Tren. Rani heard the clang of a master smith hammering out a bar of molten metal.

Beyond the candle was a carved quiver of arrows. Bon, the god of archers, made his presence known with the whinny of a stallion, heard from a distance, as if Rani stood upon a windswept moor.

Even now, she was comforted by her knowledge that she was in the hands of the Thousand Gods. As she looked at the screen, she recognized friends, companions, fellow spirits who had journeyed through all the kingdoms of the world. She remembered how she had called upon the gods when she lived in Amanthia, when she was dragooned into the Little Army. She recalled how she had felt their presence in distant Liantine, in the kingdom that held fast to the old goddess, to the Horned Hind. She thought on how the gods had become real to her in Brianta, how they had come to live within her eyes and ears, her nose and mouth, every inch of her skin.

Her struggle against the Fellowship had brought her to all those places, had led her to lands where she could learn the true source of power within the world.

For that was the lesson that she had mastered, the truth that she had learned more completely than any of her other lessons: the Thousand Gods reigned supreme. The Thousand Gods watched over the lives of men, influenced the paths that individual humans chose to tread.

The gods had not ordained those paths; they let men choose their own ways. The Thousand could be surprised by the choices that their worshipers made. Individual gods could be saddened, angered, even driven to despair, by humans' decisions not to honor them as they should be honored. Among the Thousand, some were stronger than others, some had more influence over the lives of men.

But one truth dominated among the gods. One truth controlled. Every individual god was stronger than any individual human. Every god could defeat a man or a woman. Every god could dominate a worshiper if he chose to do so.

Accepting her inferiority to the Thousand brought Rani a sense of peace. She might lose to the Fellowship now, but in the end, the gods would be supreme. In the end, the gods would control the world.

Hal tugged his arm away from Puladarati. "I can't stay here! What will my men think? What will Hamid think?"

The councilor shook his head, his long white hair flowing about him like a mane. "I don't care what they think. Your mission is to stay alive, Sire. Your goal is to survive today's battle so that you can ride back into Moren victorious."

"And what good will victory do if every man I meet thinks me afraid?"

Thinks me afraid. Safe plans all made. Ducking the raid.

Puladarati's three-fingered hand was firm on Hal's arm. "If our maneuvers are to work, you must control two separate forces. From here, you can see both the harbor and the city walls. You will guide your men in every step they take."

"I should be beside them, not hiding like the women and children!"

"Which force would you go with, Sire?" For the first time, Puladarati's voice broke. "Will you go to the harbor and watch the ships taken there, abandoning your soldiers on the field? Or will you go to the gates and ignore the brave men who walked on water for you?"

Hal shook his head. "It's not like that! I'm not forsaking any of them."

"Not if you stay here. Not if you wait for the gates to open. Not if you command the battle from this vantage point and join us in Moren when you can."

Hal's eyes filled with unwanted tears. "This is not how it was meant to be, my lord. This is not what my father would have done. This is not the manner of an honorable son of the house of Jair."

Puladarati's face softened. He swallowed hard, and then he held his hand before Hal's eyes. "Do you see this, my lord? Do you see the three fingers that remain to me? Do you know how I lost the others?"

Fingers lost. Count the cost. Lost. Cost. Lost.

The rhyme seemed too tired even to try to control his mind, and Hal merely shook his head. Puladarati lowered his voice, offering up his greatest confidence. "I lost them on campaign with your father, may all the Thousand keep him safe beyond the Heavenly Gates. We were in the Eastern March, and we became separated from the main body of our troops. Your father stayed behind, secure, while I scouted out a safe path. I found it, but not before those mongrels had launched their bloody ambush."

"You must have hated him then! You must have resented his staying safe while you came near death!"

"It was nothing like that," Puladarati said, and his voice was soft as an old nursemaid's. "He was the rightful king. He was my lord and master. I served him proudly, and the greatest day of my life was the day I led him back to safety. Back to safety, and the rest of our army, and sweet victory in the end."

Hal stared at the maimed hand, wondering at the simple devotion, the massive loss. He tried to imagine that fidelity, multiplied by the dozens of men who stood ready to fight for him, even now. Swallowing, he forced himself to meet Puladarati's expectant gaze. "Very well, then. I'll stay here and command the forces."

Puladarati smiled, the sly grin of a feral cat. "Very good, Your Majesty. May all the Thousand keep you."

Hal let the blessing hover in the air as he watched King Hamid march their soldiers toward the Moren gates.

Even as Rani felt the peace of submission to the Gods, she realized that the chamber was beginning to fill with people. Clad in black robes, swathed in dark masks, members of the Fellowship flowed into the room. First there were a dozen, then two score, then more than a hundred.

Rani looked about the room openly, no longer feigning to follow the Fellowship's absurd precepts. There was nothing to keep her from staring at their faces, nothing to keep her from trying to discern individuals beneath their dark robes.

There. That tiny form must be Glair, the Touched woman who had long led Moren's Fellowship. She walked with a characteristic limp, twisting to one side as she made her way to the dais. She stopped before Dartulamino, clearly recognizing the priest, even as he stood sheltered in his robe.

There were others that Rani knew. Somewhere in the room was Borin, the leader of the Merchants' Council, the member of her birth caste who had helped her to flee certain death when she was only a child. Borin had been friends with Mair, had extended the Fellowship's open greeting to Rani at Mair's request.

Could Mair be in this room even now? Had she followed Rani to the city, made her way inside the gates?

Rani had no doubt that Mair knew of secret passages in and around the cathedral, even as she had known the hidden corridor they had used to escape so many weeks before. Mair knew all the Touched ways to navigate Moren; she had gotten the better of nobles and soldiers, of guildsmen and merchants dozens of times over the years. It would be like her to don a black robe, to cover her face and move among her enemies, laughing, plotting, planning painful deaths.

Rani felt an itch between her shoulder blades, a nagging suspicion that a knife stood at the ready. She told herself to ignore the sensation, that she was imagining things, imagining Mair reaping the revenge that she had promised. Despite Rani's firmest instructions to herself, the feeling persisted. She closed her eyes and made herself count to ten, closing out the shimmering images of the gods at the carved screen, shutting off the whispers and the flavors and the scents that were so distracting.

When she opened her eyes, though, the sensation persisted, as if someone were holding a stinging nettle just above her flesh. She swallowed hard and let her neck turn, bracing herself for the sight of Mair's grim revenge.

Of course, the Touched woman was not there. Dartulamino was, though. He was, and in his hand, he held a whisper-sharp dagger, a blade that glinted like golden fire in the torchlight. The message was clear. The Holy Father would not hesitate to shed her blood. Not here. Not now. Not in the midst of the secret fraternity that longed for her death.

Dartulamino nodded once, and the-shape-that-was-Glair climbed onto the dais, struggling to take the single high step. She looked out over the assembly, as if she, too, were measuring who attended, as if she, too, were wondering at the members of the Fellowship that filled the chamber.

And then she pulled off her hood. Her gnarled hands managed to be smooth with the gesture, managed to remove the clinging black garment as if she were accustomed to unveiling in this company. There was a collective gasp from the crowd, and Rani felt her own muscles tighten in startled surprise.

"Enow, Fellowship. Ye've been secret fer long enow. Today i' th' day when ye may show yer faces t' all o' Moren. Today i' th' day we 'ave worked toward fer so long." Glair's voice was shaky with age, quivering between advanced years and heavy emotion. Nevertheless her words carried to the carved screen, to the very back of the crowd.

The chamber was filled with whispers of surprise, with consternation and amazement. Glair raised her voice above all of the chatter. "Aye! All o' ye! Bare yer faces! Today is th' day ye've 'eard us speak o' through all our long years t'gether. Today is th' day we are free. We come t' our power. Show yer faces 'n' claim yer prize."

The old woman lifted her mask to her teeth, settled one snaggled incisor against the cloth. The sound of ripping fabric mesmerized the room, and then dozens of fellows followed suit, sweeping off their masks, lifting away their fabric. Hoods were ripped, masks were torn, and Rani was surrounded by blinking, dazed conspirators.

Like all the others in the chamber, she found herself looking for known compatriots. She was not disappointed. Along with Dartulamino and Glair, there were other familiar faces. Yalin, the butcher she had known since childhood. Galindrino, who had served as one of her first bodyguards in the royal palace. Trilita, a master embroiderer who had represented her guild at Hal's court for as long as Rani had lived there. . . .

There were other faces, a few familiar, many absolute strangers. Each of them had one thing in common, though. Each looked to Glair and Dartulamino for guidance.

The Touched woman nodded to the Holy Father, taking a small step back while still maintaining her place of pride upon the dais. Dartulamino stepped forward, shrugging in his black Fellowship robes as if he wore the finest of holy garments.

"Greetings, Fellows," he said, and his voice carried easily throughout the chamber. "For many years, we have met in shadowed hallways. For many years, we have worn our robes and masks, we have hidden our identities from each other and from the outside world. All of that changes today. All of that ends.

"Our Fellowship now moves into a new age. It is time for us to take the power that we have earned. It is time for us to take control over the world that we have built. It is time for us to emerge from hiding and stake claim to our place in all the kingdoms of the world!"

Hal took a deep breath as he raised his spyglass. The boats on the outskirts of the harbor were at the very edge of the glass's power. Even using Davin's double lenses, Hal needed to narrow his eyes, squinting like an ancient man. The signal should be clearly visible. There were six Liantine boats, six targets for the water walkers to conquer.

Hal swore and lowered the spyglass, shaking it as if violence might better its working. He stopped only when Tovin raised a single eyebrow. "I can't see anything," he said to the player.

"They are supposed to show their colors when the sun is one hand above the horizon. We wanted to give them time, so that all the boats would be surprised together."

"I know the plan!" Hal snapped, but he immediately regretted his temper. He forced himself to say more calmly, "I know the plan, and I trust your players."

And Hal was surprised to find that he *did* trust the players. They were disciplined troops, in their own way. They had practiced using Davin's creations until any ordinary soldiers would have been bored to distraction. They had measured out the tools' limits, testing, building, creating new strengths.

Hal forced himself to say, "I understand now why Rani took up the sponsorship of your troop."

"Sire?" Tovin offered the question warily. With all the time the player had spent in Moren, Hal had never dared address him directly, had never dared to comment on the woman who bound their lives together.

"Rani. She lives for patterns." Like all the people in his camp, Hal kept the conversation in the present tense. No one admitted that Rani Trader would soon be dead, if she lived even now. No one admitted that the Fellowship would kill her, if not today, then tomorrow. If not tomorrow, then the day after that. She might already be murdered, and her body not yet found.

Hal forced himself back to the matter at hand. "You players build patterns in everything you do—acting out your pieces, performing your acrobatics. She has always been drawn to order, to logic."

Tovin seemed amused. "No one has ever called my players logical before, Sire."

Hal nodded, noting that Tovin did not precisely correct him. There were some liberties that even a player would not take with a king. "Do you miss her?" Hal asked the question before he'd thought about it, and he was surprised by the lance of pain through his own heart.

Tovin's mouth twisted into a grimace too bitter to be a smile. "I never had her, Sire." Sunlight glinted on the player's copper eyes as he visibly steeled himself to meet his liege lord's gaze. "She came to me for a while, and we both enjoyed the time we shared. But she never intended to stay with me. Her heart was never mine."

Hal forced himself to phrase an answer in the present tense. "She loves you, Tovin Player. She loves you in her way."

"She may have loved me while she was with me, but there was always another in her past."

Hal could not hear the words, could not hear the truth that he had always known, had always set aside. He swallowed hard and lifted up the spyglass again. Toying with the mechanism, he made a series of unnecessary adjustments. He blinked and told himself that the wind had brought the tears to his eyes.

When he raised the glass again, he thought he must be imagining what he saw. One, two, three, four, five, six. Six ships in the harbor. Six trails of brilliant red silk, floating on the air above each prow. "Tovin!"

The player grasped the spyglass without ceremony. "Yes!" he cried, and his joy seemed brighter than the sunlight that flooded the hillside. Scarcely taking the time to thrust the glass back into Hal's hands, he lifted up his own length of silk, tossing its wooden handle lightly in the air. He stood straight and tall as he wove the players' pattern.

Once, twice, three times, he repeated his acknowledgment to the waiting ships, waiting for confirmation that they had understood him. Then he focused on the small army of men on the plain below. That signal was simpler, a defiant pattern of looping silk, a challenge to head for the city gates with all possible speed.

Hal did not need the glass to see the army respond. Three players in their midst spun a rapid silken reply, and then the army moved out from its sheltering bushes.

Hal glanced back to the harbor. The conquered Liantine ships were already taking wind in their sails, already moving to Moren's docks. The players had control of the vessels, control of the great crossbows that were anchored to the Liantine decks.

Hal muttered a prayer to the Thousand, asking that Morenian lives might be spared. He had never wanted to see the damage that naval crossbows could inflict.

He had never wanted to see his own gates attacked, either. He had never wanted to watch fiery bolts launched at his walls, targeting soldiers who wore the holy green of Briantan priests.

And yet once Hal began watching, he could not take his eyes from the plain before him. He could not look away as Davin's engines wheeled across the plain, spinning their wooden arms and gathering speed. He could not drag his attention from Hamid, far below, from the Sarmonians who moved in ordered phalanxes across the open space. He could not speak to Tovin as the Briantans harnessed Davin's defensive engines and miniature trebuchets began to rain death upon the advancing army.

Rani felt the excitement building in all the people around her. She tried to remember how she would have felt one year before, five years before, eight years before, when she first became a member of the Fellowship. She tried to remember a time when she would have greeted Dartulamino's announcement with pride, with excitement, with joy. She tried to remember what it had felt like to believe in the power of the Fellowship, in the organization's goals, in its intentions.

It was impossible. Not now. Not when she could see the trail of the Fellowship's victims, the men and women and children—Laranifarso, her heart cried—children, who had died to further the cabal. It might have started with noble goals. It might have begun with great intentions. But like a magnificent melon on a heavy summer vine, it had grown too large, become too heavy, rotted beneath its own weight.

Rani was shaken from her thoughts by Dartulamino's rough grasp on her arm. "Fellows!" the priest declaimed, and his voice was as strong as any that he had used in the cathedral above this massive chamber. "Fellows, for decades we have awaited the Royal Pilgrim. We have awaited the one who will bring us into harmony with our brethren, into balance with the other cells of the Fellowship that await us near and far."

An expectant hush fell over the crowd. Rani saw many hands make holy signs, gesturing across black-clad chests. More than one pair of eyes blinked closed in fervent prayer, and many lips moved in quick whispered petitions.

Just to confirm her own senses, Rani brushed her thoughts across the nearest of the gods. Clain. Tren. Bon. None of them reacted with anything more than calm expectation and their familiar signatures. Apparently, the Thousand did not eagerly wait for the coming of the Royal Pilgrim.

Dartulamino continued. "The Royal Pilgrim could be many things. He could be a warrior, destined to bind together the countries of the world through battle after battle. He could be a prince, heir to one throne, husband to another, father to several more. He could be a priest, a visionary, a guiding light who shows the ways of the Thousand Gods to all the nations of the world."

The assembled fellows were growing more excited. Rani heard whispers of speculation. Pockets formed around some of the members, particularly religious priests, Rani supposed, or soldiers who were known to fight with a mean sword.

Dartulamino drew out the pause, growing the excitement with the expertise of a master. At last, he raised a single hand, commanding an almost immediate silence. "I come to tell you that the Royal Pilgrim is none of those. The Royal Pilgrim stands before you. This woman, this prisoner, *she* is the Royal Pilgrim that we have awaited. She is the one who will unite us. She is the one who will bring the Fellowship to its one true end."

The explosion of disbelief echoed off the chamber's ceiling. Rani's voice was added to the chaos; she could not hold back her own amazed, "What?" Automatically, she reached toward the Thousand, opened her senses for the gods to whisper truth, but she was greeted with nothing more than the familiar presences she had come to know so intimately. There was nothing special, nothing different, nothing that marked her as the one the Fellowship had awaited.

Dartulamino raised his voice, straining to be heard. "I tell you, this one is the Royal Pilgrim. Rani Trader, Ranita Glasswright, she has gone by many names. She is the Royal Pilgrim, and another of our brotherhood will explain to you how she will bring us glory."

The Holy Father raised a hand, as if he were calling down a lightning strike. The motion transfixed the throng; the entire Fellowship fell silent. Then, as if by some hidden magic, a path opened in the crowd.

One figure limped forward. One figure, clad all in somber black. One figure, with a withered arm, a wasted leg. One figure, who dared to walk toward Rani, who dared to climb the steps of the dais, who dared to stand before the Fellowship.

"Crestman," Rani said, and she knew that she should not be surprised. Other members of the Fellowship took up the soldier's name, whispering it, spreading it to the farthest ranks so that all knew who stood before them.

He did not bother to answer her greeting, not with words. Instead, he limped one step closer. He reached out with his good hand, and he gathered up the rope that bound her arms to her side. He moved so quickly that her eyes could scarcely follow, but she could feel his action.

She could feel the rope loop around her throat. She could feel the hemp saw across her windpipe. She could feel the sharp tug that forced her to her knees, the vicious yank that turned her neck at a painful angle. Her breath rasped, and she started to choke, but he only tightened his noose, tugging on the rope with a viciousness that confirmed that she was doomed.

The Fellowship exclaimed as one, and every person in the room stepped closer to the dais.

"Hold!" Crestman exclaimed. "Stand still, and I'll explain."

Rani could scarcely hear his words, could barely make order out of the syllables. He was going to strangle her. Here. Now. In front of all these witnesses. In front of all the Thousand. Crestman was going to murder her, and no one would raise a hand to stop him. Not until it was too late. Not until she had drawn her last, rasping breath. Not until she had collapsed beneath the curtain of red haze.

Crestman tugged again at the rope, and his voice grew stronger, as if tormenting her gave him a power he had thought lost forever. "It is said that the Royal Pilgrim will bring all the kingdoms of the world together. As you know, many of those lands are already joined. Brianta and Liantine are met in Moren herself, holding the harbor, holding the gates. Morenia holds my own homeland, Amanthia, and now it has built ties with Sarmonia. The world is reduced to two vast forces. Two vast forces that soon will be one."

Rani heard what Crestman was saying, knew that he was speaking words he believed to be true. She tried to think what he would say next, tried to see the pattern in his speech. Patterns. That was what she had mastered as a child. That was what had brought her power as a merchant, as a trader.

Mind your caste. That was the lesson that she had learned so long ago. She had been wrong to think that she could leave it behind forever. She had mastered the text, after all. It had once brought her safety and security, growth and power.

Think as a trader. Think in patterns.

She could see nothing but boiling red clouds as Crestman tightened his noose again. She forced herself to listen, forced herself to hear the soldier say, "This woman kneeling before you holds the key. She holds power over the king of Morenia, a dark power, an unholy bond. She has manipulated Halaravilli ben-Jair since the first day that she met him, shaping his reign, changing the way that he has administered his beloved kingdom.

"Rani Trader kneels before you as a merchant. Ranita Glasswright kneels before you as a guildswoman. By neither of those titles should she control the king, and yet she does."

Rani wanted to respond. She wanted to tell the Fellowship that Crestman was a jealous man. She wanted to explain that he had lost in love, and he had carried his bitterness into other battles. She wanted to say. . . The crimson clouds hovered closer, and she heard her breath rattle in her throat.

"Halaravilli ben-Jair has permitted himself to be poisoned by this one, to depend on her, to rely on her beyond all logic. There is a reason that kings are counseled to mind their castes. There is a reason that kings are told to marry queens, that royalty is meant to be with royalty."

Could they not hear him? Even past her own choking gasps, even past her pounding heart, she could hear the rage in Crestman's voice. She could hear the loss, the frustration, the jagged edge of sorrow that cut through every one of his words.

The Fellowship, though, was bewitched. They had longed for the Royal Pilgrim for so long, yearned for the one who would bring them ultimate power, ultimate prestige. They would do anything to gain the prize that they had trained for, waited for, hoped for all these endless years.

Crestman tugged on her rope, angling the noose toward the floor. Rani's hands splayed in front of her; her palms lay flat against the dais. Her belly heaved as she struggled to draw breath, and one small corner of her mind wondered how Crestman could continue to have so much power in his broken body. How strong he might have been! How great he might have proven, if he had not been eaten away by the worm of jealousy, jealousy and octolaris poison.

"And so, Fellows, it is time for us to embrace the truth. It is time for us to acknowledge that Halaravilli ben-Jair is too weak to hold his crown, too weak to do the business of a king.

"When Brianta and Liantine attacked fair Moren, what did Halaravilli do? He fled! We tested him; we tested his dedication to his men and to his kingdom. We tested his ability to maneuver from our one last challenge, from our last true measurement of his skill as king. And what did Halaravilli do? He decamped to Sarmonia and hid with his lords in a forest. He did not try to free his city. He did not try to save his people."

That is not fair, Rani wanted to cry. *Hal was regrouping. He was building his strength. He was mustering his forces so that he could free his kingdom.*

She gathered her own strength, desperate to fight to her feet, but Crestman must have sensed her intention. He twisted the rope one more time, sawing the hemp into her flesh. He forced her head to the dais, forced her cheek to the rough stone. He planted his foot on her neck, using his leather sole to grind the rope further in.

"He did not try to save his people," Crestman repeated. "Only one thing remains, one last show to prove how weak a king Halaravilli ben-Jair truly is.

"For all these years, he has hidden behind this one. He has relied on Rani Trader, on Ranita Glasswright. He has ignored his caste, betrayed his caste. He has taken the advice of a merchant, a guildswoman. And now, today, he will feel the full weight of that folly. He will recognize that he was wrong to abandon the requirements of the crown. He was wrong to abdicate responsibility."

Rani's ears were ringing. The crimson behind her eyes had darkened like drying blood, had faded to black. Her tongue was swollen in her mouth; she could barely sneak half a breath past the rope.

And yet she could still hear Crestman. She could still make out his bitter, angry words. She could still feel the hopelessness of her sorrow, the depth of her despair as the man who had once loved her said, "Halaravilli ben-Jair will collapse without this prop. He will fall over like an infant child when he is left on his own. Morenia and Amanthia and Sarmonia will all tumble, willingly, desperately, utterly, utterly completely into the arms of the joined forces of Brianta and Liantine. All the kingdoms will be united. All will be ripe for one strong leader, for one guiding force. All will be ready for the Fellowship to take charge, to take control, to lead for all the future. The Royal Pilgrim will have done her deed."

And then Rani knew the full pattern. She could see the final pieces snapping into place. She could see the direction all of them had flowed; she could read the scrolls that they had written together, through Morenia and Amanthia, in Liantine and Brianta, in the forests of Sarmonia. If she could have found the breath, she would have laughed at the simplicity of it, at the perfect, crystal balance.

Crestman completed his explanation for the Fellowship, laying out the end to any who had not yet understood. "Halaravilli ben-Jair is nothing without Rani Trader. Kill her and he will fall. Present her body to him, and he will collapse with no more struggle than a burned-out log falling to ash upon a fire. And so, in the name of our Fellowship, I will act!"

Rani heard the whisper of metal on metal, of a sword sliding from its sheath. "By Jair, I will kill Rani Trader!" Crestman lifted his foot from her neck; she felt the momentary easing of pressure against her windpipe. "By Jair, I will slay the Royal Pilgrim, and we will gain the world!" She heard the sword whip through the air as Crestman raised his blade for the final stroke.

* * *

Hal's army was being slaughtered.

Hal had watched all six ships gain the harbor, but the victory meant nothing. After all, the Liantines outnumbered their player-captors by scores; there was no way to force all the invading sailors to take up arms on behalf of the Morenian and Sarmonian liberators. Indeed, all that the players had accomplished was removing the threat of bombardment from the water. The naval crossbows were disarmed, but nothing more had been done—nothing more *could* be done—to secure success.

Looking back toward the city gates, Hal could not lower the spyglass, could not keep from watching the slaughter on the plain before Moren's gates. He had long known that Davin was a genius, but he had never hoped to see all of the old man's weapons at their work.

Yes, the moving engines from Sarmonia did their job. They spat fire where they had once flung fine ribbons. They drenched the city gates with a jelly that burst into flame upon contact.

But that was not enough. Davin had staked out defenses around Moren for years; he had fortified the city with all his wily genius.

Hal watched in horror as pits opened up beneath the feet of the advancing soldiers, traps that were sprung through narrow, strategic mines beneath Moren's own walls. Nearly a score of his men succumbed, even though they had been warned of the danger, even though they had been told of the spikes that awaited the unwary.

A dozen more fell to a deadly rain of fire, defensive engines that relied on massive bellows to splatter jellied burning oil. Flights of arrows rained down from the towers, the work of common archers, as deadly as Davin's machines.

Go, Mareka crooned. *Ride to your men. Fire or pit. Arrow or sword. Go. Find your peace. Come to me. Come beyond the Heavenly Gates.*

Hal tried to push away the ghost, to set aside the temptation.

We're waiting for you. Marekanoran and Halarameko and Marekivilli and I. All of us await you, my lord, even the lost children that we did not name. The Gates are open. The Thousand await to escort you home. Come to us, my lord. Come join your family,

Another spray of arrows took out a company of soldiers. The Sarmonians and the Morenians were reduced to clusters, mere stragglers stranded on the plain. Hamid himself hoisted his banner; his squire must have succumbed to the last assault.

Hal should have joined them. He should have led them into battle. He should have stood beside his men instead of taking shelter on a hilltop, hiding like the women and children.

The trebuchets were launched again, spraying fire upon the plain. Grass had kindled now, and smoke rose black into the late-morning sky.

It's not too late, my lord. Come to us. Ride to the Heavenly Gates.

Hal ignored Tovin's startled cry as he grasped the length of blood-red silk and hurtled down the hill, running, running, running with all his strength toward the last of his loyal Morenians.

As Crestman's sword rose, Rani realized that she must create her own escape, she must craft her own way out of the Fellowship's snare. She must move beyond the dais, beyond the labyrinth in the floor. She must move beyond the carved screen that set this room off from all the rest of Moren.

The screen.

Rani opened her eyes and focused on the closest weapon at hand, the quiver of arrows that belonged to the god of archers. "Bon!" she cried, and the single syllable was raspy against the rope that still bound her throat.

She was answered immediately. The whinny of a stallion sounded loud in her ears, and she remembered the first time that she had ridden fine horseflesh, the first time that Hal had taken her to the royal stables.

Mind your caste.

Rani had learned the power of nobility, the strength of princes and priests throughout Morenia, throughout all known lands. Ranikaleka, her brother had called her long ago, before he set her on the desperate journey of her life. She had lived as a guest of the royal family, as a noblewoman in her own right, learning to hunt hawks and rule kingdoms.

Hawks. Yot, the god of stones, spoke with the voice of a hawk.

Rani had only to think Yot's name, and the power of stone rose within her. Her cheek was still pressed to the floor; her new strength thrummed through her flesh, reverberated across the labyrinth.

The Fellowship felt it, too. They stumbled at the tremor, and some fell to their knees.

The labyrinth. It had been built by stonemasons, by guildsmen who had mastered their art as Rani had mastered her own.

Mind your caste. Ranita Glasswright she had been. She reached out for Clain, for his familiar cobalt glow. The light was blinding in the chamber; it extinguished all the torches, and the Fellowship cried out in one terrified voice.

Crestman bellowed for order, as if he were commanding a platoon of soldiers.

Mind your caste. She had been Ranimara, a soldier in the King's Men, even before she had marched with the Little Army. "Cot!" she called, summoning the god of soldiers, and the room was immediately filled with the stench of carrion, with endless, hopeless, rotting death.

Mind your caste. There were patterns here, patterns that she saw, patterns that she made. She was Rani Trader, first and foremost, a merchant who understood the value of trade. She knew the power of a bargain.

"I'm yours!" she cried to all the Thousand at once. This was the first time that she had proclaimed her faith, the first time that she had publicly, verbally, completely given herself over to the Thousand. She felt the strength grow inside her as she confirmed what she had discovered in her heart when she lay trussed in Kella's cottage. "If you would have me, I am yours!"

She thought that she had tasted the gods before. She thought that she had heard them and smelled them. She thought that she had felt them with every inch of her flesh, that she had seen every vision they could give her.

But she had never imagined the force of all the Thousand at once. She had never imagined the power that would rise up in her, around her.

Her body was fire. Her body was light.

The rope that had strangled her was burned away, disappeared into the shadows. She was untethered; she was free. She was beyond the former boundaries of her senses; she knew the presence of the Thousand with her entire body, her entire mind, her entire soul. She was freed from the constraints of sounds and flavors, sights and scents, sensations that had limited her in the past.

Without opening her eyes, she *knew* the room around her. She *knew* the members of the Fellowship, struck unconscious by the tremendous energy that radiated from the stone wall, that arced to the human body that had been Rani and roiled out above her.

She became the cathedral sanctuary above her, became the trembling walls, the glass that shuddered in its armatures, and the lead panes that buckled beneath the pressure.

She was the Pilgrims' Bell, set tolling by the shaking earth, clamoring as if all the wolves in all the world were coursing down the hills toward Moren.

She was the seawater that saturated the air above the harbor, shimmering into rainbows as it crashed against the piers, against the ships that held the warrish Liantines, that held their player-captors.

She became the fire that scorched the autumn-dry grass outside the city walls, the heat that rose in waves as Davin's defensive engines worked according to their maker's plan.

She became all the gods, all the Thousand. She marched with them out of the Fellowship's chamber. She shattered the cathedral glass, sent fragments of cobalt and ruby and emerald and lead raining down upon the cold stone floor. She swept through Moren's streets, gathering up green-clad priests who had masqueraded as soldiers, fanatics who had tainted a faith that was good and pure.

She boiled onto the plain in front of Moren, inspiring good men to take up their arms. As she passed, injured soldiers recovered from their wounds, and men who had wavered stood fast. The part of her that she had known as Tarn gathered up those who were already lost, collected the dead in a brilliant green-black cloak.

Hal was running across the plain, streaming a crimson banner behind him, stumbling like a madman. She heard the chitter of the little voices in his mind, a scattering like a dead woman's whisper, and then she felt her god-self banish the sounds forever. Hal stood straighter after she had passed, shaking his head as if his ears rang, as if silence were a separate, holy sound. He raised his silk again and continued toward the city gates, but now he walked with a measured tread, like the king he was, returning to his people.

And then the gods were gone. They swirled about the city in one final flurry, a maelstrom of sights and sounds, of scents and flavors and sensations. Rani became herself again, became a human woman, trembling and gasping from the separation.

She heard the massive chimes that indicated the Heavenly Gates were open, and she saw the souls of all the dead soldiers ascend at once. The Gates clanged shut, and Rani was left, blind and deaf and dumb, shivering and alone in the center of the Fellowship's secret chamber.

But she wasn't alone.

She heard someone else breathing close beside her, and she forced her eyes to open. Crestman had clambered to his feet. He supported himself on the tip of his sword as if he were the oldest man in all the world.

"What are you?" he gasped.

"I am Rani Trader," she said.

"What did you do?" There was no fear in his voice, no terror, as she had thought there might be. Instead, there was anger—bitter, acrid anger.

"I do not know." That was the truth. "Berylina first

brought the gods to me. I became them. All of them." Glancing about the room, Rani could see that the Fellowship was stirring. People were struggling to their knees, gasping for breath, retching.

"I hate you," Crestman said, the words as simple as a child's. Rani had never heard such truth.

"I'm sorry."

"You lied to me. You lied in Amanthia, when you said that you would stand with me against Sin Hazar." He seemed unaware of anyone else in the room, unaware that people were standing, whispering, staring at Rani in awe.

"I did stand with you. But I could not stay there. My life called me elsewhere."

"You left me in Liantine."

"I would have come back for you. You did not trust me enough."

"I loved you."

"I know." She met his eyes then, seeing the hopeless sorrow and loss and rage. "I know," she said again, and tears pricked at her helplessness, her inability to be what he had needed.

"Die, ye bairn-killin' bastard!" Rani was startled by the cry. She knew that she should move, knew that she should reach out for Crestman and pull him toward her, snatch him safe from harm. She could not make herself move fast enough, though, could not find the energy to act.

She recognized the blade, even as it whistled through the air. She knew the eight prongs that fastened the pommel to the shaft. She saw the weapon that had been stolen from Crestman himself, stolen from his hiding place in Sarmonia. She knew the knife that she had last seen in a sunny forest glade, pressed against soft flesh, spinning out a thread of blood. She knew the dagger had belonged to Mair, had measured out the depths of the Touched woman's guilt and pain and sorrow.

Rani heard the weapon sink into Crestman's chest, heard his splutter of surprise and then his sharp gasp as the point breached his heart. Even as Crestman collapsed upon the dais, Mair straddled his body, driving the knife farther into the dead meat that had been a living, breathing man only moments before. "Tha' was fer ye, Lar. Tha' was fer ye, me puir dead boy."

Mair crooned the words over and over, her face whey pale against a Fellowship robe. Rani stepped up to her side, kneeling to gather her friend against her chest. They huddled together on the dais, rocking as if they were children, as if they had all their lives ahead of them and nothing more to fear than a bogeyman in the night.

"I 'ad t' do it, Rai. By th' rules o' th' street, I 'ad t' do it."

"I know, Mair. I know." Rani looked at Crestman's withered, broken body, and a whisper at the back of her mind mourned the boy she had met in Amanthia, the boy who had given her her first kiss, beside a leaping bonfire. "You had to do it. We all did. We all did what we needed to do."

15

Rani shrugged a blanket closer about her shoulders, scarcely aware of the late-autumn breeze that broke around Tovin and gusted toward her. A some months ago, stranded in Kella's cottage, she might have reached for Purn, asked the god of dance to spread his heat across her flesh. She stood without the gods now, though, stood without their constant infringements on her eyes and ears, her tongue and nose, her flesh.

The Thousand had retreated. She knew that they were still nearby. She could sense them hovering in the shadows, soaring in the daylight. She knew that if she needed them, if lives hung in the balance, she could reach out for any, for all.

But she also knew that she was an ordinary woman. She was a simple Morenian, trying to make her way in the world. The gods had stepped back, had let her return to the life she had known and loved before the final battle, before Berylina passed on her holy power, before the Fellowship.

Even now, there were some who were forgetting how the Thousand had flowed across the battlefield at Moren's gates. Many said that the earth had moved, that a temblor had occurred, but nothing more. Some said that Briantan fanatics had fashioned stories about the gods, that the invading soldiers had invented the presence of the Thousand to explain their sudden loss to a force a fraction of their size.

Rani let the stories grow around her. She let the rumors fade. She had other missions to accomplish, other goals to achieve. Now, with Tovin watching, she reached for her closest diamond blade. "I know that I'll need a fresh one to cut the smallest pieces."

"Of course you know it." His voice was even, as steady as it had been since he first joined her in her tower chamber. "You know precisely what you're doing. You don't need me here."

"I do." She brushed a wayward strand of hair from her face with the back of her hand. "I must have a master approve my design, and you're the closest thing this land can offer."

Tovin answered her more gently than her dismissive words had warranted. "That will not satisfy the guild, you know. That will never meet your Master Parion's requirements."

Rani set the diamond blade on the table. She had avoided this conversation for days, for weeks, for the two long months since Moren had been regained. It was time, though. If she were going to reestablish her guild in Morenia, she must confront her ancient fears.

She tested her words inside her head before she spoke them aloud. "I no longer measure myself by Master Parion's rule."

Tovin nodded, as if he had expected her to say as much. "You might not. But there are others who will. There are others who will always say that you are outside the guild, that you do not deserve the commissions that you gain."

"Some of those others tried to kill me, Tovin." Her voice

was level. She had confronted her fears. "Some of those others tried to poison me in Brianta, to destroy me before I had a chance to complete my masterpiece."

He merely nodded. They had never spoken openly of Rani's cruel treatment at the hands of her guild, of how Parion had wrought his personal revenge. Rani sighed, and she tried to order the thoughts that swirled in her mind, to explain her compulsion to rebuild her guild.

"This is the end of the circle, Tovin. This is the final arc. I ruined the Glasswrights' Guild when I was a child, when I scarcely knew what I was doing. I thought that I could right that wrong when Hal agreed to grant me land and stone to build another hall. I thought that I was ready to rebuild when I learned my craft in Brianta. I thought that I could erase all that I had done by mastering skills.

"All of those actions, though, were designed to make *me* accept what had happened. All of those actions were supposed to ease *my* mind. Even my masterpiece in Brianta, my panel of the silk god, was about me, about my life, about what I had accomplished by bringing the spiders from Liantine.

"Now, though, I act for others. Now I act to restore the guild to its former power, to its position of glory and prestige among all the other Morenian guilds. With the masterpiece I plan now, I can give back what I once took."

Tovin shook his head, a small smile curling his lips. She was surprised by the expression—it seemed the look of an older man, a father or a grandfather. The player gestured toward her worktable. "I understand your thoughts, Ranita," he said gently. "I cannot say that I agree with them. I cannot say that you will be a better glasswright for finishing this project. I cannot say that guildsmen from all the five kingdoms will hear of your feat and flock to join you. But I understand that you do this thing to right past wrongs, that you act now to erase the final vestige of what was done in your youth."

He shrugged, and she was relieved to see a flash of his familiar impatience return, drowning his flowery words. Once that had been the energy that drew her to his side, that lured her to his bed. Now she remembered his restlessness fondly. She wondered if this was how a mother felt, watching her son twitch through his responsibilities.

"Go ahead, then," he said. "You've delayed enough. Is there anything left that you need from me?" Tovin's voice was gruff, and she wondered how much of her emotion he had just read in her eyes.

She shook her head automatically, hesitant to ask the question that she had toyed with all these weeks, all the months since she had returned from Sarmonia. It didn't matter, she tried to remind herself. It really didn't matter. Tovin's eyes glinted as he took one step closer. "What?" he said.

"I shouldn't ask."

"You've grown shy? Now?"

She curled a lip at his sarcasm. Very well. "Why, Tovin? Why Kella? What brought you to her . . . cottage?" To her bed, she did not say.

Impossibly, she had surprised him. Unease flickered behind his eyes, and he started to step away from her worktable. He did her the honor of meeting her gaze, though, and when he spoke, he chose his words carefully. "She had knowledge, Ranita. She had power. I wanted to learn all she knew. I wanted to collect her wisdom through Speaking."

"She was ancient!"

He shook his head and raised his chin. She braced herself for words she would rather not hear. "Not in ways that mattered, Rani. She had lessons to teach. Lessons of herbs, and other things."

Other things. Rani's mind flashed to the lavender pallet, to the bed the couple had shared. Rani had been bound on that pallet; she had waited for the Fellowship there, waited for her death.

That was past, though. That was ended. Kella had been executed in Hal's courtyard, her neck severed with one blow of the headman's axe. Kella was gone, and there was nothing to be gained by questioning Tovin, nothing to be learned by pushing for more information. The answers hardly mattered. Rani had no cause to ask. She sighed. "We're wasting time here."

He gave her a moment to change her mind, to press him for further details. When she remained silent, he said, "Very well. Let us move into the play; the first step's roughest, every day."

She smiled at the players' doggerel. She would miss the troop when she was finished here, miss their hard-driving playfulness. Later, she chided herself. There would be plenty of time for fond memories later.

Tovin lifted a piece of clear glass from the table, a curve that barely filled his palm. She remembered the first time that he had led her in Speaking. He had used clear glass then to focus her, glass that she had cut with a diamond blade.

She took a deep breath and stared at the pane, exhaling as deeply as she could manage. Another breath. Another. She envisioned a stream running beside her, swift, glittering in brilliant sunlight.

She Spoke about the instructors who had first greeted her

when she arrived at the guildhall. She recounted her introductory lessons, how the instructors had been patient at first, then increasingly sharp as Rani fumbled with easy tasks. She remembered how to whitewash tables, how to sketch out designs with fresh-made charcoal. She recalled how to scrub out those lines, rework them, simplify them, strengthen them.

She followed the Speaking stream, moving deeper into her thoughts, into her recollections. Other instructors had taught Rani how to blend sand and heat it, how to fix the perfect balance for her glass. She had measured out the ingredients, as cautious as any baker, and she had held her crucible with iron tongs. She had stirred the molten mixture, taking care to turn her face away, to breathe as deeply as she could from the colder air over her shoulder.

The Speaking stream moved farther, picking up speed as it tumbled over rocks in its bed. Rani navigated around the final craft that she had learned in the guildhall, tumbled over the Speaking rapids to truths that she had mastered at Tovin's side. She spoke of the techniques that she had mastered in exile, pouring glass across smooth stones, leveling it with iron blades.

As if she were manipulating the oars of a boat, her fingers clenched on the tools of her trade. She cradled a traditional grozing iron, curved her fingers around one of Tovin's diamond blades. She nestled tongs in her palms, closed the metal jaws around a point of lead stripping and pulled the heavy metal through a vise, stretching it, shaping it, guiding it into a supporting edge for glass. All the while, she explained what she was doing, what she had learned, how it had shaped her life.

The stream rushed forward, carrying Rani breathlessly

past all the tricks that she had mastered. She crimped lead foil around the edges of the tiniest pieces of glass, folding the covering carefully, perfectly. She soldered one piece to another, finding the tiny imperfections, setting them against each other, pressing, smoothing, easing each glass piece into place.

The water flowed faster now, and Rani could scarcely catch her breath against its riotous tumble. She told how she had learned to fashion iron armatures, great metal frames to hold the heaviest of glass pieces. She described how to anchor her designs in the iron, how to integrate the support so that it was part of the craft, part of the beauty.

The stream tumbled forward, and Rani caught glimpses of the color grinding that she had mastered, the smooth pestle in her hand, the constant, endless grinding of pigment against smooth glass surface. She folded in the image that she had learned in Kella's cottage, the carved lip of a mortar, with its symbols of Mart and Mip, Gir, and Ralt, the gods of earth, water, fire, and air watching over the process. She saw the brilliant colors that she had worked, the perfect piles of lapis and cinnabar, of lampblack and lead. She felt the muscles in her arm clench and unclench, moving in perfect, spiraling circles.

The stream became a riot, and Rani Spoke of mixing water with the pigment, adding gum arabic to some, grinding, smoothing, blending. She dipped her finest brush into the color, squeezed out excess pigment with fingers that were stained and confident. She painted the first of her designs onto glass panes, delicate tracery on some, dramatic design on others. She crafted the expressions of people, the suggestion of dramatic scenes stretching into the background. Her fingers flew across the glass like a weaver's at a loom, and designs spun out beneath her hands as if she were crafting them all in a single sweeping motion.

And then Rani could hear the thundering waterfall, see the spray as the Speaking stream reached the boulders that guarded its final precipice. She gathered together the final energy, collected up the panes that she had designed. She consigned them to the furnace, to the great brick kilns that she had first tended in her childhood. She stoked the fire and let the paint meld with the glass, let the design become one with the sand and the lead and her thoughts. She tended the kilns for hours, for days, feeding each a specific amount of hard, dried wood.

And then she caught herself against the rope that Tovin had strung across the Speaking river. She clung to the lifeline, becoming aware of the hemp beneath her fingers, soggy but firm. She gathered her feet beneath her, planted them on the rushing riverbed. She took one step toward shore, then another and another. She felt small stones beneath her feet, and she tensed her calves, flexed her knees, forced herself forward one more step. One more heave on the rope, one more surge of energy and she was safe on the shore, looking back at the tumbling riot of thought and learning and memory.

Sighing, she sat back on her stool. Her palms were spread flat on the table before her, pressing against the wood as if she were rooted to its surface. Her throat was dry with all that she had said, with all the lessons that she had relayed of her craft. She filled her lungs with another deep breath and exhaled slowly. Again. Again.

And she forced her eyes to open. She forced herself to focus on the player sitting across from her.

He studied her silently for a long moment, and then he

raised a hand to brush back the lock of hair that had fallen from behind her ear. "Thank you for the Speaking," he said. "You enrich your players beyond measure." She was not certain if he teased her, until he kept his voice somber and said, "You are ready. I will leave you."

"Tovin, don't!" She was surprised at the desperation in her voice.

"I'll be back, Ranita. When you least expect me, I'll come riding into Moren. My players and I will have new tales to tell, new plays to play. We'll entertain you and your husband and your children for days and weeks and months and years."

She caught the hand that hovered by her cheek, hovered despite the lightness in his tone. Husband. Who was she to marry? Tovin was the only man who would have had her, and he was leaving. Tovin or Crestman. She shuddered as she thought of the soldier, shuddered without thinking. Quickly, she said, "I'm sorry, Tovin."

"I'm not." He smiled, and she thought his gentle mirth might be real, might be his, might not be the product of his training for the stage. "You were good for me and I for you, but we've grown now. You have a life here in the city, and I've one on the road."

She knew that they had left each other before, that her heart had broken at his previous farewells. This time, though, his words seemed right. They seemed true. She matched the curve of his lips then, brushed his mouth with her own. "Thank you, Tovin Player. Thank you for all that you have taught me."

His embrace was quick, and then he glided toward the door of the tower room. "Use it well, Ranita Glasswright. Complete your work here, and make this player proud."

Rani turned back to the table before her, pausing for only a moment before she lifted the bucket of whitewash and began to cover the empty, eager surface.

Rani took a deep breath before she began to walk down the aisle of the mighty cathedral. In the months since the Fellowship's fall, debris had been cleared away—shattered glass, twisted lead, crumbled stone braces. The massive hall had been cleaned, but it had not yet been rebuilt. That labor was still to come. That labor might take a lifetime.

With every step, she remembered other times that she had been in the building: in her childhood, when she stood beside her mother and her father, surrounded by siblings on the feast day of Hern, the god of merchants.

She paused, waiting for Hern's salty flavor to spread across her tongue. She could remember the taste of him, remember it as clearly as the first childhood rhyme she had ever mastered. Now, though, the god of merchants kept his distance, sparing her his flavor, letting her concentrate on her current mission.

She continued to walk past the cathedral's side chapels, ignoring the throngs that filled the spacious nave. She knew that the day had been declared a feast day for all castes, not just for the guildsmen whom she represented. Hal had ordered almond cakes distributed among the Touched and wine among the soldiers. Merchants were relieved of taxes for all sales made that day, and noblemen had been summoned to a feast at the palace that very night.

A breeze picked up, and Rani was grateful for the ermine robe that covered her shoulders. It had been a gift from the Furriers' Guild, a fine symbol that she was about to be brought back into her chosen caste. She had donned the garment with gratitude, both for its warmth and for its emblematic approval.

As she walked, Rani heard the whispers of speculation growing in the crowd. Four boys carried her masterpiece on a litter behind her. The actual glasswork was hidden inside a leather-covered box, nestled in protective folds of velvet. Rani had settled it there herself, muttering a quick prayer to Clain, waiting for the memory of cobalt light to flash behind her closed eyes.

Hal waited for her on the dais, and Rani glanced at his face with a feeling akin to sadness. She remembered when he had been a slight youth, when he had stood beside his father as the King's Inquisitor. He had questioned her then, made her tell a truth that burned inside her heart, within her hand.

All unknowing, he had set them upon the road of the past eight years, for he had granted power to the Fellowship, to the Watchers as Rani had known them then. Hal had welcomed the black-robed fellows, grateful for their alliance against a nest of assassins. How different would things have gone if Morenia had not relied upon the Fellowship? Might Hal's face be free of all his lines of care?

Rani forced away the questions. She had trusted the Fellowship. They had seemed to bring peace and stability in a troubled time. Even now, the surviving members spoke fine words from their prison cells. Dartulamino had been forbidden any visitors, so smooth were his lies and so shrewd his arguments. Glair had been placed in a solitary cell, that she might not gather new allies, might not build new weapons against her king and kingdom. There would be trials for all of them, for Dartulamino and Glair and all the fellows who had gathered in the round room beneath the cathedral.

The prison cells were overflowing, between members of the Fellowship, Briantan priests who had been captured in the streets, and Liantines who had roamed the docks in the harbor. Hal had already engaged in lengthy negotiations with the weakened king of Brianta; he had sent scalding demands to Teheboth Thunderspear, with whom he'd once held peace.

Ambassadors had traveled the high roads, bearing gifts to Morenia and promises of future prosperity. Teheboth, never afraid of spilling blood to further his own ends, had sent Hal a grisly gift of half a dozen heads, leaders of the Liantine Fellowship, all.

Rani had looked upon the blackened, stinking things, and her heart had twisted in her chest. Crestman had known these people. He had brought them into the Fellowship's tent. He had lured them from a life of hopeless slavery into the engines of war.

Crestman. Even now, he was rotting in the earth. Hal had refused him a pyre, refused to recognize that the man had once been a valued captain in the Morenian army. At first, Rani had thought to argue, but her heart was hardened when she thought of little Laranifarso, of Marekanoran whom she had never met, even of Mareka. No, Crestman would rot, as if that indignity might right the wrongs of a life poorly lived.

There *had* been other pyres though, for all the men who had died upon the plain, for all of the loyal Morenians and Sarmonians who had given their lives to liberate Moren. Hal had witnessed every one, joined by King Hamid who had stood straight as an arrow in his well-tailored robes.

When the last ashes had cooled, though, Hamid had returned to his homeland. He had not dared to tarry longer in the north. As expected, his electors had called for a new king. Even now, Sarmonia's landed men were debating potential monarchs, arguing about the merits and detractions of various men. Hamid was said to ride throughout his land, bolstering his proponents.

He might regain his crown. He might be voted back to his throne. And even if he were not, his travels enabled him to root out the Fellowship, to unveil the traitor electors who had first turned against him, when he was still a legitimate king.

Rani was surprised to find herself at the base of the cathedral's dais; she could not remember the final steps that had brought her there. A strong breeze whistled down the aisle, and she shrugged deeper into her ermine robes. Here, at the front of the great religious hall, the winds blew stronger, gathering strength from every empty window that gaped above the nave. At least the doors had been repaired; the carved portals that Dartulamino had splintered had been replaced by simple oak panels.

Rani took the four steps with confidence, setting aside the memory of her last appearance in the cathedral proper, of her frantic scramble for the secret passage behind the altar. Hal helped her up the last step, taking both her hands in his.

His palms were warm and dry; his touch was steady. She bowed her head and sank to her knees before him, aware that all four of the boys knelt in the aisle behind her, carefully lowering their precious burden. Hal spoke above her bent form, projecting his voice for the people who filled the cathedral. "Greetings, Ranita Glasswright. It gives us pleasure to see you in the House of the Thousand Gods."

Again Rani felt a swirl in her memory, a whisper of the glory that she had seen, that she had summoned. The gods stood at bay, though, keeping to their unspoken promise to let her live her life uninterrupted. Rani crossed her hands over her chest, speaking loudly but knowing that her words would not carry to all. "Gracious lord, the pleasure is for this humble glasswright."

"We have been told that you would offer up a gift to us this day."

"Aye, Your Majesty." Rani looked up into his face. She could see his father's bones, the strong cheeks that had marked Shanoranvilli ben-Jair from the first day that she met the ancient king. She remembered kneeling before that man, years ago, when she had come to the cathedral as First Pilgrim. She took courage from the memory, from the thought of all that had passed since, all that she had survived, and learned, and come to master.

"Aye, Your Majesty," she repeated, and this time her voice could be heard by the entire assembly behind her. "I come to present you with a gift. I come to present you with the symbol of my guild, and to ask, if it pleases you, that you will grant us license to operate in Morenia as the refashioned Glasswrights' Guild."

"Let us see this gift, then." Hal raised her to her feet, and once again she remarked on how his touch was strong and firm.

Without bidding, the four boys climbed to the dais, balancing their burden with pride. They set the litter upon the floor and looked to Rani for further instruction. Before she could step forward, though, to open the magnificent box, Hal gestured to the man who stood closest by his side. "Baron Farsobalinti, will you give aid to Ranita Glasswright?"

"With honor, Your Majesty." Farso glided to the litter, but

he paused before he opened the box. He took the time to meet Rani's gaze, to study her face. She read that he was pleased to help her, that he was proud to stand by the side of his king. But even deeper than that message, woven into the set of his shoulders and the smoothness of his face, she read that he was at peace. He had accepted the death of his son and the madness of his wife, the loss of Mair forever. He still mourned his family, might mourn them forever, but he had renewed his mission to serve his king, to work for Hal's rebuilding of Morenia.

Rani's lips quirked into a smile, and she lowered her head in the faintest of nods. Farso bowed deeply, and then he swept away the lid of the wooden box.

Years ago, she would have been afraid to handle the glass creation nestled on the velvet. Her fingers would have trembled; her palms would have been slicked with sweat. She would have imagined her punishment if she dropped it; her knees would already ache with the embossed designs set into the benches before the altars of Sorn and Lene and all the others who had watched over her apprenticeship with exasperation.

Now, though, Rani had the confidence of mastery. She had designed the work inside the box. She had crafted it from materials of her own making, with tools that she had modified to her own needs and desires. She had foiled every seam, soldered every joint.

Her fingers were firm as she lifted out the orb. She raised it above her head, even as she sank back to her knees before her king. She heard the crowd whisper behind her, heard the stir of awe as they saw the intricacy of her work.

She had poured her heart into the glasswrights' orb, harnessing all of her knowledge, all of her craft. She had painted scenes upon the glass panes, fine drawings that captured the history of her guild. She had recreated the cathedral, with its stunning windows, now shattered and gone forever. She had drawn the guildhall that she once had known, its stalwart walls providing shelter even as they kept out the unworthy. She had shown the ruin of that fine hall, the utter desolation that had befallen the guild. And she had sketched a Hand, a mechanical tool that was used by the glasswrights who had been maimed so many years before.

The top panels of the orb were bare of any decoration, as if Rani could not guess what the future would bring, what her guild would become. Remembering the orb that she had glimpsed in King Hamid's court, the visual symbol of his uniting power over all his electors and landed men, she had kept the top level of her creation simple. She had indulged in the purest colors she could craft: cobalt and crimson, topaz and emerald, a single pane of clear, unstained glass.

The glasswrights' orb. The symbol of her guild, replacing the one that had been smashed when Rani first had led her companions to death and destruction. One king had had an orb destroyed. Now, if all the gods were willing, another would accept a replacement, would bring the guild back into official being.

She watched Hal study her creation. She watched him measure out the story of her past, of *their* past. She saw that he understood the bare panes at the top of the orb, the unmarked glass where future generations of apprentices would set their palms, would take their vows to uphold and support the guildhall.

He nodded once, and then he set his own hands atop the orb. "We see the orb that you bring this day, and we recognize it for the masterpiece it is. We declare the Glasswrights'

Guild reaffirmed within all our lands, within Morenia and Amanthia, and all the kingdoms that would call us friend and ally. We recognize you, Ranita Glasswright, as a master of your guild, indeed, as the guildmistress for all the rest of your days. We expect you to bind all of your guildsmen—apprentice, journeyman, and master—through the power of this orb, by the laying on of hands. We ask that you remember our blessing and our acceptance of your orb, and that all the members of the Glasswrights' Guild be sworn directly to us, to the house of ben-Jair, from this day onward."

Rani blinked back sudden tears, surprised by the strength of the royal acceptance, by Hal's surprise intention to bring the glasswrights under his personal protection. "Your Majesty," she forced herself to say, "you honor us too greatly."

"We honor you as you deserve." He stepped forward then and helped her to her feet, eased her toward the altar and the specially crafted stand that would protect the orb, even as the masterpiece was displayed to all the assembled crowd.

Only when Rani had nestled the work to her satisfaction did Hal turn back to the throng. "Behold!" he proclaimed. "Behold the glasswrights' orb! Let all who are present today bless the name of the glasswrights. Let all who look upon this masterpiece of their craft rejoice that the Glasswrights' Guild is returned to Morenia!"

The crowd erupted into cheers, the cries bouncing off the cathedral stonework with a force that might have threatened the windows if they still stood. Hal's smile was broad, unforced, and he took advantage of the prolonged celebration to turn Rani toward him.

"You can meet with Davin this afternoon," he said in a voice meant for her ears alone. "You can begin discussing plans to rebuild the hall. He suggests the northwest corner of the keep; he says that you'll get the best access to light that way."

She was so startled that she forgot to call him by a title. "We already have land! We'll rebuild on the old site!"

"On land that was sown with salt? On land that bears so many grievous memories?"

Despite herself, despite the joy of the day, she cast her eyes toward her feet. It was, after all, her fault that the old hall had been destroyed so thoroughly.

Hal's finger on her chin was gentle, but she could not resist the gesture. She looked into his eyes. "This is a time for new beginnings, Ranita Glasswright. We will not return to the sorrows of the past." He took a step closer, as if he were unaware of the crowded cathedral, as if he could not hear the cheers and cries of a grateful people. "We've both made mistakes, Rani. We've both acted without thought and paid the cost for our impulses. Will you set aside those errors? Will you stand beside me for all the rest of our days?"

Rani heard the words with her ears, but she could make no sense of them with her heart. "I . . ." she started, but could not find an answer. "Hal . . ." she began again, but lost the path before she could even speak his full name. "We cannot be together," she finally made herself say. "You are king of all Morenia, and I am nothing but a merchant's daughter."

"You are merchant and guildswoman. You've been soldier and Touched. You have lived inside my palace as a noblewoman for over eight years. The old orders have crumbled. They are gone, like the enemies who occupied our streets, the enemies that you drove forth with the power of your faith, with the strength of your convictions. Who am I to try to stand against that force?"

She tried to believe that he was speaking the words, tried to understand that he was offering all that she had ever wanted, more than she had ever hoped. "It will not be easy, my lord," she said. "There will be consequences."

"There are always consequences!" Before she could stop him, before she even knew what he was thinking, he closed the distance between them. She saw him leaning closer, smelled the sweet soap of the royal baths upon his cheek, and then she felt his lips brush against her own, feather soft, but promising. "I need you, Rani Trader. I need you by my side. You drive away the voices, you keep the ghosts at bay. Promise you will never leave me. Promise me that you will be my queen."

The crowd had fallen silent behind them. She felt the pressure of thousands of eyes upon her back, the power of a hundred hundred questioning faces. Hal leaned down, though, and kissed her again, kissed her with a passion that surged down her spine with more force than the rollicking Speaking stream. "I promise," she whispered when he pulled away. "I promise I will stay."

She saw tears spring to his eyes and a swell of joy that brightened all his face. She felt his fingers, firm upon her arm as he turned her back to face the crowd. She heard the breathless silence and then the solid clap as Farso thrust his hands together, repeating, two times, three, four, until all the crowd began to join him in applause.

Rani looked out over the cathedral, gazing down the long nave. Someone had opened the massive wooden doors, letting the late-autumn light flood down the aisle. For just an instant, she remembered that her brother had once waited for her outside those doors, Bardo, whom she had loved with a child's simple strength.

She blinked, as if she expected her past to stride into the cathedral. No Bardo appeared, of course. He was long gone, resigned to the mistakes of their past.

A shadow solidified in the sunbeam, though, thin and lithe. Rani could just make out the cropped hair, the narrow but muscular shoulders. She glanced at Farso to see if he could see her too, but the nobleman had eyes only for his liege lord and king.

Rani turned back to the doorway in time to see the shadow raise its hand, fingers moving in a rapid blessing. Then Mair slipped away into the streets outside the cathedral, off to whatever Touched games she would play, whatever life she would build on the fringes of Moren's castes.

Rani's heart was light as she stepped down from the dais, leaving the House of the Thousand Gods with Halaravilli ben-Jair at her side.